MW01596238

Copyright ©

Revised Edition 2015

Published by Eisele Mountain Creations and Publications

Cover Design

Courtesy of Eisele Mountain Creations.

ISBN-13: 978-1482085716

ISBN-10: 1482085712

Dedication

To S.K. McClafferty and Marcy Waldenville, the sisters of my heart, my sisters of mayhem. I could never have done this without you both. Your support was endless. Your encouragement an overflowing fountain. I am eternally grateful for your kicks to my behind, and your pats on my back. Your laughter, your guidance, and most of all, your unwavering friendship.

To Dave. You are my biggest fan, my greatest supporter, and the love of my life. I could never have done this without you, either.

And to the Most High who has blessed me beyond anything I could ever have imagined.

I am truly blessed.

When

Push

Comes to

Shove

by

J.D. Wylde

Ann,

So nice to share this
journey with you.
Live Wylde !
J. D. Wylde

Table of Contents

Table of Contents

Chapter 1

With the majestic mountains of East Tennessee rimmed in a thin veil of blue haze, Virgil Push stood before *Salvation* and knew he wouldn't find it anytime soon.

Maybe never.

At least not the Biblical kind. Not with the neatly-folded citation to cease and desist business operations for the above-named shop still stuffed in his pants pocket.

For the most part, the residents of Rodent, Tennessee were hard-working, law-abiding citizens with few violators issued citations. And his job as mayor of the small town was easy. That's why he'd taken the job. It was his part-time job as zoning violations officer – the one he shared with Officer Warren Clive and a couple other members of the town's Executive Council that sucked. But Virgil had a job to do. In this case a job he hated because he had to serve notice to cease and desist business operations to Rodent's most beloved widow.

The owner and proprietor of *Salvation*. The very hot, very sexy Miz Ruby Mae Shove.

His best friend's widow. Ex-best friend, actually.

It had been a friendship that had ceased and desisted when Virgil had—

And Ruby Mae had— or would have, if—

Virgil sighed. *Ruby Mae*. She was the one woman he'd never been able to forget. No matter how hard he tried. Even when he'd been married. *Especially* when he'd been married.

Maybe that was why he was no longer married. *Maybe*.

"Oh, hell. That was a lot of *maybes*," he muttered. Fifteen years later and his dick still twitched and hardened at thoughts of the woman. Even ceasing and desisting thoughts.

He walked up the cement driveway. Past the hulking Humvee parked there. It was Rodney Fitzgerald's Humvee. "Talk about over-compensating," he muttered, even as he ran an appreciative hand over the beefy front fender. Rodney Fitzgerald was a pencil-pushing, pencil dick. And that wasn't envy for the size of the man's penis talking, or envy for the man's stratospheric success making money with financial investments. Virgil knew from back in the day when hot, sweaty gym classes were followed by noisy communal showers. Pencil Dick Fitzgerald had been in Virgil and Willie Lee's gym class. And in their communal showers.

Enough said.

Sherianne Fitzgerald, Rodney's wife, bustled out of *Salvation*, her arms laden down with packages. "Why, Mistuh Mayuh!" her Savannah accent was thick as molasses. Her perfectly manicured hand splayed across her surgically-enhanced chest. The accent was also enhanced since she'd been born and raised in Rodent. And slumming on this side of the Shiner's Trail was as far from the affluent side of her hometown as she'd ever ventured. She fluttered her eyelashes. Also fake. "What are ya'll doin' here?"

Like he'd tell her. Sherianne was Rodent's undisputed queen of gossip. The diva of dish. And if one were unlucky enough to land themselves on Sherianne's plate, one could believe she'd enhance and embellish their indiscretion – no matter how innocent – or boring – until it was worthy of passing through her grapevine.

"We-ll?" Sherianne breathed two syllables into the one-syllable word. Her eyes bounced between *Salvation's* front door and Virgil. "Are you here to court the merry widow?"

"*Court?*" Virgil nearly choked. "Hardly," he replied, hoping none of the pent-up lust he'd been harboring for the gorgeous widow for half his life showed. Anywhere. Especially down *there*. Where Sherianne's eyes were honing in on his crotch.

She coyly fluttered her eyelashes. Like she knew something. "Ya'll do have a history, you know."

Yes, he did know. Everybody knew. That *one* damn time fifteen years ago and—

"Quite the history, Mistuh Mayuh," she gushed on. "If I recall correctly."

No question Sherianne *recalled*. The woman had a mind like a steel trap, and a photographic memory to boot. And Virgil and Ruby Mae's one indiscretion, as well as Willie Lee's wrath and retribution on Virgil were the stuff of Rodent legend.

"You courted her, didn't you?"

She was fishing. But he wasn't biting. Virgil hadn't courted Ruby Mae fifteen years ago. It had been more like he'd pursued her. With single-minded determination and intent, Willie Lee's life-long friendship be damned. Or maybe Virgil had borderline stalked her. He'd wanted her beyond reason and was going to have her. No matter what. Would have had her, too, if—

Sherianne's bags shifted and the helpless, pampered southern lady she pretended to be teetered on her classic two-inch, sturdy beige pumps.

Hoping to avert disaster and have her gone at the same time, Virgil reached for an armful of her packages. "Where are my manners?" he told her, his faux concern oozing with southern charm, as he gripped her elbow with his other hand and hustled her toward Pencil-Dick's Humvee.

"Oh my!" She wiggled in his grip, struggling to keep up. "I nevuh! Oooh! Virgil! Why I—"

Ignoring her protests, he opened the driver's side door. Tossed her bags over the console. Then with a palm to her ass, he stuffed Sherianne in behind the wheel. Whatever it took to get rid of her. When he was satisfied she was safely tucked inside, he quickly shut the door. So she couldn't escape. "Ya'll come back now, ya hear?" he told her. The sooner he got her out of here, the sooner he could get back to the business at hand.

Yeah, right. He snorted as he watched the Humvee slowly back down the drive. He held his breath as the woman tossed her perfectly coifed platinum blond hair over her shoulder. Like a beauty queen. He impatiently waited as she lifted her hand. And with her trademark Miss Georgia wave, Sherianne finally – *thank you, Lord Jesus* – pulled out onto the cinder road heading back to town.

Business his ass, Virgil thought, as he watched the hulking SUV slowly head back to town. He'd jumped on the damn citation because he hadn't wanted it served in the first place. And when it hadn't stayed buried as he'd intended, when it had resurfaced at the last Executive Council meeting, he'd quickly snatched it back because he hadn't wanted anyone else near Ruby Mae. Not Officer Warren Clive or Sonny Winfield, the other part-time violations officer. And certainly not Marilee, Virgil's mother – or rather the woman whose birthing canal he'd high-jacked without her consent – a fact his mother had never let him forget. *Ever.* He shuddered. *Mother* was way too warm and cuddly a term to associate with Marilee Push.

With Sherianne finally out of sight, Virgil walked up closer to Ruby Mae's shop. It had been renovated out of Willie Lee's three-car garage. He bent at the knees and got close enough to read the discreet white sign that hung just below the bow window that now resided where, when Willie Lee had been alive, there had been a garage door. And a big ol' beat up pick-up truck complete with gun rack – and loaded gun – safely housed behind it. Willie Lee did love his truck.

And Ruby Mae.

Virgil ruthlessly pushed aside the age-old guilt – and jealousy – that always blindsided him when he thought of Willie Lee Shove and Ruby Mae together, concentrating instead on the sign showcased in a decorative wrought iron ivy frame. Beautifully scripted letters spelling out *Salvation* confirmed to the residents of Rodent who lived on both sides of the Shiner's Trail, and to those who lived up on Mount Brandywine and even in the neighboring town of Appleby and beyond, that this was the place to indeed purchase Ruby Mae's artistic creations.

The sign was small. Inconspicuous. But then again when one was operating just beyond the legal limits of the law – in this case operating a commercial business in a residential neighborhood, it would have to be discreet. Leaving Virgil no choice but to serve notice and shut her down.

It was days like this he really hated his job.

* * *

A tiny wind chime tinkled above the door as Virgil stepped over the threshold and into *Salvation*. Sunlight streamed in through the bow window giving the shop a warm welcoming feeling. Or maybe it was just because Ruby Mae was here. Virgil swore he could still smell her sweetness. And yes, he remembered her scent this many years later. The concrete block walls had been refinished with plaster, painted a bright cottage white. His Italian loafers sank into plush carpet as he took a few more steps into the shop. He slowly turned around.

Everywhere he looked, he saw Ruby Mae. Or rather, her handiwork. She'd always been a talented artist. He just hadn't realized how talented. Or how diversified. Halogen lights shined down on pristine glass shelves filled with glass bowls and vases, each intricately painted with beautiful scenes. He picked up a plate painted with the native mountain foliage of Mount Brandywine. He glanced out the window to the mountain that stood in smoky splendor just beyond her part of town. She'd captured its likeness perfectly.

Beautifully crafted pottery bowls fired in swirling shades of iridescent blues and greens were carefully arranged on a wrought-iron and glass corner shelf. Galleries in Gatlinburg and Knoxville would fall all over themselves for a chance to display her one-of-a-kind creations, she was that good. Beside it was a small wrought-iron table with a couple chairs and an open notebook. He thumbed through pages and pages of pictures of other items she'd created from hand-painted park benches to unique hand-crafted jewelry. Just beyond the bistro table was a narrow, waist-high counter with a closed door behind it. And on the far wall beyond were Ruby Mae's signature paintings.

Virgil slowly walked toward them, in awe as he'd always been at what she could capture on canvas. She'd been good in high school. She was amazing now. Virgil's ex-wife had always considered herself an art connoisseur, and with her settlement in their divorce, she had established herself as one – and now owned the prestigious Push Gallery in Rodent. Ruby Mae's paintings were worthy of being shown in Rachel's gallery.

Virgil wasn't sure what defined realism or impressionism or even expressionism art, but he could see with his own two eyes – hell, he could *feel* it deep inside his soul all the emotion still pulsing from every brush stroke. Ruby Mae spoke through her work. She touched people through her work. Gave them a part of her.

And he wanted a piece.

A door opened. Virgil spun around. And there she was, her arms laden down with canvases. The woman he couldn't seem to forget. No matter how hard he'd tried.

"Virgil?" she softly exhaled his name.

No one had ever said it like she did.

"Ruby Mae." His voice grew thick. His throat tight as he drank her in. Curly golden brown hair framed her round face before falling down over her shoulders. Her cheeks were rosy, flushed like a ripe peach and those soft, chocolate brown eyes with their flecks of gold were the most beautiful eyes he'd ever seen. And nobody — *nobody* ever looked at him the way she did. In the old days it had fed an over-inflated ego. Today it soothed a weary soul. And stirred to life a beaten-down desire that, fifteen years later, still begged to be nurtured. Consummated. Set wild and free in a way only she could.

She turned. Bent at the waist and deposited the armful of canvases on the floor and his throat went dry. She was curvier than she'd been two years ago. When she'd stood rail-thin over Willie Lee's grave, veiled in sorrow with dark circles under her red-rimmed eyes. So fragile and frail, he'd stepped up to stand beside her. Not because he'd had any right to, but because he couldn't bear the thought of losing her even though she wasn't his to lose. She'd been nearly skeletal then when he'd cupped her arm, but he guessed watching the man she loved die from cancer was a hell of a lot harder than Virgil watching his own marriage die a slow death from neglect.

He guessed they'd both changed a lot in the last couple years.

"What are you doin' here?" she softly asked.

And Virgil's hand slid into his pants pocket, crushing that damn citation in his fist.

* * *

Ruby Mae Shove could not believe Virgil Push, the hot, handsome mayor of Rodent, Tennessee, the man she'd almost made the biggest mistake of her life with, was standing in her shop. How many times over the last two years had she dreamed of him? How many times had she guiltily thought of him over the last fifteen? The man she'd never been fully able to extract from her heart. No matter how hard she tried. No matter how hard Willie Lee tried.

It had been two years since she'd seen him last. When he'd interrupted his nearly decade-long pursuit of pleasure, jet-setting all over the world to come home to attend Willie Lee's funeral. When he'd boldly stood, bloodshot and bleary-eyed, like he had every right to stand beside her, as she'd laid her husband to rest in a cold, dank grave. And then he'd disappeared for all intents and purposes to his side of the Shiner's Trail, the old moonshine route that was now more a line of demarcation, dividing the town's affluent side from its working middle class side and the lower income mountain families living up on the Brandywine.

And now he was here. In her shop.

And he looked good enough to eat. And she was suddenly ravenous.

He'd always been Rodent's golden boy and time and his single-minded pursuit of pleasure – and his very public, very ugly divorce – hadn't detracted from his classic all-American good looks. He still rebelliously wore his blond hair longer than was socially acceptable, the golden strands touching the collar of his hand-tailored shirt. His shoulders were broader than they'd been in high school, not near as stooped as they'd been at Willie Lee's grave, but then she'd been pretty certain he'd been drinking pretty heavily back then. Partying pretty hard, too. At least that's what the gossips had been saying.

After that incident with her and Virgil in high school, Ruby Mae had tried her damndest to steer clear of gossip.

"What are you doin' here?" she asked again as she nervously rubbed her suddenly damp palms against the denim covering her thighs. Her quivering thighs.

He shrugged his big shoulder. Shuffled his feet in their Italian leather loafers. They were scuffed like he hadn't dressed to impress. Like they were regular ol' shoes and not custom made. And why would he need to impress when he had the last name of Push? One of the most impressive, weight-carrying names in East Tennessee. And probably Oklahoma for that matter.

"I, uh— uh," he stuttered. So unlike the smooth talker she remembered. And his eyes darted left, and then right. Like a rat seeking an escape.

Her brows drew together. Something wasn't right.

Then his eyes settled on her. And she suddenly didn't care, as they traveled slowly down over her body, awakening desire, painfully reminding her of everything she'd lost when Willie Lee had lost his battle with cancer. And what she'd never have with the man standing in front of her.

They were too different.

They didn't want the same things. She wanted love ever after with a man who'd stay in Rodent, preferably on her side of the Trail. And even though he'd somehow ended up mayor, he was still just passing through. The last fifteen years of his life had proven that. Yet even knowing that, she could easily fool herself into believing with one hot look that he'd changed, that he could give her everything she wanted.

He stepped closer, and her heart thumped hard in her chest. His bright blue eyes darkened with intent and wet heat flooded through her, settling between her legs. "Can I?" he asked, his voice wrapping around her the way she suddenly wanted his arms.

She slowly lifted her head up and down, not sure what she was agreeing to. He could be asking permission to rob her, or kiss her, and she'd agree to anything he asked. And didn't that make her just about the most foolish woman alive? And yet he was coming closer, until his broad shoulders were blocking out the sun shining in the window behind him, and his narrow hips were lined up with hers, and his warm breath feathered against her flushed cheek. And all it would take would be a deep breath – one she was incapable of taking right now – and her breasts would brush against his muscled chest. And she'd be in his arms where she'd found herself dreaming of being more times than not since Willie Lee had died.

Virgil brushed by her. And while she struggled to find her footing on legs suddenly limp, holding onto the counter for support, he knelt down in front of the pile of paintings she'd dug out of the spare bedroom. The ones she'd lost sleep over while she'd debated selling them. Keep them? Or lose her house? The few – namely two people – who'd seen them had both said they were her best work.

To her, they were a chronicle of her and Willie Lee's struggle and battle with the fatal disease. Each a benchmark in time from the one she'd painted when they'd found out, and every other one after when they'd foolishly hoped they'd beaten the odds, when they'd struggled with treatments, been tricked with the joy of remission and the worst one of all, the one she'd painted when she'd realized Fate had cheated them. And death was inevitable. And Virgil, with his long, slender, healthy, suntanned fingers was slowly sliding between each canvas like an avid reader thumbing through his favorite book.

Sharp, jagged pain lanced through her. It had been hard enough to make the decision to display them in her shop. They were a part of her soul. Putting them out here ripped her private pain wide open, for anyone to see. To touch. To take. She wanted to snatch them away. Stuff them back in that dark closet in the spare bedroom and never let them see the light of day. But money was tight and this shop was her only income. Any money she and Willie Lee had put aside for their forever after had gotten eaten up with rising healthcare costs not covered by insurance. And now she had bills to pay and a roof to keep over Brandon's head. *Brandon.* She sucked in a sharp breath. Her son. He'd lost so much more than she had when Willie Lee had died. And he was hurting so badly. More times than not, she didn't know how to fix it. How to fix him.

"These are beautiful, Ruby Mae." Virgil looked up over his shoulder at her, and she held her breath, schooled her features, and prayed none of the pain and anger churning inside her showed. "Can I?" he asked, holding one painting in his hand.

Her breath caught. Of all the paintings she'd brought out, why did he have to pick *that* particular one? Tears pricked her eyes as she fought panic and pain and anger and— and—

His blond brows drew together. His eyes never left hers as he slowly stood still holding that damn painting. The one she'd painted when she'd been at her most devastated. When she'd realized she'd banked all her love, her hopes, and her dreams on a promise Fate wasn't going to keep. Or let her keep.

He set the painting on the counter. Then stood close enough she could smell his expensive aftershave. Could feel the heat of his body wrapping around her chilled one. And his eyes, they were probing, digging deep. And she was so sure it was only a heartbeat, a single inhale of breath before she fell apart. And still he leaned closer. The rough palms of his hands slowly sliding up over her arms. His warm fingers gently touching the underside of her quivering chin as he lifted her head, the better to see her unchecked pain. "You okay?"

She couldn't keep her lips from trembling. Her eyes from filling. Or the pain and regret from showing.

"Aw, honey," he whispered as he dipped his head. "It's gonna be okay," he told her, his lips nearly brushing against hers. His long fingers gently cupped her shoulders and he pulled her closer still, and he held her, giving her the option to pull away. And she didn't want to. And somehow he knew. He knew. And this time his lips gently touched hers and she melted against him, her mouth opening to his and she was tasting him, stroking her tongue against his and—

The wind chime over the shop's door jangled. The door opened. Ruby Mae scrambled away from Virgil as he squeezed his eyes shut and muttered a few choice cuss words Brandon would love. And there was Sherianne Fitzgerald, in all her glory, standing inside the shop. Again. Taking everything in. "Oh, my!" she exclaimed as her hand splayed over her chest. "I hope I'm not interrupting anything."

"Oh, no, you're not," Ruby Mae lied, scooting behind the counter, putting it between her and Virgil and his overwhelming magnetism. She silently cussed her own stupidity for nearly falling under his spell again. "Virgil was just— just—" she sputtered to a stop. He was just what? Feeling her up? Picking up where they'd left off fifteen years ago? Or something else?

"I was just commenting on one of Ruby Mae's paintings. There is so much talent on this side of the Trail," he told the busy body. And the arrogant, entitled mountain boy – the one Ruby Mae had seen right after her last debacle with him fifteen years ago was firmly back in place.

She wanted to smack him.

Or maybe hug him because on second thought she wasn't sure if he was slamming her, or complimenting her. She didn't know where she stood with the man. Never had.

"She's an amazing talent. Have you seen her work?" He laid on the mountain charm as only he could. He leaned against the counter, smiling and schmoozing Sherianne. "Why, I'm so impressed, I plan on buying one." He wrapped his long, tanned fingers around the *one* painting Ruby Mae had sworn never to offer for public viewing, much less sell. "I'll take this one, Ruby Mae."

Over her dead body, she wanted to yell. But instead, with forced politeness said, "why, of course, *Mistah Mayuh*," she added, mimicking Sherianne's phony Georgia accent.

Virgil's counterfeit smile slipped off his face as he glared at her. She glared back.

"Are you sure that's all you came in here for?" Sherianne shrewdly asked, her hand fluttering in front of her chest, as she looked between them. Why her nose was nearly twitched trying to sniff out a story.

And while Ruby Mae's hand spread wide across her own chest, hoping to cover her distended nipples, Virgil's whole body tensed as he turned to Sherianne. "What do you mean by that?" he harshly asked, totally ignoring Ruby Mae's very-happy-to-see-him body parts. "Exactly what did you hear?" His voice was Northern Yankee demanding, the good ol' laid-back Southern boy nowhere to be found. His hands were fisted at his sides and the hairs on the back of Ruby Mae's neck stood on end.

"Why- why no-nothing, Mistah Mayuh," Sherianne stuttered. Sherianne *never* stuttered.

And Virgil *never* demanded. Not when he could charm the pants off instead.

Something wasn't right.

"Because it isn't true," he harshly told her, going on. "None of it is true."

What wasn't true? Ruby Mae wanted to ask. Apprehension flooded through her. He turned to her. Any semblance of the desire she'd seen hotly burning in his eyes earlier had vanished. With stiff jerky movements, he slipped his hand into his back pocket and yanked out his wallet. Opening it, he carelessly tossed down a dozen crisp hundred dollar bills.

"Twelve hundred *dollars*," Ruby Mae gasped. "For what?"

"The painting," he growled. The warm, soft lips she'd just kissed into submission were pressed so tight together they were ringed in white.

"The painting?" Was he crazy?

"Not enough for you?" He tossed down a few more bills.

She stopped him after three more. No one had ever paid that much money for one of her paintings! And probably never would again.

"*Fifteen hundred dollars*? Why Mistuh Mayuh!" Sherianne excitedly broadcast the amount like an auctioneer. "Was she really worth that much?" she added, and her double entendre hit Ruby Mae like a slap to the face. Why, if she didn't need this woman's frequent business, she'd have shown her the door. With a swift, well-placed kick to her ass!

"You know, Sherianne," Virgil grabbed up his painting. He looked down at the gossip monger with disdain. "Some things you just can't put a price on. I waited," he looked back at Rudy Mae and the disdain was gone. In its place was the hot promise of something more. Of something that still burned hotly between them, even this many years later. "I waited half a lifetime for this," he quietly added, and Ruby Mae didn't know if it was the painting he now held in his hands that he'd waited for.

Or her.

He breathed deep and she watched his impressive chest rise. His hot blue eyes locked on hers. And the pent-up lust and desire and hunger for more sparked off of them like the lightning of a harsh mountain storm. "Half a lifetime for this chance," he quietly added, as determination found a place in that turbulent mixture. "And I'm damn well gonna take it," he added.

And suddenly Ruby Mae knew exactly what he meant.

And she looked forward to the pursuit.

Chapter 2

The shop was empty, what with Sherianne rabidly chasing after Virgil for an exclusive scoop for her grapevine. After turning the "open" sign to "closed", Ruby Mae darted into the back room. Slammed the door shut and locked it. With her back to the cool wood, she slowly slid down until she was sitting on her heels. She stared straight ahead. Breathing like she'd run a marathon. Even the familiar scent of wet paint and turpentine did little to calm her racing heart.

Palms together, she pressed them to her still-tingling lips. It was too late to pray for Divine intervention. Fifteen years ago she'd made a fool of herself over that man. "*Ga-awd*," she breathed out in a moan. "What have I done?"

She'd kissed Virgil Push, that's what she'd done. Nearly inhaled the man.

She banged her head off the door. Repeatedly. She shot to her feet. Paced the middle bay of Willie Lee's garage which had been converted to a work room and storage area for her shop.

She had been so careful.

Except for those rare few times when she'd gotten tripped up, when she'd heard someone in town talking about one of Virgil's latest escapades, or one of his wild adventures, and she'd allowed herself a second or two to wonder what if... But those times had been few and far between. Her wanderings, not his escapades. And always followed by a boatload of guilt because Willie Lee had been a really good man and he'd loved her with all his heart. Loved her enough to overlook that tiny piece of *her* heart that had always belonged to Virgil.

And then when Willie Lee had died, Ruby Mae had been extra careful. Especially after Virgil had boldly stood by her side at the funeral. She'd been doubly vigilant to keep her goings-on well under the gossip radar. For two years she'd been careful! And all it had taken was one visit from that man. One hot look from his sky blue eyes and she'd been in his arms, kissing him, and tossing decorum and proper widow-hood to the four winds. And it had felt *so* good.

It had been so long since she'd been able to lean into a man's strength. The last year of Willie Lee's life she'd watched his strength wane. Not his strength of mind. No, he'd been certain he was going to beat the cancer, but it had slowly eaten away at his body until he couldn't stand. Until he could no longer be the strong one. And then she was the one to be strong. Determined she'd be strong where he couldn't. Determined she'd fight for his life when he no longer had the strength. And she'd hold their family together the best way she could.

And she had.

And Willie Lee died knowing she loved him.

And then there was Virgil... She breathed deep. He was here. After two long, hard years of struggle, he was here. And she didn't know why. And he was here on her side of the Trail. In her shop. Looking at her. Touching her. Kissing her. "Oh, *ga-wd*," she moaned again. Anytime she was around that man, she couldn't keep her hands off him.

And now everybody would know.

Everybody in Rodent would be talking about the merry widow and the playboy mayor.

Gasping for air, looking over his shoulder like a fugitive on the run, Virgil ran across the weed-infested parking lot of the abandoned Wyatt distillery toward his BMW. The one he'd left parked there earlier. Pencil Dick Fitzgerald's Humvee was nowhere in sight. Maybe Sherianne had given up on him. He could probably slow to a walk, but he wasn't taking any chances. Not with the Humvee showing up again, or with the surly bloodhound that had tried to take a bite out of his ass in the backyard of the last house he'd run through in his obscure getaway to his car.

Dropping the painting into the backseat, he was grateful he'd left the top down on the convertible. He high-hurdled the door without opening it, sliding down behind the steering wheel without decapitating his dick or impaling a ball or two. He thunked his head against the leather headrest. Squeezed his eyes shut tight. And all he could see was… Ruby Mae Shove.

Hell, he could still taste her on his tongue.

Feel her soft, sweet body melting into his as his lips had devoured hers.

"I am so freakin' screwed," he muttered, scrubbing his face with his hands. He'd be lucky to get to the other side of the Shiner's Trail, much less the courthouse, or his townhouse before everyone in Rodent knew he'd tangled his tongue around Ruby Mae's tonsils.

"You slummin' it, *Mister* Mayor?"

"Oh, sweet Baby Jesus!" Virgil shot up out of the seat. His

knees banged off the steering wheel. He swiveled his head to find Billy Ray Trainor, Rodent's resident pain in the ass – or rather *Virgil's* resident pain in the ass – palming the passenger door.

"Billy Ray, what the hell you doin' here?"

Billy Ray helped himself to Virgil's passenger seat. He glared at Virgil with narrowed dark eyes. It was the usual MO for this man where Virgil was concerned. "What the hell are you doin' on *my* side of the Trail? *That* is the question."

"This isn't high school," Virgil told him. "And this isn't *your* side of the Trail. I'm the mayor. I can go anywhere I damn well please."

"Goin' anywhere you damn well please would make you a Push. See," Billy Ray's finger waved in front of Virgil's face. "We ain't seen the mayor on this side of the Trail in three terms."

"I haven't been your mayor for three terms," Virgil told the damn fool. He'd been appointed to finish this term when Harlan had unexpectedly stepped down.

"So again I ask, what the hell are you doin' on *my* side of the Trail?"

"You know what? You are wastin' your time workin' in that iron works factory, Billy Ray. You should be a cop. You act just like one."

"What's that supposed to mean?" And Virgil knew he'd jabbed a sore spot in Billy Ray's ego with a red-hot poker. "And you say it like it's a bad thing."

Billy Ray Trainor had always wanted to be a cop. His daddy had been a cop. Hell, if what Virgil had heard was true, Billy had even gone to school for a while working toward a criminology degree.

"I might not wear the badge, but at least *I* have ethics when I do my patrols."

Virgil frowned and before he could ask what the hell the pain-in-the-ass meant by that, the pain-in-the-ass was up on his knees. Reaching into the backseat. Pulling out Ruby Mae's painting. His eyes narrowed to slits. "You steal this?"

"Give me that!" Virgil grabbed for the painting. "I did *not* steal it."

And there they were, wrestling like kids both with an eye on the same prize. But while Virgil was working up a sweat, Billy Ray wasn't even breathing heavy. And was still in possession of Virgil's painting. The one that had cost him a good chunk of his salary. And it was only the fifth of the month. There'd be a lot of days eating soup in a can.

"I know damn well Ruby Mae would *never* have sold this to you. So that can only mean one thing. That you stole it."

"I. Did. Not. Steal. It!" Virgil made another grab for the painting.

"Then why were you runnin' through everybody's backyard, duckin' and hidin' behind trees? You know how many calls I got about a suspicious character?"

"I am *not* suspicious." Hell, his every indiscretion since he'd graduated high school had been plastered across the front page of the Rodent Registrar along with his picture. He was no stranger to anybody in this hick town. "And I did not steal that painting." He grabbed the painting from Billy Ray. Quickly stuffed it back behind his seat. "And I was not running through *everybody's* backyard," he huffed out, straightening his tie. He might have missed one. Or two.

"Oh yeah? Tell that to Beau."

"Who the hell's Beau?" Virgil had seen a lot of curtains pulled back as he'd high-hurdled fences and flowerbeds trying to ditch Sherianne. He'd even waved at a few folk bold enough to come out on their back porches and stand their ground with their hands on their hips. Or their fingers on the triggers of their twelve-gauges. Those trigger-happy folk he'd done a lot of fast talking to, but he distinctly did not remember talking to anyone named Beau.

"Beau is Henry Durham's bloodhound."

"The beast who'd tried to nip my ass?"

"He was just tryin' to take a bite of crime. And it *is* a crime, *Mister* Mayor to—"

"Will you quit callin' me that?"

"—Kiss Willie Lee's wife," Billy Ray went on, "And then take a painting of hers as a departing gift."

Virgil fell back against the door. His jaw hung open as he stared at Billy Ray. "How the hell did you know that?"

"That you kissed Willie Lee's *wife*?"

"He's *dead*. Willie Lee's dead," Virgil reminded the damn fool.

"Don't matter. You think you can come in here and kiss our women?"

"How the hell did you know I kissed Ruby Mae?" Sherianne was good, but she was also selective in who she shared her gossip with. And it was only with those who lived on Millionaire's Row – the part of town where Rodent's most affluent lived. How it trickled down to the masses after that was what they dubbed *charity work*. Unless, of course, you were a Baptist.

Billy Ray reached over the console toward Virgil.

Virgil put both fists up in front of him. He'd boxed one year in college and if this pain-in-the-ass wanted to go a round or two with him, well, he would hold his own. He'd enjoy taking a swing at the man. And he was lawyer enough to call it self-defense. And get off.

Billy Ray knocked Virgil's fists out of the way like he was swatting a fly. He jabbed a finger into Virgil's jaw. Rubbed it back and forth. "You got Ruby Mae's lipstick all over your face. That's how I know."

"Sonofabitch!" Virgil grabbed the linen handkerchief from his back pocket and scrubbed his mouth with it. "How do you know its Ruby Mae's lipstick?"

"You kissin' more than one woman over here? It'd be just like you."

"What the hell's that supposed to mean?" Virgil growled. But he knew exactly what it meant. And it went all the way back to fifteen years ago. And then forward to two years ago. And maybe everywhere in between, when everybody in this town would rather believe gossip than truth. "Wait. Wait!" Virgil threw up his hands. Shook his head as if to clear it. "What do you mean by *women*?"

"That's usually what you kiss." Billy Ray's eyes did a once over, spending a little too much time staring at Virgil's crotch. "Unless you swing the other way."

"I do not swing the other way! I don't swing at all." Those days after his divorce were behind him. "I just kissed Ruby Mae, for God's sake! And what did you mean by sayin' I could come in here and kiss *your women*?" Virgil glared at the man sitting across from him. "Are you sayin' Ruby Mae is yours?"

His heart dropped into his ball sac. Billy Ray was a good looking guy. A couple years younger than Virgil, and he lived right next door to Ruby Mae. He'd been Willie Lee's best friend when Virgil no longer had a right to be it. And if Virgil remembered correctly, Billy Ray had stood by Ruby Mae's side – her *other* side when the three of them had stood over Willie Lee's grave. And he'd been shooting killer glares Virgil's direction the whole time. If those glares would have had the power of bullets behind them, Virgil's hide would have had more holes in it than Swiss cheese.

"Ruby Mae's… yours?" Virgil could barely croak out the question. Pain lanced through his chest. Serrating his hopes. *She couldn't be Billy Ray's.* She just couldn't. Yeah, way back then, he couldn't wait to kick Rodent dust off his heels. But no matter how far he'd roamed, or how far he'd fallen, he'd never forgotten Ruby Mae. Had never lost hope that maybe, just maybe…

"Oh Jesus Christ!" Billy Ray pushed Virgil's shoulder hard. "She's like a *sister* to me!" Billy Ray looked away disgusted. He backed it up with that damn judgmental finger aimed at Virgil's chest again. "You are a real pervert, you know that? Just like the other one you allow to roam over here."

"What other one?" Virgil squeezed his eyes shut. How many men did Ruby Mae have roaming around over here? He rubbed his temples where a headache was surely forming before snapping his eyes open again. "What the he-ll are you talking about?"

God! He'd just made *hell* a two-syllable word. And made it sound like it actually had an '*a*' in it. Like it was a weather phenomenon instead of a place to be char-broiled for all eternity. He'd spent years ridding himself of that hillbilly accent. Six years in Boston getting a law degree at Harvard, and another seven years roaming the world not using the damn accent unless he'd wanted to. Or if using it worked to his advantage. And one conversation with this yahoo and it all came back. As if Virgil had never left.

"What the hell are you talking about?" Virgil pressed, not giving a shit anymore if *hell* had two syllables. "First, you tell me there's *women*, which implies more than one." And there had only ever been *one* woman for Virgil – not that he'd ever say that to *this* man. Hell, today had probably been the first time in Virgil's miserable life he'd actually admitted that fact to himself.

"And the-en you tell me I'm just like the other one. Call me dumb," and God knew Virgil was. He'd wasted half a lifetime and a sixteen million dollar trust fund making that statement come true. He was broke, penniless, and if not for the grace of God and Harlan's suggestion he take the cushy mayor's position Harlan was stepping away from, he'd be jobless. And homeless. "But what the he-ll does that mean? And you damn well best tell me, or I'm slingin' you outta this car on your ass! You hear me?"

Billy Ray laughed at him.

Not just a chuckle. But a real, honest-to-goodness gut-busting belly laugh nearly bringing tears to the younger man's eyes. "Listen to you," he said as he knuckled one eye. "Soundin' like you didn't leave here just as soon as you could." The mirth vanished from Billy Ray's eyes as he narrowed them to stare hard a Virgil. Or study him. "You're soundin' like you actually care."

"I do care." And Virgil did.

About Ruby Mae. And maybe a little about this town. It had a way of growing on him. Like mold.

And Billy Ray continued to look at him. Maybe deciding if Virgil was on the up and up. Or who the hell really knew what else went on in that man's mind.

"You going to tell me what you're talkin' about?" Virgil impatiently asked.

"You don't know? I find that hard ta' believe."

"Sweet Baby Jesus! If I knew, I sure as he-ll," and there was *hell* with two damn syllables again. "Wouldn't be wastin' my time chit-chatting it up with you. So cut the crap and tell me what the he-ll you're implying or referring to."

"Pretty big words there, *Mister* Mayor. You learn them in that big fancy Ivy League college you went to up north?"

33

Virgil ground his teeth together. He deserved Billy Ray's shit. Virgil hadn't been a very nice kid when he'd been growing up. In fact, he'd been a self-centered prick. An *entitled,* self-centered prick. Or at least a prick who had *thought* he was entitled. And a cocky shit, too.

"You know what?" Virgil shoved the key into the ignition. "I don't think anything's goin' on over here. I think you just like yankin' my chain."

Billy Ray's hand shot over the console. It wrapped around Virgil's hand before he'd cranked over the engine. Not that he'd ever intended to. Billy Ray wasn't the only one who could yank a chain. "Warren Clive," he tersely said.

Virgil looked at Billy Ray. Frowning. "Officer Warren Clive? What about him?"

With his lips pressed tight together, Billy Ray stared at Virgil, and Virgil could almost see the damn wheels turning in the man's head. "You can trust me," he told him.

And Billy Ray still stared at him. Saying nothing.

Virgil might have taken the position as mayor because Harlan had said it was *easy as pie* and the only place in town where a body could get paid a hell of lot to sit and do nothing, but he was finding he *liked* the job. Well, except until now. Dealing with constituents like Billy Ray Trainor was—

"Why you really over here?" Billy Ray demanded.

And sure as Virgil knew his own name, he knew this was a test. If he lied, Billy Ray would see right through it. And he wouldn't spill what he was itching to tell. If Virgil told the truth, Billy Ray would be pissed off and would kick his ass six ways to Sunday. And Virgil still wouldn't know what was going on.

He lost either way.

"I'm here to serve notice to cease and desist business operations on Ruby Mae's shop."

"Are you freakin' *crazy*? She's not bothering anybody. We're all one hun-ard percent behind her."

"She's in violation of zoning regulations. She's operating a commercial business in a residential neighborhood. She's breaking the law, Billy Ray."

Billy Ray's eyes got all squinty. Like he was taking aim at Virgil's nuts. "And this matters to you?"

Virgil's eyes nearly bugged out of his head at the man's audacity. And blatant disregard for due process of law. "Hell, yeah, it matters." And for the cocky rich kid who'd always thought he was above everything and everyone else, that was quite a revelation. But it was true.

It did matter.

"And you served her notice?"

"You know I didn't." Or he and Billy Ray would be knocking heads instead of busting balls.

"And you didn't because she allowed you to kiss her?"

"No! Neither one of us had *allowed* the other one to kiss. It just sort of happened." Would still be happening, and who knew what else, if Sherianne hadn't barged in on them.

"So you're sayin' you didn't serve her notice for some other reason than sex."

"A kiss is not sex!" But damn if the image playing in the back of Virgil's sex-starved mind was. The two of them naked… Her on top of him… Riding…Gasping… Grinding…

"You gonna serve her that notice?"

"I have to. You know I do. It's the law. And," Virgil aimed a finger of his own at Billy Ray. "Why don't you just give me my failing grade and send me back over to the other side of the Trail and quit wastin' both our times. That's what you want to do."

"Actually, you passed."

Virgil's brow furrowed as he stared at the man. He *passed?*

Billy Ray looked out the window. Long, slow seconds passed before he looked back at Virgil. And he was all business. "You gotta problem in your police force."

"I gotta problem in my car. What are you talking about?"

"Warren Clive. When he patrols over here," Billy Ray's jaw clenched. "He patrols for young girls."

Virgil's brows scrunched together. "Warren Clive is—"

"A sick fuck who is more predator than protector."

"I was going to say Warren Clive is Chief Rutledge's cousin."

"That's your problem."

"You got proof?"

"You think I'd make this kind of shit up?"

Virgil didn't know what the hell Billy Ray Trainor was capable of. If his hunch was right, he'd say Billy Ray was capable of telling Willie Lee what Virgil had in mind for Ruby Mae that fateful day all those years ago.

"You do!" Billy Ray smacked Virgil's shoulder. Hard. "You think I made it up."

"I need proof, Billy. I can't go to the Chief and make accusations like that without solid proof. Even you know that. And why in the hell didn't Harlan do something?"

Billy Ray snorted. "As far as Harlan was concerned, his constituency stopped over there." Billy Ray pointed to the old moonshiner's trail that still divided the town.

Virgil squeezed his eyes shut. *Job's as easy as pie, Virgil. Why the town nearly runs itself.* "Shi-it," he muttered under his breath. He snapped his eyes open. "Exactly what does Officer Clive do?"

"You want a play by play?"

Virgil narrowed his eyes.

"He patrols over here, okay? And before you say, 'that's his job', he uses his *patrol* to pick up young girls."

"Maybe they're—"

"There is no maybe!" Billy Ray snapped. "He watches for them. Waits for when they're alone. Sometimes he gets lucky and finds them doin' something they shouldn't be and then he uses his position as a police officer to threaten them. Makes them do stuff in exchange for not informin' their parents, or takin' them to the police station."

"And you know this for a fact?"

Billy's lips were pressed tight together. Anger vibrated off of him at Virgil questioning his honesty. Or maybe it was leftover rage from fifteen years ago.

"*Jee-zuz.*" Virgil squeezed the bridge of his nose. "And?' he asked. He knew there was an *'and'*. There always was an *'and'*.

"And if the girls or their family make noise or confront him, then they're harassed or busted on some other trumped-up charges until they learn to shut up."

"How long's this been going on?"

"What are you gonna do about it?" Billy Ray demanded instead.

"Like I said, Billy, I need proof."

"I just gave you proof."

"Do you even go to your cop classes?" Of course, Billy Ray would go to every class. He was anal enough, and he really did want to be a police officer. "You know I need names. And dates. And I need to talk to the girls." He needed something more substantial than a wannabe cop's word. He needed someone to come forward.

And he needed somebody to watch his back when he went forward. With charges.

"They're not going to talk to you."

"Well, you better damn well make them. Or we don't have anything." And Virgil wasn't going to the police chief without proof. Solid proof. He reached across Billy. Grabbed the door handle and pushed the door open. "Get me that proof," he told Billy Ray as the man stepped out of the car. "And Billy Ray?"

"Yeah?"

"Get that damn criminology degree. If you're right about all this and we can prove it, there's going to be an opening on the force. I guarantee it."

Chapter 3

Armed with yet another newly-typed citation, Virgil left his car in the parking lot of the abandoned Wyatt Distillery and walked up the tree-lined street toward Ruby Mae's. The small, mostly one-story tin-roofed houses he passed along the way were actually old company houses from back in the day when the Wyatt's made whiskey in this mountain valley.

The houses were closer together on this side of the Trail, he noticed, the yards less grandiose than those over on the Row. And while Virgil would like to check out the neighborhood nestled at the foot of Mount Brandywine, he kept a wary eye out for any twelve-gauge shotguns – and for Beau, the wonder dog. Dropping most of his paycheck for Ruby Mae's painting earlier in the week barely left him enough money for essentials. And even if he hadn't bought the painting, a jet-setting life with custom-made shirts and hand-tailored trousers were a part of the life he'd foolishly thrown away on a pair of aces and eights. Along with what had been left of a sixteen-million dollar trust fund.

He walked up Ruby Mae's driveway to her shop. Made his way to the front door only to find the *'closed'* sign prominently displayed in the window. "Da-am," he muttered. He really needed to serve this citation. If he were being honest, what he *really* needed was to see

Ruby Mae again. To taste her would be even better. His tongue licking down her throat and lower still until his mouth greedily feasted on her perfect full breasts and… "Aw, hell." He readjusted himself. He really had to get control over his wandering thoughts. And his over-eager dick.

The slam of a door nearby pulled Virgil's thoughts out of Ruby Mae's abundant cleavage. Not wanting yet another confrontation with Billy Ray, Virgil quickly ran around the far side of Willie Lee's garage. He plastered himself up against the wall. Nervously, he craned his head left then right, before sneaking to the back of the building like a cat burglar. He crouched behind the old pickup truck parked there. He waited to be caught, before slowly rising up, but only enough to see over the bed of the truck.

The coast was clear.

He rose to his full height as he stared at the three doors that made up the back side of the garage. The one farthest away would be the back door to the shop. The one closest to the house, he didn't know what that one would be for. Plus, it was way too close to getting caught. Which left the middle one. With another quick look over his shoulder, he ran up to it, hoping it was Ruby Mae's work room. Hoping even more that she'd be in there.

He pressed an ear to the door and sure enough, he could hear her walking around. Banging things, actually. And Virgil was sure, if he breathed deep, he could smell her, too. An intoxicating combination of warm woman, flowers, and wet paint that suddenly was more appealing than any perfume he'd ever smelled.

He opened the door. Quietly slipped inside, and softly pulled it shut behind him.

There she was. The woman he couldn't seem to put out of his mind.

Not that he'd tried very hard lately. Not after their last encounter.

Her curly hair was caught up in a haphazard knot, more falling down than up. The wayward curls brushed against the smooth skin of her neck and shoulders. A bright pink tank top molded over her centerfold breasts that today weren't confined in a bra. *Thank you, Lord Jesus!* And when he dragged his eyes away from her breasts, and down further still, he found she had on a worn-out pair of cut-offs. The kind that barely covered the tops of her thighs, Leaving him to drool over her long, suntanned legs. Legs he could easily imagine wrapped around his hips as he pushed between them.

He sucked in a sharp breath at the vision.

She jerked her head up.

Busted!

Her soft brown eyes snagged on his, and for a blessed second he savored the heat he saw burning there before he realized it wasn't the heat of desire. But anger. Or something worse. With her hand clenching a tube of paint, she wasted no time with pleasantries. *"You bastard!"* she hissed, as the tube of paint whizzed by his ear.

"Jee-zus!" Virgil ducked. But not before he knocked over a can full of soaking brushes. The liquid, a weird, watery shade of greenish blue soaked into his good shirt and one leg of his pants. He pulled his handkerchief from his back pocket. Wiped at the spreading stain. It did nothing but smear it more. He glared at the woman in front of him.

"What the Sam he-ll—" And there was *hell* again with two syllable. Sounding a lot like *hail*.

"Don't you dare *Ruby Mae* me, you Benedict Arnold!"

Another tube of paint sailed past his head. Knocking over

another jar. Virgil jumped back out of the way of that spill, only to bump against a canvas. One still wet. *Damn!*

"You come into *my* shop," she yelled, as she flung yet another tube of paint at him.

"Hey!" He juked and jived as wet paint soaked through his pants. Clear down to his boxers. And the family jewels. *God!* He hoped they didn't turn green.

"Stop!" He yelled, tossing his ruined handkerchief on the work table. He dug into his front pocket. Held the citation out in front of him like a shield. "I come in peace."

Her nostrils flared. Her flashing eyes narrowed. Her arm went back and she fired another tube of paint at him, hitting him on the shoulder.

"Ow! You *hit* me!" Virgil was stunned. No woman had ever hit him. Many had wanted to. But none had ever actually gone through with it.

Until today.

"Will you stop!" he yelled.

She picked up a stretcher bar. Pulled her arm back and let it fly.

He dove for safety behind the worktable. And there, on his hands and knees, his ass was once again rubbing against another wet canvas. "*Sonofabitch!*" he muttered, as he swiped a palm over it only to pull it back and find it covered in paint, too.

He stood. "Will you just stop!" he yelled, wiping his hand on his tie. His very expensive, one-of-a-kind, Parisian silk tie. The kind he could no longer afford.

"No. I will not stop!" She fired another tube of paint at him.

His loafers slipped in the wet slime now puddled on the floor, and Virgil grabbed the work table before he ended up on his ass. Again. Wildly, he looked around for a rag while keeping a wary eye on the crazy woman in front of him.

"You come into *my* shop—" She started her rant again as she lifted the whole tray of paint in front of her. A whole tray he was certain she'd use against him.

"Whoa! No. No. No. *No!*" he yelled. Or pleaded, he wasn't sure. He held both paint-covered palms out in front of him in supplication. "Do not—"

"—And then you kiss me—"

"Hey! You kissed *me*," he corrected her. And God! His heart thumped hard in his chest. He'd had wet dreams about that kiss ever since.

"I did *not!*"

Her eyes narrowed as she tested the weight of that tray of paint like Nolan Ryan hefting a hardball before he threw it ninety-seven miles an hour across home plate. Or at some unsuspecting schmuck's nuts. Namely, his.

"Ruby Mae." Virgil held one hand palm out to her, the other holding that damn citation protectively over his groin. "Let me explain."

She sighted him in with narrowed eyes. "When were you planning on telling me about that citation?"

"Damn you, Billy Ray!" Virgil could well imagine the pain-in-the-ass wasting little time before telling Ruby Mae Virgil's intentions. And probably gleefully maligning his character in the process.

"Don't you dare pick on Billy Ray! At least *he's* honest."

"Hey! I'm honest." Most of the time.

"Oh, really?" she said with disbelief before she fired another tube of paint at him. And another. And another, emptying the tray at him. Like missiles.

"Will you stop!" he yelled, jerking left, then right. "Ruby Mae! Stop this instant!"

He'd never feared for his life, not even that time he'd nearly tripped off the mountain in Tibet. But here? He was afraid. *Very afraid.* "Will you just let me explain?"

She threw the empty tray at him.

Virgil cowered down behind the work table as the tray crashed against the wall behind him. He held the citation over his head. It was a piss-ass shield as she rained down paint brushes and sponges and whatever else she could find on him like the ancient plagues of Egypt.

"Enough! Stop!" he yelled. "Just stop!" He waved the citation over his head in surrender.

"No, I'm not gonna stop." *Splat!* "Not until you leave and—"

Splat! Another tube of paint hit the wall, this one bursting. He curled his arms over his head. It was little protection as fluorescent pink paint dripped over him.

"And— and never come back! You hear me? *Never come back!*"

Her heat-filled words sliced through him like a knife. *Never come back?*

Not caring if she coated him head to toe in paint, Virgil stood. Stared at the woman who'd spent enough time in his mind she could legally own a piece of him.

"I can't do that, Ruby Mae," he quietly told her. "I can't stay away," he honestly added, as he walked closer to her, proving his point.

He'd never been able to stay away from her. That had been the problem. Not even when he was on the other side of the world. Or married to another woman. Ruby Mae had always been with him. Inside him. She was as much a part of him as his next breath. And had been for most of his life.

"And— And—" She stuttered to a stop. Dropped the paint tray to the work table. She dropped her head to her chest, too. Her breasts heaved as she sucked in air. "And— and never *kiss* me like that." Her voice wavered when she softly added, "When I know you don't mean it."

"Aw, honey, who says I don't mean it?" he asked, as he shuffled-walked his soggy self closer to her. Close enough his paint-streaked Italian loafers bookended her worn sandals. His legs brushed against hers. And his groin… *Damn.* He could just cock his hips and his groin would be perfectly aligned with her—

"Don't," she softly pleaded, raising a shaking palm to his chest as if that could keep him away. "Please, don't," she whispered, as her fingers curled in between his pecs, hovering over his pounding heart.

"I can't do that either, Ruby Mae," he softly told her as his fingers gently brushed against her cheek. Her peaches-and-cream skin was flushed with desire and not anger. And it unleashed a firestorm of yearning and longing inside him. "I can't promise I won't kiss you when it's all I think about."

The flush spread down her throat and lower still, pebbling her nipples. And then she lifted her face to his and she slayed him with the vulnerability he saw in her eyes.

"How could you think I don't want you?" he asked. His fingers slid under the loose curls to cup her beautiful face. Her body trembled, and Virgil didn't know if it was from spent anger, or anticipation. If he was a betting man – which he no longer was – he'd bet it all on anticipation.

He leaned closer and the air surrounding them caught fire with sexual awareness. Her shallow quick breaths. Her heaving breasts one deep sigh away from his chest. Her kissable mouth and her pretty pink tongue that slid over her trembling bottom lip in anticipation of his kiss. Her eyes darkened with the same need he knew she saw in his. She leaned into him.

Unable to stop even if he wanted, Virgil leaned closer until his chest just touched the softness of her hers. And his lips brushed against the hammering pulse in her temple. And her hands slid around his waist and lower to cup his ass.

A lifetime of bad choices lay suspended between them. Yet none of it mattered because Rudy Mae sighed. Just the gentlest of exhales of breath that brushed against his chin. And then she was melting against him, her perfect breasts pressing against his chest, her soft sweet center melting over his burgeoning hardness. He slipped his hands under her tank top. Slowly slid his palms up over her quivering stomach, relishing the feel of her silky skin trembling from his touch. *His*. And his fingers slid higher still until… until they brushed against her soft breasts.

Sweet Jesus. They were perfect. Like he always knew.

And she moaned. It was the sexiest sound he'd ever heard in his life. And she was pulling him closer, her mouth kissing his jaw. And he slid his arms around her. Pulling her tighter. His mouth opening over hers, swallowing her little sounds of pleasure. And her tongue was in his mouth. And he was growling his pleasure as she devoured him. Her hands were in his hair, too, and one long leg wrapped around his calf, He pressed her against the wall. Her sweetest, softest spot was rubbing against his hardness driving him crazy.

"Just like that, honey. Oh, yeah, just like that," he was growling, ready to come in his pants.

Somewhere in Virgil's lust-filled brain he heard a door bang off the wall and a disjointed voice yell, "Mo-om!"

Ruby Mae gasped. Pushed against his chest. Hard enough to pull herself out of his arms. And while she frantically adjusted her shirt, Virgil tried to find his bearings. Dazedly looked over his shoulder. Blinking into focus a pint-sized demon with spikey blond hair, wearing a ratty tee shirt with the sleeves cut out, sporting skull tattoos on each forearm.

Before it fully registered what he was seeing, the demon from hell picked up a tube of paint. Assumed a pitcher's stance and clipped Virgil in the head with the damn tube at what felt like ninety-seven miles per hour.

The last thought he had as he went down was that at least the demon child hadn't aimed for his nuts.

* * *

"Brandon!"

Ruby Mae shot out from around Virgil – for the second time this week – and tried to corral her son before he could grab any more paint. Could this get any worse? It was bad enough her son had caught her with her hands all over Virgil, and his hands— Oh, god! Had they really been up under her shirt? Had she been— Oh, yes! They'd been there. And she'd been rubbing up against him. Against his most impressive erection – and it had felt *wonderful*. Amazingly hard and thick and long and—

Brandon lifted his leg. Bent his knee. Pulled his arm back.

"Brandon, no!" She snatched the tube of paint from his hands. Chanced a peek at Virgil. He was propped up against the wall he'd had her pushed up against. Standing under his own power, but he looked dazed. And it had nothing to do with what they'd been doing when they'd gotten caught. Brandon had thrown a paint tube hard enough the man would probably have a black eye, and her son would finally get his wish. He would be an official juvenile delinquent, most likely ending up in Juvie Hall for assaulting a public official, if the lawyer inside the man ever chose to rise up and press charges.

Virgil lifted the bottom of his tie. Wiped it against his head.

Her brow furrowed as she got a good look at him. When had he gotten so covered with paint? And... she looked down at herself. And gasped. At the paint soaking through her tank top. At the outline of Virgil's tie colorfully displayed between her breasts. At the paint impression of his penis right down there between her— "Oh, ga-wd."

"Mo-om," Brandon wiggled out of her grasp.

Virgil looked at her with slightly crossed eyes. "He hit me," he slowly told her. Was he slurring his words?

Her hands covered her mouth. Her pulse pounded. And not just from the soul-rocking kiss he'd laid on her. "Brandon, you could have given him a concussion," she scolded her son. Probably had. "I told you about throwing stuff in the house."

Standing his ground, her son was four-foot-one-inch of pure mayhem and menace. And he was eyeballing Virgil like *Dirty Harry* eyeballed a criminal. "He's a wuss if he can't take a few hits."

"I am not a wuss!' Virgil snapped out of his coma. Glared at her son. "You take that back. Right now!" Did he actually think that would scare her son? Then he lifted his chin.

"Dear, God!" she gasped as his hair fell back to reveal a big goose egg forming on his forehead!

"Brandon! You say you're sorry. Right now!"

"*No!*" Her son whirled around on her. Like she'd somehow betrayed him. She ignored the glower.

"He's sorry, Virgil. He's very, very sorry. *Aren't you*, Brandon?" She didn't really expect her son to cave. But she would. She'd crawl on her hands and knees. Grovel at his feet. Do anything else he may wish down there. If it kept him from filing a lawsuit. She clamped both hands down on her son's shoulders. Turned him back to face Virgil. "See, Virgil, he's very sorry."

Good one, Ruby Mae. Play the little-boy-lost-his-daddy card.

But she was desperate. Virgil was a lawyer. Or he was supposed to have been one. And Ruby Mae did not want to be sued. Or jailed. Or have her misguided son taken from her.

Or lose her business.

She sucked in a breath. Allowed the anger to burn away her misplaced passion and fear. *That* was why Virgil Push was really here. Not because he couldn't *forget her*. Or keep from *kissing her*. Or any of the other crap he'd spoon-fed her. With his tongue. And with that smooth mountain charm and sexy voice that always wrapped around deep inside her and tugged hard.

"I'm not sorry!" her son shouted.

"*Yes, you are!*" she shouted back.

Her son kicked a tube of paint she'd dropped earlier. It sailed across the room with amazing accuracy, hitting Virgil right in the shin.

"Ow!" The poor man bent over. Grabbed his leg. Looked up at her with an eye she prayed wasn't already starting to swell. His blond hair fell down over his forehead before she could be sure. He slowly straightened. His mouth twisted in distaste as he wiped more paint onto his thigh and stared at her and Brandon with a pinching frown.

His clothes were ruined. He'd been assaulted by a seven-year old. Attacked by a thirty-three-year widow who seemed to lose her mind and her common sense anytime he was in the same room.

"What is wrong with you people?" he asked.

"What is wrong with me? With me?" she sputtered. She'd come out here this morning to work. She hadn't expected Billy Ray to stop by and break the news that this man – this ex-infatuation of hers who'd suddenly dropped back into her life, jumpstarting her heart and shutting down her brain – and her common sense – was just serving notice on her. She'd been so angry. She'd chewed Billy Ray up one side and down the other until he'd run. And Billy Ray didn't run from anything. And then— and then Virgil had showed up here. And she'd— she'd never lost her temper like that. *Ever!* Never devoured a man like that before either. Not even Willie Lee.

She pushed aside the guilt. She'd been a good wife.

"Who the hell is that?" Virgil asked as he held the tip of his tie to a really red spot over his right eye that she hoped was paint and not blood.

"Who the hell are you?" her son fired back. His small hands planted on his hips.

"Brandon, do not swear!" How was her son going to fit in with the other second graders when he had a twenty-seven-year-old's mouth? When he was angry all the time?

"I'm the mayor of this town, that's who I am," Virgil told her son with a lot of that entitled arrogance in his voice and demeanor that only people on the Row could have. She hated it. "Who the hell are you?"

"*Virgil!* Do not swear." That's all her son needed to hear. An adult male cussing.

Her son puffed out his skinny chest. "I'm Brandon Shove."

"You act more like a badass than Willie Lee's kid."

"Virgil!" Ruby Mae reprimanded him. Again. "We don't swear." She jerked her head toward her son, but it was too late.

Brandon's eyes lit with an unholy gleam.

"Oh, no, Brandon. No, no, no! You do *not* say—"

"Badass, Badass!"

"—That," she wearily finished her sentence.

"I'm the *baa-addest* of the bad. I'm Brandon *Badass*."

"*Brandon!* We do not swear," she told him while lobbing a *thanks-a-hell-of-a-lot* glare at Virgil. Grabbing her son's shoulders, she pushed him toward the back door of the work room. "Go to your room! And do not come out until dinner."

He spun around to glare at her. "Why?"

"Because I said so." That and the fact she didn't want her son to witness her killing the current mayor of Rodent.

He lobbed his trademark version of the stink eye at her before doing as she'd demanded. But she swore she could hear him mumbling under his breath, "*badass, badass, badass*." And sounding happy. Maybe for the first time since Willie Lee had died.

She didn't know if she should thank Virgil. Or smack him upside his clueless, goose-egged head.

"Who the hell was that?" he asked her as he warily watched the door her son had disappeared through.

"Oh, *pu-leeze*," she glared at him. "Do not add stupidity to your long list of transgressions."

"What'd I do?"

She rolled her eyes. He really was clueless.

"Seriously." His tawny brows drew together in a frown. "Who the hell was that?"

Her eyes narrowed. She couldn't decide if he really was serious, or— "My son, Virgil. That was my son. Surely you remember?"

"I do. But I remember a cute little kid. Not a demon from hell."

"Hey!" That was her kid. She could call him a demon, but nobody else got to.

"Or a Hell's Junior Angel." He turned that disapproving look on her. "You let him get tattoos?"

Her motherly hackles rose up at his righteous indignation. "*No*, I didn't *let* him get a tattoo."

"You sure? 'Cause your boy there's sportin' a couple mean-ass tats."

"Are you for real?" She pushed by him. Grabbed a rag from under the work table. Tossed one at him and grabbed another one for herself. "They're penned-on," she informed him as she turned and futilely wiped at the paint covering her breasts and her... Oh, God! She tossed the rag down on the work table. She was a mess. A painted-up mess. A *hand*-painted-up mess.

"You sure?"

She turned back to him. Her hands planted on her hips. "*Yes*, I'm sure." She'd bitched and moaned every time she caught Brandon with them drawn on again. Especially after she'd just scrubbed them off the night before. Then she listened to reason, in the form of Maisey Trainor – a woman who'd make the most perfect grandma if Billy Ray would get his butt in gear and find a woman to have babies with. And from Maisey Trainor's wisdom Ruby Mae had learned to pick her battles. Getting her son to stop swearing and fit back in with the other second graders was far more important than arguing over some penned-on body art she prayed he'd grow out of before school started in the fall.

With one big hand, Virgil swiped the towel down his chest, and Ruby Mae pretty much forgot about everything. Except for the vision she had in her head now of him stepping out of the shower. Naked. Water sluicing down over his sculpted body. His big hand wiping it away. Or her mouth licking droplets of water off his magnificence.

She nearly banged her head off the work table.

He was so wrong for her! So wrong.

"'Cause they look like prison tats to me."

"What?" She drew her eyes off his impressive man parts.

"His tats. They look like prison tats."

"They're not," she snapped, irritated with her dumb ol' self. "He's a little boy who lost his father." And she was a lonely woman who'd lost her man. And was going to lose her house, her shop, her business – everything to *this* one! "Don't do this, Virgil. Please."

"I can't do that." He didn't pretend to not know what she was talking about. "You know I can't, Ruby Mae. Operating a business here in a residential neighborhood is in violation of the code ordinances."

His reasoning and his Yankee articulation pissed her off. "You can't?" She tossed down her rag. "Or you won't?" she fired back. His calm, rational ignorance of the fact he was totally destroying her world was making her crazy. "Who's betting you this time?" She couldn't remember who was on Executive Council. For all she knew it could be one of his old buddies from high school. One of the ones who'd remembered that god-awful day. One of the ones who'd thought it a great idea to humiliate and nearly destroy her. One who might put him up to that same damn bet today that he'd tried to win back then.

"Christ! Are we back to that?" And she'd hit a sore spot judging from the flush of heat crawling up over his jaw and the way his lips were pressed tight.

That was the problem. They'd never gotten around it. At least she hadn't. They'd each traveled down different paths. Had two completely different lifetimes of experience. And wedged right between them, right now, was that long-ago day.

"That was fifteen years ago, Ruby Mae. Surely, you're not still holding that against me, are you?"

Chapter 4

Virgil hadn't slept for three days. Every damn time he nodded off, he saw Ruby Mae. Saw the hurt brimming in her beautiful eyes. Didn't she know he was doing her a favor serving her that citation? Sonny would have shut her down months ago with the first citation had Virgil not purposely misplaced it. Marilee would have relished the chance to knock a widow and her child out into the street. And Officer Warren Clive, Virgil shuddered. If Billy Ray was telling the truth, the jerk-off cop would have propositioned her, or worse.

God! How the hell had his *easy-as-pie* job gotten so damn complicated?

He angled his body in his chair so he could see her painting. He had it framed and it now hung on the wall by his desk. He stared at the swirling cauldron of colors, the bold brush strokes, and he allowed her anger to resonate from the canvas and prick at his conscience. He'd seen that same anger in her eyes when he'd been trying to keep them both off of Sherianne's gossip radar. And he damned himself three kinds of a fool when Ruby Mae hadn't realized that. He damned the stupid citation that had her firing paint at him like missiles over Baghdad. And he damned that stupid bet fifteen years ago, too. It had been so dumb.

He'd been so dumb.

With the exception of Willie Lee Shove, Virgil had hung with a bunch of dumb-ass rich kids with too much time and too much money on their hands. And not a fully-functioning brain between them. What the hell should it have mattered what they thought of him back then? *He'd been one of them.* But it had. *It had.* The star pitcher could not be—

"I propose we change the name of the town to Ro*dént.*"

"*What?*" Virgil spun around. Stared at Marilee Push who was spearheading this dumb-ass proposal. And then he looked directly at every other member of the Executive Council sitting around the conference table in his office and said, "You wanna change the town's name, too?"

Davis Barnett, the only one Virgil was reasonably certain had his back, looked stunned. His owl-like gaze partially emphasized by the thick round, gold-rimmed *Harry Potter* glasses he wore. The rest of his gaze was wide in pure surprise. Sonny Winfield's mouth was pressed tight, the bulging tendons in his neck pushing against the collar of his faded flannel shirt. And of course, there was Marilee, perfectly coiffed, not a blond hair out of place. Or a wrinkle in her crisply pressed hand-tailored pants suit. Or on her face, for that matter.

She lifted a perfectly arched brow at him. "Yes, I do."

"You're doing this just 'cause I wasn't listening, right?"

Her lips thinned at his slip into Southern diction. Too bad. It seemed the more he hung around Southerners and lived here; the more he talked like he belonged.

The more he *felt* like he belonged.

Worse, it didn't bother him. Being here was starting to feel like it was right where he wanted to be. Right where he *needed* to be.

"You over-estimate your own self-worth, Virgil." She raked her cold-as-the-Arctic blue eyes over him. He knew she found him lacking. She always had. No matter what he did. "I'm doing this so we can ditch once and for all," and her lips curled with just the perfect amount of distaste, "the ridiculous hillbilly image that comes to mind when a town is named after a disease-carrying mammal."

"I'm prouda my image," Sonny told them. "And my mountain roots," he added. And obviously his missing front tooth, the one whose empty space he proudly showed off, only adding credence to Marilee's argument, in Virgil's opinion. Council members had dental insurance.

"Let me get this straight," Virgil said. "You wanna change *history?*" Everyone knew Rodent had gotten its name because of the overabundance of rats and mice which had infested the town in the 1800s. When it had been overrun and infested with fur traders and moonshiners hiding out in the mountains from the law and from the revenuers, too.

"Yes, I will change history, if I have to."

And Virgil knew she'd surely try. She'd been rewriting her own history, including the state of her marriage to Virgil's father for as long as Virgil could remember. "You planning on changing the county name, too? 'Cause Vermin County and Rodent, Tennessee kind of go hand in hand, you know."

"If I have to," she told him.

"Talk about someone over-estimating their own self-worth." Or their power. She hadn't been able to talk his father into sticking around and playing the role of dedicated oil man who put his family above his company no matter how many times she tried. Everybody knew Vincent Push had high-tailed it out of Rodent first chance he got and never looked back. Which was right after Vince got married. And the couple times every year he did come back to town, it wasn't for family. It was for board meetings. Didn't matter he had a wife, which in his dad's defense, Virgil could well understand his dad staying the hell away. But what about Virgil when he'd been a kid? Not that Virgil gave a shit anymore what Vincent Push did.

"We are not changing the name of my town!" Sonny Winfield pounded his fist on the table.

"Mister Winfield! We have *protocol*, which we follow for meetings, and pounding one's fist on the table is not it," Davis reminded the man.

It was Virgil's job to run the meeting, but Davis was doing such a good job, Virgil let him.

Sonny reached for the gavel sitting in front of Virgil.

"Give me that!" Virgil snatched it back. "As mayor, *I'm* the one who gets to pound it."

Sonny stared at Virgil with dark, beady eyes. He rubbed his fingers and thumbs together, looking a lot like… a *rodent*. And while Virgil was mentally marveling at how he'd never noticed the resemblance before, Sonny went on addressing the group. Like he had the floor. "I propose we change the '*Welcome to Rodent*' signs comin' into town." Sonny's hands framed an image only he could see. "We add a few dashes around the '*o*' so they look like whiskers. And we add a rat to stand beside the sign with his tail comin' up to cross the '*t*.'"

"Oh, *pu-leeze*." Marilee rolled her eyes in distaste at the image, but it lost any weight and bite because she was flutzing over the pink ribbon in the hair of her Yorkshire terrier. A rat dog, if Virgil ever saw one. She picked it up, nuzzled him close as she baby talked to it. "Mummy loves her Percy-Wercy, doesn't she?"

Mummy? "That dog gets to call you *Mummy*?" Virgil had never had the privilege. Then again, she'd never shown him that much affection either.

Marilee ignored him to glare at Sonny. "That, *Mister* Winfield," she added the *Mister*, but not to be respectful. "Is an image we'd rather not see." And she said *rather* more like *rahther*. "On any welcome sign or street sign in this town."

"Street signs?" Sonny's dark, marble-like eyes lit from within. "Hoo-ee! I never even thought about street signs." He slapped his palm against the walnut table with excitement.

Percy shot to his feet, a quivery ball of hair, shaking clear down to his pink painted toenails. He scrambled into Marilee's suitcase of a purse, which was currently filling the spot where the absent Edgar Wyatt usually sat.

"I can see it all now!" Sonny was still high on his vision, sighting it in, right between his wide-spread fingers. "Since them street signs is littler, we can use mice on 'em. We can have 'em scurryin' up the poles. Or sittin' on top 'em. We can even put light bulbs up their little a—"

"—Time for a break," Virgil cut in, before Sonny told the group exactly where he planned to stick those damn light bulbs. He slid his chair back and stood.

"Ro*dént*." Marilee was in bulldozer mode, completely ignoring Virgil's call for a break. "I make the motion the town's name be changed to Ro*dént*. All in favor?" She reached for his gavel.

"Excuse me!" Leaning over her shoulder, Virgil grabbed the gavel before she could override his wishes and pass her little name-change coup.

"*Ró*dent." Sonny heavily accented the *Ro*, ignoring Virgil, too. "The name of the town is and always was *Ró*dent. We ain't some hoity-toity French Village wearin' them damn cissy hats and talking funny. Ain't that right, Davis? Why we're—"

"Hey!" Virgil planted his hands on his hips. "Who the hell's running this meeting?" he asked. Obviously it wasn't him!

"Well we should be in touch with our French heritage." Marilee stood. Leaned over the table, resting her body on her fingertips until she was nose to nose with Sonny.

"Our *heritage* is hillbilly. Not French," Virgil reminded her. "Moonshining is what built this town. Hell, we had a distillery right in town."

"On *that* side of the Trail," she haughtily informed him. In her mind *that* side of the Trail was tantamount to being in the ghetto. "And it's abandoned," she added.

"And I called for a break," Virgil told them before she blamed him for the distillery moving operations to another town. "That means we take one."

"How you gonna have rat races if our town isn't called Rodent?" Sonny glared at Marilee. Like she was in charge.

"People? I called for a break. Remember?" Virgil reminded them.

"We won't have rat races," she fired back.

"*Jee-suz!*" Virgil yanked his chair out. Sank down hard enough on it to warrant a disgusted look from his mother. Good. He slouched, further pissing her off. She hated slouchers. And he could see the words in her mind flashing across her forehead: *You're just like your father.*

"The rat races are a big part of summer here," Davis timidly joined in the discussion, pushing his round-rimmed glasses up his nose. "It's been a tradition for many years. And something the town looks forward to."

"We have to have the rat races!" Sonny wailed.

"It's past time to change the image that this town is full of rats." Marilee was still trying to take over the meeting. "Why we haven't had a rat or mouse in the town proper since 1987. They don't dare cross the Trail." She lifted her chin and snared Virgil with a look. "They know better. Not like some people here."

And there it was. She might know he crossed the Trail, but there was no way she knew he'd kissed Ruby Mae. Or that he'd been dreaming about the woman night and day since. He was thirty-three freakin' years old. It hadn't mattered what she'd thought when he'd been seventeen. It didn't matter today.

But he wouldn't give her any reason to go after Ruby Mae. "Since when do rats observe unseen rules of etiquette, Marilee?" he asked. "Or know sides of the Shiner's Trail for that matter?"

"Some people know where they belong. And where they shouldn't be sniffing around."

"So rats are people now?" he asked, purposely misunderstanding her subtle threat. And he was smart enough not to acknowledge it, or give her any more reason to suspect anything. He'd gone to Ruby Mae's to issue the citation. That he'd gone repeatedly to do the same thing was beside the point. That was *his* story and he was sticking to it. "This discussion is tabled. We're takin' a break." Virgil banged the gavel down on the table.

Percy yapped from deep inside Marilee's purse. "Quit scaring my little boy!" She grabbed the bag before it slid off the chair.

"He's a *dog*, for God's sakes, Marilee. Not your little boy." Only Virgil had that dubious distinction.

Emma, Virgil's secretary, popped her head into the door. "Pizza's here." She walked in, sat two boxes on the table. How she knew it was time to break was a mystery to Virgil. Nothing got past her though. Especially not Ruby Mae's smeared handprints on his ass when he'd tried to sneak into his office to change his clothes.

He followed Emma back to her desk. Reaching into his back

pocket, he pulled out his wallet. Opened it and looked at what little was left in there. He scowled.

"Don't worry, Virgil. All food and refreshments for Executive Council meetings come out of petty cash." She handed him a bag containing the napkins, plates, and cans of soda.

"Well, since I'm not paying," Virgil eyed the gangly teenager anxiously standing at the door. Was he from Ruby Mae's neighborhood? Or from up on the Brandywine? Didn't matter. "Make sure we give a big tip," he told Emma. The kid looked like he could use some money. His shirt was threadbare and his denim cut-offs were so faded they were almost white. His sneakers looked too small for his feet, and they had holes on the side. "A really big tip, Emma," he added. "He's had to wait out here for quite a while."

And then just because he wasn't sure if Emma would follow his orders – nobody else around here seemed to – he walked over to the kid and slipped him a fifty hidden in a couple folded one-dollar bills. Seeing the dollar bill, the kid would figure Virgil was a cheap ass until he checked the tip again when he got out to this car. There he'd assume Virgil hadn't seen the fifty mixed in. And because he'd already dubbed him a tight wad, he'd figure Virgil deserved to lose the money. He'd drive off thinking he really got something. Which was exactly what Virgil wanted. He just hoped the kid put the money toward buying himself a new pair of shoes.

Virgil walked back into his office and played waiter passing out soda before making his own plate.

While Sonny and Davis tore into the pizza, Marilee walked toward Virgil's desk where he sat, a piece of pizza untouched in front of him. Percy followed, taking twenty steps to every one of hers. His long blue-black hair swaying around his rat-like body was dragging on the floor like a silky mop. "That's a fabulous painting," she remarked, scrutinizing his newly acquired artwork. The corners of her usually pursed lips lifted a fraction of an inch. She obviously liked what she saw. Recognized the quality of the painting, if not the artist.

She bent down to pick up the rat-dog. "You want to see this, too, don't you, Percy-Wercy." And there was that damn baby talk again, which set the hairs on Virgil's neck on end. And had him honestly entertaining a fantasy of bidding petition to the courts to have her legally declared incompetent. And put away. Except he'd probably get custody of the rat dog.

She'd always had it out for Virgil.

And probably the entire male population, for all he knew.

She held the mutt close, rubbing her cheek against his fur. Poor dog. "What do you think, Percy-Wercy? Do you like it, huh? Or—"

"Like he gives a rat's ass about my painting," Virgil muttered under his breath.

Marilee shot him a dagger look before turning back to study the painting. A little too intently for Virgil's peace of mind. Beads of sweat rolled down his back between his shoulder blades. He pulled on the knot of his tie. Opened the top button of his shirt. The inquisition was coming and he was helpless to stop it.

"I'm glad to see you're trying to work things out with your wife."

"*Ex*-wife," Virgil corrected her. "And there's no way in hell I'm ever going to mix things up with that woman again." Not even to talk to her on the street. If he never saw Rachel Push again, it would be too soon.

"You should be begging her to take you back."

"Hell will freeze over first, *Momma*." And Virgil almost smiled at the death glare she lobbed his way at that little slip. He'd always called her Marilee. At her insistence. He looked at the painting.

"Besides, that's a painting from a local artist. And we both know Rachel would never show it. No matter how good it is."

"Well, if you're going to acquire artwork, Virgil, you really should talk to her to see which pieces have the potential to increase in value. She's the professional. Not you."

"Oh, she's a professional, all right."

Marilee sucked in a sharp breath.

Virgil wouldn't apologize for telling the truth. Rachel had sold herself out. And not just to the almighty Push dollar. He pushed his plate aside. "You know, momma, maybe I'm not out to acquire artwork to make money. Maybe," his eyes were drawn back to the painting, to the emotion that pulsed from every brush stroke. Maybe I just wanted to have it." Like he wanted to have Ruby Mae.

Marilee's eyes narrowed further. She leaned over his desk until they were eye to eye. "Did you issue that citation to the Shove woman?"

"In case you haven't noticed," Virgil reached for his dish, pulling it back in front of him. "We're on dinner break." He grabbed his piece of pizza and stuffed the nearly whole piece into his mouth.

"Did you?"

Virgil took his time chewing though the pizza now tasted like cardboard.

Marilee's lips pursed in disapproval. "Did you?" she asked again, this time loud enough to capture Sonny and Davis's attention.

Virgil did not want to have this discussion. It was why he'd specifically left it off this meeting's agenda.

"Well, did you?" she demanded.

He swallowed the lump of dough and cheese. "No."

"Why not?" Her cold blue gaze scrutinized his every move. His every twitch, yet he could feel the pulsing swirls of the painting behind him, almost like they were watching his back. Just as he'd imagined Ruby Mae watching out for him. And then he thought of Warren Clive and the shit he was doing to young, innocent girls. Shit that would damage them for the rest of their lives. And kids like the pizza delivery boy who struggled and took on extra jobs when they should be out having fun before they had to graduate and face the day-to-day grind of the real world without a sixteen million dollar trust fund to ease the journey.

He pushed his chair back. Stood. And leaned across his desk on his palms until she had no choice but to back off and look up at him. "Maybe there's more important shit happening here in Rodent than serving citations on people who aren't hurting anybody."

She lifted her chin. "Where did you get that painting?"

"Why? You want one for yourself?"

"Don't flatter yourself, Virgil, or whoever painted it for you. It's not that good."

"Quick change of opinion, don't you think?" Virgil didn't know why he didn't let it drop.

"It's bad enough you hang out on *that* side of the Trail. Must you support them by purchasing and encouraging their pathetic paint-by-number attempts?" She sniffed in disdain. "I hope she had more to offer than that." She jerked her head to the wall.

The urge to tell Marilee to go fuck herself rode Virgil hard. No one got to talk about Ruby Mae like that! Not Sherianne Fitzgerald. And certainly not Marilee Push. On their best days they didn't have in their whole bodies one-tenth of the sweetness and love – and honest-to-God talent – Ruby Mae had in the tip of her little finger.

"Give me the citation, Virgil. I'll have Officer Clive take care of her."

"Officer Clive better not come anywhere near Ruby Mae," Virgil spit out through clenched teeth.

Victory gleaned in her cold blue eyes. "You always had a thing for that woman. I see nothing's changed."

She'd always had a sixth sense when it came to him and Ruby Mae.

"Well, you're wrong this time, *mother*." He knew it was a lie. So did she. He turned toward the group eagerly watching. "This meeting's adjourned," he told them, walking to the door to show them out.

"What about my street signs?" Sonny protested as he shuffled the pizza slices into one box so he could take it home with him.

Virgil walked over to the table. Grabbed both boxes. Pushed them into Sonny's arms and then half-dragged the man toward the door. Davis hurriedly stuffed papers into his briefcase before scooping it up and nearly running from the room. Marilee, though, she took her time. And just when he was ready to physically remove her from his office, she walked toward him.

He opened the door wider. Impatiently motioned with his hand in front of him, a sign for her to leave.

She ignored him. Stared at him long and hard. Until he was ready to squirm. "She's all wrong for you. Make up with Rachel. She's a much better match for you. More worthy of your station in life."

Virgil nearly snorted. He was broke and would be homeless after his stint as mayor. He could deal with that. But making up with Rachel? "Hell hasn't frozen over yet, *mother*."

"Quit calling me that!" Marilee snapped as she pushed by him. "And get rid of that ridiculous painting."

* * *

Day was losing the battle against night as dusk settled over Rodent. With the convertible top up, but the windows rolled down, Virgil bypassed the turn-off to his townhouse, driving instead through town until he crossed over the Shiner's Trail. Slowly, he drove up the street toward Ruby Mae's house. He pulled off onto the berm of the road. Put the car in park and cut the engine. He let the encroaching night settle over him. Allowed the warm, welcoming golden light spilling from the windows of her house to soothe the restlessness in his weary soul.

He slowly tugged off his tie. Folded it before tossing it on the console. With his arm resting on the door, he breathed deep as he settled back into his seat. The scent of fresh mowed grass filled his nose. Crickets chirped. Dogs barked. Fireflies lit up the dusky sky. And a solitary blond-haired boy slowly walked up the street dragging the toe of his shoe in the gravel. With his head bowed and his bony shoulders slumped, he looked nothing like the attitude-driven badass who'd used Virgil's head for pitching practice. Loneliness and discontent weighed heavily on the kid's shoulders and something in Virgil chest turned over.

He'd been that kid once.

Sometimes thought if he looked deep inside the man he claimed to be today, he might still find that lonely boy.

A door opened and Virgil's gaze was drawn to the woman who stepped out of the house. The bright light behind her lit the strands of her golden brown hair making them glow like the sun's rays. She turned and her curvy body was silhouetted in the doorway. Desire replaced the restlessness deep inside him. He welcomed it, sliding down further into his seat, allowing it room to grow.

She held out her hand, helping an older woman outside. The older woman stood behind her, leaning on a cane, as Ruby Mae searched her yard. She caught sight of the brat as he turned into the driveway.

Virgil sat up straighter in his seat.

With purposeful strides she quickly walked toward the kid. Seeing his mother, surly attitude shot down the kid's spine and once again, the badass was giving his mother fits. Virgil was too far away to hear what she said, but concern made her voice loud, strained her features and pinched her lush mouth. The kid was just as loud and the age-old anger was so familiar to Virgil, he felt his heart squeeze.

It wasn't fair. Ruby Mae was trying. So was the kid.

The older woman called out something to the brat and for whatever reason the kid listened to her and stopped his angry tirade. And with her hands clamped down on his shoulders, Ruby Mae herded him toward the house.

Virgil wondered where the kid had been. And what he'd been up to. He didn't have to hear Ruby Mae's words to know she'd been worried. The brat had been someplace he shouldn't have been. A kid growing up with no father could get in a hell of a lot of trouble. Virgil knew that first-hand, too.

The bright lights of a big truck cut across the windshield and Virgil raised his hand to shade his eyes from the blinding light. The immaculately clean truck turned into Ruby Mae's driveway and pulled to a stop. Billy Ray Trainor stepped out. Envy ignited a slow burn in Virgil's gut. Billy walked up to the group gathered by the front door and was greeted with warm affection. They looked like a family and Virgil suddenly felt the stab of envy. And the caustic burn of jealousy that it wasn't *him* being warmly greeted that way. That it wasn't *him* Ruby Mae was looking up to and smiling at.

Billy Ray pointed a finger Virgil's way. Ruby Mae's eyes grew wide before her brows drew together and she frowned. The older woman fluffed her curly gray hair and puckered her lips as if to blow him a kiss. And while Virgil prayed the older woman wasn't flirting with him, Billy Ray turned and walked down the driveway toward Virgil's car. Ignoring the man's purposeful strides, Virgil focused on the frown, which hadn't left Ruby Mae's face.

Billy leaned down, propping his forearm on the opened window, blocking Virgil's view. "What do you think you're doing?"

Virgil had no answer.

None he'd share. He didn't know what the hell he was doing. "Look," he wearily replied, trying to see around the pain in the ass, but Billy wasn't allowing it. Virgil looked up into Billy Ray's dark eyes. "I had a helluva day." And all Virgil had wanted was to see Ruby Mae one more time before he turned in. Was that so bad?

"So what'd you think? You'd come over here and serve the widow her citation and call it a good night?"

"No!" He pushed Billy Ray's arm aside. Saw Ruby Mae and her little family still staring at him. Her arms were wrapped protectively around the brat's shoulders. And she was still frowning, obviously none too happy to see him. Virgil looked back to Billy. "Do you know the kid's out by himself?"

Billy's dark eyes narrowed. "You gonna cite Ruby Mae for that, too?"

"No. No!" Virgil tamped down his anger. "I was just sayin'."

Too much probably. But even Virgil knew a kid that age shouldn't be out walking the road alone. Especially at night.

Billy Ray tapped a warning finger against the door. "You might be mayor, but that don't give you the right to come over here. We take care of our own."

The headache Virgil had earlier was returning. With a vengeance. He looked at Ruby Mae. "I just wanted to see her. That's all." He didn't want to hurt her. Didn't want to serve her that damn citation either.

Billy Ray stared hard at Virgil. Long enough Virgil started to fidget. Then Billy looked over his shoulder at Ruby Mae one more time before his dark eyes settled back on Virgil. "She's got her hands full. It's not easy raisin' a kid by herself. And Brandon's…" Billy didn't finish. That said more than if he had. Billy Ray stood. The conversation was over. He looked down at Virgil. "She don't need you addin' to that. Leave her alone, Virgil."

Virgil looked back at the woman he couldn't quit thinking about. He looked at the kid he couldn't seem to stop worrying over. And he looked at the older woman who right now was waggling her fingers at him in a flirtatious wave. Then he looked up at the man who'd appointed himself their guardian and watchdog and honestly replied, "I can't do that, Billy Ray. Much as I tried, I can't."

Chapter 5

Ruby Mae didn't know if she should be flattered. Or angry. Or worried. The man had been parked across the street from her house last night. *Watching* her. And when she'd realized it, she'd felt the old, familiar tug of awareness uncoil deep inside herself.

Instead of the concern she should have felt.

He'd looked so lonely. So tired. Yet even from as far away as she'd been, she'd seen the yearning hotly burning in his sky blue eyes. And he looked so hungry for her that she'd nearly crossed the road, slid into his car, and straddled his hips. Nearly pinned him to the leather seat so she could take him right there with her mouth and her body.

Why was he here, on her side of the Trail? Why was he pursuing her? And why did she even care? She should be mad at the man. He wanted to shut her down. Take away her business. He wanted to destroy her life! Yet still she wanted to kiss him. Wanted to feel his big, strong arms wrap around her. And worse, she wanted to lie beneath his healthy body as his hardness pushed into her over and over again.

She needed her head examined.

Willie Lee had been all laid-back, easy Sunday morning. Old faded blue jeans and soft, white cotton tee shirts. A good ol' boy with a big ol' heart, one who had an unwavering love for her that never faltered – never once in his entire life. He'd loved her from the time he'd been a kid in kindergarten to his last adult breath on this earth.

And Virgil… She inhaled slow and deep. He was all Armani suits and wealthy entitlement. Filthy rich, actually. She'd bet her last dollar he didn't even own a pair of blue jeans and his heart, well, she wasn't all that sure he had one. At least one big enough to take on an angry little boy more lost than found. And his obviously deranged mother, if she was even entertaining such ridiculous thoughts.

She tossed down the brushes she'd been attempting to sort on to the worktable.

Virgil was complicated. And she wanted easy Sunday morning. Her fingers curled over her heart. She missed Willie Lee. Feared she could no longer remember his face and she'd been so sure she'd memorized every feature, every nuance of his easy-going demeanor.

And she had.

For two long, lonely years she'd seen him smiling at her every time she shut her eyes. And now at night, she saw sky blue eyes instead of turquoise. And long blond hair brushing over the collar of an expensive dress shirt instead of short blond hair and a suntanned patch of skin above the collar of a soft white tee shirt.

And she wanted to cry.

Her heart beat hard in her chest under her clenched fist. She wanted to ignore the voice in her head that sounded exactly like Willie Lee. The one that said, *it's okay, Ruby Mae. It's okay to love again,* because she didn't want to love Virgil Push. Not that she did. *But she could.* Oh, she could. And that scared her to the bottom of her soul.

She gave up trying to inventory her work room, sinking down on a stool instead. She couldn't figure Virgil out. Didn't know why she even wanted to try. She didn't need any more complications in her life. It would be best to forget about his soul-stirring kisses. Or the way her foolish heart fluttered in her chest every time he was near. Or the way her palms got damp – the way other parts of her body got damp and tingly when he was near.

She slid off the stool. Walked to the door of her workshop and searched the backyard until she found Brandon. He was sitting on the bottom of the porch steps. His head bowed, his shoulders slumped, and he was picking at his thumb with a finger. It nearly broke her heart. He was such a loner now, when before Willie Lee had died, he'd been everyone's friend. A brooding child had taken over the boy who'd inherited his father's easygoing charm. He was angry. All the time. And hurting. And she was worried. Scared, really. So afraid she was losing her son and there was nothing she could do to reach him.

He pushed her every attempt away. But not Billy Ray's. That man seemed to understand her son. Reached him when nobody else could. He spent lots of time with him, too, and Brandon loved his *Uncle Billy* in return. He idolized the man, in fact. Would Virgil understand her troubled son? Would he even try?

She wasn't sure.

And why was she even wondering? She should be looking at Billy Ray. It was a damn shame she couldn't feel something more than brotherly love for the man. He'd make a great daddy. A good husband, too. He was handsome. Devoted to his family. And he was a hard worker. He gave back to the community. He wasn't a taker. And from past personal experience she couldn't say the same about Virgil Push.

But fifteen years was a long time. People do change.

She certainly had. Ruby Mae caught a glimpse of herself in the small mirror hanging on the wall. She ran an unsteady hand down over her not-so-flat stomach. Over her fuller hips. She touched her unruly hair. Virgil went for sleek, sophisticated country club women like Sherianne Fitzgerald. And Rachel Cromwell Push. Not women like Ruby Mae Shove.

And what did she care? She dropped her hand. "He's not interested in you, the woman," she told her reflection. "He's just interested in shutting down your business." And for all she knew, he wasn't above using her affection for him against her. Wasn't above using it for his own agenda. And she'd be wise to remember that.

Damn shame her body – and her heart – thought differently.

Ruby Mae glanced at the clock on the wall. It was time to check on Maisey. Her physical therapy sessions always left the older woman drained, and yesterday's session was no different. But with determination and hard work, the doctors and therapists were confident Billy Ray's momma would have a full recovery from her stroke. And until she was fully recovered, Ruby Mae would be there to help her. Just like Maisey had been there for Ruby Mae when she'd needed help. Billy Ray, too.

That was Ruby Mae's reality. Not a happily forever-after life with Virgil Push.

Maisey and Billy Ray had been her family back then when her own one had been too busy, or too far away to help out much when Willie Lee had been sick. She sucked in a deep breath. The things Billy Ray had helped Willie Lee with while Ruby Mae had cried in despair on Maisey's shoulder. It was time to return the favor. And move on with her life.

And time to bury any fantasies she may have about a future with Virgil Push.

* * *

Virgil felt like a game show contestant eager to find out what was hidden behind door number three as he jiggled the knob on the door of the third bay of Ruby Mae's converted garage. He ignored the nagging voice inside his head chastising him for breaking and entering like a common criminal. If he'd wanted to practice law, he'd have practiced it. Or done whatever the hell it was that lawyers did on a regular basis. And he'd justify his actions, if caught, by saying he'd heard voices. And he had. Ruby Mae's calling out from her work room to someone entering her shop. "Semantics, pure and simple," he said under his breath as he pushed open the door.

He stopped inside. His eyes bulged in their sockets. He'd expected a lot of things.

But not this.

He stepped further into the room, taking mental notes. Of the man-sized leather couch. One that easily served as a bed, if the sheets sticking out from under the cushions and the homey quilt tossed over the back of it were allowed to be entered as evidence into the courts of reason. Then there was the low table sitting in front of it. The one with two glasses half-full on top of it, beads of condensation pooling into the coasters. And the bowl of chips beside them. And the leather recliner that matched the couch. "Of course," he muttered under his breath when he spotted the man-sized TV. And the latest video game system hooked up to it, the controllers abandoned on the floor in front of it.

He stepped over them to the shelves by the TV. There were a dozen video games. All war games with other worlds. "Okay." He stood with his hands on his hips, pondering. "Do you have a love shack here, Ruby Mae? Or a playhouse?"

Either one didn't sit well with him.

He trolled the room. Opened a door, finding a linen closet behind it. The scent of fresh-washed towels hit him in the face. He shut it and opened another door, revealing a bathroom, complete with a small sink and a large shower. He huffed out a breath. He could live here quite comfortably. "So, Ruby Mae, who does live here?" he asked no in particular.

He turned. Opened another door to find a closet stuffed full of toys, junk, and sporting equipment and no more clues – except that the man was a messy jock judging by the amount of equipment stuffed into the small space. He kicked a straying soccer ball back in before closing the door. He prowled over to the far side of the room. "A freakin' mini-bar?" He stared at the granite counter.

He stepped behind it. Rummaged through the cupboards, looking for more evidence, or clues. Namely, who – who benefited from this love shack? All he found were glasses, bowls, napkins and a few snacks. A couple candy bars in a drawer. He yanked open the small refrigerator. Four cans of soda. Nothing else. Not a beer, a bottle of Scotch, or a vintage bottle of Franco Versailles-Deville '88 chilled to perfection anywhere in sight. And, "*dammit*," he sighed, fisting his hands, banging them against the counter top. He could use a drink.

On the corner of the bar there was a laptop. "What the hell are you up to, Ruby Mae?" he growled under his breath, as he ran his finger over the imbedded mouse.

The screen came to life. It was logged onto an internet auction house website. On the page, bidding was taking place for a pottery bowl that looked close enough to the ones he's seen in her shop to know she was selling on-line.

Her business was bigger than just the shop he knew about.

He should be happy. He should be concerned. Instead, he squeezed his fisted hands, struggled to contain the anger, the jealousy, and *dammit!* the hurt. She'd never told him. She'd let him believe she only had the shop. And if she'd never told him about her internet business, what else hadn't she told him?

Obviously she hadn't told him about this secret room, this pleasure palace. Who the hell did she entertain here?

He should leave.

He had no claim on Ruby Mae. She could do whatever the hell she wanted – and judging by what he'd uncovered, she was doing a hell of lot more than he knew about. And yet, he couldn't leave. Because he wanted this.

He wanted *all of it.*

The woman. The demon child. The little house on the wrong side of town. The pain-in-the-ass neighbor who'd drive him crazy. The cozy backyard. Even this love shack. He wanted all of it.

"What do you think you're doing?"

Ruby Mae stood in the doorway, looking none too pleased to see him. With her hands on her hips, she impatiently tapped her toe against the floor. His eyes traveled up over her long legs and toned thighs and further still over the frayed, cut-off jean shorts that encased her hips. Over her centerfold breasts where his eyes wanted to linger and then up, over her face. Her curly hair was pulled up haphazardly on her head, held there with a clip. Stray curls framed her frowning face. And with the light streaming in through the high window shining down on her, he could see the fatigue pinching her eyes. And the anger. At him being here. Unannounced. Uninvited.

"Maybe you ought to tell me what *you're* doing?" he demanded when he should have been apologizing. His hand gestured wildly to encompass the room while he held firm to his anger. And tamped down his jealousy.

"What do you mean, what *I'm* doing? *I'm* not the one breaking and entering."

"I didn't *break in*," he huffed. "The door was open."

"The door was unlocked. *Not* open." She walked over to the table. Bent over and those shorts of hers rode right up to the Promised Land. He swallowed. Ignored the bomb of desire detonating in his groin that was making him hungry and hard.

And stupid.

She picked up the bowl of chips in one hand and the two glasses in the other. Pushed against his shoulder, knocking him out of the way as she stepped behind the mini-bar. She emptied the bowl into a small trash can. Poured the soda down the drain in the sink. Rinsed out the glasses. Turned. Dropped one hand to the counter top and lifted her chin to look at him with hard, demanding eyes. "What are you doing here?" she asked again.

"You wanna know what the hell I'm doing here?" He took a step closer. Jutted his chin, because yeah, anger felt better than being stupid. "Why don't you tell me first what the hell *you're* doing here? Jesus Christ, Ruby Mae!" His hands plowed through his hair. "You have an illegal business over here." He stabbed a finger at the wall behind him. "And another business here." His finger pointed to the laptop.

"It's not illegal to run a web-based company from my home."

"This is *not* your home! This is your love shack! Who the hell was this built for?"

"*What?*" Golden brown fire sparked in her narrowed eyes as her brows drew together.

He was warming up to the anger burning inside him. It wasn't enough to drown out the desire, *dammit*. It seemed no matter how mad she made him, no matter how far apart they might be geographically and socially, on ideals and every other level that might matter, they connected here at this physical level. Hell, they were explosive on this level.

"Who the hell was this room built for?" he demanded. "I want his name. I want to know who the man is."

She glared at him. Her lips were pinched tight. Her nostrils flared. Her chest rose and fell with quick, agitated breaths. And she never looked hotter. "You think there's a *man*?" Her palm smacked against his shoulder. Hard enough to knock him back a step. "After the way I allowed you to kiss me?"

"Technically, *you* kissed me." He rolled his shoulder. Checked for dislocation. She had a mean right.

"Don't give me that *technical* crap! Or that lawyer double talk." She smacked his shoulder again. Just as hard. She stalked away from him. Stopped. Spun around and glared at him. "I can't believe you think so little of me."

Think so little of her? He thought *too much* of her. She dominated his thoughts. His actions. Consumed his every moment of every day. She was all he thought about. All he cared about. "Who's this room for then?' he growled. He had to know. "You have a house. What do you need an apartment for?"

"Escape." She ground out the word through lips that barely moved.

"From what?" She had the perfect life. A little house that was a home. People who cared about her, even if one was a pain in the ass and borderline psycho. It was perfect. Her life was perfect. Well, minus the illegal business he was supposed to be shutting down. And maybe the demon child.

She turned. In profile. She lifted her head toward the ceiling. He watched her chest slowly rise and fall, her long slender fingers curl against her trembling lips. And he battled with holding his ground, and surrendering. Walking to her and wrapping her in his arms. Holding her close. Protecting her from hurt. And harm. And from another man who might try to stake a claim where he wanted to stake his own.

"Willie Lee had been sick for a long time." Her words were soft. Hesitant.

He hadn't known that. Not when he'd been traveling the world for a good part of her marriage, while watching his own disintegrate for lack of caring. He'd just known when the man had died. Virgil had come home then. For her. If for no other reason than he had to be sure she was okay. Or would be okay… eventually.

"It was hard on Brandon."

And on her. He knew that from the funeral, but she didn't put voice to it. He was finding out Ruby Mae Shove never put herself before anyone else. Unlike his ex-wife, Rachel. Or his mother.

"At the beginning… when we all thought… there was a chance…" Her voice wavered. She pressed her lips tight as her chest quickly rose and fell. As she fought for control. And Virgil wanted to kick himself for being an ass, for making her feel bad. His hands curled into his palms to keep from reaching out.

"But toward the end," she hesitantly went on. "I just wanted Brandon… I wanted him to have a place, you know… A place where he could be himself." Her voice wobbled. She turned to face Virgil. The pain in her eyes slamming into him with a force strong enough to knock him to the ground. She rubbed a finger under her nose as she sniffled. "I wanted him to have a place where he didn't have to worry about being noisy. Where he didn't have to listen to doctors and nurses tell him what he— what, at that point, we all knew. I wanted him to still have hope."

She drew in a shaky breath. Lifted her chin. "And I didn't want people gathering in my house." Her eyes shut. "In *our* house," she corrected herself, her lids fluttering open. "Like it was a funeral home. Waiting in line to pay their respects. To say their goodbyes. To ask me if there was anything they could do." Her fisted hand tapped against her chest. "I didn't want to be reminded of that awful time every day for the rest of my life, so Billy built the apartment out here. It was bad enough that Willie Lee di—"

"I'm sorry," he said, stopping her before she said what he already knew. That Willie Lee died at home. In their bed. In her arms.

She took another breath. And another, eventually winning the struggle with control. "Life goes on, Virgil."

He supposed it did. Hell, he knew it did. His life had gone on when she'd married Willie Lee. And he'd had a pretty good one. Minus the whole miserable failed marriage, losing all his money, and coming back home broke and most likely destitute when this mayoral gig played out.

"Give it to me."

"*What?*" Virgil's dick sprang to happy attention, pressing long and hard against his fly, eager to give her what she wanted. But then she'd always had that effect on that part of his body. Hell, that effect on all his body. On him, period.

"I know you have it. Give it to me. Now," she breathed out. "Right now. Right here."

"No!" He drove his hands into his hair. There was nothing he'd rather give her than that, but even he – horny as he was, desperate as he was to sleep with her – wasn't game for rebound sex. Or pity sex. Or maybe it was sleep-with-the-mayor-to-get-the-citation-dropped-sex. "No!" He wouldn't do that. Especially that.

Sweat popped out on his forehead. He couldn't believe he was turning her down.

"Give it to me now, but know," she squared her shoulders. "I'll fight you."

"What? No!" He wasn't into kinky sex. Wasn't into bondage, or getting hurt when something should feel good. "*No!* No. Just, no. No, no, no!"

"You're turning me down?" She stared at him.

"I'm not turning you down."

"You're not handing it over."

"I just can't hand it over. Give it to you on demand. I'm not a machine, Ruby Mae. I don't get turned on," he snapped his finger." Like that."

"*What?*" She frowned. Her eyes narrowed. "What are you talking about?"

"What are *you* talking about?" he carefully asked.

Her eyes narrowed further. "I'm talking about the *citation.*"

"Oh, thank God." He let out a relief-filled breath.

Her eyes were nearly squinted shut. "What did you *think* I was talking about?"

"Nothing. Absolutely nothing," he nervously sputtered. "Nothing else at all."

"Oh, you meant something. And I think I have a pretty good idea what."

And he had no intention of telling her how far off-base he'd been. "Come with me," he asked instead.

"*Where?*" She was looking at him oddly. "And why?" she added just as warily.

And he could only stand in front of her, feeling like a geeky sixteen-year-old with no social skills. His tongue was glued to the roof of his mouth. His hard dick pushing its way through the back of his zipper.

"You thought—" She pushed a chunk of hair from her face that had escaped its clip. "Oh my God! You *did*." Her head jerked back, her eyes went wide with shock. Or horror. "You thought—"

"I didn't," he quickly replied, putting both hands up, palm out in front of him. "I swear. I didn't." He had. But she didn't need to know.

"*Yes*, you did!" And Virgil didn't think he'd ever seen a woman go from desire to disgust in such a split second of time. She even beat Rachel's record. And his ex-wife had had plenty of practice. She'd desired Virgil up until the moment he'd said, *I do*. Then he'd been fed a steady diet of scant amounts of desire and copious portions of disgust until she'd gotten all his money and everything else she could bleed out of him. Then she spit him out. In complete disgust.

Ruby Mae looked like she just wanted to spit *at* him.

"Hey! I'm a guy." Like that lame-ass excuse explained everything.

She crossed her arms over her chest. And continued to stare at him. In disgust.

"Just forget that. All of it. Okay? Let's go somewhere. Somewhere to talk." Billy Ray wasn't coming through with those girl's names and Virgil couldn't go to the police chief with supposition. He needed proof. Names. Dates. And he silenced the nagging voice blathering on inside his head that said he was using her to get what he wanted.

Just like he'd tried to do fifteen years ago.

"Let's go out on the lake," he added, as a lame-brain idea started to take shape in his sex-fogged head.

"Why?"

"We could go fishing." He liked to fish. It was also one of the things Harlan, the previous mayor, had told him he could to do a lot of. Since the town supposedly *ran itself*. Harlan's words. Not his. Which Virgil was fast learning it didn't. But that was beside the point.

"You want you – and *me*?" She stared at him until sweat pooled under his arms. "To go *fishing*?"

"It sounded a hell of a lot better when I said it, but yeah. Come on." He took a step closer. "It'll be fun." And suddenly his motives had taken an about-face. Suddenly he wanted to do something just for *her*. Something to lift the burden of responsibility from her shoulders for a little while. Suddenly he wanted to do something for her so he could see her relax. And smile. And maybe enjoy herself, with no cares.

And maybe he was asking for another chance. Or maybe asking her to forgive him for what he'd almost done fifteen years ago. He didn't know anymore. His feelings for her were all tangled up. And before she turned him down, which he could plainly see she was going to do, he rushed on. "Come on Ruby Mae. Come with me now."

"I can't leave right now."

His brows drew together. "Why not?"

"I have Brandon to consider."

He'd forgotten about the demon child. "He can come," he told her. How much trouble could the Badass be?

"And I have my shop."

"Close it."

"Just like that?" Her eyes went all squinty again and a ripple of apprehension rolled through Virgil's gut.

And he wasn't going to stand around and wait for her to

bulldoze down his plans. "I'll go home and change and be back here in an hour."

And while he was at home, he'd burn the fourth citation Emma, his secretary had typed. The one he had right now folded in his pocket. And tomorrow he'd endure her knowing looks and shrewd comments about him losing the first citation, crumbling the second one so badly it couldn't be served, and bringing the third one back to her dripping in paint. And he'd make up another lie so she'd never know he'd burned the fourth one, which he was going to do when he got back to his townhouse to change his clothes.

He was not serving this woman a citation until he could hand her a solution to her problem.

"I don't know, Virgil." She gnawed on her lip.

She was going to turn him down. He frowned. Women did *not* turn him down. And although he'd gotten more selective as he'd gotten older and he didn't jump on every offer, the ones he did the offering to did not turn him down. *Ever.*

And this woman was going to.

"I said you could bring the brat. And if it's the shop you're worried about, I'll have my secretary come over and run it while we're gone."

"Isn't that abuse of power or something illegal?"

"Probably." But he'd justify it as undercover work for the citation he had no intention of serving.

"I have Maisey to think about."

"Maisey?" Virgil frowned. "Who the hell is Maisey?"

"Maisey is Billy Ray's mother."

"He was actually born? And not hatched in a lab somewhere?"

She ignored his barb. "Maisey had a stroke and I watch out for her when he's working."

"She can come along, too." What was one more? His palms wrapped around her shoulders. "No, buts, honey," he told her. "I don't wanna hear any more lame-ass excuses, which would necessitate me being a gentleman and responding by saying something equally lame-ass like, *'no problem'* or, *'some other time'*, okay?" It no longer mattered if he got the girl's names from her. This was no longer an outing for information. Somewhere along the way it had turned into an outing for Ruby Mae. And since he was feeling pretty damn magnanimous, he added, "You can even bring Billy Ray along. Although I seriously think the man will put a real damper on our outing."

The tightness lifted from around her eyes. The corners of her mouth lifted into a sexy-as-hell smile.

"It would be hell having my every move scrutinized," he added.

"He doesn't do that."

"Oh, hell, yeah, he does. But there's always the chance he'll fall overboard."

"*Virgil!* That's awful," she chastised him, but her smile was still in place.

"I'd throw him a life preserver… After he treaded water for an hour, or two." She rolled her eyes, and he pressed his hand. "So, you'll come with me?"

She nibbled on her bottom lip. Her fingers absent-mindedly stroked over the silk of his tie before venturing beyond it to stroke his pecs. And his breath caught in his chest. And his dick got hard. And her fingers stuttered in their journey as she felt his hardness brush against her thigh. Or maybe she realized what she was doing.

Slowly she nodded her head, the softness of her curls brushing against his chin. The sweet scent of her body wash filled his nose. She lifted her soft brown eyes to his. With the tip of her tongue she wet the plumpness of her bottom lip. Desire detonated deep in his groin. "All right. I'll go with you," she shyly told him.

And his face split with a huge grin as he pulled her close and hugged her hard.

"*Virgil!*" A surprised laugh burst from her as a blush of color spread across her cheeks.

She was the most beautiful woman he'd ever seen.

He was the happiest man alive.

He draped an arm around her shoulders. Turned them toward the door. "I'll be back in an hour. It'll be fun," he added, stealing a quick kiss before turning down the road.

Besides, how much trouble could one old lady and one demon child be?

Chapter 6

Virgil had everything he wanted. The sun shining down on him. The interstate to the lake stretching out in front of him unobstructed with traffic. And Ruby Mae sitting beside him.

He also had Maisey Trainor in the back seat, her curly, gray-haired head thrown back, her arms raised up in the air like she was a pagan goddess offering herself for sacrifice, singing about being wild and free. And he had her walker. Duct-taped to the trunk of his BMW. His pristine, showroom quality BMW. His pride and joy. His last hold on a life he could no longer afford.

And he had the Badass in the other seat. Nailing him with dirty looks in the rearview mirror while attempting to behead Virgil with peanuts, gummy bears, and pork rinds. His head bobbed up and down to music blaring from the ear buds of his IPod loud enough to give Virgil a headache.

Or maybe it was just the stress of seeing his car, his escape from the mundane that was now his life being assaulted with candy wrappers, potato chips, and snack crackers. All being ground up, tossed up, and spit across his buttery soft leather seats and plush dark carpeting by a pint-sized human garbage can with a boatload of attitude and a way-too-deep goodie bag.

It was assault with intent.

It was crazy.

He had to have been crazy asking to bring them along.

Then he looked over at Ruby Mae with her head resting against the seat, her face lifted to the sun, and the peace and maybe even happiness softening her features.

As if she sensed him, she turned her head toward him, her golden brown curls wildly blowing all around her. She opened her gorgeous eyes. And she smiled at him.

And he no longer cared what the hell they did to his car.

A pork rind hit him in the ear before bouncing off the console and sliding down between the seat. Virgil slid his sunglasses down his nose. He took his two fingers and pointed them from his eyes to the glowering reflection in the rearview mirror. *I'm watching you*, his unspoken words lobbed to the backseat gremlin.

The kid lobbed him back one finger. The middle one. Pointed straight up.

Virgil swerved the car in shock.

Ruby Mae shot up in her seat. "What's wrong?"

He jerked his head side to side. "Deer," he lied, sliding back into his lane. He sure as hell hadn't seen that coming. The gesture, not the deer; there was no deer. And obviously neither had Maisey or Ruby Mae, because much as they put up with crap from this kid, they didn't abide him swearing or throwing obscene gestures.

Ruby Mae settled back into her seat and Virgil checked his side mirror. He clicked on his turn signal. Swung into the fast lane. The sooner he got the brat to the dock at the lake, the sooner he could push him in. He wouldn't. Not really. But it was an entertaining thought.

"You ever fish?" he asked the glowering reflection. Not that he expected an answer. Not with the decibel level of the music blaring out from around the kid's ear buds.

"Fishin' is for wussies."

"Brandon!" Ruby Mae tensed in her seat.

"Oh, yeah?" Virgil replied, barely holding back the urge to add, *you take that back!* The brat had a way of getting under his skin, pushing all his *man* buttons. Instead he found his politically correct voice and said all nice and conversational-like, "Your daddy and granddaddy would have to disagree with you."

The brat studied him through narrowed eyes. His lips pressed tight and for that split second, he looked exactly like his daddy. Exactly like Willie Lee had looked at Virgil that day fifteen years ago when Virgil had overstepped boundaries and had nearly taken—

"You don't know my daddy," the kid spit out.

"Oh, I do," he told the brat.

Ruby Mae sucked in a sharp breath.

"Knew your granddaddy, too," he added, all casual-like, as he passed a slow-moving truck loaded down with logs. "He taught me how to fish." Wilbur Lee Shove had been the handyman and gardener at the Push mansion. He'd also been the only one to recognize Virgil's desperate need for a father figure when he'd been a child. He pushed aside the old anger and hurt. "Took me fishin' with him and your daddy."

"You're lyin'!" the brat nearly shouted. "You didn't know my daddy."

"*Brandon*," Ruby Mae warned, turning in her seat to face her son. "Stop this now." Her brows drew together as she took in the pile of trash Virgil knew had to be nearly waist deep back there. Hell, it was probably at this very moment on the verge of overflowing over the console and into the front seats like a clogged toilet.

"He's lyin'!" the brat accused.

"Brandon, honey, don't." This request from Maisey.

The brat turned his wrath on the old lady. "He didn't know my daddy. *He's lyin'!*"

"I'm not lyin', kid." Virgil pulled the kid's anger back to him. "I went to school with your daddy."

The kid's face was pinched, blotchy red with anger. Hurt welled in his bright blue eyes. Eyes so much like Willie Lee's, Virgil had to look away.

"Uncle Billy went to school with my daddy. Not you!"

"*Brandon,*" Ruby Mae and Maisey said at the same time. Ruby Mae's voice was strained; Maisey's full of concern.

"Lots of people went to school with your daddy," Ruby Mae told him, reaching an arm between the seat to rub her palm against her son's shin. It was a motherly gesture of comfort doing little to stop the brat's other foot from kicking a hole through the back of Virgil's seat. "I went to school with your daddy," she added. "And Virgil did, too."

Her admission was enough to stop the argument. Or maybe it was the green look the kid was suddenly sporting. "I don't feel good," he mumbled, holding his stomach.

"Little wonder, brat, with the amount of junk you consumed. You should be about ready to blow and it wouldn't be pretty."

"*Virgil!*" Ruby Mae twisted around in her seat to glare at him.

"What? I'm just sayin'. If I ate that much junk I'd be hurlin'."

And then her body was pressed up against Virgil's arm as she leaned into the back seat, and he was assaulted with other thoughts. Like what she'd look like naked. Underneath him as they rocked into each other out on the water. Or—

"Oh my God, Brandon! Did you eat all this?" She held up a fistful of wrappers like it was state's evidence.

"I was hungry."

"You ate like I starved you for a month! I told you *not* to eat. That we were going out on the lake!" And then she was pushing through the opening in the bucket seats headfirst. Her body pressed close to Virgil's arm. Her hip was close enough to his mouth he could give it a little nip, which only served to further fuel his getting-her-naked-and-underneath-him fantasy.

"Look at this mess you made!"

"Oh," the kid moaned. "I don't feel good, Mom."

And to tell the truth, Virgil was getting a little sick himself, imagining what could happen to his car. Sliding across three lanes, barely missing two trucks, Virgil ignored the blaring of their horns and the squeals from Ruby Mae as he shot into a pull-off along I40.

"Mo-om!" the kid moaned as Virgil slammed on the brakes, skidding to a stop. And while the car was still rocking on its chassis and dust swirled all around them, he jumped out of the car. He grabbed the kid, ready to haul him over the side when warm vomit spewed from the brat's mouth like Mount Vesuvius erupting.

All over Virgil's seat.

And Virgil.

He jumped back. Way too late. "*Sonofabitch!*" he muttered under his breath as helplessly, he spread his arms out from his sides. Warm, wet projectiles dropped to the ground around his wide-spread feet.

"*Oh, Brandon!*" Ruby Mae's eyes were wide. Her back was

pressed against his dash. Her hands covered her mouth as she stared at them. Horrified.

That was how he felt, too.

Time slowed to a near stop as Virgil could only stare at the destruction. Of his car. Of his clothes. Of his plans for a relaxing afternoon with Ruby Mae.

And then time sped up. Ruby Mae shot over the seat trying to contain the puddle spreading over his leather seats. Projectiles Virgil knew had been specifically aimed at him that were right now seeping down between the cushions of his pride and joy. "Oh, Virgil, I'm so sorry!" she gasped. "I— I— He— he never gets sick in the car."

"That's true," Maisey added, her gray head bobbing up and down. "Billy Ray took us all down to Lookout Mountain last year. We stuffed him full to the gills and he never blew."

Of course he wouldn't blow in Billy's truck. And for a second, Virgil entertained the fantasy of Mister Anal battling the Puke Monster.

"Ain't that right, honey?" Maisey was still making conversation.

The little monster vigorously nodded his head up and down.

Virgil grabbed the brat's head, stopping him. "Do you think you should be doing that?" he worriedly asked.

"Virgil, I'm so sorry! Where's your towels?" Ruby Mae faced forward in her seat. She yanked open his console. And pulled everything out and into her lap.

Huh? "Hey!" He shot forward, too late since everything he'd had neatly arranged was now being carelessly tossed back into the compartment.

"Your napkins?" she tersely asked, turning to his glove box, opening it, tossing it the same way. Everything he had neatly

94

organized was now a jumbled heap of disarray in her lap.

"*What are you doin*?" he frantically asked as he swiped the tips of his fingers down his shirt trying to dislodge the toxic waste soaking into this clothes and contaminating his body.

"Virgil! Towels." She impatiently snapped her fingers at him. An irritating sound, if ever there was one. "Where are your paper towels? Your extra napkins from McDonalds?"

He slowly shook his head side to side. "I don't keep stuff like that in my car." Good God! Why would he do something like that? "I don't eat food in my car," he told her, too. Just to set the record straight. And hopefully set precedence for their next outing.

The kid moaned again, and Virgil tore his eyes away from her fine ass and her horrific pillaging of his car to the kid who looked like he could blow at any second. "Oh no! No, you don't." He grabbed the kid and hauled his ass over the side of the car. Holding him at arm's length in front of him, facing away from him, Virgil ran them around to the other side of the car where the little monster threw up again in the grass.

The brat stood. Wiped his mouth on his shirt and said, "That was fun."

"Fun?" It was hell. Virgil was still breathing through his mouth as they walked back to the car, fighting his own urge to throw up from the stench.

Ruby Mae scrambled out of the car, looking frazzled and ready to cry. She was all tense and anxious again. Not what he wanted for her today. He put his hand out, palm up to her. She stopped in her tracks. Her eyes were wide and wary. Her teeth sunk down into her lush bottom lip. She was clutching to her chest a small bag of trash. And he knew while he'd been tending to the reigning star of PukeFest here, she'd been cleaning up his car. Obviously, the mountain of trash he'd imagined had only been in his head. The reality of it only big enough to fill half of a small plastic bag.

He planned this day for her.

And she would get it. No matter how hard the brat tried to ruin it.

"I got this," he calmly told her. When she didn't look so sure, he put his hands on the brat's shoulders like he'd seen her do. "We're good," he added. He didn't know shit about kids. But for Ruby Mae he'd learn. And because he knew she'd never agree to sit back and let him handle things, he added, "You take care of Maisey." When she didn't move, he said, "Go on. The brat and I are good," and Virgil turned and walked them toward the back of the car.

Like he really knew what he was doing.

He opened the trunk. Rummaged through the mountain of bags Ruby Mae had stuffed in there, trying hard not to linger too long on her things. Delicate, sweet smelling girly things that suddenly fascinated him like he was a horny sixteen-year-old. He dug a little farther. Found a clean brat-sized shirt. He found a bottle of water, too. He pulled his linen handkerchief from his back pocket. Wet it and handed it to the brat. "Wipe yourself down."

The brat didn't give him a hard time. And Virgil didn't delude himself. This wasn't college where puke bonded frat boys. No, Demon Boy was just biding his time until his next assault. And while the kid changed, Virgil cleaned up his seats as best he could. Then went back, herding the freshly cleaned-up kid back into the car. He paused by his own door, wondering what Ruby Mae would say if he ditched his shirt. The stench was making him gag.

"Here you go, big boy. Use this." Maisey had taken the decision from him.

Virgil looked down at the scrap of bright yellow silk he held in his hand. His eyes grew wide as they shot to the older woman. "A thong?" he choked out, mentally marveling that it was the biggest thong he'd ever seen.

"Don't worry, stud. I have another one. On," she coyly added, with a mischievous twinkle in her eyes. "I'd offer my services to you, but I don't think you could handle me." And while Virgil choked on that thought, she added, "Plus, I don't wanna cut in here on Ruby Mae's territory."

"Maisey!" Ruby Mae's head shot up. Her startled eyes collided with Virgil's and the most beautiful shade of peach-colored embarrassment spread across her cheeks.

It was the silver lining in Virgil's puke-covered cloud.

Her hand shot up, nervously waggling between them. "We are *not*— *He's* not—"

And before she spelled out exactly what *he* wasn't, and what *they* weren't, Virgil turned and walked back to the trunk. He grabbed a bottle of water and doused the only pair of panties he was going to see today.

Or any other day in the foreseeable future.

* * *

"Brandon, do not touch anything, *please*," Ruby Mae begged. Not that her son was listening to her. He was turning every knob, poking his hands into every cubbyhole, making Ruby Mae a nervous wreck.

"Honey," Maisey patted her clenched hand. "Relax."

"How can I relax? We're on board the Tennessee version of the QE 2!"

"Not quite," Maisey replied, nestling into the cushiony seats. "But it is nice."

"*Nice*? I'm afraid to touch anything." She looked around at the plush leather seats. The teakwood tables. The polished chrome glistening brighter than the sun shining down on them. "What had ever made me think the Push's would have a little redneck boat docked along the lake like any other loyal Tennessean?"

"I don't know, dear. There's nothing redneck or ordinary about that boy." Maisey's eyebrow arched as she stared at Ruby Mae a little too close. "Do *you* think there is?"

Ruby Mae refused to comment. "Brandon. Set that down," she said instead. "Do *not* touch that stuff." He had a bag of chips clutched in one hand and a big bag of candy in the other. He was another accident just waiting to happen.

Her son's mouth pinched tight at her reprimand. "The wuss said I could have them."

"He is not a wuss. His name is Virgil. And he was nice enough to bring us out here. The least we can do is not eat him out of house and boat. Or spew all over it."

Her son's eyes narrowed in a look she was growing tired of. She wanted her happy, carefree, smiling little boy back. Not this brooding twenty-seven year old who'd hijacked his body.

"Honey, relax," Maisey told her for what was probably the hundredth time since Virgil had gone below deck. "He's not hurting anything. Besides, do you think that handsome stud of yours would have invited us if—"

"He's *not* my stud! And what's with you insinuating that earlier? That man," her arm flung out wide, her finger pointing to the hole in the deck Virgil had disappeared into, "is *not* interested in me. He wants to shut my shop down. *That's* why we're here."

Maisey patted her clenched hand. "You just keep thinking that, honey."

"I don't have to keep thinking that. It's true." Why he hadn't just served her the damn citation and ended her life as she knew it, Ruby Mae didn't know.

"I see the way he looks at you."

"He looks at any woman like that."

Maisey's head slowly moved side to side. "He don't look at me like that. And men are always looking my way."

Ruby Mae stared at her neighbor. Was she serious? With Maisey's pudgy round face and equally pudgy round body, she was hardly a sex symbol. But what did Ruby Mae know? Maybe they did.

"Oh, he's your man, all right. I know the look, honey. And he's got it."

"He's *not* my man," Ruby Mae wearily replied. But damned if there wasn't a part of her that wished he was. A part that was growing stronger, more insistent, consuming more of her—

"He could be, honey. If you'd let him." Her neighbor's voice grew soft. "Willie Lee wouldn't want you to be alone. He'd want you to be happy."

Ruby Mae fought the sudden rush of tears threatening to fall. "You sound just like him." She shut her eyes, rubbed her finger across the bridge of her nose. "Just forget I said that."

"It's okay, honey. I talk to my Ray all the time. And he's been gone for years."

Ruby Mae heaved out a heavy sigh. "Willie Lee might want me to be happy, but I don't think he'd be happy if it was with Virgil."

"I don't know, honey. From what my Ray tells me, things are different on the other side. Things that seemed to matter here, well," Maisey lifted a pudgy shoulder. "They don't seem to matter so much over there."

Ruby Mae looked at her neighbor. "But Virgil?" she whispered.

"People change, honey. You've changed. Why not him?"

Ruby Mae sighed. "I don't think Willie Lee has that much forgive and forget in him. He'd never want me to——"

Virgil crawled up out of the floor. A shirtless, golden god rising up before her.

"Oh. My. God," she breathed out the words in awe. Her hand went to her chest, hovering over her pounding heart. She gripped the edge of the leather seat with her other hand. Squeezed her quivering thighs together as he made his way above deck.

He was beautiful. A perfect specimen of a man in his prime, and somewhere with her artistic eye she registered that fact. But it was the lonely, needy woman who appreciated – and wanted – the living breathing man standing before her.

His skin was bronzed from the sun. There was a spattering of golden chest hair nestled between his defined pecs, and she wondered how a man who'd made a career pursuing pleasure could have such muscle. He didn't have a six-pack, but he was packing some flat abs that still held some definition. And there was a trail of darker hair disappearing into the waistband of the rattiest pair of faded denim cut-offs she'd ever seen. A dark trail of hair she wanted to follow down with her finger. And then lick with her tongue.

Maisey leaned closer. "If you still don't want him," she whispered near Ruby Mae's ear. "Send him my way. I'd love to work my wiles on him," she added, as she fanned her face with her fingers.

So did Ruby Mae. Want him. And fanned her face.

He wasn't as big as Willie Lee had been, but he still packed some big broad shoulders. And those ratty cutoffs hanging loose on his narrow hips were the sexiest come-on she'd seen in years.

Probably because behind all that posh and polish she usually saw, she'd found herself an easy Sunday morning.

It was an alarming – and exciting discovery.

He reached behind his back, giving her a glimpse of defined biceps. He grabbed a tattered sleeveless tee shirt from his back pocket, pulling the ratty cotton down over his head. He stuffed his arms throw the frayed holes in such a blatantly male way, Ruby Mae's breath caught and everything feminine and needy inside her caught fire and burned hot.

He ran his hands through his tousled blond hair, leaving it perfectly mussed. Like he'd just ravished his woman below deck. And Ruby Mae wanted to be that woman. Be *his* woman. Sated and satisfied. In his bed. He turned his head to her. His eyes, blue as the summer sky above them, honed in on her and her breasts grew heavy. His tawny brows drew together. "You okay? You look a little flushed."

"She's hot," Maisey quickly told him. "We both are."

He breathed in a slow breath, one that inflated his chest, and Ruby Mae was hotter than she'd ever been. Needier, too. Wanting something she was sure only *he* could give. "Ooh-kay," he slowly replied with a lot of uncertainty hanging from his words. He shook his head. Probably to clear those disturbing images Maisey's comments had evoked in his mind. "So," he rubbed his hands together. "Who's ready to fish?"

Virgil didn't know what had just transpired.

Didn't know if he should be bringing it on, or holding up a silver cross to ward it off. The old lady scared him. He'd definitely ward her off. But Ruby Mae... he wanted her all flushed like she was. Eyes dark with desire. That kissable mouth opened just enough he could slip his tongue inside – if they were alone. Which they weren't.

So he busied himself opening compartments, passing out rods and bait and tackle, tamping down a perpetual hard-on he always seem to have anytime she was near.

"Brandon and I can fish on this side of the boat," Maisey offered, and Virgil wanted to kiss the crazy old lady. Of course, she'd probably slip him the tongue if he did, so he wisely refrained. She waggled her hand in front of her. "You go over on the other side with Ruby Mae. Show her your lures. Maybe even show her how you use your pole."

Virgil nearly choked on her ridiculous suggestion.

Ruby Mae gasped, "Maisey!" Her face flushed beet red.

"What?" Maisey asked all innocent like. "Brandon and I will be fine over here. Isn't that right, honey?"

Much as Virgil wanted time alone with Ruby Mae, he wasn't about to trust the brat any farther than he could see him.

"Brandon, honey," the old lady patted a cushion beside her. "Did I ever tell you how I hold the state record for the biggest largemouth bass ever caught in this lake?"

Virgil doubted the ridiculous boast. But the brat stepped closer, obviously swallowing it hook, line, and sinker. Virgil did a quick scan of the area. There weren't all that many candy wrappers and snack-sized chip bags thrown around. And if the kid did puke again, it would be Virgil's own fault this time. He'd shown him where the goods were stashed. Gave him free rein to eat his fill. Still, he wasn't taking any chances. "Hey, brat?"

The kid looked at him with squinty eyes that would make *Dirty Harry* proud.

Or Willie Lee.

Virgil grabbed a silver champagne bucket from one of the

cubbyholes. "You feel the urge to spew," he handed the bucket to the brat. "Spew in here." Then he leaned closer. Pointed a finger at the brat's bony chest to drive home his point. "You hurl anywhere else and I'll carve you up and use you for bait. Got it?" He waited the tense seconds for the brat to throw the bucket at his head, but he didn't. Instead, he crawled up beside Maisey all docile like and Virgil wondered if she or Ruby Mae had slipped him a Drammie.

"Go on, you two." Maisey shooed them away.

And with a hand low on Ruby Mae's back, Virgil turned them toward the other side of the boat.

"Oh, and Virgil?"

Virgil turned back to Maisey and waited while she expertly attached a hook for the brat. "Yeah?" he prompted her. And impatiently waited while the old lady got the brat situated on the bench a few feet away, and involved in casting out his reel.

She looked back at Virgil, her face all business. "Be careful with them, Virgil. They're fragile."

"Hardly," Virgil scoffed. "That brat's—"

"—Just lost his daddy and he's hurting." She gave the little heathen a motherly eye of concern that made Virgil envious before looking back at him. "Much as I hate to stroke your already inflated ego, you're the only man who's caught his momma's eye since Willie Lee."

Virgil exhaled his frustration. "Is there a point to this?"

"Yeah. Don't be making plays for them if you don't really mean it."

"What's with you people?" He scowled. "You're the second Trainor to warn me off."

"Don't hurt her, Virgil."

"I'm not." He glanced at the kid. His voice was barely above a whisper when he looked back. "What she's doing is against the law, you know that, right?" Maisey was Officer Ray Trainor's widow. But she was also Ruby Mae's neighbor. And from the looks of things, extended family in some weird way Virgil could only envy.

"You planning on taking advantage of her because of that? Is that what this is all about?"

"No! *No.*"

"Because if it is and you hurt her," the older woman warned. "I'll hunt you down."

"You'll be in line behind Billy," Virgil sarcastically fired back.

"Oh, no." The woman stood and took a few tentative steps toward Virgil. "Billy will have to full-out run to catch up with me if that happens."

"Then Ruby Mae is one very lucky woman."

Virgil made his way to the other side of the boat. He found the woman he'd planned this whole afternoon around sitting on the edge of the seat like a gargoyle. Maybe he should just serve her the citation, grill her about Clive, and call it a day. "Lighten up, sweetheart," he said instead, as he wearily dropped down onto the bench seat beside her.

"I am," she told him, tensely staring out over the rippling water of the lake. Strands of her curly hair caught on the breeze, blowing around her face.

"I burned the citation."

She swung her head around. "*What?*" She stared at him. Eyes wide. Mouth open.

He pressed his fingers under her chin, closing her mouth for her. Allowing them to linger and stroke against the silky softness of her skin. Her scent, light and flowery, teased his nostrils, beckoning him to come closer. To bury his nose in her curls.

She pulled the wayward strands from her face. Bundled them in her fisted hand and held them off to one side, exposing a neck he wanted to lick and taste. "What about our talk?" she whispered.

"It can wait." Talk was the last thing he wanted to do.

"Since when?" she softly persisted.

"Since I wanna kiss you more than grill you."

"Much as I'd like that," she leaned into him, or maybe he leaned into her. Their breaths mingled, their lips a mere heartbeat away from touching. "That's not a good idea," she whispered, pulling away from him.

Virgil fisted his hand in frustration.

"Why did you do that?" she whispered, staring at her own hands fisted in her lap.

"Try to kiss you?"

"Burn the citation." Her head was bowed, her curls falling forward. "Why did you burn the citation?"

He tangled his fingers in her hair. Gently pushed it back over her shoulder. Gathered it in his hand, tugging it further down her back until she lifted her head. And looked at him.

"Why, Virgil?" she whispered, her breath teasing his chin.

"Probably for the same reason I purposely lost the first one, crumbled the second one, and painted the third one beyond recognition."

"*Three?*" she gasped. "You've kept three citations from me?"

He shrugged a shoulder. "Four, if you're counting."

Her eyes got all soft and dewy looking, and Virgil could look at them like that for the rest of his life. Her breath caught before slowly shuddering out. "We both know I'm breaking the law."

His fingers stroked up over the silky skin of her neck. "There's different ways of breaking the law, honey."

"Clive," she whispered.

He leaned closer, his lips nearly brushing against hers. "Somehow you trying to keep a roof over you and your son's head seems downright commendable—"

"Compared to Clive," she softly finished his sentence before she pulled away from him.

He didn't pursue her.

She looked at him with soft, beseeching eyes. "What are we going to do?"

"We're going to figure out a way to stop him."

"And me?"

"We're going to figure out a way for you to keep your shop. Legally." And keep her off of Marilee's radar. And somehow in Virgil's life.

"But first," he brushed a curl of hair from her cheek. "We're going to figure out how to get you to relax and enjoy yourself. Think you can do that, honey?" It's what he wanted.

"I'm just afraid we'll wreck something. My god," her hand went to her throat. "We already destroyed your car."

"It can be cleaned." He hoped.

"And then you bring us out on this boat." She slowly turned her head taking in all the opulence he'd taken for granted all this life. She lifted worried eyes to him. "What if we—"

"Honey, I trashed this boat more times in high school and college than I can count." Or remember. The wild parties. The easy women. The free-flowing booze. His pathetic attempts at getting attention and playing the big man in town were a fuzzy memory. For all his drinking and carrying on, all he'd gotten was a 'boating' schedule tacked to the wall in the kitchen.

"Nothing the brat can do will hurt it any worse than I have. Besides, Vince only left this boat docked here because he has a bigger, better one docked in the big O.K." At least that's what Virgil had heard. He'd never been to this father's house in Oklahoma.

Her shoulders tensed. Her eyes narrowed. "This isn't yours?"

The words to tell her he was broke, or that they weren't near as different as she thought log-jammed up in his throat. "No, it's Pap's," he said instead, because he knew she would never be satisfied with just *hearing* he was penniless. She'd want to know *why* he was broke, how it happened – and he was too damn proud to admit what a stupid-assed fool he'd been.

She'd never understand.

"Does money really matter?" he hesitantly asked. She was struggling to keep a roof overhead. To feed a kid. Maybe to her it did matter.

Her brows furrowed together. "Does it buy happiness? I don't think so. That comes," her fingers brushed against her chest, right between her perfect breasts. "That comes from within."

He didn't know if he agreed with that concept, but… "Are you happy, Ruby Mae?" he asked. He wanted to be the one to make her happy. That mattered more to him than money.

"Right now?" She leaned toward him, her long, slender fingers brushing against his chest. "Yes," she whispered. "I'm very happy," she told him, brushing her mouth against his. "Thank you for this,

Virgil." She slid her fingers into his hair as she leaned into him. "For everything," she added, angling her mouth over his, pressing her body closer.

And then she was kissing him. And he was kissing her back. His fingers sliding into her hair, pulling her closer. If that was even possible. And—

"Mo-om!" the brat yelled from the other side of the boat. "Come quick!"

She pulled away from him, looking as dazed as he felt. Her fingers brushed against her trembling lips. Her eyes hazy with desire.

"Mom!" the brat wailed again, and she found her bearings, shooting off the bench.

And with a beaten-down sigh, Virgil watched her depart.

Chapter 7

Ruby Mae scrambled around the deck to the other side. They were on-board a boat that most likely cost three times what her house did. When Brandon called out like he had, she had to move. *Fast.*

"Mo-om, come quick. Now!"

"I'm coming!"

"This better be good, brat." With a palm on Ruby Mae's shoulder, Virgil joined her. Together they stopped short of her son.

Ruby Mae let out a small sigh of relief. And joy.

Relief he hadn't broken anything. Except maybe that impenetrable wall he'd built around himself since his father had died. Joy because standing by the edge of the boat was a carefree, seven-year-old, gripping a bowed fishing pole in both hands. His eyes, so much like his father's, glittered with excitement. He jumped from foot to foot. "I got one! I *got* one!" he exclaimed.

And a lump of emotion clogged her throat.

"Well, *shee-it*." Virgil's curse slipped out as he slid into the seat beside her son. "You surely did."

"*Shee-it*," her son repeated the curse like a myna bird and Ruby

Mae would have corrected him – should have corrected *both* of them – except…

"Okay, son." Virgil leaned close, his arm surrounding her boy.

And her heart slid up into her throat.

Virgil's big hands wrapped around her son's smaller ones. "Let's reel this baby in."

"Ooh!" Maisey exclaimed from the nearby seat. "I have to get my camera out for this!"

Ruby Mae didn't need a picture to preserve the image in front of her.

Son. Virgil had called Brandon *son*. And Brandon had looked up at him with such innocent excitement in his eyes, his body quivering with joy, and Ruby Mae's chest hurt so bad, she could hardly breathe.

"Give it a little tug now," Virgil coached. "That's how your granddaddy taught your daddy and me."

Ruby Mae's eyes blurred with tears.

"Come on, Brandon, honey, reel him in!" Maisey called out. "I think that one's gonna break my record."

"Come on, son, just a few more tugs and he's yours."

"He's gonna get away!" Brandon cried out, frantically winding in the reel.

"You got him. He ain't goin' anywhere. You just need to wind him in." Virgil reached for the net. "Reel him in a little closer now." He leaned over the rail, snagging Brandon's fish. "Hoo-ee!" he yelled like a native Tennessean. "I told ya' you could do it!"

"I did it, Mom! I did it!" Brandon jumped around, his arms pumping wildly. "I did it!"

"It's a big one, too," Virgil said, handing the prize to Brandon. He patted him on the back. "Good job, son!"

"Get close, you two. I wanna picture."

And through the blur of tears, Ruby Mae watched Virgil wrap an arm around her son, and Brandon lean into him as he proudly held up his catch.

A father/son moment.

A bittersweet moment for Ruby Mae, because she knew Willie Lee would have wanted this for Brandon. And he'd be proud.

"Perfect!" Maisey replied, shooting off a few more pictures.

And Ruby Mae fought the emotion rolling over her. The pain of all she'd lost. The tantalizing glimpse of a future she could have. And her son happy. That one really did it.

"Mom, look! Look what I caught. Mom?" Her son's easy-going smile disappeared. His shoulders sagged. "Mom?"

Virgil's smile faded, too. His brows drew together. "Ruby Mae?"

She swiped her palms over her wet cheeks.

"Mom?" Brandon's voice grew soft, uncertain. His excitement transforming to concern.

Virgil gently took Brandon's catch from him. Stowed it as Ruby Mae turned to escape to the other side of the boat.

"Mo-om!"

"Here, honey. You stay with me," Maisey told her son. "Your mom will be okay."

Virgil followed Ruby Mae. His fingers wrapped around her arm, stopping her before she'd gotten very far. He turned her slowly toward him. "What's the matter? I thought you'd be happy."

"I am."

"You got a weird way of showing it."

"I'm fine." Ruby Mae swiped her fingers across her tear-stained cheeks.

"Yeah, I can see that. Look. Ruby Mae," he took a step closer, his solid strength beckoning to her. "This isn't what I had in mind for this afternoon."

Her emotions were out of control. As was she. "You didn't plan on Brandon erupting all over you?" She choked out a strangled bark of laughter. "Or his momma having a complete meltdown?"

One corner of his mouth curled up into one of the sexiest smile she'd ever seen. And she felt that old familiar tug deep in her body. The one she hadn't felt for two years. "She can *melt down* all over me anytime." He reached out, his fingers gently brushing a lock of hair from her wet cheek before he slid them into her hair. "You wanna tell me what really happened?"

What did she say? That seeing him with her son bonding in a father/son moment, that when he, with his blond hair and blue eyes could pass as Brandon's father nearly undid her. And how about how guilty she felt for even thinking it. Or did she say how happy, how proud Willie Lee would be to see his son acting like a happy, well-adjusted seven year old. And since she wasn't sure she even understood what she was feeling, she tilted her head. Dislodged his fingers and turned away from him. She wrapped her arms around her knotted middle. "I think I'd rather not."

"What if I beg?" His voice was soft. Rough. Sexy. Awareness rippled through her as he lifted her hair. Placed a gentle kiss on the exposed skin at the back of her neck. It sent a cascade of tingles shimmering down her spine. "I'm really good at begging," he told her, nuzzling her throat. He wrapped his arms around her. His hands slid down low on her belly as he pulled her back against his warm, solid chest.

Unable to resist, she melted against him. She dropped her head to his shoulder. "You won't like what you'll get," she softly told him, her head lolling to one side, offering up more skin.

"I like what I've got right now just fine." And he backed that up with a growl of approval as his fingers slowly spread wide and low over her abdomen and his mouth and tongue teased her neck and shoulder.

His outrageous seduction was working its magic. Or maybe it was just the man. Or maybe it was the promise of more. Whatever it was, Ruby Mae savored the contact. The feeling of comfort and *rightness* she found wrapped in his warm embrace. "Virgil," she exhaled his name.

"I know, I know," he grumbled, halting his seduction. "C'mon."

They walked to the other side of the boat. To where Brandon stood close to Maisey. Worry and apprehension pinched her son's features.

"She's okay, brat." Virgil eased her son's worry. "Just got a little dirt in her eye." And then he eased her apprehension, lifting her face in his palms. "We fish. You sit, okay?" he told her, giving her a gentle kiss before pressing her down into the soft, leather seat.

She nodded her head. Looked at her son. She should be explaining. Or apologizing. "I'm good," she softly told him, offering what she hoped was a reassuring smile. She brushed her fingers through his scruffy blond hair, and he let her.

"All right." Virgil rubbed his palms together. "Let's fish."

He handed Maisey her rod. Baited Brandon's and then one for

himself He instructed her son as he cast the line. "Like that," he said as he adjusted Brandon's grip on the rod. "Release it like you would one of those paint tubes you like to throw at me. That's it. Good job!" He patted Brandon's back, his hand lingering and Ruby Mae settled into her seat by Maisey.

A sense of contentment washed over her, warm as the sun shining down on them. Calming as the gentle rock of the boat on the water. It was the first peace she'd felt in a long, long time.

"You really knew my daddy?" Brandon hesitantly asked a while later.

"Yeah, I did. A long time ago. When we were little, we were best friends." Virgil adjusted the tension on Brandon's reel. "Your daddy could run." He chuckled at an old memory. "Nobody could catch him. He was the fastest kid in the whole town. And he had an arm on him. Bet you got your throwing arm from him."

"You think?"

"I know so. You throw a sinker just like him."

Ruby Mae listened as Virgil spoon-fed her son exactly what he needed. What they both needed to hear. That Willie Lee was gone, but not forgotten.

"He was always the catcher on our baseball teams at school. Guarded home plate like a momma bear guards her cubs." Virgil smiled at a memory only he could see.

"Was he good?"

"He was the best, kid. Nobody stole on him. Nobody got by him."

Brandon's chest expanded with pride.

Virgil dug into a box filled with lures and bait. "See this?" He held up a tiny jar to Brandon. "This is your granddaddy's secret bait.

Guaranteed to catch a fish every time. Your daddy and I caught more fish with this than anything else."

"You really fished with my daddy?"

"You don't believe me?" Virgil didn't wait for a reply. He attached his bait, cast his reel, and settled in beside her son while Ruby Mae rested her head against Maisey's shoulder. "Your granddaddy, he loved to fish the streams. Especially the Vermin Creek. But your daddy… your daddy loved this lake." Virgil looked over his shoulder at her. Gave her a reassuring smile. And a wink. "Said he found everything he ever wanted down here."

A tremulous smile touched Ruby Mae's lips as she fondly remembered all the nights she and Willie Lee had come down here. How Willie Lee would throw down a blanket in the bed of his old truck and they'd look up at the stars. More times they made out than actual star gazing, and it had been by this lake, after the fiasco with Virgil that Ruby Mae had given herself to Willie Lee.

That it was Virgil – the man who'd nearly come between them relaying that tale to her son – that it was Virgil reaching her son… She breathed deep. Could Maisey be right? Would Willie Lee not really care that it was Virgil who now made her happy? That it was Virgil bonding with his son? Slowly she breathed out.

Maybe it didn't matter so much after all.

* * *

The invitation to stay for dinner had come out of the blue.

It had been when Virgil had accepted it that all hell had broken loose. When Brandon had reverted from what Virgil had thought was a happy seven-year-old to the obnoxious brat he'd been when he'd first met the demon child.

"Mom! You can't do that. Uncle Billy is coming." The brat blocked the front door.

"Uncle Billy knows Virgil," Ruby Mae told him. Brushing by him, she ushered Maisey and the brat – and Virgil – inside. She led the way to a cozy kitchen with a round oak table. She pulled out a chair for Maisey. "Sit," she instructed. Pointed to another one for him, instructing him to do the same, which Virgil walked to but didn't obey, choosing to stand behind it. Next she went to the refrigerator. Pulled out a bunch of vegetables and a few foil-covered dishes.

It was fascinating to watch her.

When Virgil had been growing up, Marilee had employed a black cook – Marietta Wilcox from up on the Brandywine– to prepare their meals. When he'd been married, Rachel had her French chef who did all the preparations. Watching Ruby Mae do it was… erotic.

He was fascinated with her hands. God! Those talented, artistic hands were just as talented here in the kitchen as with a paintbrush and canvas. He couldn't take his eyes off them. Or off of her. How she blended and coaxed ingredients together. And how they exploded with flavor and enticing aromas when she set them over a fire. Hell, Virgil was getting high on the mouth-watering smells. Getting a hard-on just watching her chop. And stir. And lean over a pot. And shut her eyes.

He was captivated by her breasts; how they pushed up against the tank top she wore as she slowly inhaled the scents rising up between them. How she breathed in the flavors, like they were the very essence of life. And how she smiled with satisfaction. Her head slowly falling back as if she were lifting her face to the man who'd just pleased her.

It was foreplay.

It was the sexiest thing Virgil had ever seen. And he wanted it. He wanted her.

"Table's set." The brat stomped on Virgil's foot as he pushed by him.

"Ow," Virgil muttered, rubbing his insole.

Ruby Mae turned around. Loose curls framed her flushed cheeks. The heavy-lidded pleasure which had transformed her seconds ago evaporated. Her brows drew together as she stared at the table. Set for *four* people. "Brandon! I said, set the table."

"I did." A white line of displeasure ringed his pressed-tight lips, a stark white bulls-eye against his sunburned face.

"When we have guests, young man, we set them a place." She grabbed another placemat, snapped it down on the table. Dropped a plate down on top it. She followed it up with a fork, a knife, a spoon, a napkin and a glass. Then she punctuated her point by dragging the spare chair over to the table, the legs scraping against the stone floor in protest.

"I didn't invite him," the brat growled.

"No, you didn't. *I* did," she tersely told her son. She grabbed four wine glasses and a bottle of wine, which she thrust into Virgil's hands. "Open this."

"I'm not eating with him." The brat crossed his arms over his chest, his beady-eyed glare mutinous.

Virgil wondered, how did she put up with his shit day in and day out?

"Then you'll eat in your room." Her arms crossed over her chest as she stared down at the little hellion.

"What the hell's goin' on in here?" Billy Ray walked in the back door. "I could hear you halfway across the yard." His eyes narrowed to slits when they settled on Virgil.

"She won't let me eat here!" the brat wailed, throwing himself at

117

his savior. He wrapped one arm around Billy's legs, thrusting out the other one, pointing an accusing finger at Virgil. "And all because of *him*!"

"That's not true!" Virgil replied, before snapping his mouth shut. Choosing instead to watch. As Billy moved the brat toward the table and pulled out the kid's chair.

The brat climbed up, looking all smug and victorious.

Virgil's brows furrowed as Billy walked to the walk-in pantry. Rooted inside it – *like he lived here* – before returning with a snack for the kid. *Like he was the head of the house*. And Virgil knew. He didn't belong. He was an interloper.

"I think I should go." He turned to leave.

"No." Ruby Mae touched his arm. "I invited you. You stay."

* * *

He stayed. But it wasn't a pleasant meal. Not with forks banging and dishes clanking instead of pleasant conversation being exchanged. Maisey and Billy left out the back door while Ruby Mae cleared off the dishes. The brat shot out of his chair headed for the front of the house.

With an hasty excuse to Ruby Mae, Virgil followed the brat.

"Hey," he called out as the brat pushed open the front door. "You can help me get the rest of your junk out of my car." With a hand firmly clamped down on the brat's shoulders, he walked them off the porch and down the sidewalk to his car.

"I didn't leave nothin' in your car."

Virgil reached in. Picked up a stray peanut. Held it up like it was the crucial piece of evidence that would ensure him a conviction.

With a huff of frustration, the brat yanked open the car door and leaned in. "There," he growled, holding the few pieces he'd found fisted in his hand.

Virgil pointed to the steering wheel. "Under the driver's seat."

The kid glared at him, but did his bidding.

"You know, kid, if I had a momma nice as you have, I'd act the way she wanted me to."

"What do you know." The kid crawled out of the car. Slammed the door and dropped the nuts and wrappers on the ground. "You're a wuss."

And you're an antagonistic little demon, Virgil wanted to fire back, but held his tongue. He bent down and picked up the mess and tossed it back into the car. He was tired from the whole day, and in no mood to fight with the kid. They'd fought enough about dinner to ruin it. And he was in no mood to leave Ruby Mae another mess to clean up from her front yard.

"You're probably right." Virgil leaned up against the side of his car. The stench of sunbaked puke a brutal reminder he'd be riding with the top down for the foreseeable future.

The brat turned toward the road.

Virgil snagged his collar with his fingertips before he got far. "Not so fast, brat."

The kid turned. "What?" he all but growled.

"You happy you ruined your momma's dinner?" Virgil shook his head side to side. "You have no idea how damn lucky you are. Know what I think?" He aimed a finger at the brat's chest. "I think you're a brat who doesn't give a shit about anybody but yourself and what *you* want."

The kid's lip quivered, but only for a second before he rushed Virgil, knocking him back against the door of car with the force of his anger. "If you gave a shit," the brat spit out, his blue eyes blazing with rage. "You'd know my name is *Brandon*!" he yelled, as his little fists pummeled Virgil's belly.

"Enough." Virgil wrapped his arms around the kid and absorbed the blows. He hunched over the kid and pulled him close. "That's enough!" he growled, not letting go. Even when the kid stopped. With his head hanging low sucking in air, he stood in Virgil's embrace. And Virgil held onto him, none too steady on his own feet. Unsure what the hell to do.

The kid's anger had shocked him. And humbled him.

"You're absolutely right, Brandon. I'm sorry." He walked the kid back a few steps. Turned him and together they sank down on the edge of the grass. Both were still breathing heavy. "I should never have done that. And I apologize."

The kid's face was flushed red with anger. His muscles were tense and Virgil's heart went out to him.

He'd been this kid. This lonely, angry kid.

Virgil leaned forward, resting his arms on his knees. "Look, I know how you feel, Brandon. Believe me, I do." He sucked in a breath. "I know what it's like not to have a dad around."

The kid swung his head to Virgil. His gaze sharp.

"Your daddy would never have left you, if he'd had a choice." The jury was still out on Vincent Push, though. That man had a choice. And he's chosen to stay away. Virgil picked up a stone. Tossed it out onto the drive.

The kid mimicked his actions. His stone dinged off the BMW's fender.

"Look." Virgil adjusted the kid's aim. "I'm not here trying to take your daddy's place. Nobody can do that. I just wanna spend some time with you and your momma."

The kid picked up another stone. "Why?" he demanded, tossing it, this time binging off Virgil's ankle.

"Ow! Will you stop that?" Virgil rubbed his ankle. "You wanna throw something, how 'bout I take you down to the park and you can take your frustration out on a baseball?"

"You'd do that?"

The awe in the kid's response surprised the hell out of Virgil. Intense yearning burned in the kid's eyes and Virgil wondered if it had been that same look Wilber Lee Shove had seen in Virgil's eyes when the old gardener had allowed Virgil to tag along with his son when they'd gone fishing.

"Yeah, I would," Virgil told him, suddenly wanting to spend time with the kid. "We could go tomorrow afternoon. You play baseball?" he asked. All seven-year-olds played ball.

Brandon hunched his shoulders. "No," he mumbled, digging his sneaker into the grass. "Mom throws like a girl."

"She's supposed to throw like a girl. She is a girl." And a hell of a girl, in Virgil's opinion.

Anger jutted out the brat's chin. "It's a dumb game. Only wussies play."

"If that's the case, then a lot of wussies knock the hell out of a lot of balls. Your daddy included. You want to go to the batting cages, or not?"

The kid picked up another stone. Tossed it before finally asking, "Why'd you stop bein' my dad's best friend?"

Virgil stared at the kid. How the hell did he answer that? *Because we were both hot for your momma. And only I was willing to cross a line that*

121

shouldn't have been crossed to get her. Virgil picked up his own stone. Tossed it. "I guess we drifted apart," he answered. More like lust and deceit had driven a wedge between the two of them that they'd never been able to bridge.

He owed Willie Lee an apology.

He'd make it up to the man by helping his son. And maybe then, the slate would be less stained.

* * *

"Where's Brandon?" Ruby Mae asked Billy as he came in the back door from taking Maisey home.

"Outside. With Virgil."

"Oh." Ruby Mae busied herself putting away the dishes she'd washed. All the while she could feel her neighbor's dark eyes raking over her.

"You might as well turn around. I've already seen the look."

She held the serving platter to her chest like a shield against his interrogation. "What look?"

"That same look you had on your face in high school when you were ripping Willie Lee's heart out."

She dipped her head. "I don't know what you're talking about." But she did. Oh, she did. And those same feelings were swirling around deep inside her now. Pushing through her veins. Making her hot. Bothered. Making her want for something only Virgil could give.

"Yeah, you do. It was written all over your face then. It's written all over your face now. I can see it with my own two eyes. But just remember, Ruby Mae. He may be actin' like a good ol' mountain boy come home to his humble roots, but he's always gonna be Neiman-Marcus. And you'll always be Wal-Mart."

She spun around. Suddenly angry. "Thank you so much for your assessment. Do you think I don't know we're different? I know exactly what Virgil Push is."

"Do you?"

Unease skittered down her spine. Billy Ray was bullheaded when he thought he knew what was best, but he had an open mind. Did he know something she didn't?

"Look." He breathed deep. Let it out just as slow. "I don't wanna see you get hurt."

"I'm not going to get hurt."

"Yeah, you are. You're just too much in love with the bastard to realize it." Billy took a step closer. "You think he's gonna stay here?" His hand lifted, his finger pointing to her small kitchen. In her small house. On the wrong side of the Shiner's Trail. "You think he's gonna give up his fancy townhouse on the west side of town to live here? Do you forget where he comes from? Where he's been? *What* he's been? *What* he's done?"

"Is that it? You just judge him and declare him guilty?"

"He *is* guilty!"

"So am I then. Do I get judged the same way? Sentenced the same way?" God! She'd been more guilty than Virgil. She'd been the one willing to give up everything for one night with him.

"He was all wrong for you back in high school. He's still all wrong for you."

"Why? Because I'm *Wal-Mart*?"

His lips pressed down tight. Anger flushed his cheeks. "There's no talking to you when you get like this." He pushed by her toward the back door.

"Billy." She couldn't let him leave mad. She knew he was only watching out for her. The same way he had when Willie Lee had gotten sick. And every day since. And he did it with the purest of motives. He was a good man. "Did you register for your classes?"

"Yeah," he grudgingly replied, his voice gruff. "I'll be busier than hell, but I'll finally get my degree."

She slowly nodded her head up and down. "Maybe there'll be an opening on the force here in town." She didn't know what she'd do if he and Maisey moved away. They were her family. Not by blood. But in the way that mattered most. By love.

"Your boyfriend tell you that?" His dark brows drew together. "That he's going to hire me?"

"No!"

"Is that the price he'll pay for the information he wants?"

"No! But you tell me this." Ruby Mae stepped closer. "Why won't you give him the names he wants?" The names of the girls Virgil needed to take Office Clive down.

"You tell me," Billy threw her words back at her. "How do *you* know he's going to use them to put Clive away? How do you know he's not going to use them to intimidate those girl's families into forgetting what happened to their daughters? The bastard's richer than God! He could do that. Easily."

"Because I trust him," she quickly responded, suddenly realizing that she did.

"Then why didn't *you* give him the names? Huh? You know them as well as I do."

Because he'd been so sweet with her. And so good with Brandon this afternoon. And Brandon had responded.

Billy barked out a humorless laugh. "You're not *falling* in love with him, Ruby Mae. You're already there."

Chapter 8

"Did you issue that citation to that Shove woman?"

"That's not an agenda item," Virgil told his mother. "This special meeting *you* called, *without* my consent," a point that still pissed him off, "is about changing the town name."

"And it's about my mascot idea!" Sonny added, jumping up from his seat. He ran to the corner of Virgil's office. Pushed forward a large figure draped in a sheet.

Virgil scowled. "What the hell is that? Better yet, how the hell did you get it in my office?"

"If you would be on time for meeting," Marilee said, "you'd know how. And when."

"Oh, excuse me, *mother*, but I have no control over old man Patterson's cows when they're running loose on the Dinnerbell Road."

She lifted her chin. "There are other ways to the courthouse."

Not when he'd been surrounded by a hundred milling dairy cows and the Patterson boy's pickup trucks – all eight of them – blocking the road. "Let's make this quick." Virgil glanced down at his watch. He still had two more meetings after this to attend to before he'd be able to take Brandon to the batting cages.

"*This* is your job," Marilee reminded him.

"No, mother. My job is *not* to rename a town perfectly happy with the one it has."

"Wyatt?" Marilee turned toward Edgar Wyatt, Junior, the whiskey baron. "You agree with me." It wasn't a question. And it wasn't up for debate either.

"Marilee," Edgar hedged, looking suddenly uncomfortable. "I'm not so," he dragged the words out, carefully weighing them so they'd balance on the thin line he was walking. God forbid he took a definitive stand.

Virgil almost felt sorry for the man. Marilee was impossible on a good day. "Enough," he told her. "Once and for all, there's a motion on the floor—"

"No, there's not! Not yet," Marilee told him. "I haven't had a chance to state my vision."

"*Vision?* Isn't it enough you want to change our name, our identity? What vision can you add to that that would possibly make us vote, *yes?*"

"The one where we add an artist colony."

"Artist colony? Where?" Virgil demanded.

There was that viperous look in her eye. The one she got right before she struck. "A good spot would be right on the other side of the Shiner's Trail."

Virgil loosened his tie. Leaned forward on his elbows. "So you just plan on tossing those families out of their homes and setting up shops where they used to live?"

"Yes," she confidently replied.

"We can't do that!" Davis's eyes were bugging out behind his gold-rimmed glasses. "That's discrimination! Eviction without due cause."

"Marilee." Edgar leaned close to her. "You said nothing about evicting people."

Had the whiskey baron actually considered Marilee's request? Had they actually had a conversation about it?

"Where are you getting these artists to *colonize*?" Virgil asked, wondering if she'd ever see the irony of throwing a gifted artist like Ruby Mae out of her house to make room for an artist of Marilee's choosing. Not that she really could do that. Not on his watch anyway.

"Why from France, of course."

"Of course. You know you're crazy." Not waiting for an argument, he looked at the group. "Any questions? Good," he quickly added, not giving Marilee any chance to sneak through a name change. Or an eviction.

Marilee grabbed the gavel. "All in favor of changing the name of our town to Ro*dént*—"

"Excuse me!" Virgil grabbed it back. "*I'm* the one in charge here." He sat the gavel on the floor beside his chair. Passed out pieces of paper to each member.

"What's this for?" Marilee demanded.

"To cast your vote in private. That's why it's called a secret ballot."

"A simple *verbal* yea or nay is all that's needed." She narrowed an eye as she stared at each member of Council. "A simple yea from *everyone* here is all that's needed to pass it unanimously. Isn't that right, gentlemen?"

Davis didn't meet her stare, worrying the cuff of his shirt with his fingers instead. Sonny was nervously petting whatever the hell he had stuffed under that bed sheet. Edgar looked like he wanted to be anywhere but beside Marilee. She could easily bulldoze them if Virgil gave her half a chance – and half a second. He tapped his fingers on the conference table drawing their attention – and hopefully their favor to him. "Motion is out on the table. Everyone in favor of Marilee's proposal to change the name of the town, vote *yes* on the paper. Against it, vote *no.*"

Pencils scratched across the papers. Virgil collected the votes. Opened them one by one. He picked up the gavel, smacked it down on the walnut table with a resounding crack. "Three-to-two. Motion denied."

"Let me see those!" Marilee stretched across the table to grab them from Virgil's hand.

"What?" He held them out of reach. "Don't you trust me?"

Her eyes said it all. She didn't.

He didn't care. He didn't trust her either. But he showed her them anyhow. Enjoyed the tiny victory when she realized she'd been legitimately defeated. "Moving on." He glanced down his watch. "Sonny, what do you have for us?"

"Only the new mascot for the town," the man proudly told the group before pulling the sheet away revealing a hideous wildebeest worthy of a low-budget horror flick.

"What the hell is that?"

"I knew it would grab you!" Sonny hooted.

"Grab me? I nearly pissed my pants." Virgil took a wary step closer.

Sonny was a taxidermist. Apparently not a very good one. Or one with a weird, twisted Frankenstein complex because the beast that stood before Virgil was a rat, best as he could tell. One that stood nearly six feet tall. Poised for attack with outstretched paws the size of dinner plates. And a snarling mouth. With yellow fangs. Virgil sniffed the air. "What the hell is that smell?" He took a step closer. "What the hell kind of fur is this?" It appeared to be patched together. And of indiscriminate origin.

"It's Tennessee road kill," Sonny proudly announced.

Virgil snatched back his hand. "*Jee-suz!*" He wiped it down the side of his leg.

"See?" Sonny spun the hideous beast around on his wheeled feet. "He's even got a recycle and reuse emblem," the lunatic pointed out. And sure enough on its ass was painted the familiar green triangle akin to recycling and reusing.

"That's not recycling!" Davis exclaimed, his eyes wide. "He can't use that!"

"You can't be serious!" Marilee huffed out, still clutching Percy with his pink diamond-encrusted collar and matching pink toenails to her chest. And for the first time in probably forever, Virgil had to agree with her.

Sonny couldn't seriously think they'd consider this wildebeest as the town mascot. "Thank you, Sonny," he told the man. "We'll take it under advisement." Virgil returned to his seat. Smoothed his tie over his chest. "Moving on—"

"Sir?" Davis leaned closer to Virgil. His eyes darted left and right. "This could have possibilities," he spoke under his breath.

"You can't be serious."

"Not like that," Davis discreetly waggled his fingers toward Sonny's pet, his face a picture of distaste. "But something of that nature."

"What's wrong with Mickey just like he is?" Sonny demanded, wrapping a protective arm around his pet.

Virgil held up his arm, palm out. "Do not even think of copy infringing the name. Come up with something else," he told the man before turning back to Davis. "What are you thinking?"

"We could have Manchester Concrete make us a mouse mold." Davis eyed Sonny's rat with distaste. "A *cute* mouse mold."

"I like it," Virgil replied as an idea took shape in his head. "And tell him nothing more than three feet high."

"Agreed."

"And nothing scary. We'll need at least a dozen. "

"For schools and civic groups to adopt and paint," Davis added his thoughts.

"Yeah. And we can roll them out at the Rat Races."

The Rat Races were Rodent's version of a Community Day. A time when the whole town came together to enjoy rides, games, crafts, and of course, the rat races – a race where they could enter their own pet rodent, or bet on ones provided courtesy of the local pet store.

"It'll pull the whole town together."

"We are *not* glorifying rats!" Marilee slapped her palm down on the table. "We are ditching our vermin image once and for all. We're changing the name of the town. And we are going to be a French art colony!"

"Didn't you hear?" Virgil asked. "That motion got shot down." He looked at the group. "All in favor of sponsoring Davis's mouse contest and branding Rodent with a mouse image say *yes*."

A trio of *yes*'s resounded.

"All those opposed?"

Marilee opposed. Vehemently. For twenty long minutes.

When he could take no more, Virgil banged the gavel down on the table. "I make a motion to adjourn."

"I'm not finished!"

"Oh, we're finished," Virgil told her. Edgar was already headed for the door. Davis was gathering up his papers. Sonny was sulking with his rat, and Marilee was staring at him like she was sighting him down the barrel of a gun.

"Have you issued that Shove woman her citation?"

All heads stopped. And turned. And stared.

"That's not on the agenda," Virgil told her, pushing back his own chair. He stood, knowing freedom was only a few steps away. "Do I have to tell you again? Meeting's adjourned."

"Wait! We're not finished here," Marilee told the group who were nearly running from Virgil's office. She grabbed Virgil's arm when he tried to follow suit. "Why not?"

He didn't pretend to understand, nor did he want to explain why he hadn't issued that citation. "I don't have time for this. I'm late for another meeting." A meeting with Chief Rutledge. A meeting where Virgil wouldn't be able to present proof positive of Clive's misdoings because he'd been unsuccessful in getting any names. From Maisey. Or Billy. Or Ruby Mae.

"Oh, sure you have another meeting," Marilee sarcastically replied.

And before she could threaten him, or go after Ruby Mae herself, Virgil stopped. Turned toward her. "Leave a message with Emma to put the citation status on next month's regular meeting agenda. And *mother*," he stepped closer. Pointed a finger at her chest.

133

"I said *regular* meeting. No secret meeting behind my back. No secret filibustering. No special meeting. And at the regular monthly meeting we'll address the statuses of *all* outstanding citations." That should buy Virgil a little time to figure out a way to allow Ruby May to keep her shop.

And keep her off of Marilee's radar.

* * *

Ruby Mae had been enjoying a steady stream of customers. Even anticipated with the sales she had today of meeting all her monthly bills and having a little left over for Brandon. That was until the silver Lexus pulled up in her front yard and Marilee Push walked into her shop, scattering her potential customers and future sales like dandelion seeds in a strong wind. Why was she here? *Salvation* wasn't in her neighborhood. "Is there something I can help you with?" Ruby Mae asked. *Like showing you the door?*

"I doubt it," Marilee told her, as she walked through the shop. She picked up pieces of pottery, examining them with a critical eye before sitting them down with no compliment, or comment. She inspected Ruby Mae's hand-painted glass bowls and vases, too. Fingered the different pieces of jewelry on display. She obviously wasn't interested in them to purchase, which was all the more reason to question. Why was she was here?

"Well, if there is..." Ruby Mae prompted.

The woman lifted her head. And Ruby Mae shivered, suddenly chilled.

"I see you are still in business."

The shiver turned to a shudder. Ruby Mae gripped the edge of the counter. Was Marilee here about the citation? The one Virgil had yet to issue? The one that loomed dark and ominous over her happiness and life as she knew it?

But he'd said he'd burned it. Had it just been a lie he'd told to win her over? A lie, like before, to cover an ulterior agenda, this time one that included his mother? Ruby Mae had trusted him! Enough to let him have her son for the afternoon. Had that been part of the plan, too? Get Brandon away? Have mother do his dirty work?

Ruby Mae felt sick.

Marilee walked to the wall where Ruby Mae's paintings hung. She leaned in closer to get a better look. "Mediocre… at best," she said.

And then Ruby Mae felt anger. White hot anger. Burning through her veins. Firing up her own temper. "Mediocre? Really?" She wasn't great. But she was good. And she wouldn't stand here and be insulted by a woman who wielded her position in society – one she'd gotten courtesy of her husband's money – like a scepter to beat down the less fortunate.

Marilee gave her a sidelong look of disgust and Ruby Mae wasn't sure if it was a reaction to her sarcasm, or her paintings. "I've seen one of these."

"Then someone you know has excellent taste." Ruby Mae wondered why she couldn't just shut up. Be sweet. Grovel at the woman's feet like the woman demanded.

"Hanging on the wall. In my son's office."

Ruby Mae's hand went to her chest. Virgil hung her painting in his office? She'd thought his purchase had been a mercy buy, one to be stuffed in a closet somewhere to be forgotten. She was surprised. And touched.

Marilee curled her lip as she lifted those cold blue eyes to Ruby Mae. Eyes the exact shade of blue as Virgil's. How could his be so warm and caring, and this woman's so cold? "Obviously neither one of you has taste in paintings, or otherwise."

"How dare you come into my shop—"

"You look exactly like your father," Marilee talked over Ruby Mae's outrage.

"*What?*"

"Your father. Percival Randolph Stratton the Third."

"I know his name," Ruby Mae snapped.

"You look just like him."

"So I've been told." All his daughters did.

She huffed out her disgust. "You may look like him," Marilee lifted her chin. "But you are your *mother's* daughter."

"And thank God for that," Ruby Mae fired back.

"Did he give you the money for this place?"

Ruby Mae lifted her own chin. "Do you really want me to answer that?" They both knew her father. Knew how he got his money – and what he did with it – and it wasn't sharing it with his family. Even to help his daughter desperate for an income to start a shop that could save her house. "Is that why you're here? To discuss my shop? Because if it is, you can leave. Now." Ruby Mae stepped closer. "And if you want to discuss my father, you wasted your time coming here." Percival Randolph Stratton and his lack of respect for his wife and his children was something Ruby Mae was not going to discuss. Especially with Marilee Push.

"We're not through here. Not by a long shot."

"Oh, yes, we are, Marilee." And Ruby Mae watched the woman's nostrils flare as she sucked in a sharp breath at Ruby Mae's familiar use of her first name. "And you can leave. Now," she added, and warily watched as Marilee walked out the front door without another word.

"What was all that about?" Maisey asked from the back door of the shop.

"I haven't a clue." Ruby Mae had plenty of theories, but none she wanted to share. She stepped closer to the front window. Let out a breath when the silver Lexus left the driveway.

"Can't be anything good," Maisey went on.

"I agree." Marilee Push hadn't stopped in to browse.

"Maybe she thought she'd find the mayor here."

Ruby Mae turned around. Stared at her neighbor. "Why would she care?"

"You mean aside from the fact that he's her rich son and she likes to run things? Him included."

Ruby Mae walked back to the counter. "Virgil's a grown man. He can go wherever he wants. Do whatever he wants."

"Can he?" Maisey asked pushing her walker further into the store. "Maybe Mama Push isn't so much checking up on you as she's checking up on him."

* * *

With Brandon in the seat beside him, Virgil crossed over the Trail, past the abandoned distillery and a dilapidated house in serious need of a bulldozer to raze it. Three skinny teenagers in baggy jeans with chains hanging from their belt loops leaned against the side of it smoking what Virgil could only hope was a cigarette. Tattoos covered their arms. Piercings decorated their eyebrows, noses, and ears. From the insolent way they were eyeing Virgil, they were trouble. Or looking for it.

Brandon sat up straighter when he spotted them. He lifted his hand. Fisted it, moving his fingers in what Virgil could only think was some kind of secret sign. Worse, one of the teenagers signed back.

Virgil slipped his sunglasses down his nose. "You know those kids?"

"They're my friends," the brat replied. A little too defensively.

"They're teenagers," Virgil pointed out the obvious.

"So?" The kid's jaw jutted out.

Virgil frowned. They were teenagers looking for trouble. Or bringing it with them. What were they doing hanging around with a second grader? Unless they were—

"They live around you?"

"No."

"Then how'd you meet them?"

The kid's lips flattened. His body went stiff. His eyes squinted as he stared straight ahead.

"They go to your school?" Virgil knew they didn't. "They ride your bus?"

"*No*," he pushed out the one word through pursed lips.

"Then how'd you meet them?" Virgil demanded.

The kid swung his head around, his eyes burning with anger. His cheeks flushed red and not just from the afternoon spent at the batting cages. "We hang out together, okay?"

"No, it's not okay."

"You're not my dad!"

"No, I'm not." Virgil turned the car into Ruby Mae's driveway. "But I knew your dad and I know he wouldn't want you hangin' out with those kids. They're bad news."

"You can't tell me what to do!" Brandon yelled, jumping out of the car.

"Brandon?" Ruby Mae rushed out of her shop.

"Hey!" Virgil jumped out of the car. Grabbed the kid before he rounded the front bumper. He pulled him along by the collar of his shirt to the side of the car. He reached into the back seat. "You forgot this." He handed him the bat and ball and glove he'd bought him earlier today.

Glaring, chest heaving, the kid made no move to take his gifts.

Ruby Mae rushed up beside him. "What's going on?" she demanded.

"Take them." Virgil pressed them into the kid's fisted hands. "They're yours."

"Brandon?" She looked from her son to him. "You bought those for him?" she asked before looking back at her son. "Did you say thank you?"

"I hate him!" the kid growled, pushing by her.

"Brandon!"

"Let him go."

She looked at Virgil, then back at her son. "What's going on?"

And how did Virgil answer that? He knew the kid didn't hate him. They'd had a great time at the cages. Virgil had even gotten to see the happy seven-year old surface again – the one usually buried under a hard shell of anger.

"What happened?" Ruby Mae demanded.

"Nothing."

"Then why is he acting like that?"

"He's just being a brat," Virgil told her. He looked into her pinched features. "What's wrong with you?"

"Nothing," she curtly told him.

"Something's wrong." He knew enough about women to recognize the sign. And the tone.

"You just missed your mother."

Jee-suz. "Marilee was here? Did she say anything? What'd she want?" he asked, wishing the words didn't sound so rushed. So demanding. So damn *suspicious.*

Ruby Mae's eyes were trained on her son. "Yes, no, and I don't know."

He scowled. "What?"

She turned back to Virgil. "Yes, she was here. No, she didn't say anything. And I have no idea what she wanted." She lifted her hand to her hair. Pushed damp curls from her forehead. She scowled. "She just walked through the shop checking everything out."

"You sure?"

"*Yes,* I'm sure. She didn't miss anything either. Not a painting on the wall, or a piece of pottery. She checked out everything." Ruby Mae wrapped her arms around her middle.

Obviously her encounter with the Wicked Witch of the West Side of Rodent had shaken her. "Come here." Virgil opened his arms. She stepped closer, and he wrapped his arms around her. Savored the feel of her soft body nestled up against his.

Too quickly, she pulled back. Lifted her head, looked up at him with eyes shadowed with uncertainty. "Why would she come here? I'm hardly her favorite person."

"I'm sure it was nothing," he lied. He knew exactly why his mother had come. And it had everything to do with that damn citation. And he'd take care of it. He'd get Marilee off Ruby Mae's tail. But first, he had to find out what kind of shit Brandon was wading knee-deep into.

"There's a house down by the old distillery. Is it abandoned?"

"There's two or three abandoned down there." Her brows drew together. "Why?"

He shrugged a shoulder, trying for an air of nonchalance. "I saw some teenagers hanging around down there. Didn't look like they belonged over here."

Tension tightened her narrowed eyes. "We have a look now?" she asked, misinterpreting him. "A look that broadcasts to the wealthy we're from the poor side of the Trail?"

Virgil frowned. "That's not what I said."

"That's exactly what you said."

"No, it's not. I said—"

"You said they didn't look like they belonged here. So how did they look, huh?"

"Unkempt, okay? Dirty hair. Big, baggy pants with their crotches hanging down around their knees and most of their underwear showing." Kids looking ages older than any teenager should look with their souls hollowed out from having seen too much, having done too much. But he didn't say that.

She snorted. "Dirty hair and baggy pants? Wow, you just described half the teenage boys walking down *any* street in Rodent."

"Okay. I get what you're implying." He looked over her shoulder to the brat who was sulking on the porch step. He looked back at Ruby Mae. "But I think Brandon knew them."

She inhaled a sharp breath. "Well, you're mistaken."

"I saw him signal them."

"Signal them how?" Her chin jutted up. "Like a wave? Kids wave at each other all the time."

"*No,* it wasn't a wave."

"What then? Like a secret handshake?" She made it sound ridiculous. But Virgil had seen Brandon's hands when he'd responded. He wasn't wrong about this. She crossed her arms over her chest. Glared at him. "You spend one afternoon with my son and you suddenly know him better than I do?" Her thumb stabbed into her chest. "I'm his mother!"

"I know that. And I'm not questioning how your raise your child. I'm just saying those kids are up to no good. They're trouble."

"Billy would know about it if there was anything to worry about. And he'd take care of it."

"Oh, Billy, Billy, *Billy!*" Virgil was sick and tired of hearing about the sainted Billy Ray Trainor. "It always comes back to Billy Ray with you, doesn't it?" And he was pissed. Pissed she wasn't listening to him. Pissed Billy Ray was so damn important to her that she'd chose to believe him over Virgil.

"What's that supposed to mean?"

"It means how the hell did you ever have time for Willie Lee with Billy Ray right next door taking care of everything?"

"How dare you!" She smacked his shoulder with her palm. "How dare you even imply I was ever untrue to Willie Lee!"

And Virgil was blindsided by a memory of her and him behind the football field. Naked to their waists. Neither being true to Willie Lee.

She smacked his shoulder again. "He was my *husband.* The man I *loved.*"

The man she'd chosen over Virgil. And hadn't that always been the problem?

She lunged at him, angrily pushing him back with both palms. "Take your car and your concerns for my family and leave!"

"Ruby Mae," Virgil reached for her.

She pushed his hands aside.

"You know I didn't mean that the way it sounded."

And she stood, chest heaving, glaring at him. Eyes accusing. "And how would I know that? You lied to me before."

"That was fifteen years ago." He plowed his fingers into his hair. Sucked in a harsh breath. "This isn't about us. Or about then. This is about Brandon."

"No! This is about *you*. About *you* making a big name for yourself."

"*No*, it's not."

"Sure it is. Next year is an election year. What better way to get re-elected than by cleaning up the *poor side* of town."

"How can you say that?" He stared at her. Shocked. And dammit! Hurt. "This has nothing to do with getting re-elected." Christ! His mind had been so filled with thoughts of her and the problems they faced with her son, he hadn't even thought about a re-election.

"Just go."

"Ruby Mae, listen to me." He grabbed her arms. Bent his knees so he could look her straight in the eye. "We have a problem."

"We don't have *anything*." She pulled out of his grasp. Turned toward her son.

"Ruby Mae!" He grabbed her arm again.

She spun around. She slapped his hand away. "You stay away from me!" Her eyes were burning with anger, her finger pointed at his chest. "And tell your mother to stay the hell away, too."

Chapter 9

A half-dozen kids were still hanging around the old house when Virgil slowly drove by. Turning into a small intersecting alley, he parked the car, stepped out, and walked back to the side of a house that sat across the street from the one occupied by the kids. Safely concealed by shadow and overgrown shrubs, he watched as they covertly passed things between themselves. As one kid disappeared, another showed up. Who were they? The lawyer-turned-mayor inside him said this was a gang setting up shop here in Rodent, one probably selling drugs.

And Brandon was most likely involved up to his eyeballs. Probably being groomed to be a runner, or a mule.

"Christ," he muttered under his breath. That would kill Ruby Mae.

He took a couple steps closer to get a better look. It was a perfect location really, for selling or distributing, what with the abandoned distillery on one side, and the house Virgil was shadowed by uninhabited on the other. The closest neighbor was far enough down the road not to see their clandestine activities. And it had easy access for the users up on the Brandywine and Ruby Mae's side of the Trail. And contrary to what she might think of him, he knew it was easy access for the people on *his* side of the Trail, too. Just as he knew the upper-class were as guilty of buying drugs as the lower-class.

He scrubbed his palms against his cheeks. Did Billy Ray know? Or was he as clueless as Ruby Mae? Did Chief Rutledge know? How about Officer Clive who regularly patrolled here? Was this how he reeled in his girls? Offer to drop their drug arrest charges in exchange for sexual favors?

And what did Virgil do about all this?

He had to get proof. He had to— "Christ," he cussed under his breath as he caught sight of Brandon walking down the street. Headed right toward those kids.

"Yo, Badass," one kid called Brandon over to him.

Virgil shot across the road and into the yard, grabbing Brandon by the collar.

The brat spun around, his blue eyes churning with anger. "What are you doin'?" he yelled as he twisted to get away.

"I outta be asking you that," Virgil harshly replied, yanking the kid closer.

"What are you doin', ol' man?" one of the teens insolently asked, while another answered, "Maybe he's some ol' perv into little boys."

Brandon struggled against Virgil's hold. Kicked his foot out toward Virgil's shin. "You're ruinin' everything!"

"I damn well hope so," Virgil snapped, sidestepping the kick. He pushed the kid toward the road. "Let's go."

The brat spun back around, pushed against Virgil's chest. "You're not my—"

"Just get in the damn car!" Virgil pulled the door open. Pushed the kid toward it.

"Maybe he likes to play rough," one of the teens shadowing them called out, while another added, "Maybe we outta show him rough."

And that threat sounded way too close for comfort.

Virgil turned. They were surrounded. Six to one, and probably more in the shadows he couldn't see. Shitting odds for a rich boy with no street smarts.

Brandon pushed against him, struggling to escape.

"Don't fight me on this, Brandon." Virgil growled, pushing the kid into the front seat.

He turned backed to face the teens. They'd moved in closer forming a loose, wide semi-circle around him. Close enough for him to see the real skull tattoos permanently inked into their forearms. The same skulls Brandon had penned on his own arm. *Jee-suz*.

The circle of teens ebbed and flowed around him. Like jackals surrounding their prey right before the kill. Virgil held up his hands as he warily eyed them. "I don't mean any trouble. I just came to get my kid."

"Badass is yours?" the leader of the group asked, while the others lazily fingered their switchblades.

The fact they knew Brandon's nickname scared the shit out of Virgil. Almost as bad as the blades. And the guns they probably had concealed.

The teen lifted a scraggly chin to eye Virgil. "He don't have no dad."

Virgil's gut twisted. Had Brandon talked enough with these kids to tell him about his dad? Or had they assumed and preyed on the sadness of a lonely kid? And before Virgil could figure a way out of this mess without spilling blood, namely his own, from the corner of his eye he spotted Ruby Mae running toward him.

The teens spotted her, too, all cock and leering eye. "Yo! Check it out, check it out." Their eyes burned with lust that made the hairs on the back of Virgil's neck stand on end. Unmindful of what could happen, he ran toward her. Grabbed her. Shook her. "What the hell are you doing here?"

She pushed against him. Her eyes were wild with fear. "Brandon!" She grabbed his shirt in her fisted hands. "Where is he? I saw him come this way. And I saw those kids."

"He's fine," Virgil tersely told her. Giving them what he hoped was a wide berth; he dragged her toward his car.

"Who's your momma, ol' man?"

The voice was too close. Like right behind Virgil's back. Sweat ran down between his shoulder blades. He spun around. Pulled Ruby Mae up tight behind him. The group flanked him on three sides. He kept her behind him. "She's nobody to you." He put himself between her and the drugged-out teenagers. "Let her alone."

They laughed. Like he'd said the funniest thing they'd ever heard. The leader stepped closer. Cocked his head as he eyed Ruby Mae over Virgil's shoulder. "He your john, momma?" The circle shrunk around them. Like the fit of the collar of his shirt. He had no weapon. No options for escape other than talking their way out. And his heart was pounding. His eyes darted as he shifted side to side, trying to watch all six of them and who knew how many more while trying to figure out how best to grab Ruby Mae and make a run for it.

They stepped closer still, tightening up their circle, their net.

And Virgil's throat got tight with his heart stuck in it. "Leave her alone," he hoarsely pleaded, pulling her close enough her breasts smashed into his back.

Like a cat toying with a mouse, they juked and swatted at them and Ruby Mae whimpered, shrinking into him. The silver of their knives coming dangerously close to Virgil's vitals. "He your pimp, momma?"

"Maybe she's Badass's *mommy*," one of the other kids taunted as he lifted heavy-lidded, spaced-out eyes to Ruby Mae. "You come to get your little boy?"

She whimpered again and the fight left her body, leaving her trembling as the kid's words registered. It left Virgil shaky, too.

Another pimple-faced kid stepped closer. "You could be my mommy," he sneered with teeth decayed and blackened from heavy drug use. That fact Virgil knew from a TBI conference he'd attended.

"Look." Virgil spun them around so he was between her and the boys. "We don't want any trouble," he told them, wondering if the shadows he thought he saw behind the windows were reflections of the setting sun, or others in the house. Most likely others.

Ignoring Virgil, the kid trained his drug-dulled eyes on Ruby Mae. He fingered his blade with one hand, while his other hand palmed his crotch. "You could hold me to your breast. Let me suckle."

She growled something under her breath, fighting to free herself from Virgil's hold, but he gripped her tighter. Another switchblade clicked and Virgil grabbed her before pushing the teenager hard enough to knock him out their path.

And then they were running.

Drugs had made the teens belligerent, arrogant, and thank you, Lord Jesus, a little slow. He'd gotten the jump on them. And with Ruby Mae now safely in front of him, he pushed her, hauling ass for the safety of his car, all the while hoping and praying one of their knives didn't find a home between his shoulder blades.

"Let me go!" she struggled against him. "They knew Brandon!"

"You're damn right, they knew him," he growled at they reached his car.

She spotted Brandon hulking near the passenger door. *"Brandon!"* she cried out, running toward him.

"I told you to get in the damn car!" Virgil yelled at the brat. "Both of you! *Now!*" He grabbed Brandon's collar, stuffing him in the back seat.

"Mo-om!" The brat fought, kicking and yelling. "It's not fair. He's ruinin' everything!"

"What were you thinking?" Ruby Mae yelled. "Hanging around with those kids? Is this what you do when you disappear at night?"

"Can we just get in the damn car? *Now!*" He pushed her inside. Slammed the door. Ran around the front of the car. Yanked his door open. Slid in behind the steering wheel. Turned the key. Dropped it into gear. Stones shot out from under the tires as he spun around, speeding toward the crowded safety of town.

"You have a lot of explaining to do, young man! Who are those kids?" Ruby Mae demanded, as she turned in the bucket seat to face her son. The car shot over the mounded Trail, the front end bottoming out as they landed on the other side. "Who are they?" she shouted as she gripped Virgil's shoulder with one hand and the headrest with the other.

"My *friends,*" the Brandon spit out. "They were my friends. And *he* ruined it!"

"They're *not* your friends," Ruby Mae yelled. She grabbed her hair blowing wildly around her face into her fisted hand. "They're ten years older than you!"

More likely closer to five, Virgil thought, remembering the barely-there peach fuzz on their faces. His eyes darted to the rearview mirror, the side mirrors, and the open road. He had no idea what they'd stumbled upon back there. But it wasn't good. The adrenaline rush was draining from his system, leaving him weak. Thoughts of what could have happened left him shaky. He pulled back a little on the gas. The last thing he needed was to get a ticket from Office Clive.

He chanced a look at Ruby Mae. She looked brittle. A breath away from falling apart. And he looked at the brat giving her a hard time in the rearview mirror. "You mind your mother."

"They were my friends!"

"Trust me, Brandon; they are *not* your friends."

"Yes, they are. And *you* ruined it!" The kid kicked his seat. Once. Twice. Harder. "Uncle Billy's gonna beat you up."

"*Brandon!* Stop this now!" Ruby Mae cried out. She was close to tears. Virgil understood. He was pretty damn shook up himself.

"Your Uncle Billy's gonna thank me." Virgil told him, as he shot out onto the Mountain Parkway. "So everybody just shut up, okay?"

In the ensuing tension-filled silence, Virgil gripped the steering wheel with one hand and ran another over his head as he sped down the bypass around town. The cool night air blowing in from the open top did little toward calming him down. His heart still thundered in his throat. Blood pounded in his head. His skin prickled. His fingers gripped the leather steering wheel harder. *Drugs and gangs had infiltrated his town.* And he was clueless how to proceed.

She grabbed the sleeve of his shirt. "Where are you taking us?"

He met her glare with one of his own. "Home," he tersely told her.

"You're going the wrong way."

"Am I?" His voice dropped low. "Do you want them to know exactly where you live?"

Fear filled her eyes. She gave her head a jerky nod before turning away to stare out the side window at the surrounding darkness. Her shoulders slumped.

The brat stayed mulishly quiet in the back seat.

And Virgil breathed a shaky sigh of relief when he swung out onto the Dinnerbell Road without a tail.

Forty-five minutes later, up a round-about back-door route over the Brandywine, Virgil pulled into Ruby Mae's driveway. He put the car in park, cut the engine. Let out a breath he swore he'd been holding since they'd crossed the Trail, fear dogging their every mile.

The engine ticked as it cooled and Ruby Mae stared straight ahead. She hadn't said a word to him since they'd headed out of town. That was fine. He was in no mood for small talk. And that's all it would be since she'd ordered him out of her life.

Virgil turned in his seat. Pushed on the brat's shoulder. "Wake up." Somewhere on the drive home, he'd fallen asleep across the back seat. Drool pooled on the leather seat below his opened mouth.

"I'll get him." Ruby Mae pushed by him.

Virgil held her arm, stopping her. "*I'll* get him." He jerked his head toward her darkened house. "You get the door," he told her, lifting the brat into his arms.

He followed her into her house. Down the hall to the kid's bedroom. He fought the protective feelings he had for both of them while she turned on the light and pulled down the bedding. He laid the kid down and stepped away. Unable to leave, he stood by the door, watching as she removed his shoes. Pulled the covers up over him. She pressed a kiss to his forehead, hovering over him. She smoothed her hand over his spiky blond hair before shutting off the light and Virgil followed her as she slowly walked down the hall to her living room.

Ruby Mae's heart was breaking. Her son was involved in a gang! *Oh, Willie Lee, I let you down.* She'd let her son down, too. And, she turned to the man standing stiff and silent in front of her, she'd let him down, too. She hadn't trusted him. Questioned his motives. Doubted him.

She owed him a huge apology.

"It's not as bad as you think," he quietly told her.

"They're a gang, Virgil." She said the words she dreaded as fear spiked through her frazzled nerves. "A *gang.* And Brandon's involved with them!"

His lips thinned. Why couldn't she just keep her mouth shut and agree with him? Why did she have to pick up the fight where they'd left off earlier?

"We don't know that for certain."

"How can you say that? You saw them!"

"We'll figure this out, Ruby Mae. I won't let anything happen to Brandon."

Her heart pounded. She wanted to believe him. Wanted to think he had all the answers, but she'd seen him earlier. He'd been just as shocked, stunned as she'd been. Just as scared, too.

His shirt was limp. Wrinkled. His dress pants grass stained from his earlier outing to the batting cages. The lines bracketing his mouth were cut in deeper tonight, and his eyes were bloodshot. He looked tired. Weary. And she wondered how much of his job he took personally. She'd always assumed he'd slid through life on his polished silver spoon. That it was one big easy for him. But she'd met his mother. And after she'd ordered him out of her life, she'd found him, rescuing her son from those teenagers. "God, Virgil!" She ran a trembling hand through her hair. "I don't know what I'd have done had you not been there."

He shrugged a shoulder. Like it was no big deal. "You'd have done the same thing I did. Got Brandon away from them."

She wasn't so sure. She wasn't sure of anything. Her safe little part of town had gangs at the end of her street recruiting little children!

"Lock up," he quietly told her, before turning toward the front door. He paused before opening it. "I don't think they know your last name, or where you live, but don't take any chances." He breathed deep. "Call Billy. Have him come over."

For some inexplicable reason Virgil was jealous of Billy Ray. Just like for some inexplicable reason – at least one she wasn't ready to admit yet tonight – she didn't want him to leave. "Don't," she whispered as his hand turned the door knob. "Don't leave."

"Ruby Mae," he breathed out her name on a groan.

"I don't want to be alone, Virgil."

"I can't stay."

"*Please*." She took a step closer, her palm hovering over his tense shoulder. "Please."

He dropped his head to the door. "I can't."

"Why not?" she whispered.

"You know why not!"

"No, I don't." She only knew she didn't want to be alone.

"If I stay, I'll wanna sleep with you, dammit!" He turned around. His churning blue eyes were a blazing bright mix of anger, want, and need. "I won't be used. I won't be a crutch to get you through the night."

"I'm not using you!" But she was. Just like she'd used him fifteen years ago when she'd let him take the blame for her actions. She'd known the rift forming between Willie Lee and Virgil where she was concerned. She could have stopped it. But she'd liked Virgil's attention. And when they'd gotten caught, she'd allowed Willie Lee to believe it had been all Virgil's doing, when she'd been just as guilty.

They might have had different reasons for their actions, but they'd both wanted to sleep together. And they would have if Willie Lee hadn't caught them.

Willie Lee had been so angry. And she'd been so afraid she was going to lose him, too, that she'd never told him the truth. She let him believe it was all Virgil's doing. And Virgil hadn't said a thing. He'd taken Willie Lee's beating, never telling him the truth. That deep down inside she'd wanted Virgil and had been willing to throw a good man like Willie Lee aside for one night with another. God! What did that make her?

"You're scared. Confused," he told her.

"Damn right I'm scared and confused." About what she was feeling for him. What she'd felt for him that she'd never ever quite buried, even when she'd been blissfully happy with another man who'd loved her with all his heart for his entire life. A man she'd had every intention of spending the rest of her life with had cancer not taken his.

"I won't deny I wanna sleep with you, Virgil." It was little atonement for what she'd done fifteen years ago. And this was one time when she hoped Willie Lee wasn't looking down, watching over her. "But I want *you*. More than just as a crutch." She took a step closer to him. "I want the man near me who'd step between a gang to protect me and my son."

"You have me," he hoarsely told her. "You've always had me."

Tears pricked her eyes. For him. For her. For Brandon. "I'm scared." She wrapped her arms around her middle. Shivering even though it was too warm in her house for her to be cold.

He turned. Wrapped his arms around her, strong and sure, and she laid her head against his chest feeling safe for the first time since those kids had surrounded them. And she allowed his solid strength to surround her, to shore her up.

"What if Brandon's really involved with them?" she quietly asked into his neck.

"We'll get him out."

"But what if—"

"No buts, honey. We're not losing Brandon."

Still holding her, he walked them to her couch. Without letting go, he sat down and she snuggled closer. The heat of his body wrapped around her, warming her like a blanket. "What are we going to do?" she whispered as she listened to the strong, steady beat of his heart.

"Nothing tonight."

"And tomorrow?" she persisted. God? What would it bring?

"Tomorrow I do some investigating at the courthouse. Then I get a closer look at that abandoned house where they set up shop."

"We," she corrected him. "We get a closer look."

His arms tensed. "I don't want you down there."

She lifted her head. Looked into his fierce blue eyes. "He's my son."

"And you both mean too much to me to have something happen to you." He lifted his finger. Reverently brushed it over her cheek. "Let me do this. Please? For you."

She sighed. Unable to resist him, she nodded her head. Nestled closer into his body.

He slouched down into the cushions. Relaxed into the couch. Breathed in slow and deep as the quiet of the night and the stillness surrounded them.

"Virgil?" Her fingers slid into his hair, then over the sunburned tips of his ears, and down the strong column of his neck.

"Yeah?" He lifted sleepy eyes to hers.

"Emily O'Leary. Gina Dimaglio. Katie Michaelson." Her fingers stroked over his beard-stubbled jaw. "Those are the names of the girls you need to talk to if you want to stop Officer Clive."

* * *

"What the hell is he doin' here?" Billy Ray's voice carried loud and sharp into the living room.

"None of your business," Ruby Mae curtly replied.

"Hell of a way to get woken up," Virgil grumbled, as he pushed his hands into the small of his back. He rolled his shoulders, working out the kinks of a restless night spent sleeping on Ruby Mae's couch. He lifted his hands above his head, stretched his arms up as he followed the scent of freshly-brewed coffee to the kitchen.

"You just don't listen, do you?" Billy was glaring at Ruby Mae, hands on his hips.

"She don't listen to anybody," Virgil told him as he stepped into the kitchen wishing for a shower and a change of clothes he wasn't going to get. Or a good morning kiss from the woman he'd held all night in his arms.

"I listen just fine," the woman in question snapped as she slapped down flatware on the table with enough force to leave dents. She lifted her head. Looked up at Virgil and paused, fork in mid-air. And the fierceness left her eyes. And they turned soft. And warm. And sexy. "Good morning," she quietly told him, a soft tentative smile replacing her scowl.

He smiled back. "Maybe it's you, Billy," Virgil told her neighbor as he walked over to Ruby Mae. "Maybe you just bring out the worst in people." Virgil lifted her chin. She looked beat, with dark circles shadowing her eyes and tension pinching her features. She hadn't slept any better than he had, jumping at every sound.

"Well, maybe I just have her best interest in mind," her guard dog growled.

Virgil turned. Stared at the man. Willie Lee had said that same thing to him fifteen years ago. The last time they'd talked. Or argued, rather. Fought, actually.

"And maybe you should just sit down." Ruby Mae stepped away from Virgil. Her lips were pinched tight as she glared at her neighbor.

"*I* don't have to be told twice." Virgil slid into the place setting at the head of the table. He knew it was childish. Knew it was Billy Ray's seat, but he couldn't seem to stop himself. If he were a dog, he'd be pissing all over the table legs.

"Hey! That's my seat!"

"Just sit down!" Ruby Mae grabbed Billy's arm, pushing him to the other side of the table.

Brandon walked in, blond hair sticking up all over his head. A crease from the pillow case reddened one cheek. He said nothing as he crawled up on the chair by Billy.

With a skillet in one hand, Ruby Mae dished out eggs and potatoes to all of them. She sat a plate of toast on the table. Brushed a curl from her flushed cheek with the back of her hand before grabbing the coffee pot.

Virgil stood. Took the pot from her. "Sit," he ordered. He filled Billy's cup and then hers as she wearily slid onto her chair. "Drink," he told her, before taking her plate and walking over to the stove where he filled it. "Now eat," he added, sitting the plate in front of her.

"Thank you." Her smile was faint; the wattage dimmed by worry and strain. Yet even minimized, it still found a way to detonate inside him to warm him from the inside out.

He pillaged her cupboard. Pulled down another plate, which he filled, as well. He turned to find her watching him. He shrugged a shoulder. "You want me to take this over to Maisey?"

"I'll take it over," Billy told him, emptying his cup of coffee as he stood.

"I'll walk out with you then."

"But, Virgil, you haven't even touched your breakfast!"

Virgil turned toward her. "I'll take something to go," he told before leaning down and brushing his lips against hers, getting that morning he kiss he craved more than anything else.

* * *

159

Billy Ray was waiting outside the back door, looking none too happy.

Virgil wasn't sure if it was his usual none-too-happy look, the

one he wore anytime he saw Virgil hanging around, or if it was because Virgil had just kissed Ruby Mae.

"Didn't take you long to move in."

"You got bigger problems than that." Virgil pushed by him, heading toward his car.

Billy followed. "Like what?"

"We ran into a little trouble last night." Virgil looked out over the yard. At the small, well-kept houses on the other side of the road. At the kids playing carefree in the front yards while dogs barked, excitedly chasing after them. It all looked so picture-postcard perfect. And yet…

"I know."

Of course he would. Virgil buried his irritation. "I think they might be a gang."

"So tell me something I don't already know."

Of course Billy Ray would know. A superhero of his caliber knew everything.

"Brandon's involved."

Billy swore. His dark-as-midnight eyes burned as they stared at Virgil. "How much?"

"I don't know. He's mimicking their tats. And I caught him going to meet them."

"Shit."

"Yeah, shit about covers it," Virgil wearily replied. He breathed deep, asking what he really wanted to know. "So if you knew about them, thought they could be a gang moving in, why didn't you say anything?"

"You think I didn't do anything?" Billy snorted in disgust. "I told Clive. He ignored me. I brought it up at a town meeting when the police of chief was supposed to attend. But he blew off the meeting."

"Maybe he had a call. A good reason not to be there."

"Maybe. But nobody representing him followed up on what I told them. So what would you have had me do, *Mister Mayor*?"

And before Virgil could reply, Brandon shot out the backdoor and down across the yard.

"Hey!" Virgil yelled. "You get back here. Right now!"

The brat tensed. Slowly turned around. "Why?" he snarled, bristling with attitude.

"Because I said so. You don't leave this yard today. You got that?" Not until Virgil knew what the hell was going on down the street.

"You're not my boss." The kid turned to his savior. "Tell him, Uncle Billy. Tell him he can't boss me around."

"Virgil's right. You mind what he says and you don't leave this yard."

And it was Virgil's turn to stare at the man standing beside him.

"But, Uncle Billy," the brat whined.

"No buts, Brandon," Billy told him. "Do as he says." And they both watched as the kid sulked into the back yard.

Virgil turned to Billy. "Thank you for that."

"Don't get used to it. It's not gonna happen all that often."

"You don't like me much, do you?"

"I don't trust you," Billy told him.

"Look." Virgil buried the urge to have it out with this man once and for all. "I need your help. I need to get into those abandoned houses. Need to see what's going on in there."

"Breaking and entering is against the law," the sanctimonious pain-in-the-ass told him.

"So is intimidation. So is taking a woman's only child and ruining his life."

Billy's eyes narrowed. "I won't let that happen."

"Neither will I." Virgil was getting sick and tired of having to prove himself over and over. "And when we're done checking out these houses and any areas around here you think might be a hotbed for suspicious activity, you're going to take me to meet Emily O'Leary, Gina Dimaglio, and Katie Michaelson."

Billy sucked in a harsh breath. "She told you."

"Yeah, she did. And I want to meet them. I want Clive held responsible for what he's done. And you're going to help me."

Chapter 10

Late in the afternoon a few of Ruby Mae's neighbors and fellow crafters gathered in her shop. Like Ruby Mae, they were all trying to make a living. And make it outside the town's ordinances. Outlaws all of them, Ruby Mae supposed, given her present dilemma. Gwendolyn was a photographer. Shelly, a quilter. And Bitsy... well, she was a flirt. And very good at it.

"What do you think?" Gwendolyn asked, laying a couple of her latest photographs on the counter.

"They're beautiful," Ruby Mae honestly replied, as she looked down at the framed photos.

"I've sold a couple already," her neighbor shyly replied. She'd just opened her pseudo shop in the front entryway of her home. Gwyn rubbed her finger over the side of one of her frames as she gnawed on her bottom lip. "I haven't been able to convince Harry, though, to remodel our garage like you have so I can set up a really nice gallery."

Ruby Mae's converted garage was coveted space on her side of the Trail. And her success, small as it was, had been inspiration to her neighbors who, like her, struggled to make ends meet.

"We closed in our back porch," Shelly said, as she set an infant's quilt on the counter. "What do you think?" she asked, as she held it out for them.

"It's beautiful."

"Danny put a sign out at the end of the driveway pointing customers in the right direction. They don't seem to mind the walk behind the house." Shelly looked at Gwen. "Maybe Harry could do that for you."

"Arnie just sets his creations along the driveway," Bitsy added. Arnie Townsend, her husband, was a chainsaw-wielding artist who created adorable black bear lawn ornaments out of Tennessee logs. "The customers come running to see what else he's got."

"They come running to see you," Shelly teased. "Especially when you're sunbathing out there in your teeny bikini."

And while Bitsy brushed the tease aside, Ruby Mae knew Arnie Townsend wasn't above using his wife's flirtatious nature and beauty to his advantage. Bitsy was a sweet petite who knew how to bat her eyelashes and fall all over a man without tripping herself up.

"I'm thinking of setting up a table myself."

"You?" the girls all asked in unison.

"Yes, me." Bitsy pulled a piece of tissue paper from the pocket of her sprayed-on jeans. Unfolded it to reveal a beaded bracelet. "What do you think?"

Before Ruby could reply, the bell over the shop door jingled and Virgil walked in. "Ruby Mae, you in here?" He stopped short when he saw her neighbors. "I'm sorry. I didn't know you had…"

Her neighbors and fellow crafters scrambled, liked criminals, grabbing up their treasures, stuffing them behind their backs as they spun around to face Virgil. They couldn't have looked guiltier if they had neon signs flashing on their foreheads. And then Ruby Mae heard the gasps of surprise. And then the sighs. And the *oohs* of pleasure as they stared at her visitor.

Ruby Mae stared, too, because standing in the doorway looking all pressed and proper; he was the polar opposite of the men in blue jeans and white tee shirts she usually saw in her neighborhood. He was Rodent's own golden boy. And didn't Ruby Mae let out her own sigh and *ooh* of pleasure as her eyes slowly slid over him.

The dark blue trousers he wore lay with perfect pleats across his flat abdomen. The hand-tailored blue shirt he wore matched his eyes. Perfectly. An expensive silk tie hung loose around his neck. Like an afterthought. His blond hair was windblown from the drive with the convertible's top down. He should be on the cover of a magazine. Or at least standing at the bottom of her bed while she lay naked in it. The knowing grin spreading across his handsome face said he knew exactly where her mind had wandered – and he was willing and eager to fulfill any and every fantasy she might have. He took a couple steps closer. "Am I interrupting something?" he asked.

He knew full well he had.

"Of course not!" Ruby Mae shot around the counter, intent on heading him off at the pass. "What could possibly be going on here? We're just talking, isn't that right, girls?" she added, wishing she could rein in her tongue and put it to better use – like licking the man beside her up one side and down the other. As she fanned herself, she turned around.

And found her neighbors still standing in front of her counter. Brows arched, eyes wide, looking way too interested in Ruby Mae's blathering. And the proximity of her body to Virgil's hot, hard one, which was close enough to hers that his warm breath teased her neck.

She stepped away. Lifted her hand and made introductions. "Virgil, these are my neighbors." And as her neighbor's eyebrows arched even higher up their foreheads, she realized too late she should not have introduced him as Virgil and instead as—

"Mayor Push!" Bitsy pushed by Ruby Mae to grab Virgil's hand. "Oh, look, girls!" she turned toward Ruby Mae's other two neighbors, her hand splayed over her chest. "It's Mayor Push!" Like they didn't know already. "Ruby Mae," Bitsy chided her with one hand resting on her tiny hip. "I didn't know you knew Mayor Push. Why didn't you tell us?"

Virgil flashed her neighbor a big smile. "There's nothing to tell." And with that good ol' boy way he had of talking, added, "Ruby Mae and I went to school together."

"He knew Willie Lee," Ruby Mae corrected him, wondering why she was clouding the issue. Everyone knew of her encounter with the man in question all those years ago. She took a deliberate step away from him, only to catch his arched brow. She was doomed either way.

"Mayor Push," Ruby Mae looked at her curious neighbors, hoping she looked cool and detached. And not like a woman who was remembering how wonderful it felt to fall asleep against his broad chest. To feel his long fingers sliding reassuringly over her back and through her hair. Or to know the enticing touch of his fingers against her bared breast. She waved a hand in front of her heated face from that old memory. "This is Shelly Haufbraugh, Gwendolyn Dillon, and—"

Her pint-sized neighbor stepped closer still to Virgil, offering her hand. Like she wanted it to be kissed by him instead of shook. "Elizabeth Townsend," Bitsy nearly purred, fluttering her eyelashes at him. "But my friends call me Bitsy. *You* can call me Bitsy, too."

Ruby Mae's eyes narrowed. She wanted to remind her petite, way too cute neighbor she was married, but there didn't appear to be any way of tearing her attention away from the handsome man standing between them.

"It'd be my pleasure, *Bitsy.*" Virgil lifted Bity's hand. Kissed her knuckles. And while jealousy did a slow yank and twist deep in Ruby Mae's gut, Bitsy flushed and gushed like she'd just met a rock star.

Ruby Mae's fingers curled into her palms.

Virgil dropped Bitsy's hand, but Bitsy didn't drop her idol-worshipping gaze. He turned his blond head toward Ruby Mae. "I didn't mean to interrupt. I was just—"

"You didn't interrupt anything, Mayor Push," Bitsy answered. Like he'd been talking to her. She sidled up closer to him, until her chest nearly touched his. Her hand – the one that sported a huge diamond, compliments of her husband's love and devotion, appeared to stroke over Virgil's left pec – not once, but twice.

"Bitsy Jane!" Ruby Mae growled out.

"What?" her neighbor turned a way-too-innocent gaze on Ruby Mae. Her bottom lip quivered and her big brown eyes got innocent, little-girl wide. "I was just going to show our mayor the crafts we're selling."

Ruby Mae rolled her eyes and groaned.

"Crafts?" Virgil's blue eyes shot to Ruby Mae. Piercing and probing. "You never said anything about *other* crafts."

She swallowed. She hadn't said anything. And she wasn't going to do so now either.

His eyes narrowed. His mouth turned down on the corners. And he turned back to Bitsy, but not before he lost the frown and pumped up the wattage of his smile. "Why, Bitsy Jane, a woman as pretty as you, and talented, too?" he poured on the hokey hillbilly charm. "Whadaya'll sell?"

167

And while Bitsy spilled her secret and all the other secrets of the crafters on their street, he had the nerve to act interested. Like he really cared. Ruby Mae wanted to believe he did, but there was still a tiny little part inside her that thought he was only prying information so he could serve them all citations to cease and desist business operations. They were all in violation of the town ordinance. And then she felt a caustic flush of guilt.

He'd never served *her* a citation. And he'd had more than ample time. And reason.

And while Bitsy spilled all their secrets and some Ruby Mae hadn't known about, she watched Virgil. Watched his long, lean fingers gently brush over Shelly's quilt. "You made this?" he asked, turning his blond head to her other neighbor.

"Yes," Shelly shyly replied, obviously enraptured with the man.

"It's beautiful," he told her and Ruby Mae watched Shelly's face flush with joy at his heartfelt compliment. "And you make other things?" he probed. "To sell? Over here?" And just like Bitsy, Shelly spilled all her secrets.

And after he'd gotten all the information he'd needed to shut Shelly down, *if* he chose to do so, he turned his attention to Gwen's photos. "You took these?" He lifted one up. Studied it the same way he'd studied Ruby Mae's paintings all those weeks ago. His long, lean fingers slowly stroked over the glass the same way he'd stroked them over her body last night. Wet heat flooded her panties. He turned his dazzling blue-eyed gaze on Gwen. The one Ruby Mae knew could melt all resolve and good intentions. "This is up on LeClaire, right?"

"Yes!" Gwen excitedly replied. "It's off the beaten path though, Mister Mayor."

"Call me Virgil, please. It's over by the twin falls, right?" he asked, his finger brushing over the glass again and another wave of heat pushed down deep through Ruby Mae's body. "I used to hike up there," he quietly added, and Ruby Mae wondered who he'd hiked up there with. And wondered why it even mattered. She had no hold on him. He wasn't hers. Yet she felt possessive as hell of him. And angry with him for what she was sure he was going to do to her friends and neighbors.

"It's an extraordinary picture," he told Gwen after he'd gleaned all of her secrets. "I'd like to buy it from you." And while Gwen's chest filled with pride, Ruby Mae's filled with jealousy. Would he offer Gwen fifteen hundred dollars like he had offered her?

Gwen had asked a meager thirty dollars for her framed photo and Virgil paid her the exact amount. Not fourteen-hundred and seventy dollars more. Not one *penny* more.

"Mister Mayor," Bitsy slipped her arm through his. Batted her long lashes at him. "What do you think of this?" She held up a beaded bracelet in her hand.

Ruby Mae leaned forward to get a closer look.

Virgil held it up. Looped the silver chain around his index finger. The beads on the chain slowly slid down his palm and Ruby Mae remembered his hands sliding down over her body. "It's very pretty." His fingers fondled the crystals and Ruby Mae swore she could feel his touch brushing against her skin, fondling her.

"Oh, thank you, Mayor Push," Bitsy gushed, interrupting Ruby Mae's fantasy. "I wasn't sure if it was something I could sell."

"I don't think you'll have any problem there," he replied. Like he was an expert on what would sell and what wouldn't. Him! A jet-setting playboy! And then her conscience harshly reminded her, *He's been in Rodent for two years now, girl! Mayor for the last year.*

And he'd been with her for the last month. With no citation served.

"Ladies, all your things are beautiful." He smiled at his

newfound fan club. He rubbed his hands together and asked, "So, where do ya'll sell your items?"

"Oh, look at the time!" Ruby Mae pushed between Bitsy and Virgil. Quickly she grabbed up her neighbor's treasures, pushing and stuffing them into bags before herding all them toward the front door.

"But I didn't get a chance to tell Mayor Push where— Or how—"

"Another time, Bitsy," Ruby Mae cut her off, pushing the last of her neighbors out the front door. "I really have to close the shop early today." She didn't. But if Bitsy was left to succumb anymore to Virgil's charms, he'd know every single thing about their side of the Trail. And Ruby Mae wasn't sure she was ready for him to know everything yet. She changed the sign to *Closed*. Locked the door. Drew in a quick breath. And turned to face Virgil.

He was leaning up against the counter, one leg casually crossed over the other at the ankle. His arms were crossed over his chest. The indulgent, easy-going smile he'd had for her neighbors was gone. And he wasted little time getting down to business. "When were you going to tell me about your neighbors?"

She took a deep unsteady breath. Slowly shook her head side to side. "I wasn't."

His arms dropped to his sides. His blond brows drew together. "Why not?"

"You know why."

He frowned and guilt filled Ruby's Mae's chest. "You still don't trust me," he quietly replied. Like she'd hurt his feelings. And her heart gave a painful pinch in her chest.

"I do trust you," she told him.

He snorted his disbelief. "Just not enough to tell me about the little crafters loop ya'll got goin' on over here. You get lots of customers from all over? Do a pretty good business?" He pushed away from the counter and glared at her. "We spend the night together and you don't even think to mention this?"

"Virgil," Ruby Mae sighed out his name. "You have a citation to issue to shut down my business. Do it, if you have to. But leave them alone, please," she pleaded. "Gwen's husband is just plain mean when he drinks and he drinks a lot now that he lost his job. And Shelly and Danny? With Danny's alimony payments to his first wife, they're barely making ends meet. And Bitsy's husband was a logger until the mill shut down. They need the money they get from selling their crafts to keep their houses. Don't take that away from them. *Please.*"

"Ruby Mae," he stepped closer. "Do you honestly still think I'm only here to shut you down?"

And before she could answer *no*, before she could ask if he was here for the same reason she was, before she could ask if he felt the same amazing, scary things she felt when they were together, the back door opened and Billy Ray walked into the shop.

* * *

Virgil wished he could have had more time with Ruby Mae to convince her he was on her side, but instead he was following Billy across the yard and through the side door into his garage. He found three trucks sitting side by side, new to old, big to little, filling the pristine bays. "Sweet baby *Jee-zus*," he breathed out, staring at the sight in front of him. "I feel like god-damned Goldilocks."

"Then wipe your feet, Goldie," Billy ordered as he rubbed the soles of his own boots against the carpet placed just inside the door before walking across the immaculate floor, waxed and buffed to a glistening sheen. Virgil followed, stopping in front of the neatest,

171

cleanest workbench he'd had ever seen. He stared at the huge collection of tools. "Do you really line each one up and outline them?" He'd never seen anything like it.

Virgil picked up a wrench. Held it up to the overhead fluorescent lighting. "This has more polish and shine than the jewelry in the cases at Winkelman's."

Billy snatched the wrench back. Rubbed it up and down on his pants removing Virgil's prints before laying it back down inside its neatly drawn off space. "Don't touch my stuff."

Virgil tested his theory. He reached for a screwdriver.

Billy's hand shot forward to block him, his finger pointing out in warning. Yep, the man was certifiable. "You know, this takes you to new levels of anal," Virgil told him.

"Fuck you," Billy replied.

"In your dreams." Virgil turned his attention to the hulking brand new pick-up truck buffed so shiny he could see his reflection in the waxed fenders. And then further down the line to the fully restored older model pickup sitting in placid glory beside it. He walked over to it. Looked over at Billy. "I remember your daddy patrolling in this." He ran an appreciative finger over the fender.

Ray Trainor had been a legend in Vermin County. Way back in the day, all the small towns in this area had no local police forces, leaving them under state police jurisdiction with long response times for calls for assistance. Rodent had been lucky. Before they'd had an actual police force, they'd had Ray Trainor. "Before we got enough funds to buy an actual cruiser, your daddy used to patrol with this truck." Virgil chuckled at an old memory, "I remember being hauled home a few times in the bed of it."

"Don't touch it," Billy tersely ordered, wiping Virgil's fingerprints from the fender with the bottom of his tee shirt.

"Where in the hell'd you get the anal streak?" Virgil had to ask. Certainly not from Billy's momma. Maisey was a wild card. And although Ray had been straight as an arrow, Virgil didn't remember him anal.

"I'm not anal."

"*Right*," Virgil replied, watching the man pull a cardboard box from a shelf.

"What's that?"

"Stuff we'll need."

Virgil rifled through it, finding a box of latex gloves, a box of plastic zip-lock bags, a couple permanent markers, and a digital camera, and some other stuff he knew nothing about.

"Will you stop?" Billy grabbed back the box. Carefully rearranging everything Virgil had tossed. He pushed by Virgil, walking toward the last truck. The only one not buffed and polished to within an inch of its mechanical life.

"Of course you'd pick this one." It was the only one covered in mud. The only one with over-sized, knobby tires and a jacked-up suspension that put the bottom of the door level with Virgil's belt buckle.

"What?" Billy Ray turned toward him, bristling. "You think you'll be better received up on the Brandywine questioning everyone and everything, tooling around in your expensive sports car?"

Virgil's brows drew together. "No, but—"

"Just like I suppose you figured you'd get more information out of the residents looking like that."

"What's wrong with the way I look?" Virgil defensively replied, running a hand down over his French silk tie. "It's who I am."

"Exactly." Billy sarcastically replied. And the gauntlet had been thrown.

"Hey! I'm not going to apologize for who I am and what I have." Virgil was tired of apologizing. Tired of living the charade, too. And tired of having his motives questioned by the people over here. Especially Ruby Mae. "*Dammit!*" She should trust him. He aimed a finger at Billy. "You know, if I wanted to shut Ruby Mae's business down, I could have. Five different times to be exact. But I didn't. And I don't understand why you, and her, can't see that." He yanked open the truck door. Looked around for something to grab onto to haul his ass inside. Instead he saw Billy still staring at him. "What?" he irritably asked.

"I don't trust you."

Virgil stepped away from the door to glare across the muddy hood at the man. "That seems to be a running theme around here." He sighed out his frustration, suddenly weary. He ran a hand through his hair. Then down his neck to squeeze the tense muscles there. "It's because of Ruby Mae, right? Well, here's a new flash for you, Billy. I don't trust you either. You're not taking care of Ruby Mae because of some promise to her dead husband—"

"You don't know shit!"

"Knowing you, you probably did promise." It was the code of the South – and something a man like Billy Ray Trainor would do for a man like Willie Lee Shove. "But that's not the only reason. You're taking care of her because *you* care about her. Admit it."

"Damn straight I care about her." Billy's coal-black eyes burned with rage as he rounded the truck to stand toe to toe with Virgil. "I was in that damn locker room fifteen years ago. I heard you braggin' out your *grand* plan for seduction."

Shit. "You don't know what you're talking about."

"The hell I don't!" Billy spit out. "I heard you inviting your buddies to watch! You don't deserve a woman like Ruby Mae."

"You only know what you want to know," Virgil muttered as memories of that day long-ago came rushing back like it was yesterday. He'd been the star pitcher on the baseball team. The richest kid in school, too. And smart enough to only fuck out-of-town girls who didn't know that. He just hadn't been smart enough to know his plan would backfire on him.

"How do we know you're not playin' for the other team?" his friends had taunted as they'd surrounded him after showers in the locker room. *"Because I'm one of you,"* Virgil had arrogantly replied, thinking he really was. He was Virgil Push. Who were they to question him? *"We're not so sure,"* they'd told him, huddling closer, their minds as closed as the space between them. To this day, Virgil broke out in a cold sweat whenever people huddled too close.

Billy jabbed a finger at Virgil's chest. "Willie Lee was your best friend! You *knew* how he felt about Ruby Mae. Everybody knew! And you were going to sleep with her just to beat your best friend into her pants."

"That's not how it was," Virgil growled, pushing Billy's finger away. "Yeah, I wanted her." From the first time he'd seen her with Willie Lee. And the attraction and the want had only grown every time after that he saw her. "Yeah, I wanted to sleep with her, but I hadn't invited them to watch."

"The hell you didn't."

They'd come up with that lame-ass condition all by themselves. And Virgil couldn't find the balls back then to tell them to go to hell. Not that he was going to let it happen. "Look. They doubted my *sexuality,*" he ground out, feeling the old heat of anger and embarrassment crawling up his neck and jaw. He'd been a good looking kid back then. Maybe a little too good looking. "The girls in school loved me. They hung all over me. They'd have done anything to sleep with me." And he hated how arrogant that made him sound, but it had been the truth. "They'd have loved for me to knock them up just to get their hands on the Push money." And the power that went with the name, a point that had been drilled into his head from the time he'd entered puberty.

"So?"

Virgil glared at the man's judgmental tone. Nobody could ever know unless they'd walked in his shoes. "Look." He ran his hands through his hair. "I only slept with women from other towns." Towns where the Push name and the Push wealth weren't heard of. "They didn't know that. Nobody knew."

"So?"

"*So?*" Virgil angrily retorted. "*So?* They thought I was *gay*!" Even fifteen years later that still mattered in this small mountain town. Harlan, the former mayor had been gay. And when he'd come out of the closet, he'd come away for his efforts without a job. That's how Virgil had gotten appointed the position. "*That's* how it was," Virgil angrily spit out, not quite sure why it mattered that this judgmental pain-in-the-ass know the truth.

Billy stared at him with narrowed eyes. "So you threw over your best friend to prove yourself?"

"You'd have done the same damn thing," Virgil ground out, defending his stupid choice. "And you know it."

But Billy wouldn't have done that. And Billy would never have had his sexuality questioned in the first place. He was that honest, that straight – that everything that Virgil wasn't, but wished to hell he was. Everything he was trying to be. Christ! How had he fucked up such a good life? He'd had everything – and yet nothing.

"Look," he sucked in a sharp breath. "It was fifteen years ago. I was a dumb kid. I didn't go through with it. And I had no intention of ever going through with it." He didn't know how he'd have handled his so-called friends when they'd have found out his change of plans, but he knew for certain that what he and Ruby Mae would have shared would have only been shared between her and him. And to insure that, he'd told his friends they could find him in a different location. Far from the woods near the school where he'd been meeting Ruby Mae.

"Only because Willie Lee stopped you."

"Yeah." Virgil let Billy believe that. He'd allowed Willie Lee to kick his ass all over the baseball diamond, too. Allowed Willie Lee to pound on him, allowed Willie Lee to think the deception was all Virgil's doing. And he'd taken every slur, every punch to protect Ruby Mae.

He shrugged a stiff shoulder. Like it didn't matter. But it did. "Willie Lee got the girl," he told Billy. And Virgil got nothing. Still had nothing. He tamped down the age-old jealousy. And disappointment. He sucked in a deep breath. "So you're the one who told him?" Virgil had always figured as much. He hadn't known much of Billy Ray Trainor back then, except he was good enough in sports to have played with the upper classmen. And that he'd been a good friend of Willie Lee's.

Billy shook his head side to side. "No. I didn't."

That surprised Virgil. He stared at the man. Was he telling the truth? "If you didn't tell…" he paused. Then who had? "Screw it. It doesn't matter. It's ancient history." Willie Lee was dead and Virgil would never get the chance to apologize to the man.

But he could save the man's son. Maybe that would even the score a little.

"Look," he squeezed the bridge of his nose. "Will you help me?"

Billy's lips pressed tight.

"Will you stand with me on this? I need your help. I can look in those abandoned houses by myself and find what I need, but I need your help to reach these people. People who just like you don't trust me. Together we can figure out if we have a gang problem. A drug problem. A police force problem," he added, remembering the accusations against Clive he had yet to take care of. "We can make a difference here, Billy. We can make our town better, but I can't do alone." Virgil put aside his pride. And his anger, and his frustration, and looked the man straight in the eye. "I know you don't like me, but will you help me?"

Tense seconds that felt like hours slowly crept by, but finally, Billy heaved out a heavy sigh. And swore under his breath. "I'll help you. But," he lifted a finger and pointed it at Virgil's chest. "If you call me Robin or Tonto, I swear, I'll push your ass right out the door. Got it?"

Chapter 11

Ruby Mae paced around the kitchen, alternating between looking at the clock on the wall and looking out the window. The sun had set an hour ago and they still weren't back. "Something could have happened," she murmured.

"Yeah, they could have gotten lucky."

Ruby Mae swung around to face her neighbor. "You're supposed to be lying down."

"I'm fine." Maisey waved her concern aside as she walked into the kitchen. "I'm not dying."

"But you had—"

"A stroke," she finished for Ruby Mae. And pressed her index finger close to her thumb. "A little one," she added. "I'm recuperating. And I'm fine. Really. You're the one who's acting crazy."

Ruby Mae's eyes narrowed. "I am not."

"Relax honey. Billy's not going to let anything happen to your man."

"He's *not* my man!"

"Right."

And Ruby Mae was spared defending the lie when the back door opened and Billy and Virgil walked in. Her heart slid up into her throat.

His shoulders were slumped. His beautiful designer shirt wrinkled and his trademark tie nowhere in sight. His eyes were bloodshot. His face drawn. His hair was messed, like he'd repeatedly run his hands through it in frustration and aggravation. And *gawd!* She wanted him to be hers. She really did.

Billy pushed by Virgil. Dropped a bag onto her kitchen table looking no better than Virgil.

She stared at it with wary eyes. "What is that?"

Virgil sank down onto the chair at the table. He let out a weary sigh. He scrubbed his hands over his face. "Drugs. Gang paraphernalia. You name it, we found it."

Ruby Mae grabbed the back of a nearby chair for support. Her eyes shot to Virgil's. Her hand flew to her chest. Her palm pressed down over her thundering heart. "From the house down the street?"

"There," he nodded his head slowly up and down confirming her worst fear. "And up on the Brandywine. And over on the west side of town." *His* side of town.

"Well, this isn't good," Maisey solemnly replied, as she slowly sank down on one of the chairs gathered around the table.

"No, it's not," Billy added, taking the other seat. He opened the bag. Up-ended the contraband onto her table, allowing what looked like crumbled wrappers, prescription bottles, and what she hoped were cigarette butts, but feared were marijuana joints to roll out, along with a couple mirrors, a razor blade and some other stuff she couldn't identify, but, as a good mother, she should have been able to. Her heart slid up into her throat. Blood pounded in her head as the reality slapped her in the face. This was a parent's worst fear.

And her son was involved in it.

Virgil looked over at Billy. "That was a good idea you had bagging and tagging what we found."

"There's more?" she asked.

Virgil nodded his head, his eyes not leaving Billy. "I want your notes and the pictures you took, too."

"You'll have them tomorrow morning," Billy replied, and Ruby Mae waited for his flippant retort to follow. Or his usual anger that always seemed to resonate to surface wherever Virgil was concerned. But there was nothing, except what appeared to be mutual respect.

Her brows drew together. Billy was the hardest sell on the planet where Virgil was concerned. What had happened while they were out?

Virgil pressed his hands, palms down onto the table top and breathed deep. "I'll call for a special Executive Council meeting to disclose what we found. And I'll make sure Chief Rutledge is there. I want you there, too. You know more about what all this shit is better than I do."

"Absolutely." Billy nodded his head.

"I appreciate that. I checked courthouse records this morning. Edgar Wyatt owns those three abandoned houses at the end of the street here."

"Edgar Wyatt owns them?" Ruby Mae asked. Her Edgar Wyatt? The man who'd—

Virgil's head swung toward her and she snapped her mouth shut. His eyes latched onto hers, probing deep. Into places she wasn't ready for him to pry into yet. "You know Edgar?" he demanded.

"No," she hurriedly replied. "I mean, yeah. I mean *everybody* knows Edgar Wyatt," she nervously added, and Virgil's tawny brows drew together as he studied her. She wished he'd look away. She didn't have anything to hide. It wasn't like she *knew* knew Edgar. She knew him.

He frowned. His eyes reluctantly pulling away, sliding back to the contraband spread over her table and Ruby Mae breathed a little easier. She should tell him, but tonight didn't seem to be the right time to explain her relationship with Edgar Wyatt.

"I'll talk to Edgar tomorrow morning. See if I can convince him to tear down those houses. And," his eyes went back to Billy. "I want the addresses of those other houses we found up on the Brandywine. I want to contact their owners. Try to convince them to tear them down, too."

"And I'll talk to Tim O'Leary," Billy told Virgil. Tim O'Leary was Emily O'Leary's father. One of Clive's victims. "I'll see if he'll agree to a meeting with you."

"If he doesn't, give *me* his number," Virgil told him. "I'll talk to him. I want that meeting. I need her statement." His index finger tapped the table top. "I want Clive brought down."

He breathed deep. The action pushed out his chest, accenting the definition of muscles she'd have bet her house he didn't have. Except she'd seen them. Naked and toned and tanned on his boat. And desire did a slow swirl deep in her stomach, piercing the throbbing spot right between her legs that always ached whenever he was anywhere near.

She sucked in a sharp breath. Squeezed her thighs together. And prayed the flush of desire warming her skin wasn't showing on her face.

He scrubbed his hands over his cheeks, the sound of his beard scraping against his palms sliding down Ruby Mae's spine detonating a tsunami of tingles rippling out in its wake.

"We need summer jobs for these kids. Something to keep them busy. Something to give them hope." He took another breath. "I'll talk to Davis tomorrow."

"Davis Barnett?" Billy asked. "You trust him?"

"Probably the only one on Council I do."

"But your mother's on Council."

He shot Ruby Mae an odd look. One that had nothing to do with his trust of his mother and everything to do with him remembering Edgar Wyatt was on Executive Council – and her nervous blathering on and on about knowing him.

He looked away. "If anybody can find more money in the budget to pay for jobs," he went on. "It'll be Davis. These kids need them. I don't care if it's just mowing down weeds, or picking up trash, I want jobs available to them. I want them to have something to do other than hanging around with gangs or selling drugs to make money. And I want to talk to Wyatt about donating the old distillery to the town."

"Why?" Maisey and Ruby Mae both asked at the same time.

"So we can renovate it." He reached for Ruby Mae's hand. The warmth of his palm slid under her skin. His long fingers wrapped around hers and she wondered if he knew he held more in his palm than just her hand. He looked into her eyes and the sincerity shining in his was so bright she nearly looked away from guilt. She'd doubted him so many times. Justified her reasoning on a past which no longer mattered.

What mattered was right here. The man – and woman – they were right now.

"I want a place for every crafter and business over here to have a *legal* place to set up shop." He turned his head to include Maisey and Billy. "And I want reasonable rent for them, or a percentage of profit dependent upon income as their rent. I'll talk to Davis. He's good at that stuff. We'll work something out. I want these families to have a chance. I want them to succeed. I want Rodent to succeed."

"Virgil, that'd be wonderful," Maisey told him.

"I'm just doing what I'm supposed to."

"We need that kind of support. And you're the first one to understand that in years."

Virgil shrugged off Maisey's compliment, like he was uncomfortable with her praise. And another misconception Ruby Mae had about the man fell away.

"I need to talk to Chief Rutledge. I want to talk to him about opening up an auxiliary police force. I want a stronger police presence over here. And up on the Brandywine."

Maisey's hand hovered over her heart, and Ruby Mae wondered if he'd known what that meant to the older woman. Tears filled her eyes. "That was always my Ray's dream."

"Then hopefully we can make it happen," Virgil told her. "I want the residents here to know the town of Rodent has their best interests at the forefront. Same as it has for the people who live on the west side. That there are no differences. Not under my watch."

Billy sat up straighter and this time Ruby Mae knew the look he gave Virgil was one of respect. And maybe even admiration.

"And I want a community center in that building, too. A safe place for kids like Brandon to go and play video games. Or shoot pool. Or play basketball." He squeezed her fingers and Ruby Mae blinked back her own admiration threatening to leak from her eyes. He looked back at Maisey. "And I want a place there for seniors to get a free hot lunch and play cards. A place where they can hang around and socialize with people their own ages."

"That's all well and good there, Superman," Billy said.

"I believe it's the Lone Ranger, or Batman, to you."

"Don't push it," Billy cryptically warned, and Virgil smirked, making Ruby Mae wonder just what had happened between these two. "How you going to pay for all this?" Billy asked. "Nobody's going to want their taxes raised to fund something that only our side of the Trail benefits from."

"Everyone benefits from new businesses. I'll find a way to fund it. Davis and I'll comb the current budget looking for any spare money. And I'll hit up every philanthropist within a five-hundred mile radius – even some abroad, if I have to." He lifted his chin, looked at all them gathered around her kitchen table. The tip of his long finger tapped her table top. "We're going to make a difference here. We're going to send a message to any gang thinking they can set up shop here that our kids are hands-off." His bright blue gaze settled on her. Where it stayed. "And we're not losing them to drugs. Or alcohol. Or gangs. Not one kid. Not if I can help it."

His words were protective. And passionate. And she knew. With absolute certainty she was in love with him. And he wasn't leaving here tonight. Not until he knew that, too.

"That's wonderful, honey," Maisey told Virgil, "But your momma isn't going to be too happy with you declarin' a war on drugs."

"Momma," Billy growled out a low warning.

"No, Billy Ray." Maisey turned to her son. "He needs to know what he's up against."

"I need to know what?" Virgil demanded, wondering what he was missing. It was obviously something big.

"Maisey," Ruby Mae softly added her own warning, which pissed Virgil off. What did she know that he didn't?

"I think everybody's been keeping enough secrets around here. And I'm damn sick and tired of it!" He shot an accusing glare Ruby Mae's direction, before turning his hard-ass stare on Maisey. "So why don't you tell me why *my* mother, who I might add, is a member of the Executive Council, and on the boards of a half dozen banks and institutions in this town, why she would have a problem with me declaring a war on drugs?"

"Momma," Billy growled out another warning. This one stronger. Harsher.

But Maisey ignored her son, her steady gaze still on Virgil. "Because, Virgil, she's a user."

"What?" Virgil blinked, unable to believe what he'd just heard.

And Maisey didn't miss a beat telling him again. "Because she's a user, son."

"You're wrong!" Virgil harshly replied. "You're all wrong," he hotly added, catching the sympathetic – and *dammit!* – knowing looks Ruby Mae shared with Billy.

Maisey slowly shook her head side to side, the universal sign that the recipient of it was clueless. Or dumb as a fencepost.

"I think I would know my own mother!" Virgil vehemently added. "Better than you. Or you!" He glared at Ruby Mae.

Maisey lifted her chin and he wanted so badly to discredit her, to prove her wrong. But gone was the audacious woman who'd given him her thong in the car as a towel. Gone was the devilish twinkle in her eyes that had him grabbing protectively for his crotch. Instead, a sensible seriousness settled over her when she asked, "Then you know about Percy?"

"Her dog?" He snorted. And just when he was ready to fire back a scathing reply, she just shook her head side to side again. And

186

Billy pretended intent interest in the corner of his thumb, while Ruby Mae's head was bowed so low, her chin nearly touched her chest.

"Not her dog, honey. Percival Randolph Stratton, the man." The old lady said the name slowly. Like she was talking to a dummy.

"Who the hell is Percival Randolph Stratton?" Virgil impatiently asked, although he vaguely remembered the Stratton mansion when he'd been growing up. It had been the only home bigger than Marilee's. It had been the envy of the entire neighborhood. And the bane of Marilee's existence to hear her talk.

"Percival Randolph Stratton," Maisey went on, "was the man your momma had been engaged to before your father."

Virgil's head swung side to side. "I know my family. Better than anybody here," he added. And there were those damn looks exchanged again. The ones which raised the hair on the back of his neck.

"Percy Stratton gave your momma a ruby engagement ring. It had a huge square ruby in the center 'bout the size of your thumbnail. Surrounded with more rubies and diamonds, set in a wide gold band. You know the one," Maisey softly added.

And Virgil did. His mother wore that ring all the time. She never took it off. "But— but— my father— He gave her that ring."

"Did she tell you that?"

Virgil looked away. He'd just assumed Vince had given it to Marilee. Like he'd given her a house and everything else they had.

"Your mother was a LaCroy. L-A-C-R-O-Y." Maisey slowly spelled out the last name. And while Virgil was shaking his head vehemently side to side, she went on, adding, "From up on the Brandywine."

"Oh, you're wrong!" Virgil huffed out, furiously shaking his

187

head side to side now. "My mother has always been from the west side of town." The wealthy side. She'd never hailed from the mountain.

"After she'd *reinvented* herself, she was from the west side," Maisey informed him, banishing his family history as it had been told to him. "And that was right after she started working for Edgar Wyatt, Senior. The year she'd turned sixteen. And had spent a summer abroad. In France. With the man who I might add, was old enough to be her father. And her bein' Baptist? Why it was shameful!"

"And your point is?" Virgil impatiently demanded, not wanting to hear about his mother's sex life. He shuddered at the thought of what Maisey was suggesting.

"The point is that when she'd come back from that summer abroad with that old lech, she was a Lacroix. L-A-C-R-O-*I*-X. And suddenly she was French."

"She is. We are." That point had been repeatedly drummed into Virgil's head for as long as he could remember. Along with his entitlement. And how he and Marilee were above everyone else. Which he pretty much believed until recently.

Had he been fed a steady diet of bullshit? Bullshit he'd believed to be true? "God," he whispered. He'd walked around town like he was better than everybody else. Because Marilee had told him so. And Vince hadn't been around. And the few times he'd been around, they hadn't talked about family.

Virgil was an only child, his parents both only children. He had no cousins, no grandparents. No other close relatives. Except the ones Marilee told him about who lived abroad. The ones who were... "Christ," he looked over at Maisey. "You mean I'm not French?"

"Honey, with your momma being from up on the Brandywine, and your daddy from this side of the Trail, you're pure mountain common. Well, except for Vince's money when he'd struck oil. That's when you became special. And rich."

Virgil stared at the old lady.

He squeezed his head in his palms. It was going to blow. It was just a matter of time. His eyes narrowed. It was so freakin' bizarre. So outrageous. Ridiculous. Could it be… *true*? And how did Maisey know this?

"So what does that have to do with this Percival Randolph Stratton?" God! He could barely say the pussy of a name. And why did he get the sickest feeling in the pit of his stomach? His head swung to Ruby Mae.

Before she'd married Willie Lee, her last name had been Stratton. He looked back at Maisey. "What does that have to do with Marilee being a user? Not that I believe for one minute, mind you, that she is," he added, pointing his finger toward her for emphasis. "Marilee *couldn't* be a user." It didn't make any sense. "She couldn't be!"

"Oh, she is, son. She is." And Maisey said it so calmly, so matter of fact-like, the hairs on the back of Virgil's neck stood on end as a wave of uncertainty rolled down his spine. "And we need to go back about thirty-four years to start the story."

"Thirty-four years?" Sweat popped out on Virgil's forehead. "That was—"

"—Right before you were born," she calmly finished for him. And as if reading his frenzied mind, added, "And we need to go back to the party that changed all their lives."

* * *

Virgil clutched the back of the chair for support. The world was still evolving around him. Ruby Mae and Maisey and Billy were still standing in Ruby Mae's kitchen like they did every night. It was only Virgil who'd been knocked onto his ass and out of his own orbit.

He sank down onto the chair. Ran his hands through his hair. Squeezed the back of his head to keep it from exploding. And tried to understand what the hell he'd just been told.

It was impossible! Ridiculous! Outrageous! *Un-freakin'-believable*!

He looked up at Ruby Mae who was still staring at him. Concern and god-damned pity shadowed her eyes. And yes, knowing was mixed in there, too. She knew about this. "*Your* father and— and *my* mother?" he hoarsely asked, before adding, "And— and— *my* father and *your* mother?" He swallowed the lump clogging his throat. "*You*... and *me*... conceived—"

"Oh, no, Virgil," Maisey rubbed his tense shoulder. "Only *you* were conceived that night out on the front lawn of the Stratton mansion. Ruby Mae was already Percy's little bun cookin' in Vince's girlfriend's oven for a good two, three months before that night."

He pushed up out of his chair. Dislodged her hand, as he repeated what the old lady had told him. "You already told me how her momma was knocked up before that party. And not by her boyfriend, who at the time happened to be my damned father!"

"You don't have to get huffy," Maisey reprimanded him.

"*Huffy?*" he huffed out. "Well, *excu-use me* if I'm not takin' this news very well." And how could he? He'd just found out his mother and father and their respective –but certainly not respectful or faithful— girlfriends and boyfriends had been regularly getting it on before they'd all gotten busted on the front lawn of the Stratton mansion for drugs and sexual deviate behavior by the legendary Ray Trainor, Super Cop. And it appears everyone knew but Virgil!

190

What a joke he was.

"Hey!" Billy took a menacing step closer. He stabbed a finger at Virgil's chest. "Back off. My momma's tryin' to be nice here, helpin' you out. You best be mindin' how you talk to her, you hear?"

"Virgil," Ruby Mae's hand brushed against his clenched fist. "It's not Maisey's fault—"

"I know," he replied, displacing her hand. He squeezed the bridge of his nose. "I know." He sucked in a harsh breath. And looked at the older woman standing in front of him. No wonder the messenger always got shot. "I'm sorry, okay?" he apologized. "But I just can't quite wrap my mind around the fact that Marilee was engaged to Ruby Mae's daddy. The man who'd been banging my daddy's girlfriend on the sly. And that he'd knocked her up. And provided enough drugs and alcohol to get the four of them drunk enough and high enough to go at it all together on the front lawn!" Or the real biggie, Virgil thought, that his momma had tried to pass *him* off as Percy's baby. Why would she do that? Why would a woman—

He shot a look at Maisey. Searched her eyes as a horrific thought took root. "You're sure I'm Vince's?" he hoarsely asked. His head would freakin' blow if Maisey were to tell him he and Ruby Mae were brother and sister!

Maisey nodded her head up and down. "No question, honey. Look in the mirror, if you don't believe me. You're Vince's all right. You look just like him."

"But—"

"I'm telling you. You're Vince's. Besides, Percy's momma had you paternity tested as soon as you cleared the birth canal."

"*Jee-zus!*" Virgil squeezed his eyes shut to that vision. Slowly, he opened them. His hands slid down over his cheeks. He looked at

Ruby Mae. "You're Carmella Stratton's *granddaughter*?" And he knew she could read all the thoughts racing through his mind. If she were a Stratton, she would be from the richest family in Rodent. And if that was the case, why had she grown up poor on this side of the Trail? Why had he never seen her once on his side? Why had she never laid claim to her birthright?

"I would have been her granddaughter, if Carmella hadn't disowned my father," Ruby Mae softly confirmed his worst fears.

"Because of… of my mother?"

And she slowly nodded her head up and down.

"I don't understand. I mean," Virgil pressed his fingers into his aching temples. "I understand Percy," God! It was such a pussy of a name, it nearly made him gag just to say it. And it made so freakin' much sense. "I understand he was rich. But that was thirty-four years ago." He obviously wasn't now. He looked back to Maisey. "What's that got to do with drugs and Marilee now?"

"Your momma never gave up Percy."

"What?"

"Your mother and my father have been having an on-going affair for thirty-four years," Ruby Mae quietly said from beside him.

"What?" Virgil swung his head around to her. "You knew about this?"

And the look she gave him said it all. *Yes*, she knew about it. And *yes*, Virgil was indeed a dumb fuck.

He exhaled a harsh breath. "Okay, so they had an affair – are *having* an affair," he corrected himself. "I still don't understand what that has to do with drugs."

"Let me spell it out for you, college boy." Billy said. "Percy was a lazy-assed rich boy with more money than brains." He glanced over to Ruby Mae. "Sorry, Ruby Mae. I'm just saying it like it is."

She nodded her head.

Billy looked back at Virgil. "You know the type. Living off his trust fund instead of having a real job. Spending his easy money on anything he wanted." And there was that damn jab at Virgil's past which Billy was so damn good at pointing out.

Virgil held up a hand, palm out. "Spare me the editorial comments and tell me the damn story."

Billy's mouth pinched. Probably from holding back. "Long story short then, Harvard. Percy would rather be high than work. No offense, Ruby Mae."

"None taken," she quietly replied.

"And he had connections," Billy went on. "For every kind of recreational drug he wanted to experiment with. And he shared them all. With your mother. Who was more than happy to take whatever he got."

"Billy, be nice," Maisey softly reprimanded her son, but Billy wasn't inclined to obey.

With one palm raised up to his mother, the pain-in-the-ass went on. "When Percy's momma found out he'd knocked up some poor girl from the wrong side of the Trail, no offense, Ruby Mae—"

"None taken," she softly replied.

"His mommy shut off his trust fund and disowned him. But by then, college boy, your daddy had done the right thing by *your* momma and married her. And may God bless Vince for the life sentence he got for that act of decency."

"Just finish the damn story!" Virgil wasn't as inclined to make Vincent Push a saint.

"Fine." Billy went on. "By then, your daddy had already struck it rich. Richer than the Stratton's. And since your daddy didn't care what the hell your momma did since he wasn't staying in Rodent, and your momma wasn't giving up her precious Percy, and Percy wasn't giving up getting high, well, let's just say your momma found connections. And with your daddy's money, she's well connected. And she's above the current law," Billy cryptically added in disgust. And Virgil was too stunned to ask who her connection was inside the police force to give her that kind of carte blanche power. "That simple enough for you to understand, Harvard?"

"William Raymond Trainor! I didn't raise you to be mean. You apologize. Right now!"

"Hey!" Billy's brows drew together over his stormy dark eyes as he glared at Maisey. "He asked for it. I just gave it to him."

Maisey rolled her eyes, before leaning close to Virgil. "Just between you and me, your momma has a lot more *drive* than Percy ever had. She's dangerous, honey. Especially if you plan on taking away one of the two things she loves."

And it didn't go without notice Maisey's implication was Marilee's love of this Percy pussy. And drugs. Not her husband. And certainly not her son.

Maisey patted his tense forearm again. "If it's any consolation, honey, I just don't know what your momma sees in that Percy. No offense, Ruby Mae."

"None taken."

"Vince is three times the man that waste is." She squeezed Virgil's shoulder. "You be real careful, now, son. Your momma's dangerous if she feels threatened. And I like you too much to lose you. So you just be real careful now, you hear?" Maisey told him, before disappearing out the back door.

And leaving Virgil too stunned to do anything, but watch.

Chapter 12

"You knew about this," Virgil accused her as soon as the back door shut.

"Yes," Ruby Mae softly replied. Her father leaving for weekends, and sometimes weeks at a time to be with his mistress had defined their home life.

"And you didn't tell me?"

"When was I supposed to do that? When we were in high school? Or that day when we—we almost—" Abruptly she shut her mouth, unwilling to bring up the day that had changed both their lives. "Believe me. My mother paid dearly for her indiscretion."

"*Indiscretion*?" he scoffed. "That's putting it mildly."

"Try to understand, Virgil." Ruby Mae forgave him his misguided arrogance. "While your mother walked all over town dripping in rubies, opals, and pearls, the closest my mother ever got to the real thing was naming her daughters Ruby, Opal, and Pearl."

He glared at her like that peek into her home life was insignificant.

"She spent her *life* trying to keep up with your mother. And she was miserable."

"And this is my mother's fault?"

"*Yes*! It's your mother's fault. Why are you defending her?"

"The way I see it, there's plenty of blame to go around."

"Spoken like a true lawyer," Ruby Mae muttered under her breath. The man may never have practiced law a day in his life, but he could sound – and act like one, on demand.

"It's what I am," he coldly replied. "If you have a problem with that—"

"You're *not* a lawyer; you're the mayor of this town! Look," she huffed out her frustration. "You're right. There is a lot of blame to go around." Her admission seemed to pacify him. "My father jumps at your mother's every beckoned call. *You* might not have known about it, but their affair is no secret." And Ruby Mae and her sisters had paid dearly for it with town gossip, their mother's bitterness and misery, and their father's indifference and selfishness.

"He gladly left us whenever she called. And came home afterward with more money in his pockets than we'd ever seen." And before he could scoff or defend the woman who'd given it to him, Ruby Mae rushed on. "He kept it all for himself. He didn't share a dime." And maybe that was the part she resented the most. Her sisters and her mother struggling to live on what her mother made at the hair salon while her father spent his money on drugs and porn and sex toys for Marilee. "My father didn't want my mother, but he was too lazy to leave her. Not with your mother taking care of him. And my mother providing a roof over his head."

Virgil stared at her and she hated the flush of embarrassed heat spreading across her cheeks. She'd thought she'd left her twisted childhood behind when she'd married Willie Lee and saw how love changed a marriage. But here it was. Tormenting her again. And Virgil was looking at her. Like he didn't understand. Like affairs were a normal part of a marriage. "What about your grandmother?" he asked.

198

"My *grandmother*?" Now it was her turn to scoff. "My grandmother sat back on *your* side of town and watched her grandchildren struggle. And she didn't lift a finger once to help. We did not exist to her." She sucked in a sharp breath. Willie Lee had showed her how wonderful a marriage could be when two people were committed to each other, heart, body, and soul. How happy they could be even when they were scraping pennies together to make ends meet.

"Jesus," he growled jamming his fingers into his hair. He pressed his palms into his eyes. Rubbed them back and forth like his head hurt. He dropped his head back into his tense shoulder blades and stared blindly at the ceiling. "I hate this. I hate all of it!"

"It doesn't matter what they do." She told him what she'd been telling herself for years. "All that matters is… is right now." He dropped his head to look at her and suddenly the tension charging the air surrounding them shifted into something more.

His eyes ignited with a simmering fire that had been burning hotly between them for fifteen years. And the words she'd used to pacify him had taken on new meaning. And she didn't bother to clarify them. Not when he looked at her like he was now. Awareness filled every cell in her body. Anticipation arced between them. Like a blinding bolt of electricity. And desire swirled low in Ruby Mae's stomach. Spearheaded into an ache between her legs. An ache only he could take away.

"I should go." His voice was thick. Desire did that. He tore his gaze away, but not before she felt it stripping away all her clothes. He grabbed up the contraband spread across her table. Stuffed it back into the bag with jerking movements. Desire did that, too. Just like it wetted her underwear. Made her do crazy things. Like ask him to…

"Stay," she breathed out.

He jerked his head up. His hot blue gaze snagged hers. His jaw was clenched tight. His body tense with frustration, aggravation, and pent-up want. The muscles in his chest, the ones that were just as beautiful now as they'd been fifteen years ago pushed up and out. "We both know what'll happen."

"I'm counting on it," she boldly told him, tugging the hem of her shirt. Pushing it up over her sensitized skin and pulling it off over her head. She dropped it to the table. Her breasts tingled. Her thighs quivered. The spot right between her legs ached. "I need you. And I won't be happy until I have you."

"*Jee-suz*," he breathed out, his eyes honed in on her breasts.

He dropped the bag on the table. Walked toward her. Roughly slid one arm around her waist. Pulled her toward him until his thick, hard erection pressed right between her legs. Right where she wanted it. And she nearly moaned at how good it felt. The soft cotton of his dress shirt teased her breasts. And she rubbed them against it needing more. More of what only he could give. The fingers of his other hand spanned her neck as he held her head close, lifting her chin so she could look at him. "You wanna screw me?"

She sucked in a sharp breath. So the polished rich boy had a rough, guttural side. A raw crudeness about him. "I'm not screwing you," she told him. She hated that description. What she was offering was not a screw.

"It's sex then. Just sex," he told her. "But it'll be the best sex you ever had," he arrogantly added. He pushed her back against the wall, trapping her between it and his hard, tense body. His face was fierce. His jaw clenched. His eyes were jaded. Almost hard as he told her by rote what she assumed he told every other woman he'd been with.

And when he was finished she said, "This is not *just sex*." It had always been something more that burned hotly between them. She

200

also knew he always behaved badly when dealt a blow. Or a shock. And tonight he'd been handed a trifecta of blows, shocks, and surprises. "You're not even close," she added. Right before she nipped his bottom lip with her teeth. For her, it was love. She wouldn't be here otherwise. It had always been that way with her. But she also knew not to say that to him. Tonight, he wouldn't believe.

For all she knew, he might never believe.

"Oh, I'm close," he arrogantly replied, pushing his throbbing length harder against her, mimicking what she wanted so badly. "And so are you," he confidently added as he read her every gasp and moan like a *How to Pleasure Ruby Mae* manual. He lifted her heavy breasts. His thumbs slid back and forth against her tingling nipples, driving her closer. He pushed her legs wider apart making room for his body. The brush of the expensive material of his trousers an erotic caress against her inner thighs, pushing her closer still to the edge. His mouth closed over hers, claiming and demanding. His tongue pushed deeper inside, wrapping around hers, the same way his body was wrapping around her. Totally surrounding her. Totally in charge of her. And her orgasm. And she was so close. So damn close. Intense sensations quivered through her body.

And he knew what to do to her. How to touch her. How to make her body come alive in ways she hadn't known possible. And he did it with mastery, like they'd been doing this forever. She gasped. Grabbed his body. Ripped at the buttons of his shirt, exposing his hot skin. Dug her nails into the muscles of his chest needing to be closer. Needing to mark him. Claim him as her own.

He growled. Pushed her harder against the wall. Higher, too. Pressing his hard length up against her. He grabbed her leg. Hauled it up to wrap around his waist. All the while thrusting harder. Faster against her. "I wanna fuck you right now."

She thrashed against him, nearly lost in sensation.

"And it'll be the best fuck you ever had." He reached for the button on her shorts.

"No." She pushed at his chest.

He unsnapped the button. "I've been all over the world. Been taught by the best."

"No," she breathed into his mouth, trying to free herself as his mouth laid claim to hers again. She didn't want to hear about his conquests. She'd heard enough about his affairs when he'd been married. While she waited in the line at the grocery store.

"I know stuff… How to do things." His fingers were roaming again. Doing some of those amazing things she'd imaged he'd been taught. And his mouth was following right along.

And Ruby Mae was damn near close to orgasm. "Virgil, please," she breathed out.

"That's right, baby. Things that'll make you scream out my name." His fingers were… oh, God! His fingers were… *amazing*. "And I'll ruin you for any other man."

He already had.

"No, not here," she managed to say. She managed to push him back, too. Enough to stand on her own wobbly legs.

And before she could take her next breath, his mouth closed over hers again. And his arms were sliding around her waist. He was pulling her close. Lifting her off her feet. Her arms were wrapped around his neck. Her fingers clutching his hair as she sucked on his tongue. Bit his lip. And then she realized he was walking them through the living room. To her bedroom.

"No," she gasped, grabbing the door jamb.

He stopped. Stared at her. His chest heaving. His eyes dark. Turbulent. Churning with desire. And anger.

"Not here," she told him. Her angry, confused son was back here. And she wouldn't add any more to his problems by having him find Virgil in her bed. There had been no other man since Willie Lee. There'd only *ever* been Willie Lee. She jerked her head toward her son's closed door. "Brandon," she barely whispered her son's name, afraid she'd wake him. Afraid she'd add more to his turmoil if he opened the door and found her half naked, wrapped around Virgil. In front of her bedroom door. He was already ages older than his years.

"Where then?" he growled, not moving an inch away from what he wanted. His jaw was clenched. Angry blue fire spitting from his narrowed eyes.

She untangled herself. Standing on her own two feet, she reached for Virgil's hand. His clenched fist actually. Silently she turned them back toward the kitchen. Grabbing her shirt from the table, she hurriedly pulled it over her head. Stuffed her arms through the sleeves and cleared the backdoor, walking them toward the apartment.

Once inside, she turned on the outside light. For Brandon. Should he wake. It had become their code of sorts since Willie Lee had died. Her son's way of easily finding her when she couldn't sleep at nights. The outside light on by back door of her shop when she was taking late-night inventory. Outside light on by the back door of her work room when she was up late painting. And the outside light on by this door to the apartment when she couldn't sleep in her own bed. When the memories were too much to bear and she came out here to escape.

Tonight she'd be making new memories here. With Virgil.

Who the hell cared he wasn't good enough to be in her bed, Virgil angrily thought, as he kicked the door to the apartment shut with his foot. He'd heard her say the brat's name. Knew she was protecting the kid as best she could. Like any good mother would. He also heard all she hadn't said. That he wasn't Willie Lee. That he wasn't worthy enough to take his sainted place in her bed.

And then he didn't care. He just wanted to feel. To fill her. To have her writhing and screaming out *his* name the way he'd wanted her to do since the first time he'd seen her. And even when he'd been miserably married to Rachel. *Especially* when he'd been married.

"I want you naked. Now." He jerked his head toward the shirt she'd hastily pulled on. "I want your breasts in my hands. In my mouth."

The flaring of her nostrils said she wanted it, too. So did her pebbled nipples outlined by the soft cotton of her tank top.

She raised an eyebrow. "You can check that rich-boy attitude at the door."

If she only knew how rich he wasn't.

Something must have changed in his demeanor. "That's better," she told him. And then she smiled. And then her hands slowly slid down her body, sliding over the breasts he wanted to suck and fondle. And he was *this close* to coming in his pants just watching her. She was teasing him. Taunting him. Fueling his insatiable hunger for her as her fingers slowly curled around the bottom of her shirt. And she was taking way too long to bare her body to him.

"I waited fifteen years for this, Ruby Mae. I'm tired of waiting," he told her, hauling her up against him. Pushing her hands aside, he grabbed the hem of the shirt. He yanked it up over her head. Tossed it on the floor. And then, finally! His hands were touching her. Lifting her. His palms full of her soft, plump flesh. And his thumbs were brushing against the soft velvet of her nipples. And she was moaning. The breathy sound an aphrodisiac making him harder. Hungrier. He bent his head. His mouth replacing his hands. And he was sucking, pulling her deeper into his mouth. And it was he who was moaning. He who couldn't get enough of her.

"Oh, Virgil, *yes*. Just like that," she gasped as she molded her body into his. Pressing her scented flesh closer. Her hands grabbing fistfuls of his hair as she held his head right where she wanted him. Right where he wanted to be.

He wanted more. He wanted all of her. He walked her backwards to the sofa bed. He lifted his head. Covered her mouth with his. Unsnapped and unzipped her shorts. Pushed them down over her sweet ass. Heard them hit the floor with a dull thud. Then he pushed her down onto the bed. And admired all that he'd uncovered. And he could only stare at her beauty. At her perfectly rounded body, all sleek curves and softly scented flesh. At the softness in her eyes. "*Jee-suz*, woman," he breathed out. "You are beautiful."

The sweetness of her lips curved up in a smile. She was a welcome offering of pleasure. And then she leaned up on her elbows.

"Don't you dare move," he growled as he yanked free the few remaining buttons on his shirt. Still hanging from his shoulders, he grabbed the buckle of his belt, pulling it open.

"Virgil, there's no hurry," she quietly told him as her soft eyes slowly slid over his exposed skin making him harder. Hungrier. Needier.

"Oh, hell, yeah, there is." He yanked on the button of his pants. He pushed the zipper down over his throbbing dick until his pants puddled around his ankles. And he kicked and pushed one heel of his foot against the other trying to untangle them so he could get his stupid shoes off. All he'd accomplished for his effort was tangling himself up even more. "Shit," he growled under his breath as he tried to untangle himself before he fell on his ass.

"Virgil," she said his name all soft and breathy like.

And Virgil huffed out his frustration. "Just my freakin' luck," he grumbled, his hands landing on his naked hips. "I've waited fifteen years to get the only woman I have ever wanted right where I want her, and here I am, all fucked up, tangled up in my own boxers."

"We have all night, don't we?"

And the shadow of uncertainty in her eyes dropped him down to the bed's edge like a stone. His crass words earlier that *this was just sex* beat down on him. He didn't know what the hell *this* was, but it sure as hell wasn't *just sex*. If it was, he'd have never thought of her once after he'd walked away from Rodent fifteen years ago. Instead she'd dominated his thoughts for all those years. Consumed his mind. Hell, she owned half of it.

He inhaled a long, slow breath. "Yeah, we have all night." Hell, she could take a lifetime and he'd be okay with that.

"Okay then." Slowly, she slid off the bed, all sleek curves and soft, pliable flesh. Her sweet tongue moistened her lips as she looked at him, and his dick twitched. Grew harder. Her fingers slowly trailed down over his thigh as she slowly walked around him. She leaned into his ear. "I'm guessing you like fast and furious."

He would like anything she offered.

She rounded his knee, her finger still touching him. Always touching him. Driving him crazy mad with lust. "But, Virgil, there's a lot to be said for slow… and easy." She knelt down in front of him. Her finger slowly swirled around his knee and then ever so slowly down his shin, setting a chain reaction of awareness sliding down his spine. And lower still. "Like this," she added, pulling off one shoe, then the other. Tossing them off to the side. Next she reached for his clothes wrapped around his ankles. First, his pants. Then his boxers. And then…

And then she sat right there. Right between his legs, staring at his junk with such emotion softening her eyes. Approval…

surprise… Awe. And he didn't dare make any move to haul her close because it had been so damn long since anyone had stared at him like that.

Like they wanted him.

Not the persona, but *him*, the man. Never, to be exact. *No one* had ever wanted him like that. And it felt so damn good. Down there. Up here in his head. And for some damn reason right in the center of his chest.

Her eyes darkened with need as she leaned between his legs. Her fingers slowly trailed up the insides of his thighs. "You're better than I imagined," she whispered, and then her hands circled around him, her long fingers sliding into his groin hair. And his balls tightened.

"And I want inside you. *Now*." He stood, but with one palm to his chest, she pushed him back down.

"Slow and easy, Virgil," she reminded him. "I know things, too." she added, as she slid up over his body. Her hair tumbled over her shoulders, teasing his stomach. Then his pecs as she inched her naked way closer to him on her hands and knees. Until she was right between his legs, her sweet center teasing his hard cock. "Let me show you what it's like slow and easy."

And he was powerless. She was the one in control.

And she knew it. She sat on her heels. Lifted her breasts in her own hands. He got hotter, harder as she rubbed her nipples with her thumbs. Her head fell back, her eyelids closing in pleasure and he was ready to explode just watching her.

"Let me," Virgil begged, lifting his chest off the bed. And she leaned forward to allow him. And he eagerly latched onto her with his mouth, teasing her nipple, sucking it and part of her soft full breast inside his mouth. And while he tongued and tended to one breast, she thumbed the nipple of the other and softly told him with hot, wicked words what she wanted him to do to her.

"*Jee-suz*, Ruby Mae," he growled as he pushed her hand aside and sucked her pebbled nipple into his mouth. "You drive me crazy." He pushed her back down to the mattress until he had her underneath him. "You always have."

She laughed. A rich, throaty, sexy sound that slid right through him, imploding in his groin. "Slow, Virgil. And easy."

He slid into her hot, wet center. Once, then twice, and then she rolled him over. And he was on his back. And she was straddling his hips. "Slow and easy, baby," she told him.

"You like to torture me, don't you?" She was right where he wanted her. Rocking over him. All that wet, hot heat encircling and contracting around his throbbing dick. And she knew just how to drive him wild.

"You are beautiful," she softly told him as she slid down between his legs, her mouth inches from his dick. "I'd like to paint you," she whispered.

"I think you already have," he rasped out. Raising up on his elbows, he looked down at her.

She lifted her head. Her grin mischievous. Playful. And he liked this side of her, too. He liked all of her. Every delectable inch. "Not down here," she told him as her hands slowly slid up over his dick. Her fingers sliding over its engorged head. Stroking... teasing... promising more. "But I know just how I'd do it," and she proceeded to tell him every dirty detail right before she took him deep into her mouth.

Virgil groaned, his head falling back as sensation after sensation spread through his body, heating his blood, driving him higher and higher.

"Or here," she added, fondling his balls. "I have wanted to touch you since…"

That day in the woods behind the football field at high school. When they'd eagerly stripped each other's shirts off. And she'd nervously stood before him, naked to the waist, her beautiful breasts dappled with the light of the sun filtering in through the trees.

He'd thought her perfect then.

But this take-charge, know-what-she-wanted woman was so much better than the perfect innocent young woman she'd been back then. Life had tempered her. Made her stronger. And he wanted her more than he wanted his next breath. "*Now*. I want inside you now."

There was that teasing laugh again as she ignored his demand. As her hands traced over his shoulders. His pecs. His belly. And hips. "I have always loved your body," she whispered leaning over him, her mouth and tongue following the path of her fingers. "I loved everything about you. Even when I shouldn't," she whispered against his chest, as her mouth tasted and sampled a hot, wet path toward his—

"*Jee-zus*, Ruby Mae," he hissed as her mouth settled over his dick again and she sucked him into her mouth. Her finger fondling his balls. "*Jee-zus*," he hissed out again pushing her head closer to his groin as she took him deeper and deeper into her mouth. Over and over again. Faster. Deeper. And the pleasure was so intense he wouldn't last but a few more thrusts. Then he was pulling her head off of him. "When I come, I'm comin' inside you." And then he rolled her onto her back and was spreading her legs to make room for him.

"I have to taste you," he told her, as he dove for the curls between her legs that were driving him crazy. His mouth settled over her hot, wet center. His tongue licking… tasting…

209

And her hands were in his hair. Yanking him closer. Her nails scraping over his skull, the pleasure pain pushing him closer to his own release. "Yes, Virgil... Just like that... Oh, yeah.... More—Harder. Deeper." Her pants of pleasure surrounded him, fueling his own passion. And her words that followed, as guttural as his, fed the fire in his groin.

"Faster," she panted as he fitted his cock to her. She lifted her hips to take him. Her heels dug into the back of his legs. "Harder," she told him. And he was pumping faster. Harder. Deeper. And somehow she found a way to slide her hand between them. To squeeze and tug at his balls. And the most intense pleasure he'd ever felt in his entire life spread through his body. And he cried out as he came inside her, as her own orgasm squeezed him, pulling everything from him. Her cries of pleasure mingling with his.

He lay on top of her. Spent. Completely used up. His face buried against hers. The softness of her hair and the alluring scent of wild sex surrounded them. Their rough pants mingling together as he breathed her into his lungs.

He'd traveled the world. Had been schooled in the art of pleasure by the world's best, most willing, desirable women. Brazil. Bangkok, Japan. India. Thailand. But no one – not one single woman had ever made him feel the way she had. It was indescribable what she did to him.

Somehow he found the energy to roll off her. Side by side they lay together. Bodies touching. Chests heaving. They stared up at the ceiling. He couldn't stop the grin that spread wide across his face. He turned his head toward her.

She wore the same grin.

"You sucked me dry. I won't be able to get it up for at least a week."

"Oh, yeah?"

"Yeah." At least a week.

She rolled to her side. Her throaty chuckle slid under his skin, right to the spot in his chest where her fingers were now stroking. "Are you sure?" she playfully added, as her fingers moved lower still. And damn, if his dick didn't rise to attention. "We're not done here, Virgil," she softly told him as her fingers slowly slid down further still to wrap around his happy dick. "We're just getting started."

Chapter 13

"Ruby Mae, honey, wake up."

The mattress dipped and she rolled up against a warm thigh. "What time is it?" Reluctantly, she opened eyes. And feasted on the sexy man whose index finger was right now tracing lazy, erotic circles down her chest. She wrapped her finger around his. Moved it to where she wanted it. And smiled.

He smiled back and the erotic circles he was drawing were now right around her nipple.

She sighed in contentment. "I thought you were staying the night."

"I did."

She glanced up at the window. "It's still dark outside." Then back at the man sitting beside her, fully dressed in yesterday's wrinkled dress shirt and pants. Beard stubble darkened his jaw. His hair was still damp from his shower. She ran her fingers through it. "Stay a little longer."

He wrapped his fingers around hers. Drew them to his lips and kissed her fingers. "I can't. Billy saw the light on and he dropped off the papers I need for—"

"Oh, my God!" She snatched her hand back. If Billy saw the

light on that meant he'd come to the door. And then it was only a turn of the knob and a disapproving glance inside for him to have seen Virgil and her. She scrambled up off the bed.

Virgil placed a warm palm low on her back. "Isn't that like putting the horse in the barn a day late?"

"*What?*" She glanced over her shoulder as she untangled herself from the sheets. "Oh my God! Where are my clothes? My shirt? My shorts? I can't believe you let him in here!"

"I didn't let him in here. And you're getting steamed for nothing."

"Steamed?" She stared at him. "I'm getting steamed for *nothing?*"

"He knows, honey. And no amount of hiding it now's going to change that."

She sat back on her heels. He was right. She just didn't like.

He pushed a strand of hair from her cheek. Her hand flew to the tangled mess. She closed her eyes. "I know I look a mess." And probably every day – and then some – of her thirty-three years.

"You look beautiful. Just the way I like you." He brushed his lips against hers. "Naked," he playfully added as he kissed her gently on the mouth. All slow and easy. Like Sunday morning. And Ruby Mae relaxed against him. Savored what he was offering.

Too quickly he broke away. "Come on." He tugged her arm. "I'll walk you to your door."

With the quilt wrapped tightly around her, Ruby Mae leaned her head against his shoulder as they slowly walked under the waning moonlight toward her back porch and up the steps. They stopped in front of the door. His brow furrowed as he stared at it.

"Key's under the flower pot," she whispered, nudging her head toward the pot in the corner.

"A flower pot, Ruby Mae?" He walked over. Lifted the clay pot. Picked up the key. Held it out to her. "Really?"

"You do know who my neighbor is, right?" Billy Ray patrolled the neighborhood better than any of Rodent's finest.

He was still frowning. "He can't be everywhere all the time."

She took the key from him. Unlocked the door and stepped inside. She turned to face him. "He's not going to let anything happen to me or Brandon."

"Yeah, well… I care about you, too." And she knew he did. His warm, strong hands slowly rubbed up and down her arms. There was softness in his eyes she'd never seen before. One that gave her hope. One that made her think he might just feel the same way she did. He breathed deep, the muscles of his chest straining the buttons of his wrinkled dress shirt.

"Last night was… amazing," she whispered. Clutching the front of the quilt with one hand, she fished her other hand out through the folds of the soft material so she could touch him. Her fingers slipped into the silky strands of his still-damp hair. "I loved everything about it."

"I did, too," he told her, as his mouth trailed a line of kisses along her jaw and further to tease and lick her neck.

She pushed her tangled mess of hair over her shoulder, baring her neck, giving him better access to her skin. "I love what you do," she gasped, pleasure awakening inside her as he eagerly gave her more of what she wanted. More of what only he could do with his mouth and his very talented tongue. "Oh, yeah, more of that," she breathlessly told him. "Oh, God, yes," she gasped.

The quilt fell away as she reached for him with both hands. Her body melting against his as desire flamed hotter and hotter inside her. "I love you, Virgil."

And time stood still as he stood frozen beside her. His mouth still hovering over her neck, but not touching. His warm breath non-existent against her sensitized skin. And he said nothing. And her words hung in the air between them. Waiting for a response she knew she wasn't going to get. She took a deep breath. Swallowed her disappointment. "I'm sorry. I shouldn't have said that."

"Ruby Mae." His voice was gruff.

"It's okay. Really." Quickly, she bent down. Grabbed the quilt. Wrapped it around herself. She stepped further into the kitchen, hoping to escape.

"Ruby Mae." He reached for her arm, thwarting her. He slowly turned her toward him. Looked down at her. His expression pained.

And what had she expected? That he'd pledge his undying love like Willie Lee had? This was Virgil Push. And it wasn't like he hadn't told her up front that this was *just sex*. The best sex she'd ever have. But it was still *just sex*.

"I don't... I— I don't—"

"It's okay," she cut him off. "Really," she added, as she clutched the quilt to her naked body. "I just wanted you to know."

And he slowly shook his head up and down. And she waited the excruciatingly long minutes, wishing, hoping he'd tell her the words she desperately needed to hear. That this wasn't *just sex* to him. That he loved her. But he just stared at her. Emotion battling in his beautiful eyes. And her foolish heart filled with hope he'd say what she needed to hear. That he loved her.

His mouth opened. "I... I have to go," he told her, and she didn't try to stop him, reminding herself what he'd told her up front. But knowing that didn't change the fact one bit that she loved him. And it hurt that he didn't love her back.

And still he hesitated at her door. Unsure. Uncertain what to do.

"It's okay," she softly told him. She was the one who'd altered things. She was the one who'd changed the game, who hadn't played by his rules. "It's okay. Really," she told him.

And still he didn't leave.

"Just go, Virgil," she told him as gently as she could. God! She was so embarrassed.

He reached out for her. Changing his mind, his hands dropping to his sides. And he looked as uncomfortable as she felt.

"Just go," she told him again.

"I'll be back," he told her as if he were putting her on notice. "I'm sorry," he added.

"It's okay," she lied, as he turned and she slowly shut the door between them.

* * *

Virgil reluctantly walked to the edge of the porch. Dropped his head back and stared at the bleached-out nighttime sky. The craggy peak of the Brandywine was a dark shadow reaching skyward to the few die-hard stars fading in the early morning light. He sighed.

She loved him.

He scrubbed his hands down over his face. She just came right out and said she *loved* him. And he knew she meant it. Ruby Mae was not a woman to just *have sex*. "You're such an ass," he muttered under his breath. He'd seen the hurt and disappointment in her eyes when he didn't say the words back. But how could he tell her he loved her when he didn't believe in love?

He knew other people who'd claimed to be in love, but he'd never been.

He might not know how to love, or believe in it, but he could make her happy. She'd been screaming-out-his-name happy last night. Shouldn't that count for something? He walked back to the apartment. Opened the door. The scent of a night full of sex hit him in the face. She'd rocked his world. They were good together. Explosive. He could make her happy, even if he couldn't say the words she needed to hear.

They could have a good life together. Him. And her. And Brandon.

He picked up the bag of contraband. And that idyllic life started with him getting the gangs and drugs out her neighborhood. Getting them out of his town. He shut the door behind him. Looked once more toward the darkened kitchen before slowly walking down her driveway and down the road to where he'd left his car parked last night.

He keyed the remote to unlock it. Opened the door. He'd just dropped the bag of drugs onto the floor of the back seat when a police cruiser pulled up to a stop behind him. Virgil's heart did a slow thump in his chest when Officer Warren Clive stepped out.

"You're out an' about awful early this morning, Mister Mayor." Clive swiped his palm across the dew-covered trunk of Virgil's car, rubbing his finger together.

"Not really your concern, is it?"

Clive turned his head toward Ruby Mae's dark house and Virgil was glad she was disappointed enough in him and his mutated emotions not to be standing on the porch watching him leave. Clive looked back, a smug smirk curling up over his pasty lips. "Makin' house calls now, are you?"

"Officer Clive, I'm standing by my car. Last I checked nobody's living in it, so I guess that shoots down your house-call theory. Nice talking to you." Virgil reached for the door handle.

"Not often we see a car fine as this on this side of the Trail. It kind of stands out. All night long, if you get my drift."

Virgil spun around. "Is there something you want, Officer Clive? Or are you just wasting time before you clock out for your shift?"

"I do my job, Mister Mayor," Clive spit out, his face blotchy with anger, his phony grin gone. "And I do it better than these folk deserve."

Virgil barely resisted the urge to tell the bastard that these *folk*, as he called them, deserved a hell of a lot better than Warren Clive, but Virgil didn't want busted on a trumped-up drug charge in retaliation, which he was quite sure Clive would do if pushed too far. Virgil opened his car door. Slid behind the wheel and onto the dew-covered seat. The sooner he got away from the scumbag, the better off they'd both be. He pulled the door closed.

Clive stopped it. "So, Mister Mayor, is the lovely widow as good as I imagine? And trust me, I do imagine her lots of different ways."

Virgil refused to rise to the bait. And barely resisted the urge to jump out of the car and take this *sonofabitch* down. "She deserves your respect. Not your foul mouth," he told the man instead, as he jammed the key into the ignition. He turned it, and the engine purred to life. "You sadly lack knowledge in what's right and wrong."

"You cocky little prick." Clive reached in to grab Virgil's shirt. "I know what's right and wrong!"

"Ut-ut," Virgil shot a warning finger toward Clive. "You might want to think that through a little. It could bring *a lot* of charges your way. Like police harassment, intimidation, and brutality, just to name a few. And I'm lawyer enough to know all of them. You best watch your step, Officer Clive. I'm watching you," Virgil warned, before putting the car in drive and pulling away.

* * *

"Come on, you little prick, make one damn mistake!" Warren Clive snarled, as he followed the sports car traveling at a snail's pace down the road toward town. He was following close enough to see the remnants of duct tape fluttering on the scratched trunk. Hell, the little prick didn't take any better care of his car than he'd taken care of his wife. Everybody knew he'd been a lousy husband. He was a lousy damn mayor, too.

Virgil Push was not going to get the best of Warren Clive.

Clive would make damn sure of that.

The bastard was obviously not going to speed so he could pull him over and give him a ticket. Swerving into the deserted parking lot of the old distillery, Clive yanked the cruiser into park. And while it still rocked on its chassis, he grabbed his cell phone from the glove box. As he watched the little prick's taillights disappear over the Trail toward town, he called the number he knew by heart. Impatiently tapped his fingertips against the steering wheel while he waited for her to pick up.

"Do you know what time it is?" her haughty voice pierced the connection. "Decent people do not get up at this hour. But you aren't decent, are you?"

Neither was she. Clive ignored her taunt. "I have information you'll be interested in."

"Really."

Clive ground his teeth. He hated her imperious tone. But he loved the big, thick envelope he knew would await him. Money was money, and in Clive's opinion, none spent quite as sweetly as Push money.

"Well?" The voice on the other side of the connection grew impatient. "What is it?"

220

"It concerns your son."

"Virgil?"

Clive snorted. "You only have one, don't you? Or were you fuckin' more than ol' Vinnie?"

Clive knew she was. He savored her sharp intake of breath as his hand slid down behind the fly of his uniform. He knew all her secrets. "What are you wearin', Marilee?"

"None of your fucking business," she snapped, and he chuckled, growing harder in his own hand. He loved getting a rise out of her. "What about Virgil?" she impatiently demanded.

And he made her wait as he stroked his cock up and down. He had dirt on the Queen Bitch of Rodent. And she had dirt on him, which made theirs a mutually satisfying association, in Clive's opinion. She greased palms and kept the mayor's eyes off Clive's under-age dalliances. And in turn, he stole drugs from the evidence locker for her, intimidated suspects, and steered his stupid cousin, the chief of police away from Marilee's interests, illegal, immoral, or otherwise.

"I know where he spends his nights. And it ain't in that fancy place the town provides for him," he finally told her.

"And you think I'll pay for that?"

"Oh, you'll pay," he huffed out between strokes.

"Are you fucking yourself?" she demanded. "Wouldn't one of your little honeys do it better?" she taunted.

He chuckled at her balls. And her crudeness. His hand slid up and down. Faster and faster. "I could make *you* scream," he arrogantly told her, imagining it was her stroking him. Her, whose mouth was going down on him.

"Hardly," she replied, just as breathlessly, as if she were— He sat up straighter in his seat as semen filled his hand. "Christ, Marilee," he breathed out. "You're gettin' off on me gettin' off."

"Don't be ridiculous," she told him. And the line went dead. But not before he heard the breathless strain in her voice. Right before she came.

* * *

Marilee Push pulled her Mercedes in between a couple cars parked on the street near her son's townhouse. Her lips pursed in distaste at his choice of residence. If she'd had her way, he'd still be living in the mansion she'd steered him toward buying when he'd married Rachel. And he'd still be married to the woman. Rachel was perfect for him. Instead, he was panting after that Trail trash, Ruby Mae Shove. "You always were a bastard of a child."

Just like his father.

She cut the engine. Powered down the window, and watched for her son's return. She didn't have long to wait. He pulled into the driveway. Stepped from his car. Wearing yesterday's clothes. Whistling. Probably still reeking of sex.

It pissed her off.

She'd paved his way. Greased palms for him to take over the mayor's job when that imbecile in office before him had outlived his usefulness. She'd saved her son's face, too. Hid his disgrace when he'd slinked back into town broke. And this was the way he paid her back? By screwing that Shove woman. That woman he'd never gotten out of his system. No matter how much pussy Marilee had put in his path.

This was the one indiscretion she would not tolerate. Or allow.

For a while after he'd come back, he'd been a diligent son, doing what she'd wanted. Heeding her counsel on town matters, although he hadn't known it at the time. But this! This blatant disregard for her feelings where that Shove woman was concerned was irreprehensible. Totally unacceptable!

And she knew exactly how – and *who* to hurt to make him pay.

* * *

It was late afternoon. Ruby Mae had just changed the sheets on the sofa bed in the apartment when two cars pulled into her driveway. Grabbing the duster, she stashed it under the mini bar. Put the vacuum in the closet. Rolling the sheets up into a ball, she walked outside.

Virgil was standing by the opened trunk of his car. He was directing an older woman, pointing her toward the apartment. "Just put that in there."

"Excuse me." Ruby Mae rushed up to Virgil. "What are you doing?" she pointedly asked as the older woman passed by with a box to disappear inside Ruby Mae's apartment.

"Oh, hey, babe." He brushed his mouth against hers with a quick kiss. "How's it goin'?"

And before she could answer, he lifted a cardboard box from his trunk. Handed it off to the older woman when she returned. "Just put these on the table in there, too."

"No, no. No!" Ruby Mae told the woman.

At the woman's questioning look, Virgil replied, "It's okay," overriding her. The woman disappeared inside to do his bidding.

"Virgil!" Ruby Mae spun around to face him. "What are you doing?" She looked into his trunk. "Oh, my God!" she exclaimed, as she looked at the boxes filled with manila file folders, computer equipment, desk accessories, and, of course, the ones filled with clothes. "What do you think you're doing? You can't move in here. That's what you're doing when you pack up your office. And— oh my God! Your underwear. That's your underwear. Admit it! You're moving in!"

"Ruby Mae, honey," he said, his smile forced and strained. "We talked about this."

"No. No, we didn't. You cannot move in here!"

"Excuse us, Emma." Virgil wrapped an arm around Ruby Mae's shoulders in a vice-like grip. "You just keep unloading that stuff," he added, as he forcibly walked Ruby Mae away from his car.

Ruby Mae rounded on him the moment he stopped. "You *cannot* move in here! And who is that woman?"

"I have to. And that's Emma. My assistant."

"Your assistant," Ruby Mae flatly replied. "You have an assistant. Of course, you do." He was a Push. Probably the richest man in Vermin County. Of course, he would have an assistant. One who was right now adding up one and one and coming up with a whopper of a tale to tell around the water cooler in City Hall. Ruby Mae turned to find the woman standing by the door, arms full, intently watching them. She called out to her. "This is not— We're not—" Ruby Mae waggled her hand between them.

Emma's eye brows arched. A knowing grin spread across her face. And still she stood by the door watching them.

"I give up." Ruby Mae squeezed her eyes shut. She was toast. She opened them, turning back to the problem at hand. She pointed a finger at him. "You cannot move in here."

"Ruby Mae," he wrapped his fingers around hers. Lifted them to his lips. He kissed it. Added, "We talked about this last night."

She yanked her hand free. "We talked about a lot of things, but *not* you moving in!"

"Ruby Mae, I need to be closer to my people."

"Your people? Now you have *people*?"

His lips flattened. His eyes narrowed. "You know what I mean."

"No, I don't!" He spent one night with her. *One night!* And he'd said nothing when she told him she loved him, except that he had to go. And now he was *moving in*? "In case you've forgotten, Virgil, I already have one illegal business on the property. I don't need another one." Or a way too handsome, way too sexy man who she was in love with, but who wasn't in love with her under foot.

"This wouldn't be illegal."

"Yes, it would!"

"Think of it as confiscation of property for mayoral business. A seizure of sorts."

"A seizure?" *She* was having a seizure. Quite possibly a stroke, if the constant twitch in her right eye was any indication.

He silenced her with a finger against her lips. Seriousness settled over his features. "I have to have access to the people on this side of the Trail and the Brandywine. And I have to be accessible in town. So the office I'm setting up here will be after hours. Evenings. Early evenings," he quickly amended, as if he were making this up as he went. "Couple nights a week, honey, tops. And I need to have clothes."

"Of course, you need to have clothes," she told him. "Because you'll be *living* here!" she nearly shouted. "You're moving in. You are moving in! Admit it!"

"Would that be so bad?" he quietly asked.

And the tension built.

It would be awful. It would be *wonderful*. Having a man underfoot again. Making dinner for a man with a healthy appetite. Having someone her age to talk with. To laugh with. To wake up

225

next to. She sighed. "No, it wouldn't. But what about Brandon?" she softly asked. "I have my son to think about." Her son who didn't like Virgil. Her son who was angry all the time. Her son who was *this* close to being lost to her. This could put him right over the edge. And into the hands of drug dealers and gang bangers.

"I talked to Brandon."

"*What?*" Her eye was twitching faster. "You talked to Brandon. When?"

"When I stopped over this afternoon."

"You stopped *here?* This afternoon?" Why hadn't she known about that?

"He's okay with me being here."

"*My* son? *My son* is *okay* with you being here?" Was one side of her body going numb?

He shrugged a broad shoulder. "I told him what I wanted to do."

"You *told* him what you wanted to do?"

"Ruby Mae? You okay?" He touched the side of her face. "You look a little twitchy."

She slapped his hand away. "That's because I'm *having a stroke*! You talked to my son and *I didn't know?*"

"Ruby Mae. It was man talk."

"Man talk."

"Yeah, man talk," he replied. Like there actually was such a ridiculous thing! "I'm not dumb. I wouldn't do anything to hurt him. And he's okay with me being here."

"You asked Brandon," she whispered. Her hand curled over her heart. He'd thought of her son. He'd been concerned about her son's feelings.

"Well, yeah. Of course, I did." He looked affronted. "I would never do anything to hurt you. Or Brandon. I care about you. And about him."

And more tension filled the air. He cared.

But he didn't say he loved her.

His blond brows drew together. And still he said nothing else. And she knew she wasn't going to get anymore. He wasn't going to say what she needed to hear.

But he cared about her son.

Enough to ask him before he did something crazy. And moving in here was crazy. She let out a sigh of defeat. "I just wished you would have warned me," she told him, tugging on the hem of her frayed shorts. "I look a mess to be meeting people."

"No, you don't," he told her as he brushed a curl from her cheek. "You always look beautiful to me."

His phone rang. He pulled it from his pocket. Looked at the screen. "I have to take this," he told her, before walking way.

Ruby Mae turned to find Emma standing near.

"So, you're Ruby Mae," Emma said, stepping closer. "So you're the one who makes him smile."

"He's a politician. He has a whole drawer full of those smiles."

"Not that one." Emma gave her a knowing grin. "And if I didn't miss my guess, you're the one who put the spring in his step this morning."

Ruby Mae clamped her jaw shut. Wished heat wasn't flaming

across her cheeks like a neon billboard saying, *Yes! I had phenomenal, life-altering sex with Mayor Push.*

"It's okay, honey." Emma reached over and patted Ruby Mae's tense forearm. "He's a good man. Probably the best mayor we've had in ages. That bitch of a mother got him appointed, you know."

"No, I didn't know that."

"Thinks she can run him like he's her own personal puppet."

Ruby Mae frowned. The bossy, take-charge man she knew would *never* be anyone's puppet.

"You know, there isn't a nicer guy than Vincent Push. And he," Emma's chin nudged toward Virgil's turned back. "Is just like his daddy." She turned her gaze toward Ruby Mae. "Watch his back, honey."

"What? Why?"

Emma looked left. Then right. And then she leaned close, her voice soft. Like someone might be listening. "His bitch of a momma put him in this job thinking he'd be one of her puppets. When she finds out he's not, there'll be hell to pay."

"What? I don't understand any of this. What are you talking about?" Ruby Mae asked as she dogged Emma's steps back to her car. This was suggesting something—

"When Marilee gets wind of what's going on over here —"

"What do you mean, going on over here?" Did she mean Virgil's satellite office? Or them? A shiver of uncertainty washed down over Ruby Mae.

"She'll come after him," Emma went on, pulling her car door open. "And she won't be happy until she brings him down. I'm warning you, honey. Beware." She slid in behind the steering wheel.

Looked up at Ruby Mae. "Watch his back. And while you're at it, watch your own back."

"Emma." The car started. "Emma! What are you talking about?" Ruby Mae called out, as a wave of foreboding steamrolled right down her spine.

But Emma had already put the car in gear, was backing down her driveway. And with a wave, she pulled out onto the road, heading back toward town.

Chapter 14

Man talk. When had they had time for *man talk,* Ruby Mae wondered, as she prepared a snack for Brandon. Business had been slow today. She'd had one customer. She'd been away from Brandon for ten— fifteen minutes, tops. When could they have possibly *talked?* Debated? Weighed out the pros and cons of what they were about to do? Or shouldered the guilt of their actions? "Man talk, yeah, right," she mumbled under her breath, as she rinsed off the knife she was using.

As if an internal hunger alarm had gone off, her son rushed in through the back door. His face was flushed. His hand still stuffed into the baseball mitt the man in question had bought him. "I'm starvin', mom," he told her, as he jumped up to sit on the counter top. The back of his sneakers bounced off the cupboard door below as he grabbed for a slice of apple.

"Off the counter, young man," she reprimanded him.

"I'm not hurtin' nothing," he grumbled.

"*Anything,*" she corrected his grammar. "And your smelly butt is on my counter."

"You're such a girl," he said. Like his father used to, but he did jump down.

"Wash your hands. You were outside."

"So?"

"Just go," she told him, pointing in the direction of the bathroom. She finished slicing the apple she was peeling for him. Added a couple grapes and a few raisins – not that she expected him to eat those. Shriveled-up food was unacceptable in Brandon's world. She picked up the plate. Turned around.

"*Cereal,* Brandon? You're eating *cereal?*" And eating it right from the box. His cheeks filled, looking like a ground squirrel. "You just had lunch an hour ago."

"I'm hungry," he replied around a mouthful.

She set the plate of fruit in front of him before taking the seat beside him. "So… You… and Virgil…" She tested the waters.

His turquoise-eyed gaze, the one exactly like his father's, fixed on her before sharpening and pinning her to the spot. It was a warning look she knew well.

One she chose to ignore. "So, you and Virgil… You guys hooked up today and had a little talk?"

He said nothing.

She tried again. "So… You're okay with Virgil staying here? In the apartment? I mean, of course, he'd be in the apartment. Where else would he stay?" She nervously laughed. "You're okay with him here, right? Living with us. Well— I mean— Not that he'll actually be *living* with us, but he'll be here— I mean not *here*, not *right here*, I mean not exactly *right here*, but …" she wound down. Let out a sigh of defeat. "You're okay with him doing his mayor stuff here?"

His mouth had been stuffed full of cereal the whole time.

It still was.

He didn't move. Didn't chew. Didn't swallow. Didn't say anything either. Just watched her. With his father's eyes.

She nervously played with the edge of the placemat. Her finger tracing the frayed seem. "I'm glad you're okay with it. Virgil's a good guy. He's a nice man, too."

Brandon's eyes narrowed. Exactly like his daddy's had that day fifteen years ago. And any time after when Virgil's name was mentioned, even in passing.

And a tiny voice inside her head was telling her to *stop!* But she didn't. "He really is a nice man, Brandon."

"He's a wuss."

So, they were back to that again. "He's not a wuss, honey," she softly told him, not wanting to start an international incident, but needing him to understand. "He's trying to help you. And me. And Maisey and Uncle Billy and everybody over here…" She let her words die a natural death. Her son obviously had his own opinion of Virgil. Nothing she could say would change it.

He swallowed. Slipped off the chair and stood. "You done?"

Well, so much for her enlightening *mother/son* talk. "Yes," she quietly replied.

He grabbed his ball glove. Slipped his hand into the leather and pushed open the back door.

"Don't leave the backyard," she called out.

"Jeez, Mo-om, I already told the wuss I wouldn't leave," he informed her, before disappearing out the backdoor.

And Ruby Mae could only watch. And wonder how Virgil Push, a spoiled only child, a man with no children of his own, knew how to reach her son.

Better than she did.

Dusk was settling in over the Brandywine. Ruby Mae was turning down Brandon's bed when she heard voices in the backyard coming in through the open window.

"Spread your legs a little further apart. Come on, I gotta be able to hit the sweet spot."

Not exactly the usual conversation coming from out there.

Ruby Mae went to the backdoor. She quietly stepped out onto the porch to find Brandon squatted down over a makeshift home plate. He was wearing a brand new chest protector and a catcher's mask. One she hadn't bought. The price tag was still hanging off it. Shin guards – again, ones she hadn't bought – protected his legs from the tops of his scuffed tennis shoes to above his knees.

And the man in question, the one who wanted legs spread further apart so he could hit the sweet spot, was still dressed in the same navy blue dress pants and blue shirt he'd put on when he'd left this morning. The shirt was limp from a long day doing his *mayor* stuff. The top two buttons were opened. His always-present tie was still wrapped around his neck, but the knot was askew and pulled halfway down his chest. His sleeves were rolled up over his forearms. Golden blond hair brushed against his collar. Fireflies circled overhead, their neon glow blinking on and off like dilapidated lights over this makeshift field of dreams.

"That's it. Now guard the plate like I showed you." Virgil assumed a pitcher's stance. "Now I'm going to toss you one with a little pepper on it. You ready?"

Brandon snorted, but he assumed the squatting catcher's stance like he'd been doing it all his life instead of for the short amount of time they'd been out here tonight. Brandon hadn't shown an interest in baseball. Even when she'd tried to throw him pitches.

Virgil fired a pitch right into Brandon's glove like the all-star pitcher he'd been in high school. The crack of leather against leather was loud and sharp, slicing through the muggy air.

"You throw like a girl," Brandon taunted, firing a pitch right back at Virgil.

Ruby Mae's brows furrowed. When had her son learned to throw like that? And so well?

"Yeah, yeah, right," Virgil blew off his taunt. "You'll be wishing you were wearing the cup I bought you if you miss this one, brat."

Cup? Her son was old enough to wear a cup? And then she wondered how that conversation went. And did it qualify as *man talk*, too?

Virgil assumed his pitcher's stance. He fired another pitch, faster than the last one at Brandon's glove. The one he had positioned right between his legs and Ruby Mae held her breath, wishing her son wouldn't have been so stubborn – and yes, she wasn't naïve enough to think it was modesty that had kept her son from putting the damn thing on.

But her son caught the pitch! Like he'd inherited his daddy's athletic prowess. And Ruby Mae clapped. Like a proud mother.

"You throw like a girl," Brandon taunted, throwing the ball back, obviously inheriting some of his father's cockiness, too.

Virgil laughed, easily catching it. "Your daddy used to always say that, too."

And even from the porch she could see the pride in her son's stance at the mention that he was like his father.

Brandon punched his fist into the center of his glove. "You gonna throw? Or talk like a girl?"

"You didn't fall far from the tree, did you, kid?" Virgil assumed his pitching stance. "See how you do with my special curve ball." He fired a ball that had Brandon leaving the safety of the plate, stretching full out to the side, nearly falling over in the process.

"Come on. The runner's headed to home and the pitch from the outfield was shitty."

"*Virgil.*" She was going to have to give him another lecture about swearing in front of her son.

"Damn straight is was shitty."

"Brandon!" She was going to have to lecture *both* of them.

"You got to tag him, or the other team wins the game. Come on," Virgil coached him. "Lord over that plate. Nobody got by your daddy and nobody's going to get by you. You're the boss of this game. You're the badass."

"Do not encourage him," Ruby Mae called out.

"Oh, Mo-om!" her son whined, sounding very much like a well-adjusted seven-year-old. "I am a Baddass."

She rolled her eyes. *So much for well-adjusted.* "Brandon, no swearing—"

"I'm just like dad," he proudly said, and Ruby Mae swallowed the reprimand to stop swearing when she heard the pure joy in her son's voice.

"He's right, Ruby Mae," Virgil told her. Like it had been Brandon recounting Willie Lee's athletic prowess from memory instead of having it spoon-fed to him from Virgil. God! She loved the man for that alone. "You remember how we played together. You remember what he was like."

She did.

Virgil had been the star pitcher. Willie Lee the all-star catcher. Best friends taking their team to the state championship three years running. And then her coming between them in their senior year, destroying that friendship. *I'm sorry, Willie Lee. So very sorry.* She'd said those words so many times in the last fifteen years. Even knowing Willie Lee had forgiven her, she still carried the guilt.

"Come on now," Virgil called out. "Throw me one of the signs I taught you. You're the one calling the pitches. I gotta know what you want me to throw."

Brandon's hand dropped down between his wide-spread legs. One finger extended from his hand not covered with a glove. One middle finger.

"Not that sign," Virgil told him, dropping his stance.

"*Brandon!*" Ruby Mae gasped.

"And for the record," Virgil looked over at her. "I didn't teach him that."

Leaving her to wonder where he had learned it. She stepped away from the porch post. "I think that's enough for tonight."

"Aw, mo-om!"

"Aw, Ruby Mae!" they both whined at the same time. "Come on," Virgil begged. "We just got started."

"Yeah, mom. It ain't even dark yet."

"Isn't," she corrected his bad English. "And it's close enough."

"Just a few more minutes, Ruby Mae. Please?"

"Yeah, mom," her son added. "Please, please, *please?*"

"I'll make it up to you… later," the big boy added. The mischief in his eyes conveyed exactly how he planned to do it.

"Five more minutes, *boys*," she conceded to his charisma, trying hard to hide a grin. One was a little boy who could get away with that kind of whining and begging. And the other... Well, he could get away with just about anything when he looked at her like that.

* * *

The encroaching night had claimed the Brandywine, smothering it in darkness. From somewhere down the street a door slammed and a dog barked. A whole lot closer, crickets chirped and an owl hooted. And when he should pick up his glove and take his tired body to his new quarters in Ruby Mae's apartment, Virgil sat on her back porch steps, savoring the precious ordinariness of the bedtime ritual. Ruby Mae's voice and Brandon's accompanying whine floated out from the brat's window. And Virgil waited for the tension of a lousy day to leave his muscles.

A short while later she stepped through the back door. "He's finally asleep. Still wearing that chest protector," she added, as she sat down beside him on the back porch. The subtle scent of her shampoo swirled around him, teasing his nose. She looked over at him. Patted his knee. "You didn't have to buy all that stuff for him, you know."

"Yeah, I did." He wrapped his arm around her, needing to feel her close. "I had to do something good for a kid tonight." He breathed out a long, slow breath.

"It didn't go well with the girls today?" she quietly asked, leaning into him.

He shook his head. He'd finally gotten in touch with the girls and their families and had arranged to meet with them. "I guess I wanted more." His hand curled into a fist of frustration. He'd wanted them eager to follow him in his quest to take Clive down.

"They're teenage girls. *Dammit!*" Teenage girls being forced to strip in front of some old bastard who fondled them for their trouble. "He humiliates them. And he does it all under the pretense of dropping charges against them or their families or their boyfriends. "*Jee-zus.*"

He ran a hand through his hair in frustration. "Our children are supposed to be able to trust the police to protect them. Not be extorted by them." He swung his head toward her. "I talked to six girls today. And their families. Two refused. Absolutely refused to say anything. But I could see, *dammit!* I could see shame in their eyes. And they didn't do anything wrong!"

"I'm sorry." Her hand gently rubbed over his thigh, easing one tension, igniting another one in his groin. "What about the other four?" she asked.

He rubbed the tension from his forehead with his fingers. "Becca Anderson could barely talk about it. She'd be no good on the stand." He sucked in a deep breath. "Emily O'Leary, Gina Dimaglio, and Katie Michaelson talked to me. But when it came time to make a statement, Gina and Katie said they wanted time to think about it."

She rubbed her fingers over his knee again. "I'm sorry."

"And I had to sit there with my thumbs up my ass. And smile. And make nice knowing full well that bastard could be trolling the streets for his next victim if they don't agree to help me!"

"What about Emily?"

Virgil rolled the tension from his shoulders. He rubbed his thumb over her long, slender fingers, feeling better just touching her hand. He exhaled another breath of spent tension. "Emily is Tim O'Leary's daughter. Did you know that?"

Curly strands of her hair caught in his beard stubble as she nodded her head up and down.

"He was a couple years ahead of us in school, but I knew him. I knew Shannon, too. And Emily." The tension built right back up in

239

Virgil's shoulders. "Emily is this beautiful girl who looks exactly like her momma."

"I remember Shannon." She softly told him. "She was beautiful."

"They put their house up for sale, did you know that?"

"That's because Clive went after Shannon at the supermarket on a trumped-up parking violation. And then stopped her a couple times out on the Dinnerbell Road. To harass her."

"You knew about that?" His head swung toward her. Of course, she would.

She pulled her hand back. "It wasn't a secret, Virgil. When Tim came to Billy—"

Virgil put a hand up. "Spare me," he wearily told her. He was in no mood for a pissing contest with Billy Ray. Truth be told, he was jealous of the man. And enraged at the injustice being done to these girls. "I'm sorry," he told her. "I'm just tired."

"And angry."

"Hell, yeah, I'm angry. I have six girls who came forward. And probably another six – or more – who are too embarrassed, or too ashamed, or too afraid to say anything. And I got one girl's confirmation of Clive asking for oral sex in exchange for dropping charges, but she's too afraid of the bastard to come forward. And I can't blame her. She's sixteen."

"Becca?"

Virgil nodded his head.

"What are you going to do?"

"I'm going to go before the Executive Council and hope they back me on this." There was protocol he had to follow since town

240

ordinance didn't allow the mayor alone to fire a sick bastard masquerading as a policeman.

"I can't imagine they wouldn't."

Virgil wasn't as certain. His mother was a member of Council. And after what he'd learned about her lately, he wasn't sure he ever really knew her. Much less know whether she'd back him, or not.

"You know Clive is the chief's cousin."

"*Yes*, I'm aware Chief Rutledge is related to Clive," he testily replied. "I did live here, you know."

Her nostrils flared. "You don't have to get huffy."

"I'm sorry." He sucked in a sharp breath. "I'm just tired."

"No, you're mad. And when you're mad, you act out."

She knew him well. He did turn into a bastard when he was mad. And he was plenty mad.

"Do you have enough to make a case against Clive?" she asked.

And Virgil stared out over the darkness. "Provided Emily is willing to go before a judge. And provided no surprises come out in her background—"

"Emily's never been in trouble."

"She got caught spray painting graffiti on one of those abandoned houses."

"*What?*" Ruby Mae's eyes went wide with surprise.

"That's how Clive got her. Her boyfriend talked her into going down there with him. And when Clive pulled onto the scene, the boyfriend ran, leaving Emily holding the can. Clive had her where he wanted her then, and he slapped the cuffs on her."

Her hand went to her chest. "That's awful!"

"That's procedure. But it was when he offered to drop the charges if she'd strip for him that he'd crossed the line."

"And when she refused?"

"She didn't."

"No!" she gasped.

"Yeah," he confirmed. "She stripped for him. And he fondled her."

Ruby Mae squeezed her eyes shut. Raised her hand, palm out. "I don't want to hear any more."

And Virgil was glad. Recounting that girl's humiliation, remembering her tears, and her parent's anguish were images he wouldn't soon forget.

"I hate those houses! I hate that kid's lives are being ruined down there."

He wrapped an arm around her tense shoulders. "That's why we're going to make sure we don't lose any more kids down there."

She turned in his arms. "Tim and Shannon are wonderful people. They shouldn't have to go through this."

"I know they are. But Clive's attorney will be looking for anything to discredit Emily. And since I only have her statement – and there's no guarantee I'll be getting any more – I have to be concerned. But before we get that far, I have to present my findings to the Executive Council and Brett. I just can't fire Clive. There's procedure that has to be followed."

"Then what?"

"Then I can demand an internal police investigation. And if I get it, they'll check Clive's past arrest records, looking for other victims. And we'll keep digging on our end—"

"You and Billy?"

Virgil nodded his head. "Yeah, me and Billy. Who'd have thought, huh?" Him and Billy Ray Trainor joining forces. It was like the Dark Side converting one of God's own archangels.

"What if the chief doesn't buy it?" she quietly asked. Her eyes were shadowed with worry.

"He won't. No leader likes having a wrong pointed out. Especially one related to them by blood. And certainly none as illegal and immoral as what Clive's doing. Brett isn't going to like it. But, you know what?" He ran his hands through his hair. "I don't want to be mayor of this damn town if the Council and the chief of police turn their backs on these girls. We failed to protect them. I have to stand up for them!"

She took his hand. Wrapped both hers around it. "I love that you're helping those girls." She lifted her face. Looked at him with soft brown eyes swimming with emotions he couldn't even name. And time stopped. It stood still. Hovering all around him. And her. And everything else – every problem, every concern – seemed to fall away. Everything but her, and everything she felt for him shimmering in her beautiful eyes.

"I love you."

Her words were a warm caress against his skin. Her fingers slowly slid down over his chest to curl over his heart. And she smiled up at him before leaning close, brushing a gentle kiss against his mouth.

And as he kissed her back, he wondered how he'd gotten so lucky.

And what he was going to do about.

"I love you." She told him again.

"Ruby Mae." He hated that his voice sounded so pained. So desperate.

She sat back from him. "It's okay, Virgil," she softly told him. Her gaze dropping from his as she stared into her lap. She inhaled a slow, deep breath. The kind that sucked in the hurt and disappointment and pushed it deep inside.

And he dropped his gaze. Staring into his own lap.

She was asking for something he couldn't give her.

"I just want you to know."

She said that a lot to him, too. That it was okay he couldn't say the words. That she loved him anyway. And he knew she meant it. Just like he knew she staunchly believed in the emotion.

Him? He wasn't sure love even existed. But he wrapped an arm around her anyway. Held her close. More for him than her. He was that selfish. And he savored the heat of desire that always burned between them. He knew it would only take a kiss and he could have her in his bed. And he didn't know why he didn't do that.

Instead he pulled her closer. Savored her softness pressed against him. And the contentment that seemed to surround him when she could make everything all right in his world just by being with him.

"I'll take care of Brandon," he softly told her, wrapping his arms tighter around her.

"I know you will," she whispered against his neck as she laid her head on his shoulder.

"I'll take care of those girls, too." And he'd get Clive off the force and brought up on charges so he couldn't hurt another girl again.

"I know you will," she softly told him. Like she had no doubt in his abilities.

And when he got all that taken care of, then he'd try to figure out this thing between them.

This thing she called *love* that he knew nothing about.

Chapter 15

Virgil was unusually nervous as he paced one side of his office waiting for this special session of Executive Council to begin. Worried, in fact. He had so much he wanted to present. His vision for the abandoned distillery. His fix for Ruby Mae's problem. His plans for the additional police station. The community center. His undeclared war on drugs and gangs. Clive. He fidgeted with his tie while he anxiously watched his office door.

One by one, Council members filed in. Davis, who never missed a meeting. Always prompt, always first. He was followed by Sonny, and Marilee. Even Edgar Wyatt, whose duties at Wyatt Distilleries kept him more times at the distillery than in meetings here in chambers, had shown up. All who were left to show were Billy Ray and the chief. And Virgil barely resisted the urge to run out to the outer office's door and look down the hall. *They'll be here*, he kept telling himself.

"Let's get started." Marilee was the only one sitting at the large meeting table. Davis was standing by his chair waiting for the call to meeting. Sonny was trolling the snack table. Wyatt was hanging out by Virgil's desk looking way too close at Ruby Mae's painting. "Everyone's here," she told him, reaching for the gavel.

"Everyone's *not* here." Virgil shot across the expanse of rug to lay claim to it. "And *I* call the meetings to order, not you."

The door opened. Billy Ray walked in. He nodded his head to Virgil.

"What's he doing here?" Marilee demanded, and while Virgil explained as little as he absolutely could, Billy walked to the far side of the office where he fell into easy conversation with Edgar Wyatt.

Virgil's brows drew together as he stared at the two. How the hell did Billy Ray Trainor know Edgar Wyatt? And so friendly like? They hardly ran in the same social circles. Hell, even when Virgil had been rolling in money, he didn't run in Edgar's circle.

And while Sony had moved on to entertaining Percy and irritating Marilee in the process, Virgil made his way across his office only to find both men seemingly fascinated with Ruby Mae's painting. Edgar ran an appreciative finger along the lines of the paint on the canvas.

Virgil wanted to slap his hand away.

"How's your momma?" the whiskey baron asked Billy.

Edgar knew Billy Ray's momma?

"Doin' fine," Billy answered.

"Glad to hear that. How's Ruby Mae? How's her shop doin'?"

Wyatt knew about Ruby Mae's shop? Virgil stepped closer.

"It's keeping her real busy," Billy Ray replied. "She would have lost the house without your help."

What the hell? Virgil could feel his eyes bugging out. Could feel his mother's eyes boring holes right between his tension-filled shoulder blades, too. And he knew he was walking a fine line here. Any misstep and he tipped his hand. And put Ruby Mae back in Marilee's sights. A place Virgil didn't want her to be.

"It was real nice of you, Wyatt, to help her get set up."

248

"*Excuse me?*" The words spewed out of Virgil's mouth. The words to demand to know exactly how Edgar Wyatt helped set up Ruby Mae were clamoring up into his throat. "You *bent* code enforcement laws to set Ruby Mae up in her shop?" Virgil asked instead in a low, harsh voice. Edgar was one of Rodent's most prestigious, upstanding citizens. As a member of Executive Council, he most certainly knew the town ordinances.

And that Ruby Mae was breaking them.

Edgar looked over his shoulder. "I see you've got yourself a Ruby Mae," he added, totally sidestepping Virgil's question.

Well, two could play that game. Virgil stepped closer. He pointed a finger at the man's chest. "You helped set up Ruby Mae in a shop that didn't comply with zoning regulations?"

"She's an amazing talent. And a beautiful woman," Edgar slyly added. "I was just doing my civic duty."

"By ignoring zoning ordinances? By setting her up to break the law? By—"

Edgar waved away Virgil's interrogation with his hand. "I merely helped out a beautiful woman in her time of need."

"If you say she's *beautiful* one more time—"

"You want to dispute that fact, Virgil? That surprises me, what with your reputation with the ladies and all." The whiskey baron turned back to the painting. "Can you imagine all the passion, all the fire behind each stroke of her—"

"Will you forget about the damn painting!" Virgil growled.

Wyatt turned toward him. The smirk on his face confirmed that the bastard knew he was getting to Virgil. "I can't. Her paintings leave an impact. Almost as much as her beauty."

"That's the second time you called Ruby Mae *beautiful.*"

"Third," Billy Ray corrected him in a low voice.

Virgil glared at him.

"Oh, I'm sorry," Edgar went on, blowhard that he suddenly was. "I should have added vivacious, intriguing, and… sexy." The bastard was pouring it on as he tapped his knuckles against Virgil's tie. The look on his face smug. Like he knew something Virgil didn't. "Definitely sexy," he added, before walking over to join the others at the meeting table.

Virgil turned on Billy Ray. "You let him near Ruby Mae?" he growled.

Billy dark brows drew together. "He helped her," he succinctly pointed out.

"He is a blowhard! A jerk. A—"

"All right, Mayor." Chief Rutledge walked into the room ending Virgil's tirade. The police chief looked none too pleased to be here. "So what is so damn important you called me away from my regular duties?"

"Sit down," Virgil told the man. "And we'll tell you."

* * *

Billy Ray was freakin' amazing.

That was the only way Virgil could describe the man as he stepped the members gathered around the table through what they'd found. And with such authority. And attention to detail. Evidence had been bagged. And tagged. He had pictures. Statements from residents. Copies of surveillance reports he'd made on the drug houses. And background information he'd been able to dig up on gangs infiltrating in the area. He had the answers to any questions the Council members sent his way.

And he'd never lost his cool once. Nor even when Marilee had gone for his jugular questioning his credentials. Or the chief, when he'd tried to dismiss the evidence they'd presented.

Freakin' amazing.

"I never knew," Davis quietly said as he stared in shock at the pile of drug paraphernalia sitting in the middle of the table.

"Nor I," Edgar added. "I had no idea we had this kind of problem. And in Ruby Mae Shove's backyard. What a shame for such a *beautiful* woman to have this kind of trouble."

Virgil gritted his teeth. The bastard was baiting him. And he refused to rise to it.

"This is just *awful*," Edgar went on, dramatically shaking his head, "Terrifying, too." And Virgil wondered if the man had plans for an acting career after his whiskey-making gig.

"We don't even know for sure there's an actual problem," Marilee brusquely interrupted. "We shouldn't make any decisions based on one man's observations." She gave Virgil a frosty glare. "And a wannabe man at that."

"Are you for real?" Virgil growled. "*I* saw those kids. *I* was with Billy Ray when we drove all over this town and up the Brandywine. *I* was there when he talked to witnesses. He gave you their names. Their statements."

"Hearsay." She waved his defense away with the flick of her wrist.

"Fact, Marilee. They're *facts*. We need to act now." Virgil looked to each member of the Council sitting around the table. "And we need to act. Now. Before we lose another kid. Before gangs get a serious hold on our town. Before drugs are easily bought on our streets."

Before Ruby Mae lost Brandon.

"I totally agree with Virgil," Edgar pompously replied. "I will make immediate arrangements to have my abandoned company houses torn down. Emma?" He turned to Virgil's assistant. "Can you make arrangements, dear, for the newspapers and the television news crews to be on the courthouse steps at oh, say," he glanced down at his Rolex. "Three o'clock?"

"What do you think you're doing?" Virgil asked.

"Sure," Emma talked over Virgil. "But Mister Wyatt?" she went on. "In case you forgot, what with you being so busy an' all relocating your distillery from here in Vermin County up to Kendrick County, eliminating jobs down here, putting your own neighbors and fellow citizens out of work, well, I just want to remind you Rodent's a small town. We only have one weekly newspaper. And no television stations. Or crews to come to the courthouse steps at *oh, say, three o'clock.*"

Edgar's eyes narrowed at her veiled sarcasm and criticism.

Virgil wanted to applaud her.

"Call the television stations in Knoxville then, Miz Lewis," Edgar snapped. "And the affiliates in Vermin Springs. They'll race to the courthouse steps to hear anything *I* have to say."

"What are you planning on saying?" she asked sweetly, totally overstepping her boundaries as the recorder of minutes for these meetings. "Us being a small town and all, there has to be some phenomenal reason for the television crews to drive on over here."

"Why, Miss Emma," Wyatt cozied up to the prospect of a captive audience. "I'm planning on telling the world what our mayor here has informed us of. That crime is *rampant* in our streets."

"It's not *rampant*," Virgil hotly replied.

"That gangs and drug lords are takin' over our neighborhoods."

252

"I didn't say that!"

Wyatt looked at Virgil. "Yes, you did. For the last two hours."

"That's not what I said. You're twisting my words. You're twisting everything."

Edgar leaned his elbows on the table. "Mister Mayor, you can't have it both ways."

Virgil matched him lean for lean, pressing his elbows into the table top. "And you can't turn this into some kind of media event!"

"Why not?" Edgar leaned back in his chair, a smug smile hovering over his mouth. "Did you think to be happy with reporting this *breaking* news, which you insisted had to be discussed in a special council meeting, taking all of us away from our regular jobs? Did you think to be happy having it recorded in the weekly paper buried under the *Executive Council Board Meeting Minutes* banner on page three?"

"No." Truth was Virgil hadn't thought much past getting the problem taken care of. And certainly not about media coverage.

"Well, let me enlighten you, Mayor. That's not how things are done in the twenty-first century."

"And I suppose *you* know how things are done?" Virgil fired back, knowing full well Edgar would know how things were done. He was the president and CEO of Wyatt Distilleries, Tennessee's second largest producer of whiskey. Of course the man knew how to work the media.

Edgar leaned back, lifting the front legs of his chair off the rug. He tapped his palms against the arm rests. His expression smug. Like a man who knew things Virgil didn't. "Looks like we have us a virgin politician in our midst, folks."

"I am not a virgin!"

"And an outraged one to boot," Edgar sneered. "Look at him. Our mayor all flustered. And nervous." And while Sonny and Chief Rutledge snickered, and Marilee and Edgar outright laughed at Virgil's expense, Davis leaned close. His voice was hushed. His lips barely moving.

"Use it to your advantage, Mayor."

Virgil swung his head around.

"His press conference," Davis whispered under his breath. "Use it to *your* advantage."

Virgil looked to Emma, who was subtly nodding her head as if she'd heard Davis's whispered suggestion and whole-heartedly agreed. And then a germ of an idea took root.

Virgil believed in what he'd presented earlier. He believed it to be the answer to a lot of the town's problems. And he believed in Billy Ray. He knew the evidence they'd collected was not fabricated. Rodent *did* have a drug and gang problem. And if assholes like Edgar Wyatt and Chief Rutledge wanted to dismiss them, that was their right. But for Virgil, and kids like Brandon and the pizza delivery boy, Virgil wasn't willing to back down. "You're right, Davis," he whispered back. He would use it to his advantage.

Emma left the room, Virgil assumed, to do Wyatt's bidding. Or at least her version of it.

"Please excuse me." Davis stood and followed Emma out the door.

"If there's nothing else," the chief pushed his chair back and stood. "I have actual work that needs to be done."

"You might want to sit back down," Virgil told the chief. "There's a little more *enlightening* that this *virgin* mayor has to do. And this time it involves your police force."

* * *

The meeting with the Chief had gone worse than Virgil had anticipated.

"That's ridiculous!" the chief sputtered an hour later. "Pure fabrication."

"No, it's not. I have six girls who have come forward so far, Brett. Six girls who have all pointed an accusing finger at Warren Clive."

"They're out to get him," Marilee interjected, disgust blatant in her tone.

"I don't think so," Virgil told his mother. "They're from all over town. In different grades at school. There's nothing to connect them except that they are teenage girls. And they've had brushes with the law involving Officer Clive."

The Chief jumped on-board Marilee's train of denial. "It's a small school," he told the group.

"And it's a small mind that won't accept what is right in front of it." Virgil tapped the copy of Emily O'Leary's statement still lying on the table with his finger. "Did you read what he forced her to do? What he did to her?"

"I personally know Officer Clive," Marilee told the group. "And he's an asset to the force."

He's an asset to the force my ass, Virgil thought. For all he knew, Clive could be pilfering drug evidence from the police storage locker and giving it to Marilee. "She's a teenage girl, Brett. And he's a man old enough to be her father." And a sick perverted fuck, but Virgil didn't say that.

The chief pushed the statement aside. "What do you want me to do, Mayor? Fire Clive because one teenage girl with a '*daddy*' complex had her advances spurned by one of Rodent's finest, and now she's out to get him?"

"He is not Rodent's finest if he's conducting himself in this manner. And we don't have *one* girl, Brett. We've had six come forward."

"And I'm supposed to go back to my office and fire Clive? On circumstantial evidence? How do I know that statement wasn't coerced? Given under duress?"

"It's corroborated with five other girl's accounts."

"Where are their statements?"

Virgil knew this was going to happen. "They chose not to formalize them."

The chief snorted. "Probably because it never happened."

"It happened." Virgil wouldn't be forgetting the looks on those girl's faces anytime soon. And he'd fight for them so no other girl ever had to go through what they had.

"So what you're really saying," the chief leaned forward. "Is that all you have is *one* girl who's got it out for one of my officers. That's hardly enough to initiate an investigation, Mayor. Let alone the firing of a dedicated officer of the law."

"What I have, Chief, is a duty to the citizens of Rodent. Consider this a courtesy to your position as Chief of Police then and nothing more. Whether I have the support of this group gathered here, or not, I'm going to be asking for a full investigation into these claims. And I will go to Internal Affairs. And to the Police Review Board. And the Citizen's Review Board. And I will get justice for these young women."

And Brett stared at Virgil. Hard. And Virgil stared right back. Hard. The heated words hanging between them like ominous storm clouds. The air crackled between them with tension. And anger. And unspoken promises of retribution.

The chief was first to break. He pushed his chair back. Stood. Tapped the table with the tip of his index finger. "You do what you have to, Mayor. And I'll do what I have to."

"So will I," Virgil told the chief's back as he stormed out the door.

Virgil looked to the other members of Council who'd taken either an oath of silence, or a stand of neutrality. They'd disappointed him. Angered him. And even with additional items on the agenda, he wanted nothing more to do with them today. "Meeting adjourned," he told them.

One by one they filed out of his office. Except Marilee.

"What do you want, *mother*?"

"What do I want? What do I *want*?" she huffed out in disgust. "How about a little appreciation?"

"*Appreciation*?" He laughed, but it held no humor. "For what?"

"I got you this job when you came back home a disgrace. An embarrassment to the Lacroix name."

"I'm not a Lecroix. I'm a *Push*," Virgil reminded her, thankful for that small grace.

"Indeed you are," she derisively replied. Contempt dripping from every word.

"You want to talk about disgrace?" Virgil warmed up to the battle she wanted so badly to fight. "How about you? Backing that sexual predator?" Virgil's hands curled into fists. "Undermining *me* every step of the way. 'There's no drug problem,'" he threw back her earlier words. Words which still enraged him. "There's no gang

257

activity here," he went on. "And my all-time favorite, 'He's a *dedicated* police officer.'"

"He is!"

"To you, maybe. But tell me, *mother*." Virgil leaned over the table toward her. "What exactly does he do for you?" His eyes narrowed as insidious thoughts took root in his mind. "What does he do to have your unfaltering loyalty?"

"You're letting this position go to your head. You were *nothing*. I made you what you are."

"You're full of shit," Virgil growled, as another deluge of unsettling thoughts gained footing in his mind.

"You think?" She laughed, lifting her chin. "You think you got this job on your *merit*? On your sterling reputation? I put you here. I manipulated you. And this town."

"No, you didn't."

"Oh, yes, I did." She slowly shook her head up and down, a harsh smile cracking across her pursed lips. The glint of victory gleamed in her cold eyes. "I greased palms. I slid you into place. Held your hand as I stepped you through what you were supposed to do. And just like when you were a whiny little boy, when you wanted your *mommy's* approval because you were so *lonely* and wanted somebody to care, you did everything I said." Her lips curled into a sneer. "You voted the way I wanted. And I sat back. And I laughed at your gullibility. You know, you're Harvard schooled and graduated, but you're more stupid than the hillbillies that still laze around Mount Brandywine."

"You're lying!" Virgil yelled. She had to be. Because if she wasn't…

"You think?" She leaned closer. "Do you actually *think* the people of this town trotted out to vote a drunk into office?"

"I'm not a drunk." He drank his fair share in his life, especially during his divorce, but he wasn't a drunk.

"Do you actually think the people of this town trotted out to vote into office a broke, disgraced, worthless man who's never worked an honest day in his life." And the words – dammit! some of them true – hurt. And Virgil hated she had that kind of power over him. And she didn't let up. Relished, in fact, that was hurting him. "You're a disgrace who can't even keep his wife satisfied. A disgrace who has no qualms about fucking Trail trash right out in the open for anybody to see."

"Enough!" Virgil shouted. "Do not even think about bringing my personal life into this. Or, by God, I swear, Marilee, I will bring yours in. And I know a lot. A lot more than you think I know."

And she faltered. For only a second. But it was enough for Virgil to know everything Maisey had told him about his mother and Ruby Mae's father and the drugs were true.

"You have gone too far!"

"No, *mother*. I haven't gone far enough."

She quickly regained her aplomb. She lifted her chin. The blaze in her eyes was that of a zealot's that sent a ripple of apprehension rolling down Virgil's spine. "Then you will be sorry, Virgil. So sorry you ever crossed me. And you will pay for that. Mightily."

And Virgil watched her storm out of his office, unable to shake the feeling of impending doom that hung in the air long after she left the room.

* * *

"Virgil?" Emma pushed open Virgil's office door. "You really need to get downstairs. The press conference will be starting shortly."

259

Virgil dropped his foot from his desk drawer to the floor. He'd been brooding in his office since his mother had stormed out. Licking his wounds where Marilee's words and taunts had sliced into his soft underbelly. Into the unprotected spot that refused to accept his mother was evil. Hateful. And an all-round horrible person.

He slowly turned his head toward his secretary. Davis was right behind her. Virgil made no move to get up. "Do you think I'm my mother's puppet?" he quietly asked. God! The notion still rankled him. But he remembered in the beginning. When he'd taken this job. When he'd sat at this very desk, disinterested in the positions he'd recently acquired. Merely filling a chair, following Marilee's lead because he… he didn't care. He'd been biding his time back then. Playing at being the big man around town. All the while waiting out the time until he'd be cut free or fall back into a shitload of money that would allow him to do what he wanted. Which was doing anything, anywhere but here. "Do you think I'm self-serving?" he quietly asked, forcing the words up from his dry throat.

"Honestly?" Emma asked, stepping closer to his desk.

"Of course."

"Maybe in the beginning," she quietly told him, and Davis nodded his head in agreement.

Virgil winced. He'd never known his mother had greased palms to get him the job. He should have assumed it. What other plausible reason was there for him to be appointed mayor when Harlan had conveniently resigned? And back then he'd been still reeling from his divorce. Stinging from Rachel's fleecing of his bank accounts and his own stupid actions. Afraid he might actually have to work for a living, that when Harlan said the job was *easy as pie*, that the town nearly ran itself, well, Virgil jumped at the chance.

He'd never known he'd been Marilee's puppet.

He was as dirty as she was. And it disgusted him.

"Maybe in the beginning, Virgil," Emma's voice cut through his soul bashing. "But not now."

"Not for a long while now," Davis solemnly added.

"But you knew? You both knew my mother had gotten the position for me?"

Emma slowly nodded her head up and down. So did Davis.

Virgil winced. He breathed in a long, deep breath. Tapped his thumb against his lip as he stared at the top of his desk. "I must have looked pretty stupid."

"You never looked stupid, Virgil," Emma told him. "Not when you care about the people of this town. Not when you care what happens to this place. And *you* do care." She rubbed his shoulder. "You've cared for a long time. And that's why your mother is so angry at you."

"Because she has her own agenda for this place?" Her art colony. Changing the name of the town. Allowing drug pushers and gangs and sexual predators to roam freely.

"Yes," Emma replied. "Marilee has always had her own agenda. She has always thought she was above the law, too," Emma added, making Virgil wonder if his assistant knew about Marilee's drug use. Why wouldn't she? The woman knew everything. She should be mayor. "And Marilee has connections all over town, Virgil. You know that."

He did now. And he wondered about a few more.

"She thought putting you on Council would guarantee her getting her way on every issue brought up in meetings," Davis solemnly added. "And that you'd vote her way no matter what."

"But I haven't." Virgil stood. He rolled up the cuffs of his shirt to his forearms.

261

"No, you haven't," they both answered.

"And I'm not going to start now," he added, regaining some of his old self-confidence, reviving his wounded self-esteem.

"No, you're not," Emma replied, dusting a palm over his shoulder, straightening the collar of his shirt and then his tie.

"I'm taking my ideas to the people. I'll ask them for their support."

"That's the mayor I work for," Emma said, as she handed him a sheaf of papers.

"What's this?"

"Copies of your press release to hand out."

He hadn't thought of hand-outs. Hadn't thought much about what he'd say. Until now.

As if reading his mind, she added, "Just tell them what you told us this morning. About the summer jobs. And the auxiliary police station. About waging a war on drugs. Tell them about your vision for the old distillery and for this town."

"I don't pay you enough money, Emma."

"No, you don't," she cheekily replied, "But I wouldn't be happy working for anyone else."

Virgil made his way to the door.

"You'll need this, too." Davis handed him a poster board drawing about the size of a large picture. It was covered with a sheet of white paper.

"What's this?" Virgil asked, lifting the protective sheet.

"Architectural plans – hastily drawn up. I didn't have much time to finish them after I left meeting this morning."

Virgil stared at *his vision* for the distillery, sketched out in perfect detail. He stared at what he hoped was the answer to Ruby Mae's problem. And her neighbor's problems. And hopefully, some of Brandon's problems. "You did this for me?" he asked.

Like all the other members of council, Davis had a full-time job. He was an architect. Sonny, a welder and a taxidermist. Wyatt, a whiskey distiller. And Marilee, a ball buster.

"They're your ideas, Mayor. I just put them into drawing form. I've been working on them since we did the walk-through."

Virgil looked at the only two people he trusted in this whole damn building. "You did all this for me?"

"We did it for our town."

"And our mayor."

"Edgar Wyatt is a blowhard," Emma added, working up a fine head of steam. "One who's going to take this press conference he called to make a big deal about him tearing down a couple houses which should have been torn down when he turned his back on his hometown and moved his distillery to a neighboring county so he could make more money with tax credits and paying a labor force less money. He doesn't care about the people of this town! About the jobs he took away from them. If he did, he'd have kept the distillery here. He'd have made the few necessary upgrades on the building. He'd have kept the people he's supposed to represent employed. But he didn't."

"Like I said, Mayor," Davis picked up the cause when Emma wound down. He tapped the drawing. "Use this press conference to *your* advantage."

And Virgil did exactly that.

Chapter 16

It was early morning and while Virgil still slept in the bed in the apartment, Ruby Mae stood by the kitchen counter. He'd come home in a mood last night. Quite the opposite of the charismatic man who'd stolen the spotlight from Edgar Wyatt when the whiskey baron had tried to turn the simple razing of a couple abandoned houses on the poor side of town into a major media event.

She looked at the pile of newspapers currently delivered to her home now that Virgil had taken up residence here. She scanned their headlines. The *Vermin County Dispatch* had a front-page banner that read, *Small Town Mayor with Big City Vision*. The *Appleby Gazette* had one that read, *New Mayor Breathes New Life into Abandoned Landmark*. And the *Rodent Registrar* with a bold two-inch headline that read, *Mayor Push, No Pushover*. All carried his picture and his announcement as front-page news.

She'd caught the coverage on television, too. He'd been amazing. Totally in his element as he'd bantered and parried against Edgar's one-upmanship when the whiskey baron had tried to take credit for Virgil's vision for the Distillery Shops on the Moonshiner's Trail. And Virgil's vision for raising the funds to renovate the building had been well received. She'd especially loved when he'd pledged half his salary. And then challenged Edgar and anyone on Council to top it.

The newspapers and television stations and the crowd gathered had loved it. They'd loved him, too, much to Edgar's annoyance. The anything-but-humble mayor had stolen the show. Had probably garnered a re-election to the position in the process. And relegated Edgar to second-page news. And he'd amassed a hefty amount of money for renovations.

He should have been on top the world when he'd come home. Instead he'd retreated behind an irritating wall of indifference. One word replies to her questions. A terse damper to her exuberance over his achievement. The only time she'd caught a glimpse of the real man had been when he'd made love to her. And then it had been frantic, almost to the point of frenzied. Moving over her like a man staking his claim. And as he'd poured himself into her and she'd shattered in his arms, he still held a piece of himself back. And not just the three words she needed to hear.

There was something more.

Something she was determined to uncover.

The back door opened. Ruby Mae slowly turned around.

"Good morning," she softly told him as he walked toward her. She drank him in like the coffee long forgotten in her cup. "You're up early," she whispered.

He wrapped his arms around her. "I didn't sleep all that much." He nuzzled her neck in a way that had her breasts tingling and her blood pushing thick and needy through her veins. With his morning arousal pressed long and hard against her, he reached around her to grab a cup. And with his arms still encircling her, he filled it, kissed her temple, and turned toward the table. He pulled a chair out and sank down onto it with a weary sigh.

Ruby Mae followed, sitting down beside him. "What's wrong?" she quietly asked. "I know there's something, so don't deny it."

He slowly scrubbed his palms over his cheeks, remaining stubbornly silent.

Okay. She'd try another tactic. She tapped her finger on top the pile of newspapers. "You're the top story. Everywhere." The headlines had been the stuff of dreams for a man who lived in the public eye. "You should be happy," she told him. "The Virgil I know, the one who usually resides in your body, would be tearing through them, sucking up the attention."

He pushed the papers aside. "Maybe I'm not that guy."

"Oh, you're that guy." And more. "You love the attention of an adoring public. You love feeding that adoration with anticipation of what the wild boy from Rodent would do next."

"I never did that."

"Oh, yes you did." And he'd delivered in spades. "And you still do. So what's wrong?"

He stared into his cup. And before she could ask him again what was wrong, he breathed deep. He lifted his head, and looked at her with searching eyes. "What's with you and Edgar Wyatt?"

She sat back in her chair. "What?"

"You heard me."

"I did. I just don't understand your question." Or why he could possibly think there was something between her and Edgar Wyatt, Junior.

"All right. I'll make it clearer." His hand fisted on the table. "What's your relationship – past or present – with Edgar Wyatt, Junior?"

Ruby Mae slowly shook her head side to side. "There is no *relationship.*"

"There must be, because he thinks you're beautiful."

Ruby Mae's brows drew together. "You're wrong." He had to be. There was no way Edgar Wyatt would ever say such a thing.

"Oh, I'm not wrong. I was with him. I heard him."

"Virgil." She leaned closer to him. "There is *nothing* between Edgar and me other than he helped me set up this shop."

"Why?" he wearily asked. There was no anger in his voice, which meant he'd already known Edgar had helped her.

"Is that what's been bothering you all night?"

"Why did you have to go to him, Ruby Mae? Why *him* of all people?"

"I didn't *go* to him," she softly told him. "Not like you're thinking."

"Then how?"

"I ran into him."

He sat back. "You *ran* into him." His mocking disbelief dripped from every word.

"Yes," she replied, tamping down her own irritation.

"Where?"

"What's with the twenty questions?" She barely knew Edgar. Other than that one time in the courthouse and one or two other times when he'd stopped by to check on her progress. She never saw the man. And back then she'd been one-half walking zombie, the other half a frantic crazy woman who'd given up eating out of worry and distress. She'd been a hollow-eyed bag of bones. Hardly memorable. Or *beautiful*.

"I want to know how a man who you *claim* to have just *run into* thinks you're beautiful." He shot out of his chair. He paced back and forth, jerking movements beside her.

"Virgil, you're making it sound… "

"Like you had an affair?" he growled out the words she dreaded. And then added, "I'm not the one who's making it sound like that." He pushed his hands through his hair in frustration as he glared at her. "He is."

Ruby Mae leaned toward him. "Virgil, I honestly ran into him in the courthouse. I smacked right into him rounding a corner."

"What were you doing there?"

"I don't know." She tamped down her rising ire. "At the time it seemed like a good place to start."

"What he did was wrong."

"Was it?" She didn't state the obvious. That she was still living in the home she'd have lost if she'd have waited for someone or something else to happen.

"He set you up to be on the wrong side of the law, Ruby Mae. That's no kind of friend."

"I never said he was a *friend*."

"Well, he sure as hell thinks he is!"

Which gave her reason to pause. And to wonder. And question motives. Was Edgar's unexpected generosity a cover for something else? Now *that* was crazy. What man waits three years to collect on a favor?

"He was a member of Executive Council, Ruby Mae. He knew what was legal and what wasn't. And knowing that, he still set you up to fail. Doesn't that make you wonder?"

She frowned at his interpretation of the events, and Edgar's motives. Something she hadn't done when she'd been so desperate to save her family and her house and keep Willie Lee as comfortable as possible in the end.

He sat down. "Why didn't you come to me?" His eyes were shadowed with hurt and regret.

"I could never have come to you, Virgil. You know that," she softly told him as gently as she could. Not with Willie Lee still breathing. Still fighting. And her loving her husband to his end.

"Yes, you could have. I was Willie Lee's friend."

Not since that day in high school when she'd betrayed Willie Lee. But it no longer mattered. "You weren't around," she softly told him instead. She pushed her cup aside like she wished she could push aside this whole interrogation.

"I would have helped." He reached for her hands. Held them in his own. "I would have."

"I know you would have." There was no doubt in her mind he would have come to her aid. "But you… and Rachel…" Ruby Mae gently pulled her hands back. Just the mention of that woman's name still had the power to prick her pride and infuriate her own jealousy. "You were traveling," she told him. Living the life they'd chosen. And she had been living the one she'd chosen. And in hers, Willie Lee had been getting sicker and weaker. And she more worried. More afraid than she'd ever been in her entire life.

He reached for her hand. His long fingers stroked over hers, sliding gently over her ring finger – the one that no longer wore a wedding band. "Tell me," he quietly asked. "Tell me what it was like."

"I was afraid," she honestly told him. Her voice grew thick. She looked away. At a past only she could see. "Willie Lee hadn't worked in a long time. And he was getting sicker… Weaker." And she, more desperate. She swallowed the painful lump of hurt.

He squeezed her fingers tighter. A reassurance he wasn't going anywhere. He lifted his other hand to her temple and pushed back a strand of hair. His fingers lingered. "And?" he softly asked.

And she went on, her voice strained. "We had bills we couldn't pay. Expenses we never imagined. And our savings was gone. And the bills kept coming." Their nest egg for their future depleted. She rubbed a finger under her eye. "And I had Brandon. I couldn't leave him alone to take a job in town."

"What about your family?"

"Maisey and Billy Ray were already helping out as much as they could."

His lips pressed tight and she knew he didn't like her referring to Billy and Maisey as *family*. But they were. With a sigh she answered, "They were busy. My mother has two jobs as it is. And my father, well," she inhaled a deep breath, and didn't bother to finish.

He squeezed her fingers. "I would have been here for you."

You were married, she wanted to come right out and state the obvious, but didn't.

"One day I just couldn't take doing nothing. Couldn't take sitting around waiting… So I went to the mayor's office." She sat back. Still holding onto his hand, she shrugged a shoulder. "I don't know what I thought Harlan would do for me, but on my way to his office, I ran into Edgar." She'd plowed into the man, actually, as she'd rounded a corner, nearly knocking him over. "He told me he was a member of Council. And he listened to me." She shrugged a shoulder again as nefarious thoughts seeped into her brain. Had Edgar's reasons for helping her been as altruistic as she'd originally thought? Or did he have other motives? Ones that were connected to his thoughts of her being *beautiful*? "I was at the end of my rope and Edgar offered me a solution." She breathed deep. "One I grabbed with both hands."

"It was still wrong."

"I guess I was happy for a solution. Happy that somebody actually cared to help."

"He didn't care. Not really."

"Maybe." Ruby Mae didn't want to argue. Not when she knew for a fact Edgar Wyatt, Junior would never be interested any way in her. A woman from the wrong side of the Trail. "I guess I was just happy to have someone in my corner, Virgil. Someone helping me not to feel so helpless. So desperate that I willingly did whatever Edgar said without even thinking it through. It was my choice, Virgil. I did it. I made the decisions." And unlike that time fifteen years when she'd made an impulsive, irrational decision, this time she was the one left to face the consequences. The one left to take the blame.

"I would have been there for you."

"I know you would have." She brushed her fingers over his ring finger. The one that no longer wore a wedding band either. Her fingers lingered as she looked into his turbulent eyes. And she searched for the words to soothe his irritation, and maybe salve his ego. "But, you have to know," she softly said what needed to be said. "That could never have happened."

"I would have come back, for you," he persisted. He leaned closer. The light in his eyes burning brighter. More intense. More determined. "I would have done *anything* for you, Ruby Mae. *Anything.*"

"And that's why I could never have asked. Or taken anything from you. I was married. And so were you."

There. She'd said what needed to be said.

He sucked in a sharp breath. Like her truth had pricked his pride. Or his heart. Or something else. Thoughts of what that *'something else'* might be made her heart pound.

"It was always you, Ruby Mae. *Always* you. And for *you*, I would have done *anything*."

"And that's why I love you, Virgil." He *would* have done anything for her. Including ruining his own marriage. And distressing hers.

"I married Rachel because I couldn't have—"

"Shhh." Ruby Mae pressed her fingers to his mouth, silencing him before he said something he couldn't take back. Something she didn't need to hear. Or know. They'd both done what they'd had to do at the time. "We can't change the past," she softly told him.

And he stared at her. Their unchangeable pasts lying between them like litter from a train wreck. And still he looked at her. And she could only wonder what he was thinking. What he was seeing. What he was feeling.

Ruby Mae had always assumed he and Rachel had been perfectly suited to each other, and that she had been just been a distraction for him. Worse, a deceitful betrayal of his best friend. He and Rachel were two of Rodent's richest. Two beautiful people getting together, living a beautiful life and living it to the fullest. Wildly beyond the common and the ordinary of normal life in Rodent, Tennessee.

He and Rachel had been inseparable in high school after he and Ruby Mae's debacle. All over each other at their lockers – hands, mouths, bodies pressed close. Even when they'd gone off to Harvard with Virgil's arm possessively slung over his girl's shoulders. And married before he'd entered law school in the biggest wedding Vermin County had ever seen. And then there were the kaleidoscope of pictures that followed over the years of them in the local paper. The cold-hearted Cinderella and her golden-haired prince. Pictures from all over the world, taken on their many travels mixed in with the few times they'd come back to their hometown to attend some social function on their side of town. Always pictures of the perfectly-posed couple with their practiced smiles. Ones that never reached Virgil's eyes, or lit up his face.

Ruby Mae knew the difference between them now.

"You were happy?" she asked. She wanted him to be. As happy as she'd been with Willie Lee.

And the seconds ticked off the clock hanging on the wall as he stared at her. Not saying anything. Not a, *'yes, for a while we were'*. Or even a resounding, *'Oh, hell no.'*

He said nothing.

And even though a voice inside Ruby Mae's head was yelling, *you can't change the past*, she pressed on. "I wanted you to be happy," she softly told him. "As happy as Willie Lee and I were."

His lips pressed tighter together and she couldn't read his mind. Couldn't even venture to guess what he was thinking. Yet, this driving need to know made her reckless, impulsive. Had her asking, "You were happy, weren't you? I mean, you loved Rachel, right?"

There. She couldn't have said it any plainer.

"Ruby Mae," he let out a deep sigh, shaking his head side to side. "Don't go there."

"Go where, Virgil? It's a simple question. Did you love Rachel?" Did he live each day happy to be with her? Did he wake up every morning beside her and fall asleep every night with her in his arms? Even if it was only for a little while, did he need her more than he needed his own breath? Did thoughts of her consume his every moment?

"Did you love—"

"I don't want to talk about Rachel."

"But—" she persisted.

He leaned closer. His fingers gently stroking over her cheek as his eyes looked deep. "Maybe things happen for a reason, Ruby Mae."

The man cared. She knew he did. She'd heard it in his voice when he'd told her he'd have done anything for her. She felt it every time their bodies joined. Every time he was near, touching her like he was right now. She saw it every time he looked at her with hot hunger blazing in his eyes.

Why couldn't he say it?

"Like this?" she asked, her finger tapping his picture under the banner headline. He had so much compassion for the people of his town.

He sat back. Stared at the picture of him and Edgar. Undeclared rivals on the front page facing off, and his mouth turned down in a frown. "That's just doing what's right. Capitalizing on an opportunity."

"No, it's not." She refused to believe he was so opportunistic. So calculating. "That's caring, Virgil. About your hometown. About the people who live here. That's being a compassionate human being. Showing affection for Maisey. And concern for the kids up on the Brandywine." She ignored the voice of warning sounding off inside her head. The one that said she was pushing. That she should back off. Let things happen as they were meant to be.

"That's caring about Brandon," she recklessly went on. "And me. I love you, Virgil. For all those reasons. And a whole lot more."

His lips were pressed together tight. His eyes, turbulent blue orbs.

"You do care," she pressed on, and Ruby Mae didn't know who she was trying to convince. Him? Or her? And the air surrounding them crackled.

He breathed in a slow, deep breath. Let it out just as slow. But he didn't say the words she wanted to hear.

"I love you, Virgil." She said the words again. More urgently. More determined than ever to make him say what she desperately needed to hear.

"I know you think you do," he slowly and quietly told her.

"There's no thinking it, Virgil. I love you."

And still he stared at her. Withholding what she needed. And Ruby Mae's heart pinched in her chest with every second that passed and he didn't say what she desperately needed him to.

She straightened her shoulders. Looked deep into his eyes. And she went for broke. "Do you love me?"

"Ruby Mae," he breathed out her name in a pained sigh. "What do you want me to say?"

"How about, *yes, I love you!*"

Anger flushed over his face. And when she should be tabling this discussion, she was slamming down ultimatums.

"Haven't I shown you how I feel?" And his voice rose. Tension erupted in the air between them. "Why do you always gotta have everything your way?"

"*What?*" She stared at the alien who was inhabiting his body this morning. "I don't have to have everything *my* way."

"Oh, yes, you do. You had to have your shop."

"Keeping my family from living in our car is why I *had to have my shop!*"

"And instead of going through the right channels, you jumped on Edgar Wyatt's help. And look where it got you."

And before she could ask him exactly where he thought it got her, before she could straighten him out once and for all on her relationship with the man, the front door opened and just as quickly slammed shut.

"Brandon!" Ruby Mae shot out of her chair. "Where are you off to?" No good, most likely this early in the morning. She rounded the table intent on going after him.

Virgil grabbed her arm, stopping her. "I'll get him," he told her.

"Why? So you don't have to tell me what I want to hear?"

His eyes narrowed. "How about so he doesn't get too far?"

"We're not done here," she told his back as he walked across the kitchen.

He stopped. Looked over his shoulder at her. "Contrary to popular belief, I know you well enough to know that," he told her, before disappearing down the hall, dragging her hopes and her dreams along behind him like discarded toilet paper caught on his heel.

* * *

Virgil rounded the corner of the house feeling like he was being chased by a black bear. Something he'd rather face than the disappointment he'd seen in Ruby Mae's eyes every time she said she loved him and he said nothing in return. He banged his head off the side of the house in frustration. Ground his palms into his eye sockets.

She wanted something from him. Something that didn't involve money. Or endless travel. Or even giving up his left nut. It was simple. And free. And if he were still that crass, opportunistic bastard he'd been for the better part of this life, all it involved was him lip-synching three words. He turned. Pressed his back into the siding. He should be dogging the kid. Instead, he dropped his head back. All he had to do was utter three freakin' little words.

I. Love. You.

How hard could it be?

It's what she wanted. It would get him what he wanted. Which was her off his back. And the guilt of his silence off his shoulders. And who knew what else he'd get.

So why in the hell couldn't he do it?

He exhaled a long breath.

Because he was no longer that man.

The one who'd do anything, or say anything just to get what he wanted. The one who'd lie. Cheat. Try to steal his best friend's girl. The one who'd make promises he had no intention of ever keeping for the sole intention of getting what he wanted.

And then he was mad, *dammit!* He banged his fists off the wall. He should be enough just as fucked up and messed up as he was.

Why in the hell did he have to say three freakin' words he didn't even believe? He'd given her his body. She had his sole attention. Hell, she'd *always* had that. And his devotion. He'd been more faithful to her than to his ex-wife!

And as quickly as his anger boiled up inside him, it dissipated. Virgil sighed. It wasn't her pressuring him. It was his own damn conscience riding him hard.

The real truth was he didn't believe in love. Didn't believe in the fairy-tale notion of it. And he didn't want to face her and tell her that.

And now he had one more thing he was keeping from her.

Because how long would she stay with him, how long would she continue to '*love*' him knowing he didn't believe in the emotion?

Not very damn long.

And that's why he could never tell her. That was one more reason to, "Shut the fuck up and find the kid," he muttered under his breath.

He pushed himself off the wall. Headed around the house. Quickly crossed over the back yard. He snagged the collar of Brandon's tee shirt before he'd ventured into Billy's backyard. "Where you going?" he demanded.

The kid jerked his shoulder. Pulled away. "None of your business."

"It damn well is my business when you set your momma to worrying about where you're off to without telling her."

The kid was nervous. Fidgeting. Like he'd gotten caught at something. And he was hiding something behind his back the same time his turquoise eyes flashed with the fury at getting caught.

"Don't give me that look. I invented it," Virgil told the kid.

"Like you were ever a kid."

"I could say the same about you," Virgil fired back, as he reached over the kid's shoulder and snagged the paper he had clutched behind him.

"Hey! Give me that."

"No." Virgil danced away from the kid's jumping attempts to snag back the paper.

"You give me that back!" The kid launched himself at Virgil.

"Not until you tell me what it is." Virgil eluded the kid's attempts. Turning side to side, he unfolded and smoothed out the paper. "Well… shit." He paused. Looked down at Brandon. "This is an invitation to the father-son sleepover up on the Brandywine."

It was a rite of passage for any second-grade boy and his father in Rodent. Camping up on the mountain. Guys doing guy stuff. Sitting around a campfire. Eating crap out of a can. Not having to say words that meant nothing when a man's actions should speak louder and should dam well be enough.

Or so he'd been told.

"It's dumb," Brandon told him, but Virgil could hear the longing in the kid's voice.

"No, it's not." It was anything but dumb to the kid who no longer had a father and desperately wanted to go. "Brandon," Virgil put his hand on the kid's tense shoulder. "If you want to go, I'll take you."

Brandon jerked his shoulder. "What do you know about mountains anyhow?" The kid ran a critical eye down over Virgil.

"Hey! I know mountains. I climbed Kilimanjaro."

"Where's that? North Carolina? That don't count."

"Try Africa, brat. And I did some ice climbing in the Alaska mountains, too." Back when he'd been wild. Or crazy. Or maybe he'd just had a death wish when he thought of the risks of avalanches and blizzards he'd faced just to climb some frozen waterfalls.

"You're not my dad."

"Are we back to that? *Jee-suz*. I know I'm not your father. You remind me every damn day."

"So I can't go." The kid kicked a stone in frustration.

Virgil jumped like a girl to avoid getting hit by it.

And he understood how hard it was to be a kid without a dad.

"You can go, Brandon," he quietly told him. "I know I'm not your dad. But I am a lawyer. And as a lawyer, it's my job to find loopholes in legalities."

He laid a hand on Brandon's shoulder. Turned them toward the back steps of the house. Sat them both down on the bottom step and looked at the invitation again. "See here?" he pointed to the top of the paper where *Father-Son Weekend* was prominently displayed in big, block letters. "And here?" he pointed to the bottom of the page. "Where the only requirements listed are to bring a sleeping bag and a flashlight?"

"So?" Brandon mulishly replied.

"There's nothing on here that says you have to have *your* father to attend."

"But it says," Brandon leaned closer, his finger pointing to the wording on top. "Father, son."

"It does. But it specifically does not state *your* father, or *my* son as conditions of the outing. It's what we lawyers call a technicality."

"Tech— tack-na— what?"

"Loophole. It means I'm not your father, but I am somebody's son. It means we could go together, as two sons. With no fathers between us. What do you think?"

Virgil was already warming up to the idea. Although it was still three weeks away, it was a weekend away from the pressure of saying, *I love you.* And having to explain what he knew she'd never understand. Because she believed in the fantasy emotion of love – and all the faux security she thought came with it.

And he didn't.

And she should know that, too, because hadn't love already let her down? Broken her heart? Left her at the mercy of assholes like Edgar Wyatt?

"What do you say, Brandon? I never got to go as a kid." Vince had been too busy in the oilfields. Too busy staying the hell away from his family.

Brandon cocked his head and looked at him. "On the kinda your dad is in heaven like mine?" he asked.

Virgil sat back. Stared at the kid. Stunned. "No, son," he quietly replied. "My dad is…" He paused. Inhaled a deep breath.

"Is what?" the kid persisted.

Virgil ran a reverent hand over the invitation the same way he'd ran his hand over the one he'd received all those years ago when he wasn't able to attend. "My dad is very much alive. Living in Oklahoma, actually." Like he'd been back when Virgil had received his own invite.

The kid's blond brows drew together. "Is that far away from here?"

"Might as well be." On the other side of the world for all the times Vince had ever come back home for his son. He sucked in a deep breath, brushing aside the old memories, the old hurts that no longer mattered. "So what do you say?" He slapped his palms down on his thighs and looked at Brandon. "You want to go with me, or not?"

Chapter 17

Rodent's Community Park was packed, teaming with people streaming in for the Rat Races. Balloons tethered to poles near the entrance bobbed in the breeze while a warm sun shined down on them as Ruby Mae, Brandon, and Virgil made their way through the park's wrought-iron gates.

"Mayor Push," an older woman and her husband rushed up to Virgil. "This is the best festival ever!"

"Thank you, ma'am, but it's not my doing."

"Oh, Mayor, you're so humble." The woman gushed.

"Just tellin' the truth, ma'am," he told her with a smile. "But I'll be sure to pass your sentiments onto Davis Barnett. He's the chairman of the committee. He's the one who made all this happen."

"Very humbly done, Mister Mayor," Ruby Mae teased, as they pushed their way further into the crowd.

"I'll give you humble," he playfully replied, nipping her ear with his teeth as he pulled her closer. His arm slung possessively over her shoulder.

"Yuck," Brandon muttered, walking beside them.

"Someday, honey, you'll understand," Ruby Mae told her son as she affectionately brushed her hand over his spikey hair.

"No way. I am not ever gonna like girls. Girls are dumb."

And while Ruby Mae and Virgil laughed at her son's innocent naiveté, a grandmotherly sort rushed up to them. "Mayor Push!" She exuberantly shook Virgil's hand. "I told you it was the mayor!" she told the group of gray hairs gathering behind her, jockeying for position to get a few moments of the mayor's time. Everyone was calling out to him.

Ruby Mae smiled at how kind he was. How accessible he was to his constituents as he patiently fielded their questions and accepted their compliments. He might think this was *just a job*, or the *right thing to do*, or any of the other excuses she'd heard him utter over the last few months, but he *was* the mayor. The best thing to happen to this town.

And the best thing to happen to her since Willie Lee.

"Just wanted to thank you for findin' those summer jobs. My grandson's workin'. You're keepin' him outta trouble. And that makes his momma and me real happy."

"I'm real glad to hear that, ma'am," Virgil replied, warmly patting the older woman's liver-spotted hand.

"My nephew landed one of those jobs, too." A middle-aged man joined the growing crowd. "Thanks for findin' the fundin' for them. We gotta keep our kids off the street."

"Away from those shady characters down at the end of ours. Ain't that right, Ruby Mae?"

"That's right, Dalton," she replied. Dalton Pierce was her neighbor.

"When they goin' to start workin' on renovatin' that ol' distillery?" another man asked.

"We have to get all our funding in place first," Virgil told the group.

"You buy a brick over at the mayor's tent yet?" Ruby Mae asked. It was one of the ways they'd come up with to get the community involved.

"Not yet," Dalton replied.

"Better get on over there then," Virgil added. "Davis has his architectural sketches on display. And Emma, why she's taking reservations for crafter's space in the renovated building." His hand slid down low on Ruby Mae's waist as he pulled her close. Their hips and thighs touched. The softness of his forest green pullover brushed against her breast. Her insides quivered. "Why Ruby Mae here already has her space reserved. Isn't that right, darlin'?"

"That's right," she replied. A chance to keep her shop, and make it legit, while still being close to home for Brandon, it had been a no-brainer decision. That he'd gone up against Council and his mother to make it happen spoke volumes about the man he was.

How could she not love him?

But did *he* love her? Now that was the question. One he refused to address.

"That right, Ruby Mae? You signed on?" Dalton asked, intruding on her troubling thoughts.

She turned toward the group gathered around them. "Yes, I did."

"*Salvation* was the first shop to reserve space," Virgil proudly added.

She smiled up at the man, whose hand was riding low on her hip. Whose fingers were sliding under her shirt, drawing erotic circles on her back. Making her skin tingle. "The mayor has a great vision for our town, setting all us crafters up under one roof." All the crafters on her street had eagerly signed on to rent space in the distillery. There'd been a line forming down her driveway the day after his press conference.

"Thought Wyatt donated that building," another man asked, as the crowd continued to grow around them.

"Mo-om." Brandon was growing restless, eager to move on.

"Hang on, honey, we're just about finished here." Ruby Mae squeezed his shoulders. Her son had changed so much since Virgil had moved in with them. All for the better.

"He did," Virgil answered. "And we're grateful for that. But we still need to raise additional funding for renovations."

"What are you going to do about it?" another man asked. One who'd obviously not fallen under the mayor's charismatic spell, judging from his disapproving tone.

"I'm looking into trying to get some grants. Maybe some government money. And if that doesn't pan out, I'm looking at other avenues."

"Gonna raise my taxes?"

"That's not my plan," Virgil calmly replied. "I've been in touch with some national and some international foundations that specialize in community renewal. I'm hoping to get them interested enough to—"

"We don't need no Arabs and communists over here buyin' up our town."

"I don't plan on sellin' the town, Hoyt. But I do plan on making it a better place to live in." And Ruby Mae heard the steel hidden behind the charming country suave. "For my family." His hand rested protectively on Brandon's shoulder. "And yours. You buy a brick yet, Hoyt? Emma has lots of things over at the mayoral tent you can purchase. Do your part."

Hoyt's beard-covered chin jutted out. "Why would I do that?"

Virgil shrugged a shoulder. Like it didn't matter this man was crapping all over his parade. "Maybe because all proceeds from the brick sales are going to the new Community Center that'll serve your kids. As well as mine. The proceeds from the auctioned items she's got over there go into a renovation fund for the building. And the proceeds from the bake sale go toward the Senior Center."

"Be nice to have a hot lunch for us seniors," one of the older gentlemen said. "Any chance you got some transportation ideas in your plans? Some of us could use a ride to the Center when it opens."

"Not yet," Virgil replied. "But I'll check into it."

"You're doin' a fine job, mayor," another man added, shaking Virgil's hand.

"Mo-om," Brandon whined. "I wanna go. *Now*." He was hanging off her leg, scuffing the front of his new sneakers in the dirt. Clearly unimpressed and uninterested in the machinations of small-town politics.

"Soon, honey," Ruby Mae softly replied, not wanting to take this opportunity away from Virgil.

But he had noticed Brandon's impatience. He slipped one arm around Ruby Mae. Placed a hand on Brandon's shoulder and told the group, "Now if you'll excuse us, I'd like to spend some time with my family."

* * *

Most of the town was too busy enjoying all the booths and socializing with one another to bother with him much past the initial

287

outburst, which suited Virgil just fine. Hiding behind a pair of Oakley's, he and Ruby Mae threw darts at balloons – she was much better at it than him. And he now wore a ridiculously large plastic chain around his neck to prove it. They chucked quarters at plates until his pockets were emptied. And watched with pride as Brandon lobbed hardballs at the firemen manning the dunking booth, dropping them into the barrel with every throw. They gorged on French fries and placed bets on Sonny, confident he'd win the hotdog eating contest.

They made their way to the mayor's tent.

"I want some cookies, mom," Brandon told Ruby Mae right before he made a bee-line for the table where the bake sale items were displayed. It was laden down with every conceivable cookie on the planet and the badass appeared to be sampling all of them. With both hands.

"You sure that's a good idea?" Virgil asked Ruby Mae, keeping a wary eye on the brat.

"He'll be fine."

"I don't know." They walked to the other side of the tent. "I seem to remember another time…"

"Don't worry," she patted his arm. "He mixed his junk food last time. This time it's straight sugar. He'll be fine."

He lifted his glasses to his forehead. "You're messin' with me, aren't you?"

And the sexy smile she gave said it all. He was crazy about this woman. And the kid. And she gifted him with a kiss to confirm it.

With the lingering kiss behind them, they made their way to the back of the tent where the cement mouse figures were lined up waiting for their "adoption".

Ruby Mae got one look at them and spun around to face him. Her eyes sparkled, doing weird things to the inside of his chest. "They are *so* cute. Your idea was brilliant!"

He wasn't brilliant. But he sure as hell liked that she thought he was. That he was a good idea for her. And Brandon.

"Did you get a lot of them adopted?" she asked Emma.

"Ten so far. And we have our mayor to thank for that."

"I didn't do anything."

"You stood up to your mother," Emma told him, and he wished she wouldn't make it seem like a big deal.

"Who knows where this town would be if you hadn't," Davis added. "We'd probably be an art colony. No offense, Ruby Mae."

"None taken," she replied.

"We have this whole gathering because of you," Davis added.

"Oh, no." Virgil put his palms out in front of him. "Don't be giving me the credit."

"Yeah, don't be givin' him the credit." Sonny waddled up to the group wearing a plastic crown in the shape of a hot dog, and a hell of a lot of attitude. All of it bad. "It was *my* idea for the rat. But is anybody thankin' me?"

"You're right," Davis heartily agreed with him. "Thank you for the great idea."

"Damn straight it was my idea," Sonny muttered as he followed the cookie Emma was waving in the air at him.

Virgil looked at Davis. "It was *your* idea. Why give him the credit?"

"Guess for the same reason you're not taking credit for what you've done for our town."

"Mom, I wanna go shoot. Uncle Billy's over there!"

The Rodent police department was sponsoring an air-shooting gallery. And, sure enough, Billy and Maisey were there. As Officer Ray Trainor's surviving son and widow, both were doing their part to make sure the police department collected as many donations as it could for the auxiliary police station to be housed in the renovated distillery.

"Let me go with you," Ruby Mae told the kid, eying the long line of people waiting to try their luck, and make their contribution.

"I can do it by myself." Brandon impatiently shook off her hold, taking off toward the front of the line.

"Brandon!" Virgil called out.

"What?" The kid turned around.

"Here." Virgil reached for his wallet. He handed the kid fifty bucks.

The brat's eyes went wide.

"Don't give me that look. You've been emptying out my wallet all day. Might as well finish it off."

The brat clutched the money in his fist.

"You are spoiling him," Ruby Mae told him as she stood beside him.

The brat squeezed the money and did a little victory pump with his fists before pushing to the front of the line where his Uncle Billy was working.

"You didn't have to do that." She was looking up at him with her soft brown eyes. Like he was some kind of superhero. Like he was everything she needed and wanted. He liked the feeling. And the warmth spreading inside his chest.

"Think it's wise given' that boy a gun?" Virgil asked, leaning close. The curls near her temple teased his nose as he breathed in deep her flowery scent. His mouth marked a trail down the side of her face until he nuzzled her neck, and the sweet spot below her ear.

She breathed out a sexy sigh, right before she moaned and pulled back, putting a respectable distance between them.

He leaned into her again. Tasted her one more time because he couldn't resist. "I've seen what he can do with a hardball," he added, before licking her ear lobe into his mouth.

She squirmed like he knew she would. She turned toward him. Her lips were close enough to kiss. And she smiled, her hands resting on his chest. "He gets his pitching arm from his daddy. Maybe he gets his shooting arm from him, too."

Virgil laughed. "Everybody knew Willie Lee couldn't hit the broad side of a barn." Willie Lee Shove would always be a part of her, Virgil knew that. And somewhere over the past few months, he'd lost his envy and his jealousy of the man.

"I love—"

Virgil touched a finger to her lips, silencing her. He brought his lips to hers and kissed her. Slow and easy. Savoring the honeyed warmth of her mouth as he plundered it with lazy abandon. And she sighed out her contentment. And he savored that, too. And the feel of her hands as they slowly slid up his arms to his shoulders. The feel of her breasts as they pressed against his chest. The slide of her tongue as it stroked against his, making him hot. Horny. Happy. And... *content*.

Like he'd never been in his life.

Too quickly she pulled back. Her cheeks were flushed. Her eyes were dark with desire, something he'd take care of later tonight. Her fingers brushed against her bottom lip before pointing to a spot over her shoulder. "I better go check on Brandon."

"He's okay," he told her, giving a quick glance over to the kid standing with his surrogate uncle. It was selfish, he knew, but he couldn't get enough of her. Not in fifteen years. Not ever. If he lived to be a hundred, he'd still not have enough.

"I really need to," she quietly told him. And he reluctantly let her go because she would feel the need to check on her son. Even though he was standing only a few feet away from them. And he watched as she made her way to the front of the line. To her son. And he felt… special that she'd allow him into her life.

"Still slumming it, I see."

Virgil swung around to face his ex-wife.

"Still lusting after that Trail Tra—"

"Don't even think about finishing that, Rachel," Virgil warned, in a low growl. He bared his teeth in what he hoped would be misinterpreted as a smile. "Leave her out of this."

"Why, Virgil?" Rachel taunted, stepping close. "She's been between us since the first time I sucked you off behind the bleachers in high school. She has *always* been here." She waggled her hand between them. The expensive jewels she'd bought with his trust fund glittered off her fingers and wrists.

And like his life flashing before his eyes, the images shot across his mind. The things Rachel had done back then. How she'd led him around by his dick. And he wondered. Who'd coached her before him? She'd known a hell of a lot more than he had back then. And he'd been pretty experienced.

"She was always right here between—"

"Don't," he warned. He wouldn't give her the satisfaction of

292

being right. He had kept Ruby Mae between them. All through his marriage. All through his life. Hell, she'd been between him and *any* woman he'd ever been with. Married, or not.

"You haven't changed one bit." Rachel looked down her nose at him.

And his ex was right. He hadn't. When Willie Lee had won Ruby Mae, he'd been devastated. Pissed as hell. Competing for Ruby Mae had been the only thing he'd ever lost. And Rachel had been his rebound lover. His choice specific because she was the one woman Ruby Mae didn't like. Now he had to wonder... And suddenly it hit him. "You're the one," he growled. "You're the one who told."

"Of course, I was, you fool." Rachel didn't pretend to misunderstand. She knew exactly what he was talking about. That day fifteen years ago when Willie Lee had interrupted Virgil's seduction. When Willie Lee had found them half naked in the woods behind the school. Rachel lifted her chin. Stared at him like the dumb fuck he was. She curled her lips up in a cold, feral smile. "You were *my* ticket. You were promised to *me* and I wasn't sharing you."

"What?"

"You didn't know that, did you? She pointed a long, bejeweled finger at his chest. "You were promised to me. And no little prissy-assed piece of Trail trash was going to get between me and my money."

"*My* money, Rachel," he ground out. "It was *my* money." It was his fucking trust fund. All sixteen million dollars of it. Promised? *To Rachel?* He glanced beyond Ruby Mae to the other woman who'd been dogging his every step.

Marilee.

His eyes narrowed. Had she bought Rachel, too? Had she promised a seventeen-year-old heartless bitch his money in exchange

293

for getting rid of Ruby Mae? His heart pounded at the possibility. Had Marilee set him up, even back then? She hadn't cared what he'd done all his life.

Except for when he'd pursued Ruby Mae.

Then she was all over him. And Rachel, who'd never ever shown an iota of interest in him before was suddenly hotter than hell for him. Was it possible? Could his mother have been that heartless? That calculating? She'd claimed to have set him up in the mayor's position. Could she have set him up with Rachel, too?

It was absurd. Outrageous! Too ridiculous to think possible. Which made it… most likely… *Jee-suz!* And if Marilee had done that, what else was she capable of?

"The money is all mine now," Rachel coldly went on as the sun glinted off the jewels draped around her neck. "*I'm* the rich one now," she taunted. "And you," her finger trailed down over his chest. "Are still lusting after Trail trash."

He grabbed her finger. Wrapped his fist around it. And squeezed it hard. Until she winced in pain. Disgusted with her, and himself, he thrust her hand aside.

She leaned close, her eyes blazing. "Enjoy your little *piece of trash* while you can, Virgil. You won't have it for long," she cryptically replied. "Trust me."

"Like I'd ever do that," he growled, as she walked away.

* * *

It was a disgusting job, Marilee thought, trailing after her son as he showboated his way through this ridiculous sideshow he called a community day. Him, parading around. Like a big fish in a small pond. And with that Trail trash at his side, no less! It was repulsive. Despicable.

Him, pandering to the locals like they actually cared. Like they actually had put him in his current position. She had been the one who'd done that! She, the one who'd seen to it he wasn't an embarrassment to her good name. And how did he repay her? By turning on her with his traitorous decisions while playing at being mayor. And his belligerent insistence on publicly flaunting his affair with that woman for all to see. "You will pay, Virgil," she whispered under her breath. "Oh, you will pay."

Most definitely for that.

Both mother and daughter actually foolishly believed they had a right to men from Marilee's side of the Trail. Marilee hadn't been able to stop Ruby Mae's mother from sinking her talons into Marilee's precious Percy, but she would stop the daughter.

"Everybody's talkin' about your little boy over there."

Marilee turned. Warren Clive stood close enough his onion-laden breath blew hot against her face. Her son was introducing a bunch of brats and the rats they planned to run on a hokey race track complete with checkered flags at the finish line.

"Do you have to stand so close?" she pointedly asked as she stepped away from Clive. "I've really had my fill of Trail trash for one day."

He laughed. Like she hadn't just insulted him. The stupid fool.

"Everybody's talkin' about his new girlfriend. Even talkin' about the cute little family they already got stared. So, you gonna be joinin' them for Thanksgiving dinner?"

"Don't be ridiculous!" she hissed as she glared at the imbecile. Her brow furrowed. "Where's your uniform?" she demanded. "Why aren't you working?"

Clive's jaw hardened. "I've been put on indefinite leave pending an Internal Affairs investigation."

"For what?" She'd talked to Chief Rutledge after Virgil's grandstanding at the last Council meeting.

"Sexual allegations. Like you don't already know."

"They can't do that!"

"Well, they did," he snarled. "And all because of that *sonofabitch* you call a son! He got that new prosecutor all riled up, too. Hell, I'll be lucky to…" his voice trailed off as he honed in on the jailbait sashaying by him in tight cut-off shorts exposing half her ass and a midriff shirt exposing her stomach and a belly button ring. She was licking an ice cream cone like it was a rock-hard cock.

And the stupid idiot standing beside her was ballsy enough to follow after the teen.

It had been Edgar Wyatt, Senior, about the same age as Clive was now who'd taken Marilee when she'd been fifteen and taught her how to get down on her knees. She'd been a fast learner, too. Soon she'd been leading the old bastard around by his cock. Tactics she'd passed onto Rachel to snag Marilee's son when he'd been hot to trot for the Trail trash he was still sniffing around.

And she'd set Clive up, as well.

Except her bastard of a son had found the one girl who didn't realize the power she had between her legs. And he hadn't turned a blind eye to her. Or a deaf ear, the stupid fool. For more than fifteen years. And for that, he'd pay.

Clive was her conduit to Chief Rutledge. Her key to skimming off confiscated drugs stored away in police lockup. If he was charged, he lost all his value to her. And she lost all her connections inside the force.

Her son needed to be stopped. Knocked down. Forced out of the game. And she knew exactly how to do it. And who to hurt to take him down.

And he would go down. He most certainly would.

* * *

The community day's activities wound down as dusk fell over the park. Virgil walked with Ruby Mae back to his car. Brandon was leaning his head against her hip. His eyes heavy-lidded with exhaustion.

"Virgil?" She grabbed his forearm. "That's your mother," she softly told him.

He shook his head up and down, not stopping. Or acknowledging his mother's ominous presence.

"How long do you think she's been watching us?" Ruby Mae worriedly asked.

All day, he wanted to say, but said instead, "Don't worry, honey." He pushed away a wayward curl from her cheek and hopefully the tension tightening her features, too. "She can't hurt us. With you signing the lease to move your shop into the distillery shops, you're legit now, honey. The citation is null and void. And she can't do a damn thing to us."

She lifted those beautiful eyes to his and he felt the impact clear down in his chest. "You're sure?"

"Yeah."

Her features relaxed. A small smile touched her mouth. The one he wanted to kiss. "Thank you."

"You don't have to thank me."

"I do. I love—"

He pressed a finger to her lips. "Let's make today about actions instead of words, okay?"

They'd established a pattern of sorts over the last few weeks.

She said she loved him every chance she got. And he held tight to his silence. He wasn't as successful at ignoring the disappointment he saw in her eyes when he did that. Or the stab of guilt that pricked his conscience when he couldn't give her what she wanted. They were just words, he kept telling himself. Words he wished he could say to take the hurt away from her eyes.

He wasn't used to being inadequate.

He wasn't used to being broke either.

Or keeping secrets from someone.

Someone so *in love* with him.

The time to come clean with her about his non-existent wealth and how he felt about her and this thing she called *love* was bearing down hard on him like a semi. And it was in route to roll over and flatten him and all his good intentions if he didn't come clean. Soon. But for now, he just wanted a chance to let his actions speak louder than any damn words he could string together.

And still she looked at him. Deep into his mutant soul. And she lifted her hand. Her fingers gently stroking the side of his sweaty forehead. Lingering in his hair. She breathed deep and even breast man that he was, he was so far under her spell that he couldn't look away from her incredible eyes to her other equally incredible assets.

"Okay," she quietly told him. As if understanding his insufficiencies. Or maybe she just understood him better than he did.

Whatever it was, he was grateful. And aroused. And as a coral sun was sinking low in the gray-blue sky, slowly sliding down behind the tree-covered mountains that surrounded their town, Virgil hefted a near-sleeping Brandon further up onto his shoulder. And just because he could, and maybe because he knew he'd never get enough, he leaned down and brushed his mouth against hers. Tasting her. Touching her. Savoring her. "Thank you," he softly told her. His forehead rested against hers. "For being with me today. For having my back. And for standing with me."

And maybe for loving him in spite of all his damns faults.

* * *

It didn't take Marilee long to put her plans into motion. Just like it hadn't taken long for her son to disappoint her. And that had been from the moment she'd found out he was Vincent Push's child and not Percy's.

She turned over this morning's special edition of the local paper. The one with the half-page picture of Virgil kissing that Trail Trash at sunset. Holding her son on his shoulder like he was her baby daddy. She pursed her lips at the banner headline above it.

Sun sets on this year's Rat Races, but not on Mayor's Vision for Town.

The headline was wrong.

The sun was indeed setting on her son. He just didn't know it yet.

The door of her home office opened. Maxwell Thomas walked toward her desk. "Marilee, good to see you, as always." He was impeccably dressed – as always – befitting a man of his stature. Unlike her son. Or her husband.

"Maxwell," she replied, motioning him to sit down. "Thank you for coming. I know it's rather early."

"No problem." He crossed his leg over the other as he sat in the chair in front of her massive desk. "What can I do for you?"

Direct, and to the point – she liked that.

299

"There's a balloon mortgage on a piece of property that needs a demand for immediate repayment sent out."

He uncrossed his leg. Leaned forward, brow furrowed. "Is it late?" he asked. "I know the market is down, the economy is in the tank, but I don't remember seeing any new mortgages being flagged for foreclosure for non-payment."

She was part of the same five-member board as Maxwell, along with Vincent, not that her husband paid attention to board business around this town like she did. And he'd vote against her just on principal, he was that belligerent. Why, if Percy would rid himself of that trashy albatross wrapped around his neck, she'd divorce Vincent in a heartbeat. And take his fortune, his precious oil company, and half his soul just to repay him for impregnating her and ruining her life. She needed Maxwell's support. With it, the other two members would follow his lead and vote her way.

And Ruby Mae Shove would lose her house.

"What property are we talking about, Marilee?"

"The Shove property."

"Ruby Mae Shove's property?" Maxwell's face paled. He actually looked sick. "She's— I mean— I'll have to check with the other board members. Vince—" Sweat popped out on his forehead. "Vince set up that mortgage personally. Backed it himself when nobody else would. He won't go for this."

She didn't care what her husband would go for. He wasn't around. He was *never* around.

Thank God.

"The other members," Maxwell pulled a linen handkerchief from his back pocket and blotted his sweat-dampened forehead. "The other members will—"

Marilee pushed an envelope across the smooth surface of the walnut desk toward him.

He swallowed as he stared at it. His fingers twitched. She wasn't the only one in the town with vices. Maxwell had a gambling vice. A rather large one. Horses and on-line poker. He stood. Reached for the envelope with unsteady fingers, and Marilee tasted victory.

Chapter 18

It was a thick vellum envelope.

The news inside it was as devastating as when she'd found out Willie Lee's cancer was not in remission. And that their lifetime together would be measured in months instead of years.

"This can't be happening," Ruby Mae whispered, as she stared at the official letter from her mortgage holder. She had ninety days to come up with the balloon payment. The one that shouldn't have been due for years.

Due with money she didn't have.

They were terms she couldn't accept, yet had no choice. Wanting the house, eager to start their family, she and Willie Lee had both signed the papers, knowing full well the terms. Which were highlighted in yellow on the papers she currently held in her trembling hands.

The floor had fallen out of her world, and once again, she was freefalling. Terrified of what would happen. Of where she'd land. What she'd do.

They could take her house.

She had no nest egg to protect them. Her heart twisted painfully in her chest. She'd lose everything. She and Brandon would have to move. But to where?

"Ruby Mae? You back here?"

Virgil walked around the corner of the house weighted down with sleeping bags, backpacks, lanterns, flashlights, and a tent – all in one arm. In his other, he held a camp stove, an air mattress, a couple folding chairs, and a rope. Two pair of binoculars crisscrossed his chest. Aluminum pans and plastic bottles hung off his leather belt.

He dropped the massive pile at her feet.

"What is that?" she asked.

He dusted off his hands as he proudly stared at his stash. "Some of the camping stuff Brandon and I will need for the campout."

The father-son outing her son had talked non-stop about.

"Some? *Some* of the stuff?" she warily asked. "How much *stuff* did you buy?" How much *stuff* did two guys need, she wondered, to go up and sit on a mountain top?

"Just some," he vaguely replied. And she knew if she had the strength to walk around her house to his car, she'd find it loaded down like Santa's sleigh on Christmas Eve. He spoiled her son. Her, too.

"Virgil," she eyed the pile again. "Who's going to carry all this stuff?"

His brows drew together. "What do you mean *carry*? We're driving."

"To the drop-off spot. Then you're hiking." She looked at the man who'd been the envy of every kid in school. Had he never gone on the father-son campout? She tried to think back. Every boy in Rodent went. It was tradition. A rite of passage. Yet with this much equipment lying at her feet, she had to wonder. "You have to carry everything in," she told him.

He frowned. She could well imagine him mentally debating whether to leave the mattress or the camp stove behind. "What's wrong?" he asked, jerking his chin toward the envelope clenched in her fist.

"Nothing," she lied, sliding the wrinkled envelope under her thigh.

"You're a terrible liar, Ruby Mae. You know, I could kiss you senseless then lift that and find out for myself, but I'd like you to tell me."

And when he looked at her like that, asked her like that, she couldn't deny him. Divert him. Or even lie to him. Without another word, or protest, she slid the envelope out from under her leg and handed it over to him.

"Jee-suz," he sank down on the step beside her. "What the hell is this?"

"It's pretty self-explanatory, Virgil," Ruby Mae wearily replied. "The mortgage company is calling in their balloon payment."

He gave her a sidelong look. "Why'd you sign a mortgage like this?"

"Oh, I don't know," she found herself snapping out her frustration and anger. "Maybe because we wanted the house and it was the only mortgage offered to us." They'd been young. Just married. Tired of living in an apartment over Willie Lee's parent's garage. And Willie Lee had just come home from his job with Vincent Push's oil company. The one that took him off-shore to work on a drilling rig for months at a time. It paid good money, but Willie Lee's heart was in these mountains. And so was she.

And she'd been pregnant with Brandon.

And Willie Lee wanted his little family under their own roof no matter what the terms. Or the cost.

"This is the kind of mortgage usually offered for business mortgages. Not residential ones." He bent his head. Read a little further. Looked up at her. "These mortgages usually have a reset option. You could remortgage. It would be at the current rate, but-"

"I can't." She looked away as embarrassed heat filled her cheeks. "I was late on a couple payments." She swallowed, dreading revealing the rest of her stupidity.

"And," he softly prompted.

She pushed a sharp breath out. "I have a lien against the property from when I set up the shop."

He shot up off the step. Glared down at her. "Edgar Wyatt's suggestion, no doubt?"

And she shut her eyes. Rubbed her forehead, too weary for another argument with him about Edgar and his out-of-the-blue help that suddenly seemed to be more trouble and with more loopholes than she'd ever thought possible. In hindsight, it appeared the man had set her up all right. Set her up to fail.

"I don't know. I don't remember." She sighed, opening her eyes as she thought back. "It seemed like a good idea at the time. It was the only way to get my shop off the ground." She didn't have the Push wealth behind her. Like he did. "I don't have a trust fund," she said. Like he did. And she didn't have the security that his name alone carried.

His lips pressed tight.

She refused to apologize.

He paced. And his agitated movements matched the stuttered

beating of her heart. He stopped. Looked at her. "Do you have the money to make this payment?"

She choked out a sob. "If I *had* the money I would have *paid* it!" She'd be right now burning the mortgage book instead of shredding her hopes and dreams on it. Her throat constricted. Tears pushed into her eyes. "Virgil, what am I going to do?"

He reached for her. Wrapped his arms around her. Held her close. And Ruby Mae held onto him. The only stable thing in her life. Her hands fisted into his shirt. Her nose pressed to his neck.

"Marry me," he said into her hair.

"*What?*" She jerked back. Looked up into his eyes. "I can't marry you!"

His brows drew down over his narrowed eyes. "Why not?"

"Virgil," she sighed out his name in frustration. All their time dancing around the issue, it had finally come full circle. And would most likely bite her in the butt. But she had to ask. She had to know.

Her future, her life, her happiness depended on it.

"Do you love me?"

Tiny lines radiated out from his squinted eyes. "I have a job, Ruby Mae. I can get a mortgage. I can save your house."

And her heart twisted at his side-stepping dance.

"I have a job, too," she told him. Not one that would get her a second mortgage. And he was avoiding her question. As he'd done the last time. And the time before that.

"You'll get to keep your house."

No *we*. No *us* other than the two of them in a twisted business transaction to save her home. And no mention of *love*.

"I'll take care of you and Brandon."

And deep down in her heart she knew he would. He could give her all that. And more. And they'd probably be happy. But he wasn't giving her the *one* thing she needed. The *one* thing she had to have.

"Do you love me?" she asked slowly. Her voice strained. And she hated that she was putting him on the spot. Hated that *she* was put into this position. Hated that—

"We're good together," he told her, and a little piece of her brittle heart splintered off. "We can be happy, Ruby Mae." He pressed his stand. His eyes were bright, burning with intensity and promise. And maybe something more. But what, she didn't know. He grabbed her cold hands in his. Squeezed them. "We can make a good life together. You know we can."

And still there was no mention of love.

And Ruby Mae wouldn't be happy for long without it. There would be no good life together. Not without love. Her parents were proof of that. His, too.

And then she got mad. Fiercely angry.

She yanked her hands from his. Ignored his frown. And the stiffening of his body as he pulled back. As his own anger flashed in his eyes.

"You have money," she told him, hating how hard-hearted, how crass, how Rachel Cromwell Push-like she sounded. "Why not just float me a loan? Why marry me when you can't say you love me?"

And Virgil knew the semi that had been barreling down on him for the past month had just run over him. And it pissed him off that he hadn't been given more time. Even knowing a lifetime wouldn't have been enough.

And here she was. Eyes flashing. Misinterpreting his intentions. Demanding more of him than he was able to give. And she was refusing to compromise. Refusing to accept him as he was. And him, knowing that his mother, sweet bitch that she was, was probably behind this whole balloon repayment fiasco. Marilee and his father both were on the board of directors for this financial institution. And Vince, how the hell could his father have let Willie Lee sign such a damn agreement?

"Lend me the money," she told him. Her chin jutted out. Her lips pursed together. "Then you don't *have* to marry me."

And he could only stare at her. And get angrier. And then the avalanche of insecurities he'd kept stuffed deep down inside him sprang free, leaving him to wonder. To question. To second guess. Was Ruby Mae just like Rachel? Only interested in him for his money? He was offering to *marry* her. Did that not mean *anything* to her?

Did *he* not mean anything?

"Lend me the money," she pressed on. Just like he knew she'd done when she'd foolishly followed Edgar Wyatt's suggestions for her shop. Another man he was pissed at. Another wildcard that could be a player in Marilee's grand plan, if there was such a grand plan. And he knew – as well as he knew his own name – Marilee was behind this. She had to be.

"I won't," he growled, as he glared at her. Disappointed. And hurt, *dammit*! Really hurt. "I won't lend you the damn money."

And she reared back like he'd slapped her.

And he felt like an ass. The biggest jerk on the planet because he wasn't being honest with her. Truth was he would lend her money. Hell, he'd give it to her. *If he had it*. But he didn't.

And it was time to come clean.

"I see," she stiffly said through pinched lips. She wrapped her arms around herself. Her eyes were suspiciously bright. Like she was holding back tears. Hell, he felt like crying himself.

"It's not that I won't," he told her, pushing the words up around a boulder-sized lump of regret in his throat.

"It's okay." She pushed by him. "Forget I even asked." She hustled up the steps and into the kitchen.

"Ruby Mae!" He quickly followed on her heels. Grabbed her arm to still her from whatever busy work she was pretending to be doing at the counter. "I would give you anything," he barely choked out. "*Anything.*"

Chest heaving, she bowed her head.

He wanted to reach for her, to pull her against him, but he had no right. Not with everything he hadn't told her wedged right there between them.

His grip loosened on her arm, but his fingers refused to leave. They slowly slid up, over her soft skin. Up over her thundering pulse and clenched jaw to gently push a wayward curl from her cheek. And there they lingered. "If I had it," he softly told her, opening himself up like he'd never opened to anyone.

Only for her would he peel back the protective layers he'd built around his soul.

"If I had the money," he slowly pushed the words up out of this tight throat. "I'd give it to you. But." He swallowed his ego, and his pride. "I'm broke."

"*What?*" she breathed out in shock.

"I'm broke."

"You *can't* be!"

Oh, but he was. He was. Every time he yearned to look at the eight-figure account balance he'd taken for granted for too many years, his stupidity slapped him in the face. "I live month to month on what I make as mayor."

"That's impossible!" She pushed her bangs back with her palm. Her eyes were shockingly wide, searching his.

And shame washed over him like acid.

"You can't be broke!" she whispered. "You're a Push. You're one of the wealthiest men in town. Probably in all of Tennessee."

"Was. Was the wealthiest."

Her chest heaved as his confession permeated her shock. "I don't understand."

"Sometimes I don't understand it either."

"How?"

Embarrassment joined his shame.

"How, Virgil? How can that be?" she softly asked, as pure concern and that damned love of hers she had for him filled her eyes.

And he couldn't lie. He couldn't do anything but tell her the damn truth.

"I blew it." His eyes skittered away. It hadn't just been him. Rachel had her greedy hands in the till as much as he had, Maybe more. But it didn't matter. Bottom line, he'd been the one to allow it. "I blew it on trips around the world. Living like a playboy. Buying anything and everything I wanted. And a lot of things I didn't want."

And then there was Rachel who'd been amassing items for her gallery and padding her bank account. Virgil had been trying to forget Ruby Mae, the one woman he couldn't seem to put behind him, or out of his mind.

No matter how far from Rodent, Tennessee he'd wandered. She was always with him.

And she was staring at him now. Like she didn't know him.

And she didn't. Not really.

"Sixteen million dollars," he quietly told her. She might as well know exactly how far he'd fallen. Might as well know exactly what he was. Not that he even remotely thought he had a chance with her.

His chances today were less than they'd been fifteen years ago.

Her mouth gaped open. She grabbed the counter behind her for support. *"Sixteen. Million. Dollars?"* she gasped. "You spent *sixteen million dollars?"*

"Spent?" he choked out. She made it sound… okay… Normal. And it wasn't.

It was stupid. Foolish. Selfish. Arrogant.

And he was angrier than before. "I *blew* it! I ran through it like it was water. Like it was a never-ending supply of happiness!"

"How could you do that?" she hoarsely gasped.

"Believe me, it was easy." Like everything in his life had been. Except for that day fifteen years ago. And this one today.

"How could you not tell me?" She rounded on him. Anger flashing in her eyes, replacing the shock. "How could you keep something like that *from* me?"

"Jee-suz!" he nearly shouted as he rounded back on her. "You're worried about me keeping *that* from you?" He plowed his fingers through his hair. *"You're* the queen of keeping things from me! *You're* the one who kept your little shop a secret. That hurt, Ruby Mae."

And he was warming up to his hurt. It was what was going to keep him company tonight. Along with his anger. And he was plenty mad. Pissed, in fact. *"You're* the one who kept your neighbor's craft businesses from me. You're the one who kept those girl's names from me, *dammit!* When you knew I wanted to help. And you're the one who kept your little *association* with Edgar Wyatt from me!"

And that was her one secret that bit the hardest.

"And *you're* the one who's keeping words from me," she slowly told him.

And those words hung between them, along with her hope that he was something more than he was. And they were hovering over the anger crackling in the air. "They're just words, Ruby Mae," he wearily told her.

Words he couldn't say.

Her eyes grew moist. Her hand curled over her heart. He knew he was breaking it. And there wasn't a damn thing he could do about it. Because he couldn't give her what she wanted. She lifted her chin. "They're words I need to hear, Virgil." She softly confirmed what he already knew.

And he'd never seen her look so sad.

Except maybe the day of Willie Lee's funeral. When she'd buried another man that she'd loved.

"Words I *have* to hear." Her voice wobbled. "I can't go on without them."

And there was the ultimatum.

And they stared at each other. Her heart shimmering in her eyes. His rage churning through him. Their future hopelessly broken beneath their feet.

"Well, I can't give them to you," he told her, as his anger won the battle, and he tossed out his own ultimatum. "I've given you all I can."

She'd have to accept him the way he was. He had nothing more left. She owned his body, his mind, and his soul. And she'd had it for the last fifteen years. It was either enough or...

"Then I need for you to leave," she quietly told him, her voice breaking.

And Virgil's world imploded.

"Fuck it," he growled, pushing past her. Out the back door. And down the steps. He kicked the camping equipment out of his way as he stormed toward his car. He turned the ignition. Spun the car around. Tires squealed as he punched the gas down and headed across the Trail.

And Virgil knew he was leaving half his soul behind with a woman who didn't want it.

* * *

Leaning against the frame of the floor-to-ceiling windows in his townhouse, Virgil stared out at the darkness. It had pretty much been his routine since he'd stormed out of Ruby Mae's house. What the hell had he been thinking? He inhaled a deep breath. *He hadn't been thinking.* He'd been reacting. And badly.

He'd really blown it this time.

And even knowing that, he'd spent the better part of two days trying to find out what the hell was going on. The mortgage company wouldn't talk to him, and he'd hurt Ruby Mae too much already to lie to the company and say he had her power of attorney so he could get more information. He pounded his fist off the window frame. Dropped his head to the glass and sighed.

Marilee was behind this. He knew she was. The only one he cared about was going to lose her house on the other side of the Shiner's Trail.

And there was nothing he could do.

He pushed away from the window. Walked through the expensively-furnished townhouse. He was cold from the inside out. Empty. Like someone had taken a big chunk out of him and crushed it into dust.

And he didn't know how to fix any of it.

* * *

One week later, nine-hundred and forty-seven miles away in Dunstin, Oklahoma, Vincent Push was going down on his woman when his private line rang. With a muttered oath, he rolled off. Took the call. It was his source in Rodent. The woman who kept him apprised of things going on in his hometown. The woman who should be running the damn place, she was that thorough. And the news she shared wasn't good.

He cussed. Tossed the phone onto the nightstand.

"That was Emma, and you have to go." It wasn't a question. Rita, the love of his life, pulled the satin sheet up over her breasts as she studied him. She sat up, her back pressed against the headboard.

"Yeah, it was." Vince slid from their bed. At five-foot-ten, with long dark hair and a centerfold body, Rita Murphy was everything Vince's wife wasn't. Rita was kind. Passionate. Caring. Giving Vince her unwavering love and support when he'd been unable to give her his name.

He pulled his long, gray-blond, shoulder-length hair back into a pony tail. Pushed one leg, then the other into his faded 501s. Buttoned the fly. The mattress dipped as he sat back down. Rita's big toe drew erotic circles over his lower back as he leaned forward; stuffing his number twelve's into his battered boots. He turned. And in her hot dark eyes he saw the same want and need he knew burned in his. Unfinished want. The air crackled with left-over desire. He grabbed her foot. Ran his fingers between her toes before slowly sliding his hand up over her calf to stroke over the sensitive spot behind her knee. The spot that turned her on like a light switch. He kissed her arch as his hand slid further up her thigh to disappear under those satin sheets, slipping into the Promised Land.

And she moaned his name, just like he knew she would before reluctantly slipping her foot off his shoulder. Silently calling a cease-fire to his foreplay.

With a sigh, Vince watched her foot disappear between the sheets. He looked into her hot, dark eyes. "I really do have to go," he told her. He didn't know why he tried to explain. She understood him better than he did. And she deserved so much more than he was able to give her.

But he couldn't change the past.

Rearranging his guilt on his broad shoulders, he bent over. Scooped up the tee shirt he'd tossed on the floor earlier. He sniffed the armpit before pulling it over his head. And while Rita watched, he tossed some toiletries and a change of clothes in a bag. He set it by the bedroom door. Grabbed a leather vest from his walk-in closet. And a leather jacket. Tossed them on top the bag. Then he walked back over to his woman. Bent down. And with one hand on one side of her glorious body, the other stroking over her breast, he brushed his mouth against hers tasting her deep.

She pushed herself up, into his embrace. Slid an arm up over his shoulders to wrap around his neck as she kissed him back. Their tongues melding, dancing, parrying. She brushed her breasts that slipped free from the satin sheet against his chest and just like that, he was hard and hungry for her again. Like he'd been every day since the first day he'd laid eyes on her all those years ago.

He'd been wild when he'd been young. Still was. Wild, that is. Even corralled in the gilded prison of his own making. He'd tried to divorce Marilee way back, but she'd threatened his son.

Just like she was doing today.

"He's not going to want your help," Rita told him.

"I know." Virgil would resent his interference, but Vince didn't care.

"I should have found the balls years ago and fought Marilee for my son." But she'd threatened to take half of what he'd had back then, and it had been a lot. And he'd been too greedy to give it up to her. He'd already set up her with more than she'd ever had, even when she'd been masquerading around as a rich girl with that Percy piece of shit. He'd set Virgil up, too. And he'd paid his alimony every month, and all the boy's expenses until he'd turned twenty-five, when Vince had given the kid sixteen million dollars.

"You did what you had to do, Vince." Rita smiled as her finger slowly stroked down over his chest. "And you'll do what you have to do now, too."

She was right. And through it all, she'd be by his side. Vinnie, too. And the urge to make them his in every way possible had Vince doing daily battle against the urge to make things right with Virgil and end things once and for all with Marilee, no matter what the cost.

But he'd never gotten around to it. Had never grown a big enough set to take on his wife.

"I gotta go."

"I know you do. Be safe."

With a long-suffering sigh, Vince rearranged the ever-present guilt. It was his steady companion as he walked through their house to their enormous garage out back. It was time to ride. He secured his bag. Pulled his helmet down over his face. Slid his leg over the gas tank. Started the engine and with a deep-seated rumble, he pulled the custom-built chopper out onto the main highway, heading east toward I-40 and Tennessee. And the mess he'd never quite cleaned up.

Maybe this would be the time he finally made things right.

Chapter 19

Ruby Mae needed to quit crying. Needed to quit running to the window hoping every time a car pulled into her driveway that it was Virgil coming back to say he loved her. She needed to quit mourning a relationship that had obviously been one-sided.

And she needed a show.

That was the only way to save her house.

And she had about as much chance of getting one as she had of getting Virgil to say he loved her.

God, she hurt. Felt so empty. So raw. So emotionally ripped apart. No one should have to feel this depth of pain twice in their lifetime. With Willie Lee she'd known. Cancer had taken him. But Virgil? All he'd had to say were three words. And he didn't. Or wouldn't, or couldn't, she didn't know. She'd gone over that day a hundred times in her head, and… She squeezed her eyes shut as she drew in a shuddering breath.

It had been a week since he'd left. Seven long, lonely days. And longer, lonelier nights. Nights when she'd been so distraught she'd been unable to sleep.

And so she'd painted.

Some of her best work. Amazing how the pain in her heart and her soul transformed on canvas. But none of it mattered because she had as much chance of getting a show at the Push Gallery as she had of growing a second head. Not with Rachel Cromwell Push running it.

Ruby Mae had no contacts. She'd never needed any before. She'd sold her paintings in her shop. One or two, here or there, each bringing in a little extra income.

She needed to sell a lot to make a dent in her debt. She needed to sell the entire collection to meet the terms of the mortgage letter. And fast. She pushed her paintbrushes aside. Sat down on the stool in her workroom. Wearily leaned her forehead against her hand. "What am I going to do?" she whispered to no one but herself.

When she wasn't manning her shop or taking care of Brandon, she was on the phone, or driving all over the county and beyond trying to find someone – *anyone* interested in her paintings. Anyone interested in taking a chance on an unknown artist. And doing it before the mortgage company foreclosed and took her house.

She rubbed her bleary eyes. She should have swallowed her pride. Buried her deepest desire, forgot about her dream, and accepted Virgil's offer of marriage.

Her hand curled over the ever-present ache in her chest.

God, she missed him so much. Brandon did, too. He walked around with a boulder-sized chip back on his shoulder. His turquoise eyes, so like his daddy's, burned with silent accusation, and she could no more explain to him what happened than she could explain it to herself.

She sighed, pushing her hair back from her face. "You really screwed up this time, girl." She'd let her anger and her disappointment stomp all over Virgil's good intentions. And he'd reacted just as badly. But she'd always known that about him. She should have been more understanding, more lenient. She squeezed the bridge of her nose. Let her heavy, scratchy eyelids shut. He'd always reacted badly to shock. Now she knew. She didn't react any better either.

What she would give for a do-over. A chance to have him ask her one more time. How different her answer would be. She swiped the tears pooling in her swollen eyes.

Life didn't offer do-overs. She wouldn't get another chance. She'd been the one to ask him to leave. A rash decision she regretted with every fiber of her being.

Outside, the stillness of the late morning was shattered by the deep, growling rumble of a motorcycle crossing over the Trail. Dogs yapped in her neighbor's yards as the rumble drew closer.

Ruby Mae stood. Walked through Virgil's apartment, training her eyes on the front door and not on all the things he'd left behind. Which had been everything. And she held her breath, knowing she could still smell his cologne in the air and she'd changed the sheets a week ago. She'd dusted and swept away all traces, and yet he was still here. Lingering… taunting… teasing her with what would never be.

And she walked faster until she was nearly running out the front door.

Just in time to see a candy-apple red, custom-built chopper with glittering wheels and handlebars slowly pull into her driveway. The driver revved the engine one more time before shutting it down.

He stood. Rocked the bike back onto its stand. Two faded denim-clad muscular thighs straddling a custom-painted gas tank. Chrome exhaust pipes snaked down around the engine behind one long leg of his still straddling the bike. Big black tires were wrapped around custom-cut chrome wheels, if the oil derricks cut into the polished metal were any indication.

And before she saw the face revealed behind the tinted visor of the matching custom-painted helmet, she knew by the long gray-blond ponytail hanging out over the back of his battered leather jacket who'd come a callin'.

Vincent Push. Virgil's daddy.

"Whoa!" Brandon shouted as he ran from the house, down the steps toward their unexpected visitor, showing the most excitement she'd seen from him since Virgil had left.

"Stay back, honey." She grabbed him by the shoulders. Held him close so he wouldn't drool all over the polished metal.

Vince yanked off his helmet, swung a leg over the bike, and stood before her. Tall and broad and Ruby Mae's breath backed up in her throat because in front of her stood a rough-cut version of Virgil. Eighteen years further down the road of life.

"What are you doing here?" she asked, as she struggled to contain her squirming son.

Vince ignored her question.

Of course, he would. It was an irritating Push trait.

He stared down at Brandon. And then he smiled. One exactly like Virgil's. And Ruby Mae's heart squeezed tight in her chest. "So you must be the Badass."

"I am!" her son proudly declared. *"Badass! Badass! Badass!"* And the chanting began.

"Don't swear in front of him," Ruby Mae told her unexpected visitor. "And you, Brandon," she squeezed his shoulders for attention. "Stop swearing, too." They'd had that problem pretty much taken care of. And she winced.

There was no longer a '*they*'. Or a '*we*'. Or a '*them*'.

"Badass, you're what, seventeen now?"

"Oh, please," Ruby Mae rolled her eyes. "Do not encourage him." That was another problem they'd almost gotten under control, Brandon acting his age.

Vince cocked his head to one side. Rubbed a big, callused finger against Brandon's smooth chin. "Got a little peach fuzz growin' here, I see."

"He does not!" Ruby Mae gasped. "And *you* didn't answer my question."

He looked up at her. And smiled. And God! Could it hurt any worse? "Good to see you, too, Ruby Mae."

And just like the son, the father apparently avoided what he didn't want to talk about either.

"Look." She stepped around Brandon.

"Badass." Vince tossed his leather bag to her son.

Brandon scooped it up, wiggling like a puppy at Vince's feet. Touching everything. His questions rapid fire. "This is yours? Can I ride it? Can I drive it? Huh? Can I? Can I?"

"No, you cannot!" Ruby Mae told her son.

"Sure," Vince told him at the same time.

"Vince!" she gasped at him.

He ignored her outrage. Set his helmet, visor up, over Brandon's head. "Take my stuff to my room. Then I'll take you for a ride."

She rounded on her unexpected guest. "*You* don't have a room here! And you are *not* taking him for a ride!" Was the man crazy? That's all she needed. Her son riding motorcycles.

"*Yes?*" Brandon pumped his fist in the air. "Yes! When can we go, huh? Huh?"

"*You're* not riding on that bike, young man!" Ruby Mae told her son.

And like his new superhero, her son ignored her, as well. "You're gonna stay? Right? Huh? You're really gonna stay? Right here? Right?" Excitement dripped from every word.

Vince chucked Brandon on the chin. "Well, hell yeah, I'm stayin'."

"Hell yeah, you are!" Brandon exclaimed.

"Brandon, do not swear! And you," Ruby Mae rounded on Vince. Again. "You are *not* staying here!"

"Sure I am," he told her, his eyes following her son who was running Vince's stuff into the garage apartment like a dutiful valet.

He turned back to her. His blond brows drew down together as he studied her. "You look like hell, by the way."

"Well, nice to see you, too," she snapped. "I know *exactly* what I look like." *A mess.* A broken-hearted mess, she thought, wondering why she even cared. "You're not staying here," she told him again. "Go stay with you son."

"Now why in the hell would I do that?"

Vincent Push eyed the woman standing in front of him. She did look terrible. Fragile as he'd never seen her. Eyes swollen from crying. Face pale, drawn. If his son were standing here in front of him, Vince would kick his ass.

"Oh, I don't know." She crossed her arms over her chest, narrowing her puffy eyes at him. "Maybe because he's your *son!*"

Vince hid the grin. Even hurting like she was, she still had that feisty, fighting streak he'd always admired in the woman. "I thought he lived here," he replied. And when she looked away, he knew. Virgil had. But he didn't anymore.

Things were as bad as Emma had said.

"Go stay with your wife," Ruby Mae fired another round at him. For a cupcake she was pretty feisty. But he guessed she had to be raising a boy on her own.

"And run into your father? Not a chance." Vince pushed by her, walking toward the door the kid had disappeared into. "I'm stayin' here," he called over his shoulder.

She was the one who needed him.

"You *cannot* stay here!" She rushed by him to block the entrance.

"I'll pay you rent." She needed the money. Especially after what the Board of Directors at the mortgage holding company had done. Without his consent. And at his wife's request, damn her miserable hide. And he knew Ruby Mae wouldn't outright accept his help. Or his check. Paying her outrageous rent was a good way to give her the money she needed.

It was a good plan.

Her lips pressed tight. She was still glaring at him. And the battle was still raging in her eyes. She sucked in a sharp breath. Maybe even breathed out a sigh of regret "I will *not* take rent from you."

"Damn pride and honesty," he muttered under his breath. Well, so much for Plan A. No worries though. Vince would have to come up with something else. And she was still glaring at him. Blocking his way. Reciting silly reasons why he should be far away from her. He lifted his index finger to stop her.

"What?" she warily said.

"You have a lot of rules, cupcake, you know that?" He gripped her arms and proceeded to lift her out of the way. "But I'll get used to them," he told her, as he marched by her into the apartment.

325

"You're not staying that long!" she yelled at his retreating back, but Vince just smiled as he made himself comfortable.

He was staying for as long as it took.

* * *

Virgil hadn't thought it possible, but his life just got worse. He shouldn't care. He was past the point of caring, but *dammit!* It pissed him off. He grabbed the special edition of the newspaper Emma had left on his desk. Glared down at the headline.

Push Backs Dupree for Mayor in Newly-Declared, Early Special Election.

Virgil read out loud the exclusive. Like he hadn't already read it three times! "In a shocking turn of events, Marilee Push stunned the citizens of Rodent by publicly backing Connor Dupree at last night's Town Hall meeting over her son, and current mayor, Virgil Push. There's nothing stunning or shocking about that," Virgil muttered, tossing the paper down on his desk. He'd known she'd be laying for him. Waiting to take him down for what she'd consider traitorous behavior instead of being proud of him for taking a stand.

He just hadn't counted on how hard she'd take him down. First, Ruby Mae's house. Now, his job, and subsequently, his house.

"Dammit!" he growled. He had another year left to serve in Harlan's original term. And he hadn't counted on Marilee getting Sonny on her side to make this happen. Sonny always voted with Virgil and Davis. He wondered what it had cost her. Or what she had on the man. It could be anything from extra cheese on his pizza at Executive Council meetings to naked pictures of the man and his Monster Mouse. Who knew?

Certainly not Virgil.

It had been their usual Executive Council meeting. The one where Virgil had officially declared Ruby Mae's citation cleared, null and void. It was while under new business when Marilee had struck. And now it was confirmed, right there in black and white on the front page of the *Rodent Registrar*. "Executive Council votes three to two to hold a special election for the position of mayor immediately."

Emma walked in. "You okay?"

She'd been looking at him funny since he and Ruby Mae— He rubbed the ache in his chest. The one he knew would be there for the rest of his life. He'd blown it with Ruby Mae and he didn't know how to fix it any more than he knew how to stop Marilee.

"I should sue this paper." He picked it up. Shook it at Emma. Savored the burning sting of anger, misdirected as it was. "For not specifically specifying which Push was backing that asshole Dupree in their headline."

"Oh, I think they know all right which one," she told him, taking the paper from his clenched fist. "No one's going to vote for Connor Dupree."

Virgil wasn't so sure. Marilee had a lot of power in this town. More than he'd thought, or known about. And Connor was a spineless rich boy with enough ghosts in his closet Marilee would have no problem having her pick of what to hang over his head to get the man to do what she wanted.

"*Da-amn!*" He was pissed. He didn't want to have things end like this. Didn't want to go out this way. But there was little he could do, if anything. He'd been an ass with Ruby Mae. Again. And—

"They've already called for a debate," he told Emma. "And according to page three," he jabbed the paper she still held in her hands. "She's already scheduled a time." He couldn't even say his mother's name anymore!

"I haven't confirmed it," Emma calmly told him. Like his life wasn't imploding. First, Ruby Mae. Now this.

"Well, we'll look like asses if we don't show up."

God! He hadn't even thought about running again. His mind had been consumed with Ruby Mae. And Brandon. And getting rid of a crooked cop preying on teenage girls. And a gang of drug pushers infiltrating the rest of his town.

"Do you want to run for re-election?" Emma asked.

"Hell, yeah," Virgil replied, if it meant beating Marilee at her own game. But could he stand four more years in this town with things the way they were between him and Ruby Mae? And worse, what if she found someone new? And he had to watch her from the sidelines blissfully happy. *Again.*

God! He'd done that once. That had been what had inspired schooling at Harvard. Far away from Tennessee. And trips around the world. Again, far away from Tennessee. He sure as hell didn't want to do that again.

Nobody should have to suffer like that twice.

His lifted his chin. "I'm pissed, Emma."

"I know."

"Itching for a fight, too." And that it just happened to be his mother and the man who his ex-wife had regularly slept with while still married to Virgil, the man who he'd be knocking heads against, well, all the better. Besides, it would take his mind off Ruby Mae and the mess he'd made there. And Brandon. "Christ," he muttered, running his hands through his hair. "I need another term to clean up this town and make it safe." For Brandon. And kids like him. He lifted his head to his assistant. "Confirm the debate. In fact, move it up a week. I'm ready."

"Good." His secretary smiled at him. "So are Davis and I."

Virgil's brows drew together.

"Don't look at me like that," she told him. "Consider us your re-election committee. Marilee's not going to win this. Not with us in your corner."

Virgil pushed a breath up through his tight chest, asking what he really wanted to know. "Any word on Ruby Mae's mortgage?"

Emma's smile slipped as she slowly shook her head side to side. "Nothing yet. But I'm sure help is on the way and should be here soon."

Virgil frowned. He didn't know what kind of help she was talking about. He'd exhausted all avenues he could think of and hitting nothing but roadblocks for his efforts. He ran a hand over his head. Squeezed the back of his neck where a headache was forming. "There has to be something I've missed."

"I'm sure things will work out."

He stared at his secretary. "What? Do you think some fairy god mother's going to ride into town and save the day?"

"Something like that," she cryptically replied.

"The final payment is due by the end of next month. Maybe I can get her an extension on the loan." He wasn't without a few connections of his own.

"Is Ruby Mae going to like you butting in?"

Of course, she wouldn't. Not with her asking him to leave because he couldn't say three damn lousy words. But he could string a whole mouthful of other ones together if it would save her house. "At this point, I think Ruby Mae will take help from anyone."

Even him.

"The lovely widow needs help?"

Virgil jerked his head toward his office door. Gritted his teeth.

Edgar Wyatt filled the entrance, leaning casually against the jamb. Leaving Virgil to wonder how much the whiskey baron had overheard.

And how long it would take before the man was sniffing around Ruby Mae again.

* * *

"Will you quit throwing money at me?" Ruby Mae snapped as she picked up the hundred dollar bill Vince had tucked under his breakfast plate. He'd been living with her, driving her crazy. "I'm not taking it!" She stuffed the offending bill back into the front pocket of his jeans, knowing she was three kinds of a fool for not taking it.

Vince grinned. "You always this bristly in the morning, cupcake?"

"You always throw your money away? I told you." She pointed a finger at his chest. "I'm *not* taking rent money from you. So quit leaving it tucked under your pillow. And I'm not taking tips for serving you breakfast either!"

"Can I tip you for serving me lunch and dinner?"

She growled as she pushed by him and Vince laughed. Actually laughed at her! And she wanted to smack him. And herself. He'd offered her enough money in the past month to make a healthy dent in her debt. And still she couldn't take it from him.

Pride wouldn't allow her to take another handout.

He reached for her arm, stopping her. His brows drew together as he studied her. A little too closely. "You sleep much last night?"

"Did I keep you up?"

There was a closed door between the apartment he'd commandeered for his visit and her workroom where she regularly spent her sleepless nights painting. But the man either never slept, or woke up at the drop of a paintbrush.

"Why don't you just take my money?" he quietly asked.

"Because," she wearily replied, looking away. She did not want to have this conversation.

"Because why?" he persisted. "It's not like I'll need it. Or miss it."

"And wouldn't it be nice to have that kind of endless supply." She sighed, rubbing her forehead. "I'm sorry. My money problems are no one's problem but my own."

"Just take the money, honey. I'm giving it away. Just take it."

"I can't." And when he opened his mouth to argue, she talked over him. "I can't be somebody's charity case. Again." She'd already been there. "I'll find the money. Somehow," she added, as her anxiety level shot off the scale. The days were ticking by and she was no closer to getting the money than when she'd gotten the letter.

"Why are you bein' so stubborn?"

"I'm not being stubborn," she tiredly replied, wishing he understood. His son would have. She rubbed the tender spot over her broken heart. How it still beat, shattered as it was, she didn't know.

"Yes, you are," Vince went on. Like she hadn't just thrown up a brick wall in his face.

And here she was. Punching through it. Trying to make him see. "No, I'm not being stubborn. When Willie Lee was so sick, you were there for us, helping us out." She swallowed the painful memories. "And even before that. When he graduated high school and couldn't find a decent job, you gave him one."

"I gave a lot of kids from this town decent jobs."

And he was right. He employed a lot of people from Rodent. But… She lifted her chin. "Did you pay them all like you paid Willie Lee?"

She'd never quite been able to believe how much money Willie Lee had made. Or all the reasons he'd recited for the huge paycheck. The work was dangerous. That she could believe, but, "Did you pay all your employees more for being taken away from their family like you paid Willie Lee?"

And when he didn't answer right away she plowed on. "Did you pay them good money to keep good help? Because I find it hard to believe you did." And then she added one more to her case. "When we couldn't get a loan for the house, you pulled strings and got us one."

He shrugged a shoulder. Like it was no big deal. Just like his son did when *he* thought something wonderful he'd done was *no big deal.*

"And when *you* needed help with your shop, *you* went to Edgar Wyatt." Vince's lips thinned in disapproval when he said Edgar's name. Just like Virgil's did. "You should have come to me. I would have helped you then, too, Ruby Mae."

"I know you would have." She breathed out a heavy sigh of regret. "You're the most generous man I know, except for maybe…" She blinked back the tears. Swallowed down the regret for what could have been. "Have you even seen your son since you've gotten back to town?"

He frowned. "Virgil?"

"*Yes*, Virgil!" How many sons did the man have?

And again he looked at her. And it hurt to look back; he looked so much like the man she loved.

"You think I should go see him." It wasn't a question.

"*Yes*, you should go see him. He's your *son!*"

He seemed to mull that over. "If I go, can I pay you?"

"For what?"

"For suggesting it."

"No, you can't!" she told him. Not when one of the reasons she wanted him to go was so he'd tell her when he came back how Virgil was doing. How he was getting along. Because despite everything that happened, she still loved him. And always would.

"Anything you want me to tell him?"

Only that she loved him. That she missed him. That she wanted him back anyway she could have him.

"No, not a thing," she quietly replied, knowing it was the biggest lie she'd ever told.

* * *

Virgil was in no mood for company, yet someone was banging a hole through the front door of the townhouse. He yanked the door open.

"What the hell did you do to Ruby Mae?"

The last person Virgil expected to see on his doorstep – his father – was glaring at him from the other side.

"What the hell's wrong with you?" his father went on and Virgil's already dark mood went black.

"I could ask you the same damn thing, dad." Virgil turned. Stalked back into the living room. Picked up the crystal tumbler half-filled with Jack. No way in hell would he ever drink Wyatt whiskey again. Even if it was touted as Tennessee's finest.

"There's nothing wrong with me." His father followed Virgil into the room. Made himself at home, too, grabbing a glass. He dropped a few ice cubes into it before adding the Jack. He lifted it to his lips. Took a taste and hissed out his satisfaction.

"That's debatable." Virgil picked up the conversation where they'd left it, taking a sip of his own whiskey. Neat.

With the bottle in hand, his father moved to the couch. Got comfortable, slouching down into the white leather.

Virgil arched an eyebrow. "You plannin' on stayin'?"

"Looks that way. Guess we're going to have us a little chat."

"What for?" Virgil took another swallow. At this rate, he'd be drunk before they got the formalities out of the way. "We've never done that before."

"Guess there's always a first time." Vince took another swig of his whiskey before refilling the glass. "Consider this a little father-son bonding."

"Oh, yeah." Virgil slumped down into the matching leather chair facing his father. "'Cause we've had so many of those in the past." He crossed his right ankle over his left knee and jiggled his foot.

"Not for lack of trying on my part." Vince took another sip from his glass. He crossed his leg. Left ankle over his right knee and his big black biker boot didn't jiggle. Not once.

"Oh, yeah, you tried so damn hard." Virgil dropped his foot to the carpet.

"Are you still holding that one time against me? You were in second grade."

The father-son trek up the mountain. Virgil tamped the old hurt down inside. "*One time?*" he snorted, taking another big swallow of his whiskey. There'd been a hundred times.

Vince dropped his booted foot to the floor. He leaned forward. Dressed as he was in faded, ripped jeans, wearing a holey tee shirt with the sleeves cut out, he should look out of place against the plush surroundings of Harlan's townhouse. Instead Virgil was the one who felt out of place. What he'd give to be living in a little house on the wrong side of the Trail with the woman he couldn't get out of his mind. Or out of his soul.

"I did try." Vince sat the crystal down on the glass table that separated them. It might as well have been nine-hundred miles of Tennessee-Oklahoma dirt. They were that far apart. Always had been. "I asked your mother for summer visitations every year... Until the year you started to act just like her."

Virgil frowned. He hadn't known that about Vince. He did remember acting like his mother though. It had been his senior year in high school.

"Then I quit askin'," Vince told him.

And a part of Virgil couldn't blame him. Virgil hadn't liked himself much back then either.

"Do you love Ruby Mae?"

Virgil's brows drew together. "*What?*"

"It's a simple question, Virgil. Do you love her?"

"How many people are going to tell me that same damn thing! *It's simple.* There's nothing *simple* about it!" Virgil shot up out of his seat. He paced back and forth. Stopped and glared down at his old man. "How the hell do I know!"

"You should." Vince leaned back into the leather cushion. And Virgil found he couldn't take his eyes off his dad.

And he stood there. Wondering... Waiting... Wishing he'd impart the wisdom Virgil desperately needed to make things right with him and Ruby Mae. Praying he wouldn't be disappointed like he'd been most of his life where his parents were concerned.

"Does she consume you, son? Is she your every waking thought? Your every dream at night? Do you need her with every breath you take?"

"Like you need Marilee?" Virgil lashed out. And he waited the tense seconds for his taunt to reach its mark. For Vince to react the way he'd always done in the past, which was to do nothing. Allowing Virgil to feel justified in his actions. God! He was one messed up fuck. His whole family was.

"Like I need Rita," his father quietly replied.

Which only made Virgil madder. "Who the hell is *Rita*?"

"My woman." And the possessiveness, the pride resounding in Vince's voice shocked Virgil. "We've been together for more than thirty years. And I'm still hungry for her."

Ignoring the "*ick*" factor associated with his father getting it on with this *Rita* person, Virgil could only stare at his dad. At the contented smile that transformed his face.

"I still need her in every way I can get her."

"Oh this is just great! Just great!" Virgil agitatedly paced back and forth. "And I wonder why I'm messed up." He stopped. Glared at his father. "You have a wife. And you have a— a— *Rita*. What the hell else do you have?"

"I have happiness. And a son."

Virgil sucked in a sharp breath.

"Another son. His name is Vinnie."

"Who the hell is Vinnie?" Virgil nearly shouted. "Besides your freakin' *namesake*?"

"He's your step-brother. And consider yourself lucky. Your mother wanted to name you Percy."

"Oh, *Sweet Jesus*! I have a step-brother. Of course, I'd have a step-brother. Which you conveniently *failed to mention*. Like *ever!* Let me guess. He lives with you and this *Rita*—"

"Don't," Vince growled, but Virgil wasn't listening.

"And you're all one *big* happy family, right?" he went on. "Well, what about me, dad? Did you *ever* care about me?"

"I gave you sixteen million dollars. Which you promptly blew."

"Forget the freakin' money! You left me with her!" And this time Virgil couldn't stop the hurt from filling his voice. "You *left* me with her, dad, and you *never* cared. You want to know if I love Ruby Mae? Well, how the hell would I even know what love is? I never had any."

"That's not true, son," Vince quietly replied. "I always loved you. And I never regretted having you. You were the first best thing I ever did."

"Well, it's nice to know I'm *number one* in something."

"Thirty four years ago, I was a wild-assed kid who didn't care about anything but having the next good time. Having you made me grow up. Made me be a man."

"Some man you turned out to be. You *left* me with her." Virgil hated the weakness in his voice. Hated the vulnerability he was too weary to hide. "Do you know what I would have given to be with you?" How many times he wished his dad had given a shit about him.

And the air grew thick, pulsing with a lifetime of bad decisions. On both their parts.

"I'm sorry," Vince quietly replied. "I truly am." And something in his eyes told Virgil his father was telling the truth. "I tried to get you from Marilee, but she wouldn't give you up. Not without taking everything from me. And she had my nuts to the wall, what with me living with Rita. And I wasn't willing to give your mother everything. I'd already given her more than she deserved. More than she'd ever had – no matter what she had the people in this town believin'."

"So you just left me behind. Moved on."

"I paid alimony. And child support. Every month. I bought every single thing your mother said you needed. And more. I bought the roof over your head. Your first car. Your Harvard education."

"Did that make you feel better? Because it sure as hell wasn't working for me!"

Vince's eyes narrowed. "I wanted you to come work with me after you graduated, but by then you'd already married your mother."

"*Jee-suz*," Virgil hissed. But it was true. He had married a woman exactly like his mother. A woman Marilee had put directly in his path when he'd lost Ruby Mae to Willie Lee. A fact recently confirmed by Rachel.

"You know what?" Vince stood. "I don't want to talk about this anymore."

"That suits me just fine." Virgil didn't want to talk about it either.

"We've both done what we had to do. The only difference," Vince looked down at Virgil. "I learned from my mistakes. Will you? Because letting the woman who loves you get away from you is the biggest mistake you'll ever make. And you'll regret it for the rest of your life."

"Like you?"

"I regret not divorcing your mother. Even if she'd have taken everything, Rita would still have had me. She isn't with me for my money. Or for what I could get her."

Virgil winced. His father had just described Rachel's motives for marrying him. Worse, this Rita woman sounded exactly like Ruby Mae. Ruby Mae had still wanted him, even knowing he was broke. And obviously an idiot.

"Rita knows exactly what I am and she still loves and wants me, even fucked up like I am. Just like your Ruby Mae. I regret not marrying Rita. Not being able to give her my name. But I never, I *never* regret lovin' her.

"Get your head out of your ass, son. You can call it whatever the hell you want, but you've loved that girl since you first saw her with Willie Lee." His father nudged Virgil's shiny loafer with one of his scuffed-up boots. "Back then, you couldn't wait to kick the dust of this town off your shoes. I was like that, too. But you," his dad's eyes slid down over Virgil. And they were filled with... pride. "It looks to me like you're planting roots in all that dust. And you're thrivin' here.

"You deserve Ruby Mae. And you deserve to be happy. To be in love. And to love. Don't blow it, son. Find a way to make things right," Vince added, before turning and walking out the door.

Leaving Virgil with an odd, warm feeling in middle of his chest.

And the ragged edges of his tattered soul all sutured up.

Chapter 20

The house was too quiet what with Vince and Brandon up on the Brandywine for the father-son campout. It gave Ruby Mae too much time to think. Too much time to worry. And too much time to miss Virgil. Her breath caught. It had been a month and she hadn't heard from him. Not one word. Anything she learned about him she'd learned through the newspaper and Vince.

It hurt, but she pushed it aside. She had bigger problems at the moment.

She counted the day's receipts one more time. She'd run ads in all the local papers. She'd advertised on-line, offered discounts to first-time shoppers, and she had one of her biggest months in sales, but… She entered the numbers into her laptop and her heart sank.

"Damn," she said. It wasn't enough.

She closed down the program. Shut the lid on her laptop. Pushed it aside. Sighed. Even if she drained what little she had in her savings and the one with Willie Lee's life insurance money set aside for Brandon's college, scraping together everything she had, and pawning what she could, she'd still come up short.

She'd still lose her house.

She and Brandon would be living out of Willie Lee's truck.

She rubbed her chest. Tamped down the panic. She searched her mind. Prayed for a miracle to come walking through the side door, but like her house, her workshop was dishearteningly silent. And empty.

The chimes above the shop door jingled.

Running a hand over her hair, Ruby Mae quickly walked across the workroom to the door that separated it from the shop. And prayed whoever was on the other side had a miracle stashed in their pocket.

"Edgar?" She paused just inside the shop, surprised at her visitor. "What are you doin' here?"

He turned from her wall of paintings. "Ruby Mae." He smiled. "How are you?" His eyes slid down over her.

"I'm fine." She wasn't. Nowhere close. But he didn't need to know.

His eyes ran over her again. Any other time, she wouldn't have thought twice about it. But after hearing Virgil's take on the man, she was now finding herself feeling uneasy. Uncertain.

Edgar turned back to her paintings. Like he couldn't get enough of them. "These really are very good." He glanced over his shoulder at her. "You're very talented."

"Thank you." Why was he here? Since she'd officially opened her shop two years ago, she hadn't seen him once. "Is there something I can help you with?"

Her fingers wrapped around the scooped neck of her shirt and she subconsciously tugged it up. She didn't know why. This was Edgar Wyatt, Junior. He'd never given her any reason to feel uncomfortable in his presence, yet… Suddenly, she was.

"I have something for you."

She took an involuntary step back, bumping into her counter.

He laughed. "I don't bite, Ruby Mae. Not unless you want me to."

His voice grew husky and a shudder of unease ran down her spine.

This was all Virgil's fault. Everything he'd said about the man had her questioning his motives.

He stepped closer. Rested an elbow on the counter, and she wondered if it was her wild imaginings, or had he leaned closer than was necessary? "I have something for you." He reached a hand into the inner pocket of his suit jacket. He pulled a large, creamy white vellum envelope, which he laid on the counter between them.

She could only stare at it. Lately it seemed, she'd developed an aversion to thick vellum envelopes.

He chuckled. "Well, aren't you going to open it?" He pushed the envelope closer to her. His fingernails were buffed and polished. His face was youthful, although she knew him to be pushing fifty. His perfectly styled hair was sprinkled with gray at the temples making him look distinguished. He was a nice looking man. But, excluding Virgil, she wasn't interested in any. Especially ones bringing her thick vellum envelopes.

"It won't bite," he told her, and that was the second time he mentioned *biting*. "Go on." He motioned with his head.

"What is this?" She carefully picked up the envelope.

"Open it." With both elbows resting on the counter, he leaned closer. His smile seemed genuine, yet she couldn't ignore the hairs rising up on the back of her neck.

Thank you, Virgil Push, for destroying my faith in mankind, too!

He jerked his head toward the envelope. "*Open it.*"

And before he could tell her again it didn't bite, she carefully lifted the flap. Pulled out what looked like… "This is an invitation." She looked up at him. "To an art show."

"I know. I set it up for you."

"But—"

He talked over her. "You'll share space with three other new artists, but it will be your show."

It wouldn't really be *her* show if she was sharing it, but she didn't point that out. He was offering her a show. And from it, she might be able to make enough to save her house! Or at least get an extension of the deadline with a decent attempt at payment. And a whole lot of groveling.

His long, lean fingers brushed over the knuckles of her hand that lay fisted on the counter top. "I made all the arrangements."

She pulled her hand back. "I don't understand. This is at the Armstrong Gallery. In Dawson Falls." Where his distillery was now located. "I— I can't go—" She stuttered to a halt as her conscience did silent battle with her checkbook balance.

"Sure you can." He curled his fingers over hers until he held her hand in his. A ripple of apprehension slid down Ruby Mae's spine and she resisted – barely – the urge to pull her hand back again. "We'll go up Thursday night. And stay until Monday. Maybe Tuesday."

"I can't." She tugged at her hand.

He didn't let it go. "We'll make it a long weekend. You and me. Together."

"Edgar." This time she retrieved her hand. And stared at him. And everything he was offering her. A show at the Armstrong Gallery. Even one shared with three other artists was more than she had now. But a weekend with him was more than she was willing to pay for it.

"I can't do this." She pushed the invitation toward him.

"Sure you can." He stopped it with a finger. Pushed it back. "I've rented a suite for us."

"You're not listening. I'm not spending the weekend with you."

The edges of his easy-going demeanor cracked. His jaw tensed as anger replaced the heat of desire in his eyes. "You think you're going to get something better? *Here?*" he sneered. "You think Rachel Cromwell-Push is going to give you a show?"

"I know she's not." And Ruby Mae resented that he thought her stupid enough, or naïve enough to even think such a thing.

"Do you really think you have other options? Better offers?"

She knew she didn't. She resented his attitude. His arrogance. But even desperate as she was… "I'm not sleeping with you."

"You owe me!" he spat out as he leaned closer. His face was blotchy red with rage. The tip of his index finger pounded the counter top. "You think I helped you out of the goodness of my heart?"

She sucked in a sharp breath. She had. But not anymore.

Virgil had been right.

His body vibrated with rage and not for the first time, Ruby Mae wished she wasn't alone. She heard a rumble, but knew it was most likely her heart thundering in her chest. Vince was up on the mountain with Brandon. For the weekend. And she was here. Alone. In her shop. With a man she wanted rid of.

"You think I helped you out of some misplaced sense of Christian charity?"

"No!" she fired back. "There is nothing Christian or charitable about what you're offering."

"You think I allowed you to cry on my shoulder because I actually cared?"

"I *never* cried on your shoulder!" She'd cried all over the place back then. She'd been so desperate and so weighed down with the expenses of Willie Lee's illness and their life crumbling all around them, for all she knew, she had cried on his shoulder. But she wouldn't admit it now. Not when he'd use it as a bargaining chip in a game he was never going to win. She'd gladly live in Willie Lee's truck than sleep with Edgar Wyatt to keep her house.

He stood to his full height. Slapped his hand down on the counter top hard enough to make her jump. "If you want to save your house, you'll sleep with me. You don't have any other choice."

"And if you want to save your face from needing plastic surgery, you'll leave."

Ruby Mae nearly jumped out of her skin at the voice coming from right behind her.

"Vince," she gasped out his name as she spun around to find him standing in the workroom doorway like an avenging angel. Gray-blond hair wildly framing his clenched jaw before falling over muscled shoulders bunched tight with anger and rage.

Wyatt snorted. "Still cleaning up after your boy, I see."

"I don't clean up after my boy," Vince corrected him. "He's his own man." He took a menacing step closer, "But I will clean up the floor with *you* if you don't apologize to this lady and then get the hell outta here before I really lose my charm."

Wyatt turned angry eyes on her. No words of apology left his mouth. Instead, he pointed a finger at her and said, "We're not done here."

346

"Oh, yes, we are," Ruby Mae told him, feeling pretty brave with Vince watching her back. She picked up the invitation. Ripped it in two. Laid the pieces in his palm. "Leave," she told him. "And don't ever come back here."

Edgar spun on his heel and quickly left the shop, slamming the door behind him.

Ruby Mae sank down onto the stool, suddenly feeling weak. And drained. "Thank you," she whispered.

"You're welcome," Vince gruffly replied.

"Is anybody what they seem?" she whispered.

"He's like his dad," Vince told her. "They use women anyway they can."

She rubbed her fingers against her forehead. Tried to suck in a calming breath, but it did little to settle her. She looked up at Vince. And frowned. "Why are you home early?"

He shrugged a shoulder. "Half of the group rolled in some poison ivy."

"My half?" That's was all she needed. Her son itching and scratching.

He shook his head side to side. "No, we're both fine."

He included himself in her half. Like his son used to. She let out a deep sigh. "Thank you, Vince. For everything." For being here for her. And for her son. She thought of the show she'd never participate in.

Vince stepped closer. "Ruby Mae, tell me what I can do. I'll do it."

Tomorrow she'd put everything on the internet. All her work. All her tools and equipment. Everything in the house she could sell but their beds. Willie Lee's truck. Her engagement ring. Her wedding band. She'd sell everything. And then—

Vince touched her shoulder. Turned her around and she looked into eyes that were so full of concern – and caring – she nearly broke down. "You won't take my money," he quietly told her as he studied her. "What can I do? Tell me. I'll do it. Whatever you need, honey. It's yours."

"Give me a show," she quietly told him. "And while I'm wishing for the impossible, give me your son, too."

"One wish at a time, cupcake."

And she smiled… until he pulled his cellphone out of his back pocket.

Her smile slipped. Her heart started to pound. "What are you doing?" She tried to grab it, but he juked faster. "If you're calling Virgil—"

"I'm getting you a show. Jeez, woman," he held up a hand, palm out. "I can only handle one crisis at a time."

"What?"

"I said I can only handle—"

"*I know what you said*! Who are you calling?" Blood pounded in her temples. He'd only punched one number on the keypad, which meant whoever he was calling he had on speed dial.

She hoped to God it wasn't Rachel.

"Giovanni? *Vincenzo* here. *Saluto*."

There was only one Giovanni in the art world. Giovanni Arturo. And he had the most affluent, successful shop in all of Tennessee. Maybe the entire south. That Vince knew him… Spoke to him on a first name basis…

"Gotta favor to ask," Vince said, before slipping into fluent Italian. Words like *bella*. And *artista molto talentuoso* flowed from his mouth.

"You speak in English when you're talking about me!" she nearly shouted. She had a right to know what people expected of her. Not that Vince would ever propose such a sleazy deal as Edgar had.

Vince grinned. The smile so like his son's. And while her bruised heart recovered from it, he switched back to English. In time for her to hear, "She's an amazing talent . And I'm giving you first chance to show her work. Yeah… yeah… Okay… And I want only the most affluent, influential there. And it has to happen immediately." He paused while Giovani spoke. "Yeah… yeah." Then Vince added, "You'll be here tomorrow? Good. *Grazie*. See you then, my friend. *Ciao*."

He hung up the phone.

And Ruby Mae could only stare. She'd hoped for a miracle.

"That was easy," he told her. "Now, let's get you my son."

"No!" Ruby Mae quickly covered his hand with hers before he punched another number into his phone. "One miracle a day is more than enough."

Besides, she wanted Virgil to come on his own. Not because Daddy had ordered him to.

* * *

Vince grabbed a beer from the small refrigerator behind the mini-bar in Ruby Mae's apartment. Held the cold bottle with two fingers as he walked over to the couch. He sat down with a satisfied sigh. Propped his feet on the low coffee table. Crossed them at the ankle as he took a long swallow before lifting the bottle in a mock toast.

By tomorrow morning Marilee would know that in six weeks Ruby Mae would headline her own show. With Giovani Arturo, no less. And she'd make enough money at that one show to more than cover the balloon payment his wife had forced the bank to demand.

He wondered what Marilee had on Edgar, Junior to keep him loyal to her. And how much of Junior's manipulations had been Marilee's scheming. God knew she'd manipulated Edgar, Senior for years. Fucking a fifteen year old was a crime in this state. But instead of pressing charges, she had blackmailed the old man, recreating herself after a trip to France that the old man had taken her on for her sixteenth birthday. And she'd been doing okay for herself. Until Vince had made the mistake of fucking her for his eighteenth birthday.

Their history was ugly. And better left in the past.

He wondered what Marilee would do when she found out Vince had foiled her plans to have Ruby Mae tossed out of her house after Virgil had foiled her plans to take down Ruby Mae's business. And all because their son loved a woman Marilee didn't approve of. A woman she had never approved of.

"Push men don't take to being pushed around," he told the shadows of his past lurking in the room. "And nobody messes with my family," he added, taking another swig of his beer.

Especially Marilee.

Ruby Mae was his future daughter-in-law. Well, she would be when his son finally realized he loved the woman. And he would. Vince would make sure of it. They were making progress with their shouting matches over the phone. And then there was the Badass. Vince took another sip of his beer. He already loved the kid. Couldn't wait to spoil him rotten. Maybe even get him his own bike. Maybe even bring him out to the ranch for a summer. He was the grandson Vince had always wanted. One well past the stinky diaper stage and not yet ready for the smartass, know-it-all puberty stage.

The kid was perfect.

Vince couldn't wait for all of them to meet Rita and Vinnie.

Just like he couldn't wait to see what Marilee would do next.

He sat his empty bottle down on the table. Leaned back into the couch. He laced his fingers behind his head. And smiled.

Not bad for a month's work.

* * *

One week later, Virgil stood on the second floor of the high school auditorium where the debate between him and Connor Dupree was scheduled to take place. With an arm resting against the wall by the window, he watched the parking lot fill. Watched the people of his town slowly file in. Surprised and humbled by how many came out to hear what he had to say.

He also watched a black limo pull up to the curb. Marilee and Connor stepped out of the back. Cameras flashed from the crowd of reporters gathered near the entrance. They waved and smiled as Marilee answered questions fired at Connor. Then she raised her palm and the questions ceased. She slipped her arm through Connor's and they walked inside, a united pair. Against him. Her own son.

He should feel angry. Hurt. Betrayed. But Virgil felt... nothing. He hadn't for a long, long time. Backing Connor had been the final straw that had broken the thin filament binding them. And he knew it wasn't love. He'd been doing a lot of thinking on that. A lot of soul-searching, too. He was coming to understand a lot of things.

Even love.

"You okay?" Emma came up beside him. She rubbed her hand across his shoulder.

"I'm fine," he told her, unable to take his eyes off the parking lot.

"She's wrong, you know." His secretary squeezed his shoulder.

He nodded his head, not correcting his assistant's misconception he was upset about his mother's defection. He was scouring the parking lot looking for Ruby Mae. Would she show up? Did she even care? And if he got the chance to talk to her, what would he say?

"Ruby Mae will be here."

Virgil swung his head to his secretary. Narrowed his eyes. How did she know?

"You might have hit a rough spot," she rubbed her hand across his shoulder again. "But she hasn't given up on you."

And before Virgil could question how she knew that, Davis burst into the room. "Are you ready?" He pushed his wire-rimmed glasses up his nose. "Did you go over the questions I left with you?" He'd taken his position as joint-campaign manager very seriously researching issues, taking opinion polls. Even canvasing door-to-door. "Do you have your responses written out? Here," he pulled a clipped pile of papers from his briefcase and pushed them toward Virgil. "Take mine."

"I don't need them."

Davis frowned. "You have to have responses."

"I have them. Up here." Virgil tapped a finger against his temple. "Don't worry. I know what I have to say." It was what he believed. And he didn't need cue cards to say that.

And maybe when this was all over, he'd apply that same

philosophy to Ruby Mae and what he had to say to her.

Two hours later, Virgil stood at the same window on the second floor. The one that overlooked the parking lot. He watched as the black limo pulled up to a side door and his very angry mother dragged a dumbstruck Connor into the car behind her.

The debate hadn't gone well for Connor.

Or his mother.

And with the special election two weeks away, Virgil had a damn good shot of getting a second term.

He should be happy.

All he felt was hollow. Like something was missing in his life. He knew what it was.

Ruby Mae. Brandon, too.

"You okay?"

Virgil spun around. Maisey Trainor stood in the doorway looking him over with motherly concern. "Why does everybody keep asking me that?"

"Oh, I don't know." She walked further into the room, stopping in front of him. "Maybe because we all care about you." She reached up. Straightened his tie. "She was here, you know."

He didn't pretend to not know who she was talking about. The tightness in his chest was gone. But not the hollowness. "Ruby Mae was here?" he asked. She'd come to hear him? Even after he'd walked away from her?

"Yes, she was. Real proud of you, too."

Warmth spread through his chest. Excitement and eager anticipation spurted through his veins. He looked past her. "Is she still here?"

Sympathy filled Maisey's eyes as she slowly shook her head side to side. "No, honey. Billy took her home." And the knife of disappointment carved a little more out of Virgil's chest. "She's gone door to door campaigning for you."

"Not to sound arrogant, but her neighbors love me. I'm saving all their asses by converting the old distillery into a craft mall."

"She went door to door up on the Brandywine. And over in *your* old neighborhood. Where they don't love you."

"My neighborhood?" There was that damn warmth radiating from the center of his chest again.

"Marilee's street, in fact. And don't give me that look," Maisey quickly added. "Billy was with her. And Percy was with your momma. And everybody knows to stay away when they're going at it. Especially his daughter."

Virgil winced at the mental picture.

Maisey slipped her arm through his. "You can walk me to my car."

"You don't have a car."

"Walk me to your car then. I'll be your date for the evening."

And Virgil gave a sideways glance at the woman beside him, not sure if she was teasing, or serious.

"You are so easy." She laughed again. "How are you and your daddy getting along?"

"Is there nothing private in this town?"

"No, pretty much not."

They walked out across the nearly empty parking lot.

"We're okay," he answered her earlier question. He talked more to his dad in the last month and a half than in his entire life – If he could call the two-sentence shouting matches over the cell phone conversations. The last one he'd asked about Vinnie. And Vince had told Virgil about Ruby Mae having a show with Giovani Arturo. Virgil wasn't sure yet how he felt about Vinnie. He wasn't sure how he felt about a lot of things. Namely, Ruby Mae, but he was working through it.

He opened the door for Maisey. Stashed her cane in the back seat. He crossed in front of the car, slid in behind the wheel, and started it up. The stars shined overhead as they slowly pulled out of the parking lot and onto the Mountain Parkway.

"Ruby Mae got a show, you know," Maisey told him as they rode toward town.

"I know." Virgil was grateful to Vince for making that happen. And for taking Brandon up on the Brandywine for the father-son weekend.

"You want to meet your adoring public? Emma's got the whole backroom at Possum Charlie's reserved for well-wishers."

"I think I'll pass."

He wanted to see Ruby Mae. Tell her that what they had was something pretty special. Something that transcended time. And family. And differences over money and social standing. And that he'd felt this way about her for fifteen years. And he knew he'd feel it for the rest of his life.

But would it be good enough to win her back?

Or would he be too late?

Chapter 21

Ruby Mae did a slow, complete circle as she stared in awe at the paintings hanging on the alabaster walls of the Arturo Gallery. Halogen spotlights shined down on her paintings. Her pottery. And her jewelry creations.

And it was as if she'd flung wide open the doors and windows of her heart and soul. Allowed the public entrance into her private world. Every emotion was captured on canvas. Moments of ecstasy hanging placidly beside moments of deep, dark despair. Kernels of hope captured on one canvas mingling with misplaced dreams captured on another. Canvases filled with joy. Others brimming with sadness. And devastating loss. And still others filled with love beyond all measure.

It was her life.

It was amazing. Exciting.

"*Cara?*" Giovanni walked toward her in loose fitting linen slacks and a black silk shirt which complimented his olive skin and dark wavy hair sprinkled with gray. He kissed her on one cheek and then the other. They'd graduated from a kiss on her hand. "You like?" he asked, watching her closely.

"It's a lot to take in," she whispered. "It gives new meaning to seeing my life flashing before my eyes."

He slipped her arm through his. Slowly they walked around the rooms of his gallery. "You like though?"

"My paintings displayed on every wall?" Her shop magnified a hundred times over, only better? "I love," she whispered. "I don't know how to thank you enough for what you've done. This—" she looked from wall to wall. "This is beyond anything I could ever imagine. I just—" Words failed her. She lifted her shoulder. "I don't know what to say."

"You don't have to say anything." Giovanni stopped them in front of one of the paintings she'd created when Willie Lee had been so sick. When it had been so hard for her to accept he wasn't going to get better. That the bills weren't going to stop anytime soon. And she would lose the man she loved. And that life, as she knew it, life as she loved it, would cease to exist. "This says it all."

Giovanni lifted his head and gazed up at her painting, allowing the emotion pulsing within the brushstrokes to wash over him. "It lives. And breathes. And it cries real tears."

She had to look away. It reminded her too much of loss. Of Willie Lee. And now Virgil.

"Cara?" He turned her back toward him. Studied her with his dark chocolate eyes.

"I'm sorry." And she tried to thank him. Tried to say what would be so easy for her to put on canvas. And she couldn't come up with the words. All she could say was, "I can't thank you and— and Vince enough for this."

That Virgil's father had made this happen for her. After the way she'd treated his son. She had so much to thank him for. There was a very good chance because of his kindness she might save her house. The first hope she'd had since she'd asked Virgil to leave it – and her – two long, lonely months ago.

God, she missed him so much.

"Ruby Mae, even if Vincenzo hadn't brought you to my attention, if you'd have walked into my gallery with just one of your paintings, I would have still given you this show." He lifted her hand and squeezed it. "You're that good. *I'm* that lucky you chose *my* gallery. Now," he kissed her fingers in Old World fashion. "Let's go meet your guests."

He walked them to the foyer where Billy, Maisey, and Vince were already gathered.

"I'm so proud of you." Maisey was first to greet her wearing a very matronly, very attractive pale blue suit. She gave her a hug. "This is your night, honey." Her eyes were surprisingly moist. "You deserve it so much," she softly added, blotting the corners of her eyes with a handkerchief.

If it really were her night, Ruby Mae thought, getting a little teary eyed herself, Virgil would walk through those doors. He'd be here with her. She swallowed the hurt. She had no one to blame but herself. "Thanks for coming, Maisey."

"You know, honey. We wouldn't have missed this for anything."

"That's right." Billy Ray stepped close, wearing a beautiful charcoal gray suit that a GQ model couldn't have worn any better. A bright white shirt emphasized his dark tan, and a conservative tie perfectly defined his straight-as-an-arrow personality.

"You look pretty handsome," she teased him, hugging him with brotherly affection.

"You don't look so bad yourself." Holding her at arm's length, he gave her the once over. "Nothing Wal-Mart about you tonight."

"You sure?" Tonight she could tease him about the comment he'd made all those nights ago.

Heat crawled up his jaw. "I was wrong to have ever said that to you. You have always been Neimen-Marcus. Willie Lee knew it. And asshole did, too."

"Wow." She ignored his jab at Virgil. Her heart filled with brotherly love for this man and his protectiveness of her family. "Was that an apology?"

"Don't get used to it. It doesn't happen very often. Mostly because I'm not wrong very often," he added with a grin that showed straight white teeth. The action transformed his usually stern face to sinfully handsome. Someday some woman would see that. Would see what a good man he was. And she wanted to be around to see it when he finally fell into love.

Just as quickly as it appeared, the grin was replaced with his trademark watchfulness. He looked down at her with those dark-as-midnight eyes. Always her protector, he was looking for a crack in her veneer, ready to shore her up if need be. Or whisk her away if all this was too much.

"I'm okay," she softly told him, taking in a deep breath. "At least as okay as I can be." The butterflies in her stomach were rebelling tonight more than fluttering. She pressed a hand to her abdomen to soothe the slight nausea that lately came and went without notice.

"I'll be right here," he told her.

"I know you will. And I'll be fine," she told him, giving him a hug. She wished he'd find someone to be there for *him*. Someone who'd love him like he deserved to be loved.

"Well, cupcake." Vince stepped up to her next, looking dashing in a black tuxedo and bright white shirt with a large diamond stud for a top button. His gray-blond hair was loose, falling over his shoulders. He gave her the same once over he'd given her when he'd ridden into her life two months ago. "You clean up real nice."

She laughed in spite of her nerves. "Thank you." She pressed a palm to her chest. She'd chosen a bright red, sleeveless, knee-length satin dress with a mandarin collar. It had tiny red satin-covered buttons that went down one side from her neck all the way down to her thigh. There was a slit from there down to her knee. It was new. It made her feel pretty. It had been a small extravagance she'd allowed herself in spite of her financial woes.

Vince had called her frugal and offered to fly in half a dozen designers and their creations for her to look at. She guessed it was Father Push's version of home shopping. She'd declined.

The man was outrageous.

And she looked up into his smiling face. "You clean up real nice, too." Vince's tux was neither old, nor rented, nor off the rack. It was custom made, probably hand-tailored. Perfectly fitted and hand-couriered to her house, allowing him to look as comfortable here in this black-tie event as he did crawling off his bike in his faded Levi's.

"Thank you," she told him. "For this show. For Rita." He'd flown Rita in on his private jet to look after Brandon. Ruby Mae was quite sure her son had a crush on the statuesque brunette who had captured Vince's heart and was now spoiling her son rotten. "Thank you for being so kind to Brandon, too."

Giovanni walked up to the group. He clasped his hands together. "You ready, family?"

Ruby Mae looked at the group gathered. Vince. Billy. Maisey. They were her family in all ways that mattered. And she loved them all so much. And she got teary eyed telling them.

"*Jee-suz*, Ruby Mae," Vince groaned. "No tears. I can't take that."

"I'm sorry," Ruby Mae whispered, blinking back the moisture while accepting his offered handkerchief.

"Are we ready now?" Giovanni asked as she blotted her eyes. "Your fans await."

And looking beyond his shoulder, Ruby Mae could see the crowd of very well dressed people waiting outside the glass doors. The line snaked down the sidewalk and around the side of the building.

She swallowed. "I'm as ready as I'm going to be."

And Giovanni opened wide the front doors, letting the crowd in.

* * *

She was undoubtedly the most beautiful woman Virgil had ever seen.

He moved with the crowd that filled the Arturo Gallery to overflowing. He didn't look at the stunning paintings adorning the walls. Or at the A-List of *Who's Who* surrounding him. His eyes were solely for her.

The dress was bright red. The sleek satin hugging every curve. The slit showed off a healthy amount of thigh, which was sexy as hell. More amazing was the woman.

But he'd always known that.

The overhead light spilled down onto her, catching the gold strands of her curly hair making them glow from within. Like she did. The curls were pulled up tonight, a few wild locks escaping their hold to frame her beautiful face and brush against her slender neck. Her cheeks were flushed. With excitement. Her hands – those talented hands – were animated as she talked about her work. Her voice, the husky, sexy timbre grew soft when she shyly accepted a compliment. Humility radiated around her in a soft glow.

She had no idea how beautiful, how talented — how *perfect* — she was.

He did.

Now.

As if she could sense his presence, she turned. Found him amid the sea of guests surrounding them. And the noise of conversation, the clink of crystal goblets, the brush of linen and silk as the patrons walked by all faded away. And Virgil's heart – yes, his heart – skipped a beat.

Her mouth parted in surprise at seeing him here. And her eyes – her gorgeous eyes – softened as they connected with his. And he felt whole. Complete.

She turned back to the couple she'd been talking to. Said something to them and slowly turned back to him. The red satin of her dress flowed over her body, sliding over her hips and legs as she walked toward him.

And his heart kicked again, beating harder in his chest.

She smiled. And his heart beat faster still. And he smiled back, unable to stop himself. Feeling hope for the first time in months. And she stopped in front of him. Just out of his reach. And he pushed his hands deep into the pockets of his trousers to keep from reaching out and touching her. From pulling her to him and asking her what he wanted so badly to ask for. Forgiveness… and—

"Virgil." She said his name. It was a husky caress, detonating deep in his belly. Her smile grew, the warmth of it radiating out, warming the hollow spot in his chest. She stood close enough he could smell the flowery scent that was so trademark her, he'd never forget it. Swore he smelled it in his dreams. And knew he had for the last fifteen years. Knew he would smell it there for the rest of his life. "You made it," she softly added.

Like he'd ever miss this.

"You look beautiful," he told her, his fingers pushing a wayward curl from her cheek.

She dipped her head, a pretty blush stealing up over her cheeks. His hand slipped to her neck, then down her arm.

He had no right to touch her.

He dropped his hand back into the pocket of his trousers. The warmth of what he'd brought with him in that pocket, burning hotly against his thigh.

This really wasn't the best time. Or the best place, but...

She looked down to his trousers, then back up to his face. "You have another citation in your pocket?" Her eyes sparkled with mischief. "You've had four or five in there."

"No," he laughed. "You're free and clear." And his smile slipped. She was free of *him*, too.

She brushed a hand up his arm, her fingers lingering on his bicep. "And you're mayor again. Congratulations on your special re-election," she softly added, leaning into him. She brushed a chaste congratulatory kiss against his cheek.

And he held her close. Like he'd wanted to since that day. That stupid day he'd walked away from her. "Can we go someplace and talk?" he asked.

"Right now?" She looked around. At the room filled with people who'd come to see her and Virgil knew how selfish his request was.

"I'm sorry— I shouldn't have—"

"—Sure," she said at the same time. "Let's..." She turned

toward a side entrance and Virgil placed his hand at the base of her back as he walked beside her.

"Ruby Mae! *Cara.*" Giovanni Arturo rushed over to them. "I have someone I want you to…" He stopped mid-sentence. He stared at Virgil. Cocked his head to one side. *"Vinnie?"*

"Oh, no! No." Ruby Mae looked from Virgil to Giovanni. "This is—"

"Virgil," he finished for her as he held out his hand. "I'm Virgil Push."

"I'm so sorry," Giovanni said as he shook Virgil's hand. "I apologize. You look… exactly like Vincenzo. I just assumed you were Vinnie."

"I'm Vince's other son," he told the man. He'd made his peace concerning Vinnie. Just like he'd made his peace with his dad. Vince was entitled to a happy life. Anyway he could get it.

"The mayor! You're the mayor. Vincenzo has mentioned you quite often."

Virgil nodded his head. Surprised – and pleased Vince had mentioned him.

"*Cara.*" Giovanni turned to Ruby Mae. "I have someone who wants to meet you."

"We were just going to take a break." She looked at Virgil, the unspoken apology swimming in her eyes.

"This will only take a minute, *Cara,*" Giovanni told her. "State Senator Armstrong wants to meet the artist who'd choose my gallery over his wife's."

Ruby Mae shot a worried look to Virgil.

"Go," he quietly told her, jerking his head toward the entourage slowly sweeping their way through the crowd. What Virgil had to say... Well, it could wait. "This is your night, honey."

"Are you sure?" She searched his face.

He nodded his head up and down. "Go."

Malcolm Armstrong and his group walked up to Ruby Mae and Virgil. Giovanni made the introductions. "Senator Armstrong, this is Ruby Mae Shove."

The Senator took Ruby Mae's hand. Held it longer than Virgil thought necessary. "Miz Shove." And he stood too close, too. "So very nice to meet you." The senator looked over at Virgil. "Mayor Push."

"Senator Armstrong, good to see you, again." Virgil shook the man's hand.

"Congratulations on your re-election, Mayor. You've been doing some great things in your town. It's garnering a lot of attention. You could go far, Mayor. Right to the state capital, if you wished."

"Thank you." Virgil felt good about what he'd accomplished. Not because he'd garnered attention in Nashville and could pursue a political career in the capital city. But because he'd found a home in Rodent. A real home. A place where he felt like he was doing something other than wasting his trust fund. And his life. And if there was a chance he could make things right with the woman still standing beside him, he'd have everything.

"That was quite a police scandal," the senator went on. "The chief pushing for a suspension. You pushing harder for a firing." And Virgil had won that round with the support of Internal Affairs and the Police Review Board and the Citizens Review Panel. Clive had been fired with no severance, or pension.

"Will you be prosecuting Officer Clive yourself?"

"I'm a public official, sir, not a practicing lawyer." District Attorney Stephanie Zatalla would be prosecuting Clive when his trial came up. The list of charges was long. Bribery, official oppression, deviate sexual behavior, indecent assault, coercion.

Clive was facing serious jail time.

"We're not here to talk shop and politics I hope?" Giovanni interjected.

"No, we're not," Virgil replied. He turned to the woman still standing by his side. "This is Ruby Mae's night," he told the group as he lifted her hand. He kissed it.

This was her moment. Her time. Her life.

And he stepped back. Away from her. And watched as Ruby Mae was ushered by the Senator and Giovanni, taken away from him, swallowed up by an adoring crowd.

Leaving him alone. Again.

* * *

The night was officially over. Like a modern-day Cinderella after the ball, Ruby Mae watched the red taillights of the long black stretch limo as it pulled away. She turned. Looked up. Beside the silvery-white crescent moon, there was only one star in the midnight-blue sky that shined down on her. It almost seemed to follow her as she slowly walked up her driveway. Toward her home. The one she'd own free and clear once she met with the mortgage company next week and presented her check. The amount due was a fraction of the receipts from tonight's show. She lifted her arms high. Dropped her head back. And slowly turned in a complete circle.

She was a success!

She dropped her arms. Breathed in a slow, deep breath. With Vince's help, she'd made it. Arturo would represent her work. She'd build a clientele and she would have a steady income for as long as she wanted. She had it all… Except the one thing she wanted the most.

Virgil.

Despite everything between them, he'd come to her show tonight. He'd kissed her and had looked at her with the same hunger in his eyes. That was still the same. Just like her love for him. It would never change. She dropped her head back. Looked up at the dark night sky. At the one star that seemed to shine down on her.

All I ever wanted was for you to be happy, Ruby Mae.

It was Willie Lee's voice. Ringing loud and clear inside her head as the lone star overhead seemed to burn brighter. And her breath caught because that star was pulsating with brilliant light and Willie Lee's voice was still ringing in her head.

It is all I ever wanted for you.

It was like they were carrying on a celestial conversation that spanned here… and there. From her heart to Heaven's gate.

This was probably how it started with Maisey. A lonely night. A single star. A voice inside her head. And before Ruby Mae would know it, she'd be wearing a thong, talking regularly to her dearly departed, and ragging on Brandon to give her grandchildren like Maisey did to Billy.

Ruefully, she shook head.

Be happy, Willie Lee's voice inside her head said. Clear as if he were standing in front of her.

And then she saw the BMW parked by Willie Lee's truck. And in the illumination from the porch light, the man still dressed in his tuxedo, sitting on her bottom step. His blond head was bowed as he stared at his hands, laced together between his wide-splayed legs. His

shoulders were hunched as if he carried a heavy load as he waited…
for her.

Be happy.

It was Willie Lee's voice again. And she looked up. And there
she saw it. That shining star and the bright streak of light trailing
behind it as it shot across the sky to disappear behind the dark
silhouette of the Brandywine.

And her heart squeezed tight in her chest.

Was it possible? Everything about this night had been mystical.
Why not Willie Lee giving her his blessing? And then there was the
man sitting on her porch. Waiting for her. Did she dare hope for
more? "Virgil?" she whispered his name.

He raised his head. And in his eyes she found the familiar heat
burning there. It matched what burned in her heart.

"What are you doin' here?"

"I had a lot of time to think, Ruby Mae."

And she waited for the man who was never at a loss for words
to come up with a few.

"You know where I came from."

She did. She knew how vicious his mother could be. She knew
his father, too, and although she loved Vince, she truly felt he'd done
his son a disservice leaving him with Marilee. And she understood
how a child raised like that could be lacking in some of the most
important things.

Money didn't buy everything.

"You know who I married."

She knew that, too.

He looked up at her. "I never loved Rachel." And in his eyes she saw the honesty, the sincerity of his words. And her heart broke for him.

Anyone looking at him would think he'd had everything. Yet he'd been deprived. Cheated out of the most basic and important things in life. Love and happiness.

He stood. And a wrinkled tux, rumpled, open shirt and mussed hair never looked so good. He walked toward her. Stood in front of her. "You asked me once." He took her hand. "If I loved you." His thumb slowly brushed over every one of her trembling fingers.

"Virgil, you don't have to..." He might never have said the words, might never be able to say them, but, "I know," she whispered. She knew he loved her. "You've shown me a hundred different ways."

His mouth curled up in a small smile. "You might be willing to let me off the hook, darlin', but I'm not that obliging." His fingers gently pushed a strand of hair from her cheek. "The man you marry needs to be able to say he loves you."

"Virgil, you don't have to say— *What*?" Her heart missed a beat. "What did you just say?"

His palm slowly slid down her arm. His fingers wrapped around hers. And he held them between them. His thumb gently rubbing over her ring finger. "The man you marry needs you to know that you are everything to him."

He gave her fingers a gentle squeeze and her heart kicked around in her chest as his words sunk in. "And you need to know that the man you marry can think of nothing but you." He lifted her fingers to his mouth.

"And that he is happiest when he's with you," he added, pressing a tender kiss to them. "That he is only happiest loving you."

"Virgil," she whispered, as tears filled her eyes.

"I'm that man, Ruby Mae. It took me a while, but I figured it out. I'm miserable without you. And—" He reached into his pocket.

She gasped as she stared at the most beautiful round diamond solitaire that sparkled up at her. Like that star had earlier.

He lifted her hand. Slid on the ring, but only as far as the first joint. "When Push comes to Shove, honey, he comes asking one thing."

"Yes, Virgil." Yes, she would marry him!

He held up one finger. "Let me finish," he told her. And she waited with her heart pounding in her chest and love.

"I have loved you since I was seventeen. And I will love you every day forward until all that's left of me is a speck of light in the nighttime sky. I love your son, and I want to spend the rest of my life with you. The kindest thing you could ever do for me," he pushed the ring up her finger to the second joint, "is say you love me—"

"I love you, Virgil."

"I'm not finished yet, my love."

"I'm sorry." She pressed her trembling lips together to keep from smiling. To keep from blurting out, *yes*! To keep from crying through the most romantic proposal she'd ever heard. Her other hand was pressed between her breasts. Right over her thundering heart. The one he'd had since he'd walked back into her life for a second time all those months ago.

"The kindest thing you could ever do for me," he started over, "is to say you love me and that you will marry me. Ruby Mae Shove, will you do me the honor of being my wife? Will you allow me to make you happy for the rest of mine? Will you let me love you and take care of you, and your son? And allow me to spend the rest of my life with the only woman I have ever loved?"

And Ruby Mae gleefully replied, "Yes!"

Chapter 22

Ruby Mae and Virgil were married three weeks later at Vince and Rita's home in Dunstin, Oklahoma. It was an intimate gathering of family and friends. Ruby Mae's sisters, Pearl and Opal, and their husbands and kids made the trip. They stood for her, while Billy and Vinnie stood for Virgil.

Marilee was noticeably absent; mainly because she hadn't been invited. With Vince's help, Virgil's insistence that Marilee was behind the balloon repayment scheme was confirmed. And Maxwell Thomas was no longer on the board of the mortgage company. Neither was Marilee. And she was no longer a member of Executive Council having been removed from her position by the mayor-elect.

Ruby Mae's mother and father were noticeably absent from the nuptials, as well. Her mother had taken to her bed with yet another bout of depression. Which meant Ruby Mae's father had chosen a weekend with Marilee over attending his own daughter's wedding.

Nice guy.

Maisey served as honorary mother of the bride – *and* mother of the groom, the latter an honor she willingly shared with Rita. It was an awkward situation, Vince and Rita's, but Virgil was handling it surprisingly well. And Rita was very understanding. And very gracious. And very easy to like.

Giovanni came for the nuptials with his beautiful wife who could have been Sophia Loren's twin when the star had been young. Emma made the trip, as did Davis. Ruby Mae didn't know what Virgil would find at next month's Executive Council meeting. Edgar Wyatt had inexplicably relinquished his seat. He'd also put the family mansion up for sale shocking the whole town, stating he was leaving Rodent to be closer to his distillery. Another special election was slated to fill his vacancy and that of Marilee's.

Vince walked Ruby Mae down the aisle before taking his seat by Rita on Virgil's side. And while the sun shown down on the small group gathered, Ruby Mae and Virgil, with Brandon standing with them, pledged their love to each other.

After the wedding, Vince announced he and Rita were giving them their honeymoon. "Anywhere in the world," he'd said. "Name it and we'll send you there."

It hadn't taken long for Brandon and Virgil to form an alliance, casting their votes together, which explained how they'd traveled halfway around the world – to Africa, no less! And while Ruby Mae had envisioned a safari honeymoon with lions and zebras, she was now here in Tanzania with the two men she loved most in all the world, part of a twenty-man entourage of guides and porters, climbing up the rocky-edged mountainside in the dark hours after midnight hoping to reach the summit of Mount Kilimanjaro before dawn's early light.

"We made it," she wheezed out, falling to her knees and rolling onto her back. She threw her backpack aside. She was gasping for air, which was pretty thin at nineteen-thousand- three- hundred-and-forty-one feet above sea level. "I can't believe we made it."

"We sure as hell did!" Virgil replied, a little out of breath himself. He knelt down beside his bride – the most phenomenal women he'd ever met – who was now sprawled out across the frozen rock like Tennessee road kill. Her breaths were coming out in short, fog-filled pants. Her body was layered in enough thermal that she looked more like the *Stay-Puff* marshmallow on steroids than the curvy brunette who'd turned his world upside down.

It was a hot look. *She* was hot. And she did it for him – rocked his world in every conceivable way. And a few he hadn't counted on.

Brandon was jumping up and down, pumping his fists up in the air like Rocky Balboa when the boxer had made the infamous run up the steps of the Philadelphia Art Museum. And he was chanting. "I am the Badass! The baddest. The *baa-aadest* of the bad!"

"Brandon," Ruby Mae gasped, her eyes still closed. "Do… not… swear," she huffed out. Her eyes flew open. Her hand went to her throat. She made a couple weak attempts at swallowing. Her face grew a sickly shade of greenish pale. And Virgil settled in while she rolled to her side. Then up onto her hands and knees, quickly scrambling to an outcropping of rock barely within the faint circle of light surrounding the spot their porters had set up for their camp.

"Yuck," Brandon muttered, before wandering over to tell their guides he was the badass of the world.

Virgil sat on the cold ground, his knees bent, crossed-legged in front of him. Leaning against a rock, he patiently waited for Ruby Mae to return. He didn't have to look at a clock to know what time it was.

She returned a short time later, looking only a little less green, and Virgil said, "Now might be a good time to talk about kids, don't you think?"

Still feeling queasy in her stomach, Ruby Mae carefully sat down on the shards of rock that made up Kilimanjaro's summit. The icy cold of the frosty ground seeped into her clothes as she stared at her husband.

It had taken them fifteen days to reach the summit, twice as long as the average climber. His usually clean-shaven face was covered with a thick, dark blond beard. The *Indiana Jones* hat he'd chosen for the trip, now a lot more dusty and tattered than when they'd started, sat at a rakish angle on his head. His hair curled over the back collar of his thermal vest. He looked hunkishly handsome. And hot. Even with his eyes shadowed with exhaustion from the relentless climb and restless attempts at sleep. And like he'd done the whole climb up the mountain, he was patiently waiting for her.

Only this time she didn't know what to say. Didn't know how he'd feel about this latest development.

"I love you. And Brandon, too. You know that, right?" His ability to read her mind was obviously not impaired by the high altitude and thin air that muddled other people's brains.

"I would adopt him," he quietly went on. "Make him officially my son, but," he inhaled a short breath. All they were able to really suck into their lungs this high up. "Much as I want that, I don't want to take Brandon's name from him. He's Willie Lee's legacy. And I don't want to take that from either of them."

"Thank you," she managed to say through a thick lump of emotion jammed up in her throat. "I know that would make Willie Lee happy."

"Do you want more children?" he solemnly asked, searching her face, and she dropped her palm to her stomach where there was a 99.9 percent chance she had another child.

"The better question, Virgil, is do *you* want children?"

"Do you mean do I want the little muffin you got bakin' in that oven of yours?" A slow, sexy grin curled over one side of his mouth.

"*Might* have baking," she corrected him. She didn't know why she was being stubborn. She knew the signs. She'd had them before when she'd been pregnant with Brandon. Maybe it wasn't her inbred stubborn streak, but wariness instead. They'd never talked about kids. Or about a blended family. Or even what they'd do once his term as mayor was up. "Do you want kids?" she asked again, much as she'd asked all those months ago if he loved her.

And it was a good question. One Virgil would expect her to ask, considering his past. "I want you," he told her as he stood. He clasped his hand around her forearm and pulled her to her feet. He turned her so her back was pressed to his chest. Pulled her close until his groin pressed into her perfect ass. And his hands slowly slid down over her gorgeous breasts to rest over the tiny little life he hoped with all his heart was growing down there under his fingertips. "I want this little muffin. And a half dozen more."

"A half dozen, Virgil?" she laughed. The sweet airy sound was the most beautiful thing he'd ever heard. She shook her head, the fuzz of her wool hat teasing his nose. "You go over the top for everything, don't you, Mister Mayor?"

"I went over the top for you." He nuzzled her neck. Kissed that sweet spot just below her ear. The spot that had her uttering his name in a breathy exhale of desire that drove him crazy. And she didn't disappoint him.

"Oh, Virgil," she whispered, leaning her head against his shoulder to give him better access to the sweet, smelling skin exposed just above the collar of her jacket. They'd been on the trail for two weeks and she still smelled wonderful. And she cocked her head giving him access to more of that silky, sweet smelling skin.

"I love you," he quietly told her as the dark gray clouds surrounding the summit turned to the bright orange-red of molten lava.

She turned her head to look at him with soft eyes and he knew she understood. Accepted even, his stunted emotions. But he was getting better at saying what he felt. And he was pretty sure it didn't make him a pussy.

She slowly turned her head back to the indigo sky that surrounded them on all sides, the one now turning a deep shade of purple. "Tell me about the last time you were up here."

"I was hung over," he honestly told her. "Half hoping I'd fall off." He pulled her closer.

He'd been a mess back then. In a loveless marriage that was one signature away from being finalized with a divorce decree that left him with nothing but unhappy memories. What fortune Rachel hadn't secreted away from him, he'd blown in a high-stakes poker game so she wouldn't get any more of it. He'd been a shitty person back then with no direction, no purpose. The best advice he'd ever taken was that of the guide who'd said, *"Go home."*

And he had.

She turned her head back to him. With eyes soft with compassion. And pussy or not, he told her the rest. "It was the darkest day of my life."

"And," she quietly prompted.

He shrugged one shoulder. "And you want more?"

She smiled. It was a soft, sexy smile that made him want to do a hundred other things than spill his guts. "I want all of you. And I know what you're thinking," she added, her brown eyes sparkling with mischief.

"Wouldn't you rather do *that* instead of listening to me spill my guts?" He sure as hell would.

"Well." She turned in his arms. She gripped the front of his vest as she settled her soft body against his. "If you wanna do *that* again.

That being what you seem to want to do above anything else, my love," she teasingly added. "You might wanna spill."

"We'd have more fun doin' the other. And come to think of it." He teased the corner of her mouth with a kiss that almost had her surrendering to his charm. Almost.

"Isn't that how we got to this conversation in the first place?" her lips teased his.

"What conversation?"

"The one where we have a half a dozen little *muffins* as you call them?" She playfully nipped his bottom lip.

And before he could drag her behind a rock and have her quick and nasty up against it, Brandon ran toward them. "Mom! Dad!"

And that was something else Virgil would never get tired of hearing. *Dad.*

"Look!" His son in every way that mattered pointed toward the sun breaking through the thick blanket of clouds that clung to the mountain top, streaking the mauve-colored sky with fiery beams of coral and orange, illuminating everything in golden light.

And while they *oohed* and *aahed*, Virgil remembered.

He'd been golden once himself. He'd had everything. Money, a name that opened doors. A silver spoon allowing him to sample the infinite buffets of the world. Yet he'd been starved for the one thing he'd never had. The one thing his money, his power, his name couldn't give him.

"It's beautiful," Ruby Mae whispered in awe as she watched the sunrise.

"It is," he quietly told her as he looked down at the woman he held in his arms. "It's the most beautiful thing I've ever seen."

Ruby Mae turned her head. She looked up at the man who completed her in every way, who made her happy. The man who loved her. "You're not looking at the sunrise," she quietly told him.

He smiled. And his eyes, his gorgeous blue eyes were full of love, brimming with promise. And she knew he'd give her that forever after she wanted. And it would be filled with love. And probably a little craziness, too.

"There's nothing more beautiful than the woman standing in front of me." He settled his arms tighter around her. "Nothing more perfect than my life right now. Nothing better than the family we have. And," the palm of his hand slid over her stomach. "The one we're creating."

And while the golden light illuminated the golden boy of Rodent, he kissed the woman he loved. The woman who made him *believe.* The woman who'd healed him and made him whole.

"Yu-uck. You're kissing her and she just puked."

Virgil smiled down at his son. He grabbed the corner tassel of his wool hat and tugged it, pulling him close. "Maybe I like pukey girls."

"I am *never* gonna kiss a girl. *Ever!*" their son staunchly replied.

"Yeah, right."

And with Ruby Mae tucked under one arm and his other arm locked around Brandon's head, they watched the sun continue to rise.

Contentment settled all around Virgil settling deep into his soul. It seemed like a lifetime ago when he'd gone to her house to serve her that citation. He'd expected an argument, expected a fight, but he'd never expected what he'd gotten.

He'd traveled all over the world, yet he'd found everything he'd ever wanted – and more – in his hometown nestled in the mountains of East Tennessee.

He'd found love.

And happily ever after.

About the Author

I hope you enjoyed Book One in my Second Chance Series. Virgil and Ruby Mae are a special couple; their story a catalyst in making dreams come true. Not only for them, but for me, as well. Their story cemented a life-long dream for me of being a published author.

I thank you for making that happen, as well.

If you liked my story, please let me know. I'd love to hear from you. If possible, leave me a review at **www.amazon.com.** It really is the best way a writer can be promoted.

Be sure to catch *When Law Met Disorder*. It's Book Two in the series, where Officer William Raymond Trainor meets his match with the very sexy, Anna McFadden. Enough said!

And now a little more about me, the author.

I have always loved a happy ending. And dreams that come true. I love weaving tales where the boy gets his girl, laughter abounds, and they find all their dreams come true as they live happily ever after. That's how it is in the Land of "Wylde".

A misplaced mountain child, I live in the rolling hills of Western Pennsylvania with my husband of more than thirty years. My very own superhero. How cool is that?

Visit me at my website at **www.jdwylde.com.** Or "like" my fan page on Facebook (**j.d. wylde**) where you can keep up to date on all things "Wylde". You can follow me on Twitter, too, **@jdwylde**.

I look forward to hearing from you.

And as always... *live Wylde !*

Other Books by J.D. Wylde

Sweet Romances

The Journey

The Dream

Sexy Romances

When Law Met Disorder

Karma in Camo

Cupid in Camo

Beyond the Checkered Flag

Holiday Wish

60148871R00212

Made in the USA
Charleston, SC
23 August 2016